Dear for

BONES & RUNES

thank You for
All your work
and energy

Stephen
london 15/9/22

BONES & RUNES

BOOK 1

STEPHEN EMBLETON

Abibiman
Publishing

New York & London

First published in Great Britain in 2022 by
Abibiman Publishing
www.abibimanpublishing.com

ISBN: 978-1-7397747-0-7

Cover design by Gabriel Ogungbade & Stephen Embleton

Printed in the United Kingdom by Clays Ltd.

To Treycin & Kaylin,
For being the beautiful young adults you are.

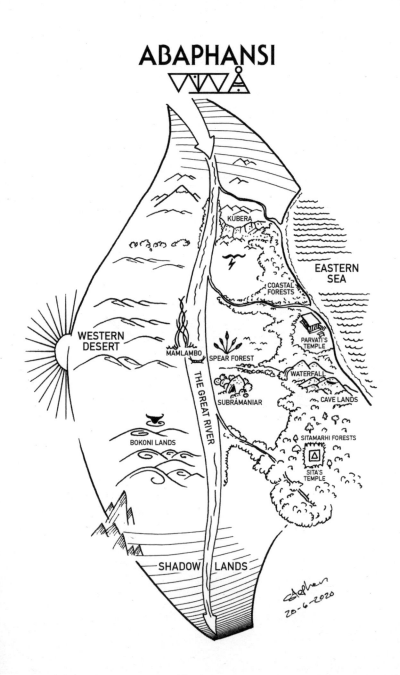

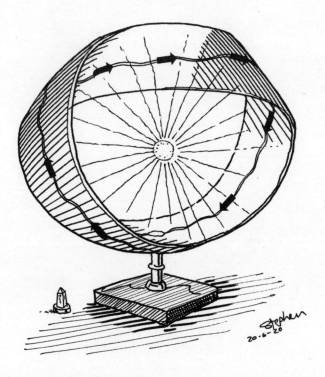

"A flat plane had been joined, end-to-end, in a twisted loop like a contorted orbital in space." (Chapter 21)

CHAPTER 1

"I just need one," Mlilo snatched a rib from the steaming cardboard box held by Dan, meat glistening in the streetlamp light. The red and black "One Stop" logo was already oiling into obscurity.

"Bru, I thought you were hungry and that's the best mutton biryani you'll find in town."

He pointed the fleshy bone at his friend. "I said I needed you to bring me something, Dan."

Dan's eyes narrowed at the subtle trembling of Mlilo's fingers. He quickly withdrew his hand to his mouth. "Mlungu mfowethu wami," Mlilo mumbled over a bite of the sauce-soaked bone, "I didn't say I was hungry." He spat a chunk of meat onto the stained concrete entrance of the shadowy alleyway. Mlilo paused, disgust visible as he stared into the stretch of darkness before him. He shook off the shiver that ran through him as he recalled his ordeal moments before he summoned his friend, and took another gnaw on the bone.

"Well, excuse *me*, Mlilo," Dan cleared a wisp of stray light brown fringe behind his ear. "I assumed you meant you needed food. What the hell else does someone want at this time of the night and what the hell happened?"

Ignoring Dan, Mlilo pivoted and stepped off the pavement onto the empty street. "I called you way after three AM and it's now," he stopped in his tracks in the middle of the three-laned road and looked up at the inky sky, "three thirty-four." He spat another mass onto the tar. "You were cutting it a bit fine. It's nearly four AM." He proceeded onto the opposite pavement towards a side road, sporadic light from the surrounding buildings mottled the path ahead.

"I'm here, aren't I?" said Dan trailing behind. "Some of us come a bit more prepared than others, even if we're rushing out the door." He stared down at the oily meat slicing the road. "What the hell. I bring you shisa inyama–"

"uMnganam," Mlilo said between licking his lips. "I don't need the meat, I need the bone. Ithambo. With my sack gone, my request to you was simply

1

following the instructions from my ancestors: *Dan will bring what is needed for you.* And I don't think they meant your clever wit."

"Whatever beating you received to your head has obviously made you more obtuse than normal."

"That beating," he paused, removed the crumpled and torn black button-up shirt protruding from his jeans pocket, and dabbed at the drying blood crusting his hair and forehead, "was a wakeup call. Some clarity on this sweaty Durban night."

Dan came around and stood in his friend's path. Mlilo shoved the shirt back into his pants pocket. "Hold up," said Dan and looked quizzically at his right forefinger. "Damn, forgot my ring."

"Hmm. Not so prepared," said Mlilo.

"Let's just take a moment, Mr. Witchdoctor."

"Isangoma," Mlilo retorted, sidestepping Dan and picked up his pace; the street inclined down, the oily, humid scent of the harbour, now visible between the buildings, wafted up towards them; Mlilo felt his gut turn. "You're the one with witchdoctors, druids and Getafix magic, not me," he glanced back.

"Merlin," Dan yelled, "for gods' sakes."

"And swearing," he sucked his greasy fingers.

"Then you're welcome. I brought you an actual bone. But what the hell is a shinbone going to do to guide you?" Dan trotted up beside him.

"A guide. A key."

"Key?"

"To step through the door."

"You called me here for something you could've gotten in that back-alley dumpster. What the hell, oke."

Mlilo flashed an image of blue-green meat, followed by the moist, oozing sounds of maggots, into Dan's mind. He followed up with a smell and taste that hit the back of Dan's throat, sending him doubling over and heaving onto the tarred road.

"Can you *not* do that," stuttered Dan between spits.

"Firstly, my ancestors are the ones who guide me to find the right amathambo, my 'bones' for divining. Why they picked you to be the bearer of it, I'm not sure, but maybe I'll need backup along the way. Secondly, no amathambo, no access to the other side. They guide me. And thirdly, you want me to use some maggot-infested scrap or some other infected artefact off the street?" He thumbed over his shoulder. "Are you ignorant? I'm not stepping through the door that a vrot object like that guides me to. Thanks anyway."

"I keep telling you, runes. Runes and Runemal are the way to go. Scratch a runic symbol somewhere, anywhere; on the tar," he gestured his arm behind him up at the concrete wall in shadow, "or the goddamn wall, and they work. Bones?" Dan clucked his tongue.

"We are not doing this again."

"Whatever."

"You have your methods. I have mine." Mlilo gestured at some rubble. "Hey, there are some bricks. Why don't you build a quick Stonehenge and wait for the solstice while I clean up this bone. Okay?"

"Funny oke. I thought your snakeskin boots were meant to protect you?"

Mlilo glanced down at his pale yellow and brown boots sticking out his skinny black jeans. "Against bad umuthi, chop. Not those troglodytes that got the jump on me and took my toolkit." He patted the four strings of black, red and white beads, crossed at his chest over his leopard-print vest; the two sets of strings draped from each shoulder to the opposite hip.

Dan glanced at his bare right ring finger and said, "You do realise you caught me off guard. Glad my cowl always has my runes and tarot in it because I left my damn obsidian ring back at my apartment." He pictured the thick, solid silver band topped with a flat, square chunk of obsidian and the engraved triskele on either side lying next to his bedside. He found his hand go to the small, gold pinkey ring on his left hand. "My grandfather's ring will at least give some protection. Where the hell does this door go, anyway?" Dan slowed as, one after the other, they emerged from the gloomy street onto the quiet, empty main road. "Have you got your GPS running on your phone?"

"Enough," Mlilo swung around to face his friend who nearly collided with his outstretched hand and bone. "Have you been chewing on umlomomnandi root again?"

"I don't need your umlomomnandi to be quick witted, bru. I have it in spades."

Mlilo shook his head. "More like a shovel. Now, either you're with me and you're going to shut the hell up, or you're turning around and going home, and shutting the hell up."

"Fine," he sighed.

Without hesitating, Mlilo crossed the empty double-lane road and onto the grassed centre island.

Dan took a moment to get his bearings, looking at the wide expanse of lights and the thin inky waterline visible further ahead. He glanced back over his shoulder at the dark street they had walked down; a shiver ran through him. He deftly darted over the road to catch up with his friend.

Mlilo was already over the other road and onto the bricked pathway leading towards a peeling white painted structure a few metres ahead.

"Bru!" Dan shouted and took a few bounding strides to get to his friend. "The harbour?"

"No," Mlilo replied and stopped in front of a gated entrance. Dan felt his stomach lurch as a gust of piss-soaked air pushed up from the underground pedestrian walkway.

"We are going to Abaphansi. And this," he held up the bone, "this says we need to enter here."

Dan looked at the rounded design of the old entrance. The paint and repaint were peeling, showing varying colour tastes over the past decades. He tried to see down the stairs and to the tunnel he knew veered off to the left under the train tracks above, but the pitch darkness gave no hint at what lay beneath. He took out his mobile phone, clicked on the torch and waved the light slowly, glinting faintly off the once white ceramic tiled passageway. "Eesh," he whispered and turned the light off. He looked past Mlilo, locked in a stare at the rusted metal gate ahead of him, and over the waist-high stone wall separating them from the train tracks and the mirror image exit leading into the harbour.

"Why can't we just jump the friggin' wall?"

"Pay attention: we're going to Abaphansi, mfowethu. We are not crossing a railway line."

"Ah, 'underneath'," Dan air-quoted.

Mlilo rolled his eyes. "Abaphansi is not under, it is everywhere, always."

"And why the hell would we want to go there?" Dan waved his hand in front of his nose.

Mlilo glanced at his companion, and then pointed at the base of the entrance. "Because this is where they went."

For the first time Dan noticed three porcupine quills on the broken concrete step. Two long, black and white spikes, and one smaller shiny solid black quill lay together.

Dan snorted. "A porcupine stole your bag?"

"You could say that."

"Well, unlike you," continued Dan, "I'm prepared. I've got the magic of my people right here." He smacked his left forearm, "and my backups when I need them." He stroked the sides of his knee-length blue-grey coat. Mlilo could picture the pale wooden wand, sheathed in a neat black leather strap around his friend's arm. A few months ago, he'd witnessed a barefooted Dan, pacing up and down his loft apartment lounge, a few blocks from where they met up earlier, flicking the neatly crafted wand out from his coat sleeve. With a grin, he's thought of the stage illusionists and their sleight of hand pretending they were performing magic.

Mlilo took a final suck on the clean bone, and held up the neat ring of the marrowless shinbone and smiled a greasy smile. "Time to get back the stolen magic of *my* people." He looked up at the morning sky, already a deep blue. "Amadlozi!"

"What's that?"

"Not what. Whom. The ancestors. They reside in KwelaBaphansi, the land of the ancestors. But that is a region of Abaphansi, to the West, we only visit if invited."

Silence.

"Now what?" asked Dan. "Do you add that trinket to your bag of goodies, if you ever get them back?"

"This?" Mlilo lifted the bare bone and looked through the middle like a keyhole, "Maybe." He looked back up at the night sky. "Think of it like a burner phone. A temporary solution."

"A burner bone," Dan chuckled to himself, then let out a deep yawn. "What the hell?" Dan waggled a finger in his ear and worked his jaw. "What's that sound?"

"You may feel drowsy, and possibly a little like you're dreaming. It's all part of crossing over."

Dan rubbed his eyes.

"Here comes the blood," Mlilo stood, arms out and eyes closed to the sky.

Plock.

Dan noticed a red splotch appear on his bright white sneakers. He glared up at his friend. "These are brand new, bru." The sound grew louder like blood rushing in his ears. In an instant a crimson downpour engulfed them.

The warm redness soaked through their hair and clothes; a tingly feeling penetrated their skin. Dan looked around. Red liquid poured down the sides of the buildings; a steady stream flowed from the main street and gutters up onto the pathway, heading in their direction. He tried standing on tiptoes as it pooled around them and soaked into his shoes, reaching his ankles in seconds.

He turned back to Mlilo, feeling the blood drain from his face. "Do we need to hold hands for this?"

CHAPTER 2

It took Mlilo a moment to get his bearings and steady himself in the soft warm light of the new landscape. He traced his fingers along his hairline; the dried blood and muck gone, the aching and swelling skin and muscle no longer pulsing pain into his eye-sockets. He moved his hand down to the six strings of bead hanging from his neck. The black, white and red plastic beads crisscrossed like a safety blanket from shoulder to waist around his chest.

He turned back to see his friend doubled over, blindly trying to find a support with one hand as he retched onto the red sand at his feet, and trying to keep his hair out of his face with the other. Finally, he placed his feet squarely on the ground and held his thighs. Spit slimed down his chin and darkened the sand.

"Some kind of warning would've been great, bru," he wheezed.

"You'll be fine."

"My goddamn takkies are gonna be -," Dan balanced awkwardly from one foot to the other. "Wait, what?"

"It's metaphysical, Danny boy," chuckled Mlilo and returned his gaze to their surroundings. Looking at his feet, he knelt down and grabbed a handful of the fine soil, then let it fall gradually through his fingers. "Everything is rejuvenated here. It's not going to stain your precious Pumas. And you can chill; it's ochre, not blood. The first-timer experience."

"Bastard." Dan gathered his shoulder length hair and quickly tied it back in a loose ponytail.

Mlilo stood back up and took in a deep breath. The Underworld's humid air beat anything Durban could offer at the peak of summer. Although the ground was dry and dusty, the scent of damp soil after a rain hung in the heavy air, always taking him a moment to adjust his breathing. His hands and face felt like they were in lukewarm water but without the wetness lingering.

"What the hell is with the air down here?"

"I told you we aren't 'down' anywhere," Mlilo replied. "We are everywhere.

What you feel all around you is Life with a capital 'L'. It's what binds everyone. It's just that you can feel it more profoundly here than you ever will in the real world."

"It feels humid but I'm not sticky or sweaty." Dan staggered towards Mlilo.

Giving his friend an up and down look, Mlilo said, "I don't know how you wear that bath robe, even in Durban's climate."

"Cowl, goddamnit." Dan adjusted his loose, charcoal-grey coat lapels. "It has a hood. Modernised with a few pockets, seen and unseen, for all my goodies."

They now stood side by side; Dan wiped his mouth and gave his whole face a few slaps as if trying to wake himself up. "What's with the horizon?"

Dan had noticed the lack of horizon. Not that it was obscured by anything but rather that it seemed to blend into the sky. Almost losing balance, Dan tracked the landscape upward.

"What the hell's that bright wavy line curving up into the sky?"

"It's really curving down towards us. That's *the* Great River."

"You mean the Umgeni?"

"I mean the Great River with a capital G. The flow of life to and from the Source. But it's all relative. If you were standing on that snowcapped mountain looking at us," Mlilo pointed out a ragged star-shaped blemish on the vertical surface, "you'd think it was flowing upward."

Dan reached inside his coat and removed his mobile from one of his pockets and began poking its screen.

Pling.

"I'm not sure how we got here," Dan addressed the device. "Our esteemed guide is a bit slack with his guiding at this stage. But we are in some alternate world."

He turned, slowing his pace, to point the camera to his right.

"Way off in the distance, over the river, past those hills, you can just make out the ocean on the dark horizon. It seems to be further away than where the actual ocean is in the real world. It's as if it's blending into," he caught his breath. "Yasas, how's those stars?"

He pointed the phone downward as he turned back.

"The sand here is typical Durban city sand - deep red and fine." He paused for a moment. "Mlilo! Come on, man," he shouted to his friend nearly thirty metres ahead of him. "Are you sure that was mud and not blood?"

Dan decided to follow his friend, continuing to hold his phone up.

"There is what you would expect to be the hilly landscape around the city. Except no city. Just these thick bushes and trees."

"It's how the land was before we built the cities; before we lived in it."

Dan stopped in his tracks, and jiggled a finger in his ear.

"You are at least twenty metres away from me and I can hear you as if you were

7

right next to me. And yet my ears feel like they are filled with water." He used his phone to pinch-zoom in on his now stationary friend up ahead. The grainy and shaky image of Mlilo on the screen looked into the camera, shaking his head.

"What do you think you are doing, umnganam?"

"Um, documenting this world, *friend*." Dan zoomed back out and turned the camera on himself, waving at the device with a smile. "You can't expect me not to, bru."

He turned the camera back on Mlilo who had resumed walking and gave Dan a dismissive wave over his shoulder. "I'm communicating with you, directly. While you are in this world, a part of this world, you can communicate with anyone, here or the real world. The problem is those in the real world aren't always listening or willing to hear."

"Yes. I prefer regular divination to hearing voices. That would freak me out. Kind of like you are doing right now."

"Signs, symbols and bones involve interpretation. With the voices, the Amadlozi, there is no grey area."

"But you use both."

"Yes. For when I'm unable to hear."

Dan pointed the phone up at the deep orange-red sky. "It seems like either sunrise or sunset. But, damn, those stars." He pressed the red record button to pause, swiped around his screen and then *Click*; took a photo.

Back to his video recording. "No clouds in sight, just this insane view of outer space, really. So many questions."

Movement in the sky caught his attention. Rotating his phone, and a quick pinch-zoom, he tracked the graceful path of a flock of large black and white birds. "Sacred ibises," he whispered to himself.

"It's not just hornbills and hadedas here, umnganam."

Dan stopped his recording and jogged to catch up to his friend.

"The stars are in the middle, right? The land seems to curve up all around but fades up into blackness where the stars begin."

"Something like that."

"Hey," said Dan as he shut off his device and grabbed Mlilo's shoulder, "can you give me some kind of idea where we are going? And at least what we are dealing with here."

"We are following those," said Mlilo taking a few more steps and bending down to pick up a single black and white porcupine quill. "This is who we are tracking right now and we seem to be tracking them north."

"A porcupine?"

"In essence, yes. But imagine everything you know about a porcupine, personified or rather bestialized into a rage monster that will snap you in two."

Dan took the quill from Mlilo. "Snap you like a quill," he quipped but failed to break the quill as he bent it.

"A bit more resilient than you think," said Mlilo and snatched back the now deformed quill.

"At least tell me what I'm dealing with in here. Are we inside the earth, or what?"

"As I said, we are everywhere. We didn't step into somewhere else. We stepped into a place that is everywhere all the time, no matter where you are in the real world; or space for that matter."

"Holy crap. Like Tír nAill."

"If you say so. But this isn't some seven stages of hell, *Danté*. These are African gods. The hero doesn't always survive. Forget heaven and hell. We've got no time for the devil here. Here, in this land, on this rock, we've got so many aspects of evil that one being doesn't suffice to hold its might; it's true strength. Maybe in your western worlds where everything is black and white, where you can afford one evil being to hurl your hatred at; one place that is good and one that is bad. This is Africa, baby. Here the good can be both bad and good at the same time. You have to figure it out. Play their game. Rules were made because of us, not before us. We have no rules. And it's not always a happy ending. You don't just complete five simple tasks and go home. We might not get out of this alive. Getting in is easy; there are many ways to get here. One way is to use the gateways available. But there are two things to keep in mind here: time and space."

"Physics? Greek for knowledge of nature."

"What do you know about it in the real world?"

"I've watched enough science fiction and read enough comics to know gravity and time are a thing."

"Good. Here, time acts like it would in the real world the 'deeper' we go," he air quoted with his fingers, "although here it's to the extreme. Keep in mind what you know about physics but also forget real world physics. You know how an astronaut, floating in the space station at a high orbital speed around the earth, experiences time slower than those on the planet?

"Right," Dan said, unconvinced.

"Simply, the astronaut ages slower than the people on Earth. But more importantly, when he returns to Earth, his clock is slightly behind the one on Earth."

"Are you saying that if the astronaut experiences one second of time, the person on the Earth's surface has experienced one minute of time?"

"Yebo. Abaphansi is the one minute while back in Durban is one second. The deeper you go into Abaphansi is the less hold time has on things, and the closer to the source you get; that primal era of the ancestors and the world. Down there, it has run for millennia while you've been messing around with questions. At the same time, just when I think I understand this world, it throws a curveball."

"How long have you gone?"

"Only a day or two. This world tries all that it can to prevent you from going deeper into it. It will grind you to dust before it lets a living person in."

"And yet, here we are."

Mlilo glanced at his friend. "But for how long will they allow it?"

"And the second thing? Space."

"Again, think of us in the middle of the Earth, on a smaller more compact globe. When we walk ten metres here, it's equivalent to a kilometre in the real world. We can travel the world in a day, on foot. Speaking of walking." Mlilo gestured to the ground ahead. "Shall we continue?"

Dan fell in behind him, engrossed in his surroundings.

After a few minutes, Mlilo stopped and picked up two loose quills in the sand. Dan hovered over him, looking around for any more.

"Maybe a third aspect to remember here," Mlilo said, sliding the quills into his belt and patting them. "Don't mind if I keep these ones intact?"

Dan rolled his eyes. "You were saying about a third thing?" as they both resumed walking.

"Information."

"What kind of information?"

"In order to be granted exit from here you have to pass on a message or information to someone in the real world. You don't get given access without there being a purpose for the ancestors who dwell here."

"And if you don't?"

"You remain here. My people understand, a person who has drowned was brought to the ancestor's place, water, but were not able to pass on messages. And so, they died."

"What information and to whom?"

"That's what you have to figure out yourself."

The world around Dan continued to fascinate. A random bushel or rock would catch his attention, as if seeing them for the first time in his life. He would track them as he passed by, half expecting them to morph into something else or disappear like an object in a dreamscape passing into the periphery. He found himself staring intently at the ground a few feet ahead, like any earthen path he could think of in the real world.

The atmosphere on his body was less noticeable now, but his hearing was something that remained a constant sensation.

Movement in the soil three or four strides ahead caused him to slow his pace. Sounds like cracking glass grated through the air, emanating from the soil.

"Mlilo?" he said to his friend in the distance.

"I see it," he replied, standing dead still and looking at the path ahead of himself. "Intulo".

"What?" asked Dan. The sand began to form into a swirl about half a metre wide, as if the earth was liquefying. Dan looked up for a moment at his friend. He could see a similar formation in front of Mlilo.

"The messenger is coming. To both of us."

Placing his hand on his left arm, Dan shifted his wand underneath his coat and took a step to the side, attempting to move around the mass that now pulled down into the ground like a whirlpool. His step was countered by the whirlpool moving the equal space along the path, back directly in front of Dan.

"There's no use avoiding him," said Mlilo. "Just wait. Don't do anything stupid."

A thin stream of dust particles rose like a mini tornado, wavering near the base within the receding hole, but forming a perfect stripe in the air in front of Dan, and Mlilo, fading off around head height.

The crackling in Dan's ears intensified, becoming more like a flat nail-on-chalkboard tone. A popping in his eardrums cleared the dullness that had accompanied him since entering this world, and the sound stopped.

Like a sheet of glass, thin edge facing Dan, pivoting ninety-degrees in place, the line of dust became a flat surface of vivid colour and rough texture. The vertical form of a blue-headed lizard, in two-dimensions, hovered above the swirling hole in the ground. Its rough grey tail extended up into the air, curling slightly at the tip, while the flecked brown, scaly body and cerulean blue head pointed at the ground. A spot of light on the edge of the single black, unblinking eye staring up at Dan, gave the impression of a round orb on an otherwise flat surface.

The head of the being split in a line as the mouth slowly opened to reveal serrated white teeth on pale pink gums.

In a soft but clear whisper like the rustling of dry grass, the figure stated rather than asked: "Fire-bringer, you are here on a quest."

Dan could make out the gist of the isiZulu phrases being spoken to his friend.

"Yebo, Intulo," Mlilo replied to the duplicate being hovering in his path.

Dan looked at the lizard in front of his friend, confused and disoriented, then back at the one in his path.

"You accompany your companion on his quest." Dan snapped his head to the flitting eye he realised was now addressing him, while sizing him up. Though the pupil was a black vertical slit, the iris was a translucent turquoise, like it's skin colouring, but undulating like water.

"Are you asking me or telling me?" Dan's gaze was held by the shimmering eye.

"No question is asked for the answer we already know."

"Okay," Dan replied, unsure of the situation. He realised that the eye's iris, rather than giving way to the background sand and landscape, as you would expect with any stained glass, he caught glimpses of images, scenes, running like a film.

"You do not desire to remain here. Not this time."

Mlilo remained silent.

Dan felt himself drawn closer to the eye, trying to discern the shapes. A flicker of light burst through, and disappeared.

"You will assist your companion. His time for this world is not now. Your journey must also bring atonement for your people. Your threefold death must be endured."

"I don't plan on staying here," said Dan, "or leaving my friend. Or dying three ways for that matter." The eye seemed larger now, filling his vision.

"You are from the other world. You do not belong here." The being's words seemed muffled, like Dan was underwater.

Dan heard Mlilo sigh. "You've said this before, lizard."

"And yet here you are."

"Who are you," asked Dan. A deep blue-black shape began to make sense to Dan. It looked like a person hunched on a chair, a spotlight ahead of them obscurring any detail in their silhouette.

"I call on those who are ready to remain. I call on those who are not. I take from your world. I do not give back."

"Death?" asked Dan. He was no longer in the same world as Mlilo. Dan was using his arms to push himself through the undulating space of light and shape, like he was swimming in thick water. The urge to get to and reach out to the person in the chair became everything. The light was brighter, coming closer. Dan writhed and kicked, voiceless, trying to get closer to the figure. Inch by inch he used every ounce of his energy to move forward, narrowing the space between them. Just as he thought he was progressing, a vortex of energy like a whirlpool began pulling at Dan's thrashing feet and legs. At the moment that the light enveloped everything, his hand touched the person's cool shoulder. He was ripped backward.

Dan gasped for air, shocked to find himself back in the warm light of Abaphansi.

"Dan?" he heard Mlilo say.

"You are granted permission to pass through, to utilize the portals. Nothing more."

"As you said, this time I am on a quest to retrieve what is mine, what is my family's."

"A desire to remain in this world has consequences."

"Not this time, I said," snapped Mlilo.

"I give you guidance."

As if inside his head, Dan heard two voices say, "Don't follow the red-bricked road," followed by childish laughter.

"What the hell," said Mlilo.

The figures of the lizard, and their swirling soil, silently moved past each of the men. Dan turned to follow them. "Whoa. Where'd they go?"

Nothing remained of the soil or the dust to suggest they had been visited.

"He is allowing us through."

The soil had become a course red black, appearing to Mlilo to be more nutrient rich and nourishing for plants and animals. The foliage seemed to reflect this in the taller trees and thick green bushes.

Dan, waving his mobile around, tried to check the GPS map.

"What are you doing?"

"I can't seem to get signal." He gave his device a rough shake. "I keep getting this error message: *Senqaba ukuhlonipha isicelo sakho. Lo mlayezo ubonakala iselelesi, noma labo abazama ukuthola imithombo evinjelwe ngaphandle kokugunyazwa.* Seriously?"

"You're an idiot. There's no signal for that toy here."

"Bra. If you get lost don't come crying to me to connect to Google Maps. Right?"

"You might get lost in your world," Mlilo paused and threw the shinbone and three quills on the soil. "I'm not about to get lost here."

Dan pocketed his device with a sigh and peered over his friend's shoulder. "And?"

Mlilo fingered the black, red and white beads at his chest while considering the bones at his feet. "Something about water. We are headed in the right direction, though."

"Water?" Dan removed a small leather pouch from his coat, pulled open the drawstring and knelt beside Mlilo. He tipped only a few of the contents onto his open palm, taking a moment to feel their warmth from being close to his body. The small, wooden, oval pieces, rune stones, clearly showed the burnt-in symbols on their matt surfaces. Dan closed his eyes, took in a deep breath, then gently let them fall from his hand into the soft dirt with a muffled clatter.

He took a moment then said, "Water, apparently. And that way." He pointed the way they both were facing.

"Helpful," said Mlilo who gathered up his tools and got to his feet. He eyed out the markings his teeth had made on the bone, then considered the bent quill. All qualities that made his reading of the bones unique.

Dan stood up and plopped each wooden piece carefully back in his sack. "I assumed it was my phone earlier, but what the hell is that whistling sound?"

Mlilo eyed his friend suspiciously, and smiled. "Sounds like your ancestors telling you that you're a dick."

"*Helpful*," said Dan.

They both set off again, but this time, side by side.

Dan stopped suddenly in his tracks. After two paces, Mlilo stopped and looked back at his friend, Dan's face screwed up in confusion.

"What's it, mfowethu?"

"What did the blue-headed lizards mean earlier about your desire to be in this world, or whatever?"

"I like it here," Mlilo shrugged his shoulders and continued walking.

"Okay, but," Dan followed on, "it was implied to be more than that."

"Who doesn't like it here," Mlilo gestured to their surroundings.

"But, if everything is trying to kick us the hell outta here, then, as far as I can tell, the only way to remain here is if you were to die."

Dan slowed his pace as he considered Mlilo's lack of response.

"Bru," Dan tried to change the tone as he caught up to his silent companion, "you need to socialise more. Sitting in your hovel doesn't do you any good."

Mlilo grunted his response.

"How about that invite I texted you a while back? A flipping thumbs up from you and then nothing. I didn't see you at my jol at my place.

No response came from Mlilo.

"You just need to get out more." Dan looked around. "And I don't mean out here."

"Don't you get it?" Mlilo confronted a startled Dan. "It's getting out that doesn't work for me. Small talk. At the end of an evening, I feel drained. You seem to soak it all up and go for hours more. It's a bloody chore for me."

"Then hang with those who don't drain you. One on one, for god sake, rather than nothing."

"I've become sullen and antisocial. Who wants to be around that," he sighed.

"I like sullen and antisocial."

"Rather than the product of some crazed scientist, I feel like life's made me the monster hiding in the forests and shadows. I like being self-sufficient."

"Self-sufficience only gets you so far."

"Someone once wrote, 'There is peace in being a stranger.'"

Dan thought for a moment, then said, "There is no life in one either. And didn't they also say, 'Let us go and be part of the living'?"

Mlilo waved a dismissive hand and stormed off, leaving a bewildered Dan watching his back.

They had been walking for a while when Dan began sighing. "I need a break. I'm tired."

"You don't get tired in Abaphansi." Mlilo remarked flatly without breaking stride.

"Ok, then I need water or some food."

"No hunger or thirst in Abaphansi."

"For f-fine!" Dan stifled the other word.

"Are you sure we're supposed to be here? Isn't there another way to get your bones back?"

"If we hesitate, they'll be gone. So, no. No other way."

"Then, how about giving me some idea of what the objects in your amathambo are. Why would they have been taken?"

"I've been racking my brain about that one," Mlilo slowed his pace. "Remove or lose one, and you can chalk it up to the ancestors having a hand in it. After all, they are the ones that lead me to them in the first place. They select what they know will aid me. But to remove the whole lot in one foul stench by this porcupine beast? That's significant. And while each one is special, there are only a handful which mean something."

"Such as?"

"Take the two actual bones in there, for instance. One of my distant relatives was attacked by a hyena that came into her kraal and took her by her head, while she slept in her rondavel one night. Even with her jaw crushed, through pure will to survive, she managed to fend the scavenger off as it tried to drag her to its den, but not before inflicting a major wound on it. One of the bones is part of her jawbone. The other is the fragment from the hyena's breast bone."

"Holy crap. A hyena, hey?"

"Yep. Pretty hard core."

"Did she die from her wounds?"

"Apparently not."

"What?"

"Yebo, mfowethu. She became isangoma and lived into her nineties."

Dan sized him up. "Who would've thought you had those genes running through you, bru."

A minute passed, then Dan asked, "Bru, how come you never ask me about my bag of tricks? Or my wand?"

"Because I know about your bag of tricks. Everyone knows about your bag of tricks. It's been plastered across pop culture for the past hundred years."

Dan feigned shock. "It doesn't mean everyone knows everything about it. There's lots of bullshit out there."

"Don't care." Mlilo placed his hand above his head. "Up to here with your 'bag of goodies' and magic wands."

"Well, I don't give a shit about yours then."

"Don't be a child. And I don't care that you don't care. But you do, otherwise you wouldn't ask." He took a deep breath. "And the reason I don't care if you or anyone else cares or not, is because we've been able to fly under the radar for the past few centuries based on the assumption that we practice hocus-pocus, vodou, superstition crap. This has allowed us to successfully dodge the burnings at the stake by that other superstition your people brought here like the flipping plague."

"*My People* didn't bring that shit here. *My people* only got here fifty years ago."

"Pfft. You know what I mean."

"And anyway, runes are an ancient art form. You perform a Runemal, and you listen to what they say."

"Ancient? They date to the first century BC. That's younger than the Bible! Whatever you do, please don't go throwing your tarot cards around like you're Gambit, mon amie."

"Tarot and runes, the practice of sortilege, are used for seeing, not as a weapon. Besides, Gambit used *Tally-Ho Circle Backs*." Dan shook his head, bringing himself back on point and felt for the lump in one of his cowl pockets. "Don't knock my Petit Etteilla cards, bru. Some say they originated in ancient Egypt."

"'Some say'? Some say the earth is six thousand years old. And you just admitted they originated in Africa."

Mlilo felt the energy in his friend change, Dan slowing his pace. Mlilo stopped and turned to Dan. "I'm not trying to knock your abilities or where they come from."

Dan screwed up his face and folded his arms. "We all access the other side in different ways, Mlilo. We all access magic in different ways. It's the same but different."

"But your ancestors, your Amadlozi, are there helping you whether you ask for it or engage with them or not. uMuthi, spells, incantations, it's all methods to get us where or what we need."

"Cast a spell? You couldn't even cast aspersions."

Mlilo rolled his eyes.

"The power you put onto any object," Mlilo held up the bone in his hand, "like a shinbone, is what counts. With the backing of your Amadlozi you can create the means to hold the true power of the other side. You're infusing your cardboard with your own soul's power. If you could only realise that your ancestors are there waiting for you to acknowledge them and those that came before you, you'd harness the full potential of the other side."

Dan's pale face went bright pink as he whipped out the stark white piece of wood from his sleeve, pointing it at Mlilo. "That's what my wand is for, arsehole."

Mlilo held both palms up in surprise, then said calmly, "This is my point exactly: you think you need that thing to harness anything."

"If I didn't it would be all over the place. This allows me to focus the energy pulsing through me into a single controlled beam."

"Controlled," Mlilo waved his hands in exasperation. "Harnessing isn't the same as controlling." With his hands at chest height, Mlilo concentrated on his upturned palms. A soft red glow began to emanate from the surface, growing steadily over his entire palms and fingers, wrapping slickly around the backs and coming to a stop at the copper bangles and goatskin isiphandla at both wrists. He looked up at his friend and grinned. "Gives me chills every time."

Keeping his eye on Mlilo's hands, Dan returned his wand to his sleeve and stood in wonder for a moment.

"Harness," whispered Mlilo and the glow began to generate a stream of heat, distorting the air around it as it shimmered upwards. Flickers of orange light pulsed and dimmed. In seconds, the air above Mlilo's hands wavered and misted, reaching inches higher than his head.

"How about," Dan raised his voice above the crackling sound, "instead of measuring dicks, we actually talk strategy and skills for when we are finally face to face with the Spiky One."

CHAPTER 3

"Goddamnit."

"What?"

"The trail's headed east." Mlilo stood from his crouch position and looked right toward the darkened horizon.

Dan looked back over his shoulder, the ever-present sunset glow hung in the western sky. "So?"

"It means she's crossed the great river."

"Then we cross the river." Dan carried on walking ahead.

Mlilo followed behind his lithe friend. He watched him, how he carried himself, surefooted on the uneven ground. Light on his feet. His square, sharp shoulders protruded from beneath the folded hood draped partway down his back. His soft coat moved in unison with his body, fluid and flowing. He wondered how his friend would match up when the time came.

"It's not a simple river crossing," said Mlilo. "You need to know some things before we get there."

"We've been walking for hours now; you can fill me in as we go. But a river is not going to stop us from getting this porcupine what-what."

"Crossing a river is one thing, but it's the personification of the river, Mamlambo, and the boatman whom we need to concern ourselves with first. There'll be no friendly hippos to waddle us across."

They came over a gentle rise and the audible surprise of Dan catching his breath told Mlilo where they were.

He stopped alongside his companion to take in the view of the hillside dotted with more than a dozen low, oblong mounds of stones, and sweeping gently down into a green stretch of thick foliage in the distance.

"What would graves be doing in this world?"

"The graves of Haiseb," said Mlilo beginning the decent and heading to the nearest formation.

18

The foot high grass became dotted with rocks and gravel, disappearing on either side of the slope, making Mlilo's steps more cautious.

He stopped and said, "Not his actual graves."

"Cairns?" asked Dan.

Mlilo nodded and bent down to select a small stone between the grass. He tilted his head to Dan who did the same.

"We'll need as much help on this journey as we can get."

One after the other, both men gently placed their stones on the mound, silent in their respect of the rite, and paused for a moment.

Mlilo was first to break the silence, pointing ahead. "Through the mangroves."

"What else do I need to know?"

Mlilo took a moment to consider the question.

"Mamlambo may look like an old hag, but she's no fool. Her eyes seem to be mere slits on her lined face. But they are slit from filtering out all the bullshit she's seen in the world. She'll look at you. She'll look right through you," he turned to point at Dan." All this." He gestured up and down. "She'll filter out all the crap the world sees of you and look into what is really there."

"Hey, this," he flicked his coat collar, "takes no effort at all. She won't need to filter anything. I'm a flawless diamond."

Mlilo winced. "mFowethu, please let me do the talking when we get there."

The smell of salty air breezed passed them as they neared the thicket of trees a few hundred metres ahead, Dan's voice a low mumbling behind Mlilo. "Do I look like I know how to wield a sword? I know ceremonies and incantations. I know how to read bones and where to go next and how to do what needs doing. I'm a man of the new millennium, not some violent right wing nut job waving a gun around. I'm a lefty. Give me a flower and I'll stick it in that man's machine-gun barrel but I've never fired a weapon or sliced a melon with a blade. The only thing I know how to cock is my-"

"Jesus! We get it. You're a naff. Now, can you keep your voice down."

The open rocky clearing had levelled off with pockets of thick grass now bunched on the pale, cracked ground, losing its previous dark colouring.

"If I can't use my mouth to get out of any situation then I resort to my other skills," he clicked his tongue.

"It's your mouth that gets you into the situations in the first place."

Within fifty metres the grass became taller and more difficult to navigate, the two men parted it as they walked to avoid tripping over unseen obstacles below. They could feel the ground softening as they penetrated a section of tall reeds and dead branches and entered the quiet, humid mangrove forest. They took a moment to adjust to the dim light, barely bright enough to illuminate the muddy trail. Despite the light, the leaves of the trees above were bright green, dotted with the odd yellow leaf here and there. Mlilo kept his eyes fixed on the floor ahead, noticing the pocked holes below the tree trunks. The ground began to soften and moisten. Scuttling sounds, pronounced in the muffled forest, missed movements in their peripheral vision, caused them to startle and slow their pace.

Over his friend's shoulder, Dan could make out a clearing ahead as the floor sloped gently down. The roots of the trees became more and more exposed.

As they made out the water's edge just beyond the opening trees, they saw what looked like an expansive fallen tree a few metres across, lying on the shoreline.

Mlilo raised a hand and they both came to a stop. He took two paces and tilted his head to see more clearly. Dan did the same, and noticed a figure sitting on top of the tree, back to them.

They both stepped quietly towards the bank of the estuary, not quite ready to leave the seclusion of the trees, and stopped.

They surveyed the area.

The dull green-brown water barely moved. The figure seemed to be a woman; long matted hair falling down her exposed back, arms outstretched reclining on the massive mangled tree. The trunk was almost horizontal with the bank, at least five metres across and the side, where the woman remained motionless, a metre from the ground. Like a giant twisted body, a trunk of muscle and bones contorted, while the gnarled and disjointed roots dug at all angles into the mud and briny water on the one end. Almost impossibly elevated inches above the water. The branches and leaves at the opposite end grew out and up.

A giant kingfisher, sitting alongside the woman, twitched its head, leering at the reflective waters below. The two men now became aware of the variety of birds all along the length of the wooden structure: there were two giant kingfishers on either side of the woman, with white speckled black upper parts, and rust-coloured underbelly, their large shaggy crest and black bill giving a regal air to them. Among the roots, closer to the water, the dagger-like bill and head of an African darter peered skyward. Its extended inky black, damp and dripping wings limply extended while its webbed feet held it steadily in place. At that moment it gave off a slow *chack-chack-chack* warning to its mate, only the neck protruding as it silently slithered through the water below, then disappeared from sight with only a small ripple on the surface.

Mlilo indicated to Dan with a nod of his head and they emerged from the trees. The short stretch of muddy bank sloped off into the brackish water. Mlilo tracked the path of the estuary, disappearing around the bends to left and right. The far bank, nearly five metres away, was a wall of bright green leaves.

"Hardly '*the great river*'," whispered Dan and picked up a pale object from the soil. "It seems muddy but simple enough to cross." He pressed hard on the cone-shaped spiral shell, bits breaking off the thin opening walls.

Mlilo shot his friend a look while Dan continued to handle the object, unaware of the glances.

The figure on the tree turned her head and, in a fluid motion, her legs and body to face them. She gently placed her hands, one over the other, face up in her lap.

Her face, although at first glance seemed smooth, had drying clay, the same tone as the mudbank, smeared over her forehead, her hooded eyelids, nose, cheeks, lips and chin. Deep cracks appeared on her brow and cheeks as soon as she smiled at the staring men. The ends of her thick black hair were clotted with dried mud clumps. And from where they stood, her skin at the neck seemed to have a condition - the pigment lacking - pink and milky-white patches scattered down to her shoulders and right arm. One area spread from below her square jawline around her lean neck and back over her left shoulder, sweeping around under her left breast, over her belly, and disappearing around her right hip, reappearing between her legs on her right leg and finally disappearing beneath the mud caking her knee and shin.

Leather cloth covered her waist and one thigh, with another emerging from under her hair and over one shoulder, covering her breasts. Even though they couldn't clearly make out her eyes, they knew she was locked on them.

"Did she pass by this way?" Mlilo called out, breaking the deathly silence, and tension.

"She?" asked Dan. "We are tracking a woman?"

"This world isn't some European fantasy of delicate fairies and sprites with a smattering of weathered and wiry old crones." He turned to the crone. "No offense".

The fingers of her topmost hand twitched towards her.

Without hesitation both men stepped a few paces closer.

Now they could clearly see the details on the woman's body. Her 'clothing' was textured like crocodile or snakeskin but the next detail had both men wide-eyed. The skins grew from her own, in a seamless morphing, like a reptile shedding. The skin from her knees down, covered with mud, had the shimmer of fish scales.

"Did she pass by this way?" Mlilo repeated, his voice rose through clenched teeth.

The birds on the tree startled and all disappeared into the water.

She raised a bony finger to her lips, "Shh."

At the sound of rustling behind them, the two men turned to see the trees shiver in a breeze, releasing some of their yellowed leaves. Silently they glided to the floor.

A second or two passed and suddenly dots of red appeared in the entrances of the small black holes in the mud below the trees. Masses of flame-coloured crabs darted out and each snatched the leaves before disappearing again.

"Don't play games with me, boy." They turned their attention back to the woman. "I don't answer to you and so your question is invalid."

"Do I address you as Mamlambo?"

"I'm your crone, your guide, your guardian, your old woman. I couldn't care less what men have named me. Your names do not make me.

"As crone, my crown, of wisdom shines, a halo from my head. I am the rivers, the river mother. I am this river of hatred. I am the river of fire. I am the thrashing river of wailing, and your river of woe. And I am the river of unremembering. I am Mamlambo. I am Amokye. As Dôn I am fertile. As a river I run and flow as Danu, goddess of primeval waters, mother of Vritra, Inkanyamba, and Kelpie. I have tamed those river serpents," she paused to stroke the pale patch of skin along her belly. In that moment Mlilo realised the dull pattern of a snakelike creature was slithering as a tattoo in the whiteness of her skin. He knew of the legends of Mamlambo. She reigned in the rivers, stretching from their icy source in the jagged mountains, down to where the waters churned to brine in the salty waves of the sea. The serpent Inkanyamba was a formidable force or foe, feared by so many of Mlilo's people, particularly in areas where using the rivers for both sustenance and ablutions meant daily contact, never mind the raw might of the storms in the highlands of the Drakensberg Mountains. Going back to the nations of the Namalaen, the !Orakhoesib and ǂNūkhoen !Haos, and others now gone, those people who contained and controlled its power for millennia, the rain bull evolved into the Inkanyamba as peoples migrated and clans merged, and ultimately losing control of the serpent. Inkanyamba was loosed in full force, snaking up and down the rivers, lurking in the deep, dark pools of the mountains and lakes of the lowlands.

Summer would bring further terror down on the countryside. In the form of the tornado spirit, Inkanyamba would take to the skies, partly to seek out a mate but mostly to spread its wrath and torment for being so long contained, raining down in storms of hail and wind and electricity.

Clashing in their common domains, tales of the rivalry between Mamlambo and Inkanyamba, was spread across the land. Epic battles reverberated through the air and the soil, wreaking destruction in their paths. Craggy mountains toppled, swathes of land shifted down hillsides, villages were buried or vanished forever. Before Mlilo's time, his grandparents would tell of the final battle that shook throughout the land. Most did not believe that the serpent had been tamed. Some hoped. Destruction returned but nothing like before.

"I am Coventina, for these waters," she stretched out her arms, "emerge from the eternal spring, my well at the source of everything.

"I am here. I've always been here. Since this place was created, I have been here. No matter your gods. No matter your trinkets. No matter your disbelief in me, I am here.

"I was created with the world. There was the creator, now far out of reach. They made themselves, consciously. Then they created the mother. Through her they seeded their worlds, their beings, their animals, their plants and their waters. Air was breathed.

"They the singular. Vast, but one. None but the mother has ever seen them. None but the mother has suffered in seeing them. None should and none shall.

"We were all birthed from mothers. Our world was birthed from a mother. And those mothers are powerful, regal and most importantly," she glanced down at the men, "can kick the excrement out of your bowels." Mamlambo noticed a drop of blood running down her forearm, and with the tip of her finger, wiped it up into a wad of mud and mingled the redness into the mass.

"Christ," said Dan under his breath.

Mlilo took a moment and a breath. "We need to cross your river," he said evenly.

She gave him a steely look. "You do not belong in this world. Not yet."

"I was guided here. I am after what is mine, what has been taken from me." The memory welled up in Mlilo.

"You tell me what I know! Your Amadlozi and the seer have informed, asked and are waiting. And they said you should bring your friend."

Her head moved almost imperceptibly towards Dan, looking him over. He felt her gaze return to his friend.

"The seer told he would be important on your journey. Reasons, the three did not divulge. And here you are. You may not like it that you require another, but for this you do. Even if he dies, he will have served-"

"Hang on a second," Dan raised a hand. "Even if I die?"

"Do not," the woman's voice simultaneously hit a screech and a rumble, pulsing through their bodies, "let my appearance deceive you." Their vision became shimmered and dizzying as an icy wind hit them. Their bodies continued to feel her rage through their core, and in an instant Mamlambo's face seemed to fill their field of vision. Her eyes wide, no longer hidden under hooded lids, shimmered like tiger's eye gemstones. Their yellow-brown and silky lustre sliced down the middle by a striking black pupil. "We beings who dwell here are ancient beings. We are simultaneously gods and monsters. I tempt humans into my waters and draw them in to be eaten and destroyed and yet here I am," everything suddenly quietened, "welcoming, guiding, advising, and warning you both. We are neither one nor the other. There is no good god here, or evil god there. With our golden light we can incinerate and heal."

23

Shaking their disoriented heads after the stunning display, they looked around at the undisturbed tranquility of the mangroves.

"Respect," she sneered.

In seconds, the water level of the estuary receded, exposing more of the sodden mud bank and roots of her tree. The moist soil erupted in popping, prickling sounds as hundreds of small crabs emerged from hidden burrows, scattering along the bank. Fiddler crabs. In unison, they immediately came to a halt and began a rhythmic swaying of their single large pincer, creating a mesmerising fluid-like wave.

"That's pretty cool," Dan rubbed his eyes.

"That's a threat," murmured Mlilo. "And those are tokoloshe."

A scuttling noise at their backs caused them both to swivel around, guarded. The forest floor was covered with flame-red mangrove crabs standing perfectly still outside their holes, facing them. "Remember I posted about the tokoloshe and you druid-splained that they sounded like-"

"Korrigan," Dan's eye widened.

"Whether they are Zulu gods, Druidic gods, or water sprites with Santa Claus hats; everything here wants us gone."

"Noted," says Dan, lowering his hand from his wand beneath his coat sleeve. He looked at the shell in his other fist and tossed it as hard as he could at the mass of crabs. It bounced and disappeared from sight.

They turned their attention back to Mamlambo, seated in the same position on her massive trunk, as she raised her voice, echoing out over their heads:

Kunengxabano.

Umhlobo uhlangana nomunye. Abahlobo bayaxabana. Nabaphansi bona bayaxabana.

Abahlobo ababili bahlangana nomunye. Bese badelana bonke, omunye nomunye ahambe ngokwakhe.

Ukuhamba wedwa ngukubona.

Omunye unikezwa umhwebo olingayo.

Uwela wedwa ukufika phesheya, omunye nomunye ngokwakhe.

Abahlobo ababili bahamba bayofuna umhlobo wabo.

Abahlobo abathathu baphuma kude babonke, kube ukuthi babe munye.

Bangene babonke empini.

She paused, then spoke to the two stunned friends. "Each branch has a unique requirement. To cross this river, you must pay the river with something you value." She held out her hand. "If you cannot pay-" She lifted both arms skyward. The birds, hidden under the water until now, burst out and up in a spray of water. The scuttling fiddler crabs barely made it back into the moist soil as the water engulfed the bank. The sky, from edge to edge, lost its deep blue and red coloring as it lightened; the stars disappearing in the midday brightness. The surrounding trees and opposite banks were wrenched below the surface, submerged in the rush of sound like a thousand waterfalls. Air and spray pushed against everything as the horizon opened up, expanding outwards for as far as the eye could see. They were no longer in a claustrophobic mangrove but at the banks of a mighty river.

With the sounds and mayhem subsiding, and the sky gradually returning to its evening hues, they realised Mamblambo no longer sat atop the tree. In the process of flattening into a platform, the branches and roots were expanding outward and upward. And, almost in the same place she was before, the woman was instead seated on the back of a black and white mottled Nguni cow, at least half a ton in weight. Taken aback, they noticed on their bank of the river, as far as the eye could see, were cattle grazing and drinking; the river's edge butting against grassland.

"–you shall remain, as these souls do, not knowing the path to take and so trapped for eternity on the shores of my river, unable to pay for passage. Or, like most," she pointed to the southern horizon, "move on into the shadow realm beyond to fulfil the soul journey to Source."

Her massive tree continued to grow, reaching up, entwining with reeds and other shoots from the waters below. Like an outward explosion, it stretched and contorted in opposite directions, its branches and roots took the form of two structures on opposite sides of Mamblambo.

"It has been an age," said Mamlambo, stroking the thick neck of the horned cow. Statuesque, with a shiny coat, it turned its head to look at the two men. Mamlambo gestured with the flick of her finger for them to approach, and held out her left palm.

Mlilo took a breath and stepped forward, descending lower down the bank with the woman towering over him. The platform, just below his knees, didn't budge as he stepped up, over the shallow water's edge, and calmly approached the cow. He thumbed the now dry shinbone already in his grasp and raised it up, having to stretch to reach Mamlambo's hand.

Her eyes closed as her gnarled fingers enveloped the pale bone. After a moment, she opened her palm up again but the bone was no longer there. She opened her eyes directly at Dan. Mlilo took a step back and gestured for his friend to do the same.

Startled out of his stupor, Dan fumbled in his coat pocket and removed his small bag of runes. Taking a moment to close his eyes and breathe, he dipped a forefinger and thumb inside and withdrew a wooden rune. 'R' "*Raido*," whispered Dan. "Journey."

He returned his bag to his coat and stepped up onto the platform while reciting in a low whisper, "I will to will thy will", and passed the piece to Mamlambo. She repeated her earlier motions; Dan watched reluctantly as his rune stone disappeared.

The two men jumped back when the cow suddenly shook its head and snorted. With a loud boom it stamped a foreleg on the platform, turned and strode off down the wooden structure towards the river ahead. Mamlambo remained seated sideways on the massive beast, gently swaying as it ambled along what they realised was a long jetty.

Mlilo and Dan followed at a distance, taking in the still-growing structure above; both ends had joined hundreds of feet in the air, creating a teardrop shaped space between where they walked. The crevices and holes were like windows and large doorways to obscured spaces within. Fifty feet above, a small flock of white egrets swooped around a wayward branch winding through the air, and alighted on the edge of a nook. Just as suddenly, they started and flew off.

Cathedral-like, it could house thousands of creatures.

The cow came to a stop, standing steadfast near the far-right side of the platform. Another boom rang out with its hoof hitting the wood, and in seconds the water below the platform erupted with thick green reeds rising rapidly from the shallows.

Mlilo and Dan watched from a distance as a long form began to take shape parallel to the jetty. The waters foamed and splashed with the movement of the foliage.

Moments passed and the base of a boat took form; the reeds tightened and wove up, creating walls and railings. Both ends, forming a bow and stern, narrowed and coned to curved points double the height of a person.

The chaos in the water was momentarily disturbed by a command from Mamlambo, out over the river, "ǂXãib !na khãi re, Haisetse!"

The movement around the boat began to subside, just as the river, a few metres from where the two men stood rigid with anticipation, exploded in a spray.

A dark figure landed lightly with a slosh on the jetty, river water streaming from his patchy hair, beard and clothing.

"Hõxa-e! Hamti kx'ontsẽbe hã, Tarase?" The figure addressed Mamlambo, with a nod to his right.

Quickly turning his head to the two stunned men, who couldn't fathom the image before them.

The left side of his body facing them had a tattered and black muddied coat; its edges at his knees uneven and torn. A wide foot with knobby toes and yellowed nails held him in place; and what looked like leather starting at his ankles, clung damply to his leg forming pants and seamlessly covering his waist and belly, parting at a low 'V' at his chest. But where the oddity of the being became apparent was that his entire right side was missing. A ragged edge, beginning at the top of his head, ran down his forehead, nose, lips, chin, over his abdomen and ending at his groin.

His dirty grin a sneer as he shuffled wetly to face the two men fully. To Dan, the movement appeared to catch a shaft of light, and for an instant he saw the figure's invisible half shimmer in and out of sight.

"What the -" Dan said, wide-eyed.

"Courtesy of our Namalaen and Hailom brothers and sisters," whispered Mlilo. "One half of his body is in this world, the other in the real world."

Haiseb was a master trickster, a deity with dual personas. His origins murky, the ancients called him Haitsi Aibeb and the earliest evidence, found in Namalaen mythology, had seeped into all local beliefs from the Xhosa to the Zulu. His more pleasant persona is also known as Qamata. Depending on which side of the coin you flipped, he was both a saviour and a devil, affecting those living in the lands he roamed like a scavenger. By no means was the partly visible man-eater at a disadvantage, agile like a springbok and quite capable of leaping metres into the air when in pursuit of his victim. Humans. Those caught in his slippery, yet iron grip were dragged into his domain, the underworld.

"Your transport," Mamlambo gestured with the sweep of an arm. "And your boatman." Haiseb promptly turned and bowed flamboyantly to the woman. "A hāts hē khoekhara mũ!namāsi."

"A a!"He nodded and turned back to the two men, arm behind his back, legs what would have been set in a wide stance but gave an unnaturally suspended body in space.

The cow snorted and turned, in a wide arc back towards the shore.

Mamblambo pointed to the sky in the far distance, "The seer will watch over your journey, your guardian of sorts." Haiseb grunted at this. "And meet you on the other side." It took a moment to realise the grey cloud undulating kilometers away from them was a murmuration of birds, too distant to identify.

"Ĩsa !ũ, dao!ũsikx'aosab," she waved over her shoulder.

CHAPTER 4

"Follow my lead. His job is to question us. Whatever I answer, you answer for you. He doesn't ask twice."

"Last time I checked I don't speak !Orakobab, or ǀXam, or the Khoekhoegowab languages, bru."

"I'll give you cues."

The ragged man remained where he was, staring at them. He turned to look at the vessel floating alongside him.

He looked back at the men. "ǀĀmas?"

Mlilo nodded to Dan. "Mhm." Turning back to Haiseb he said, "The name of the boat is *The Evening Reed Boat*." He looked at Dan.

"Uh, The Evening Reed Boat?" he said tentatively.

Haiseb grunted his irritation and swung around towards the boat.

"What did I say?"

"Nothing," whispered Mlilo. "We have to watch this one. He wants us to slip up."

What they assumed would have been his right leg, Haiseb looked as if he had stepped onto the side of the boat and paused, leaning on no visible knee to observe the deck below, without affecting the delicate balance of the vessel on the water. Seemingly satisfied he stood and brought his visible leg over into the boat, causing it to rock and splatter as he made his way to the bow.

Mlilo tapped Dan on his shoulder and indicated to proceed. After a wobbly and awkward boarding, they both stood opposite each other, holding the railing and with all eyes on the poking and prodding man fussing about the boat.

Haiseb gripped the railing on the side that Dan stood with both hands, twisting and testing the woven reed-work; he edged closer to Dan, half a metre at a time until he was within reach of the startled druid. Dan could hear the give of the reeds under the strain of Haiseb's wiry hands; he got a glimpse of the true power within them and the force needed to squeeze, to any degree, the taut materials making up the same railing he felt rock hard in his grip.

"Hē !arib," Haiseb whispered, almost inaudible alongside the lapping waters, "Taeb ka?"

"This is The River of Hatred," said Mlilo, raising his voice to get the figure's attention, but rather causing Haiseb to slide up to Dan with his wide grin oozing a liquid stench.

"The R-River Hatred," repeated Dan taking a step back but not losing his grip.

The figure thrust his left arm out over the river, hand wide, palm down. In a second, a dark wooden pole grew straight up, bumping his hand as it grew a metre above their heads. He grabbed at the stem just as it began to slow its rise from the water; submerged at the bottom. He gave the pole a quick twist and pull, snapping it off somewhere below the surface with a muffled crack.

"Hamlxī?" He flipped the pole out the water and into his invisible palm, testing the weight between both hands.

"We travel to the Field of Rushes," replied Mlilo, eyes fixed on the pole and what it might do.

In a swift motion, Haiseb slammed the one end of the pole down centimeters from Dan's feet; the entire boat vibrated with the force.

"Field. Of. Rushes." Dan repeated forcefully. His eyes narrowed as he considered the other man's body language, and fixed on the other man's visible eye. Malice dripped from the being before him, like the water falling from Haiseb's coat and chin.

Flicking the pole up, missing Dan's face by a hair, he manoeuvered around as it arced back and up over his head. The air whistled as he caught it fluidly with one hand and effortlessly put it into a spin, first in front and then just above his head; finally coming to an abrupt stop under his unseen right arm. He stepped into the middle of the vessel and faced front.

Dan looked to Mlilo with a shrug.

Mlilo raised a hand for Dan to be patient.

Haiseb looked to his left, in the direction the water was flowing from, and took a deep breath.

"Ti dīb. Taeb ka?"

"We shall not touch what you oversee, your duty to Mamlambo," said Mlilo.

Dan repeated Mlilo's line.

"Ti dīb?" Haiseb repeated with more force.

Mlilo thought for a second, then replied, "The river. Your duty is the river."

Dan looked around at the smooth beige liquid surrounding the boat. "The river," he said.

Haiseb faced front once again and the pole passed from being suspended by nothing on his right into his left hand and slammed it into the deck with another boom.

"Hē laib. Taeb ka?"

"Water. Ngamacam–" Mlilo stopped himself. "I mean, ǀAmma ke a," Mlilo turned and deliberately enunciated for Dan.

Dan's eyes widened and then he attempted the sounds, "Kammageia."

Both men jerked backwards as the boat began moving along the water.

"This feels like hours, Mlilo." Dan slouched over and rested his elbows on his knees, idly rotating the torc bracelet clamped around his right wrist. "How much longer, bru?" He squeezed the two open ends of the brass design to almost touching distance. A faint blue spark arced in the space between.

"Still a way. Relax."

Dan's eyes narrowed as he focused on the ever-damp and dripping figure at the bow of the boat. Apart from the occasional movement of the staff in the water, Haiseb was firmly planted on the wooden deck. His matted clothing and hair gave no indication of drying since they departed.

"Who the hell are you?" asked Dan.

A slight movement of Haiseb's head showed he had heard Dan's question. He glanced over his shoulder at the two men.

"Must you provoke?" Fumed Mlilo at Dan, who only shrugged.

Turning back to river, Haiseb continued in his own tongue, "Tire tje lāmakxʼaosab—"

Mlilo translated:

I am the boatman. I travel the waters of fire, and hatred, where the traitors' screams drown out the rush of the rising waters, and your heartache will make you want to forget.

"Vague much?" whispered Dan to Mlilo. "What does he mean by 'Rising waters'?"

Mlilo pointed to their left. "Imagine that is north. The water comes from the underground. It flows up in Abaphansi."

"Like a fountain?"

Mlilo thought about that term. "More like a reverse waterfall."

"A water-rise," said Dan with a smirk.

"It rises up from the source and," Mlilo turned and pointed 'south', "back down again."

"There's a source?"

"Sores tje," said Haiseb.

"The Sun?" Mlilo looked at Dan. "Its source is *the* Source. Imagine Abaphansi as a hill with a gentle incline down to the south, going back towards the source, but rising up from the source you are reborn: the further you go into it the deeper and closer you approach the Source. But this has the effect of stripping you of your recognizable self, removing everything that is wrapped around your own source, your soul. By the time a soul reaches the Source they are the Source. They are perfectly matched to become one, once again, as they were before they were born into the real world. And therefore, from that point, a Soul can return, reborn."

"It's an infinite loop?"

"More like a Möbius strip. You saw us enter Abaphansi in a state of sunset. This is the start of the soul's journey. That journey takes it into dusk and the deep blue of the coming night, stars the only light to see by. Midnight is the sheer terror of the absolute blackness of the Shadow Lands where not even the stars guide them or tell them of their journey to come, a darkness so terrifying few made it through or out or back. This is the hardest part for any soul to pass through. The purest of souls knows of no fear and so fears nothing; and is able to pass through. Hope is the first star they see sparkle in the blackness as the sky again turns the blue of dawn, reassuring them of their destiny. The first rays of sunrise hit their readied soul as they begin to feel the connecting light of the Source pull them closer to midday; the zenith of the journey. The white light of midday engulfs them in the Source energy or they pass through into the real world and a new life cycle begins."

Dan turned and looked past the stern of the boat and the ripples on the surface of the water behind them.

"Why not just travel west, towards the sun if that's the Source?"

"You don't chase the sunset to get to the sun, just like you cannot outrun the speed of the spinning Earth; rather, you pass through the darkness to get to the inevitable rising sun. Like Mamlambo's cattle," he thumbed over his shoulder, "traveling west means roaming in a world of a continuous sunset without hope of ever reaching the Source."

"But so too is the journey East." He paused and looked to his right, downriver. "It is south that one must travel, as the soul travels easefully along the natural path of the river, flowing north to south. Again, if you are to follow the real world's compass points."

"And if you travel north, back up there?" Dan pointed to their left.

Mlilo kept his gaze fixed ahead. "You go back in time."

"Back in time?" Dan swivelled his body. "Seriously?"

Mlilo flexed his fingers and clenched his fists tightly. "You can't change the past."

Dan settled back in his place and wiggled a finger in his ear, opening and closing his jaw.

Mlilo frowned at his friend, then looked up at the starry sky. "The birds seem closer than before." Trying to discern against the gloomy background of the inky sky, Mlilo finally said, "They look like pied-crows. White markings on their neck and breasts."

31

With his finger now jammed in his other ear, and with some thought, Dan said, "Crows?" He removed his finger, gave the tip a look and wiped it on his pant leg. "Who the hell is this seer, anyway?"

The dark mass undulated in the sky, no discernible lead animal directing the flow. Mesmerised, they both sat in silence for a time.

Shocked out of their stupor, Haiseb sneered another question at them.

"Who are we?" Mlilo took a moment to consider the context. "I think he wants to know what we can do; our abilities."

"Magic?"

"Not your witty tongue, that's for sure. Tell him what it is you are capable of."

Dan took a deep breath and pulled at the sleeve over his left forearm, revealing the black leather sheath holding the ivory-white wooden wand.

Mlilo saw, only taking the time now to notice, the detail carved into the side of the wood; markings running along a single line two-thirds the length of the wand. The same script almost, but not quite, mirrored on the tattoo on the outside of Dan's same forearm. The ogham script Dan had told him about.

"I am Daniel. God is my judge. Which god?" He looked around. "Which god truly rules?"

He looked back at the wand in its black sheath. "This is Fagus. Though not optimal in the muggy city of Durban, it brings focus and protection to the magic I draw from the Earth, up through my feet placed firmly on its surface and focused out." He stroked the wand all the way down its shaft and stopped for a moment at the tip.

Mlilo smiled and nodded at his friend. "I am fire. Umlilo." He held his hand out cupping the air, a subtle haze began to shimmer around his fingers. "But my true power resides in amathambo ami."

"Ats ǂxōkua. ǀAmmākua," Haiseb emphasized the last word.

"Yes," replied Mlilo and lowered his hand. "My bones *and* ancestors. Amadlozi." "ǀNūgaǂnūsas."

"What is he saying?" asked Dan.

"Something about a hyena."

"ǀNūgan di ǂNūsas!" Haiseb shouted.

Both men jumped to their feet, startled by the force of the word uttered.

"He can't be talking about *the* impisi. uNosithwalangcengce?"

"Ā!" confirmed Haiseb. "ǀNūgan di ǂNūsas."

Stunned, Mlilo slowly sat back down, now deep in thought. Dan followed suit.

"Who is uNosithwalangcengce?"

Haiseb tensed his grip on his staff as the sound of a thousand wings crackled in the sky above. All three shot a glance at the black cloud of birds, now undoubtably closer.

The ferryman turned to face both men.

"*!Ora'aris tama tje a. |Nũgas tama tje a. |Nũgan di ‡Nũsas tje a.*"

"The Queen of the Hyenas," whispered Mlilo.

Haiseb stepped closer and placed the staff directly in front of himself. A low hum resonated through the wood of the deck, reverberating up through their feet and legs. His narrowed eyes flitted between Mlilo and Dan as he murmured.

Mlilo said, "I am you. You are me. Imagine my mind. And you will see."

CHAPTER 5

The smokey mphepho haze of the room shifts imperceptibly. I pause to listen. It was as if a body had moved past one of the openings: the roof opening where the smoke gently drifts upward into the night sky, or the low entrance archway.

I crouch on one knee, on the hard dung-coated floor, and peer through the waist-high opening leading into the night. The moonlight falling through the doorway casts an undisturbed shadow inside. No movement.

The rolled herb in my hand cracks and splutters for my attention. I look at the dimming embers and give it a gentle blow, cupping the warmth with my free hand. The smoke recedes for a second; the orange light brightens. I stop and the smoke returns, heady and fragrant.

I stand and turn away from the entrance. The sensation returns, but my reflexes are too slow.

The sharp pain engulfing my ankle shoots up my tensed body, my fists clench suddenly and the mphepho snuffed out in a solid grip. A rasping growl fills my ears as my leg is yanked; my body pulled down and out through the entrance. All within a split second, I now feel time slowing as I stretch out my arms and grab the braided reeds framing the doorway to the hut

Free myself and drag to a kneeling position inside.

The light from the entrance is blocked out completely as a ragged mass of hair and muscle drags itself awkwardly into the hut.

"This is our umsamo, inja! You are forbidden in our ancestral place!" I sit back, holding my shaking frame up by my weakened arms.

The pale light returns to the room as the creature nears me. The mottled pattern, blacks and dirty yellows, visible on its coarse fur.

A ringing in my ear is followed by a subtle, then all-engulfing muffling of all sound.

I blink my eyes as the shape of the hyena seems to expand. At first it looked like muscles flexing, but now, as she steps forward and raises her forelegs up, her arms and paws more like hands, she is growing in height and width.

I notice how the room has receded into darkness, fading away and revealing the starry night outside. But not the sky I know should be above our village. The polished floor is now soft and a powdered soil. My hands grab uselessly.

"Dog?" The word rumbles out her throat.

I know her name.

"uNosithwalangcengce," I whisper. The creature standing poised before me is no dog, no hyena. The spotted pattern seems more defined, the browns of her coat a more vibrant mustard and the dark patches a solid black. Although her face and snout remain canine-like, her arms are more human, but mammoth in thickness; her squat hind legs bend back at the knees, giving the impression of a beast about to pounce on its cowering prey. Her neck at the throat has a pale dusting of fur with a thicker, ruffled mane starting at her crown, tumbling down the spine and thinning down her back. Her eyes, not the dead, black eyes of a hyena, have a shimmering tiger-eye glint.

A whooshing sound follows the downward movement of the being above me, as she reforms herself into the solid mass of muscle, fur and rage. The last things I see are the wet, white rows of fangs as her jaws envelope my face and head. Sound is dulled. Pain is all I feel.

I'm dragged.

My jawbone crunches and the cool night air hits the rest of my body. I cannot breathe. I cannot cry out in pain.

My skin and clothes are shredded by the rough bark and broken off branches as she wrenches me through the outer stick-fence of the umuzi. Through my terror and the sounds of my now muffled battle, I cannot sense whether anyone in the village has heard the commotion.

But I dare not scream. I cannot cry out, in pain or for aid. This is my fight. No one else need be taken trying to defend me.

If I enter her den, it will be over.

My fingers grab, at earth and bush and fur. I need something. One hand edges into the gaping, heaving maw, weaving between teeth and protruding bloodied bone. My power is failing, but I feel the warmth grow from my palm and wrap around my fingers. Will it be enough? The other hand, dragging helplessly over the rough ground lands the cool, solid shape of a stone, a rock, a weapon.

Whether it is hope or rejuvenated energy, I feel my hands pulse with fire.

The mass dragging me gives a moment of hesitation. That is all I needed.

The jaw is blown open as my hands blaze with light and heat. The stone, a blunt but effective point, slams into her chest, crunching bone. My body thuds to the dusty ground and one breath gives me the strength to get into a crouch.

A moment of disbelief, and she is lunging herself bodily in my direction. I do the same and we collide. My forearm snaps in her jaws, but I land the stone in the tender spot on her breast. And again. This time bone scrapes my knuckles. Out and in again.

Her grip on my arm weakens. I kick. I bite. And through my gnarled and battered jaw I scream. My fire burns.

Her fur is singed. I smell her, now only a few feet away.

We crouch, wheezing and panting. Her golden eyes hold mine in a rage I can feel through the soil.

She steps back and a rumble begins to emanate from inside her thick and bloodied chest.

The rasping roar, hitting me in a wave, causes me to stagger backward, but I hold her in my sight.

A cloud of dust and dirt erupts as she turns and bolts into the shadows.

I slump to my knees and catch my breath. I can feel my limp and shattered jaw hanging from my face. I nestle by broken arm against my chest and bring my other hand up to my face. The shredded hand, caked in blood and sand, holds a bright white bone shard.

For the first time I notice my surroundings. The air is warm, even for what should be a cool evening. The stars above reassure me that I never made it to her den. I turn slightly, pain piercing my neck and head, and take in the sun on the distant horizon.

"Abaphansi."

CHAPTER 6

Mlilo found himself kneeling on the deck of the boat, clutching his arm and panting breathlessly. At the sound of retching, he looked to see Dan dry-heaving over the side, hands gripping the railing.

Mlilo looked at his empty palm, vividly seeing the bone in his mind's eye and for the first time realising the nature of the two bones now lost to him and his family in the underworld:

Her jawbone fragment, a connection to his past, her life and abilities, and his people supporting him both in the real world and the other side; the hyena breast bone; not simply a cool trophy of a wild animal attack, but recognition of what or who she overcame and a small fragment of the power of uNosithwalangcengce in Mlilo's amathambo.

In a state of bewilderment, Mlilo stood to survey the distance ahead. Now, more than ever, he was determined to retrieve his family's bones. But, for the first time since entering Abaphansi, he felt a chill of expectation, knowing who he was truly up against.

A splashing sound brought him back from his thoughts. Dan, gripping the railing, wiped river water with his free hand over his ashen face and neck.

"No," whispered Mlilo.

His friend blinked through the dripping liquid with a frown.

Immediately, they were thrown forward. The boat came to a dead stop in the water and Haiseb leapt at them, staff coming around in a wide, arcing swipe as a rage-filled scream erupted. A hail of flicking, indiscernible shapes and screeches filled the air around them; the pole was stopped inches away from Dan's face by the undulating mass.

The surprise was visible on Haiseb's half-face. He took a moment to restrain himself while the vortexing stream of crows gravitated inward, the shape of a figure gradually emerging.

Dan looked up at the back of a woman, her one hand holding the staff tightly at her waist. Mlilo had fallen backward into his seat and watched, bewildered as the crows had coalesced into the expressionless female before him.

Her pale white face, contrasted against the almost blood-red hair and black robe covering her loosely from shoulder to bare feet placed squarely on the deck.

Haiseb, startled by the sudden shimmering of the woman before him, stepped back and pulled his staff against his torso. As if sliced by two invisible planes, the figure separated into three silhouette-like shapes; microvasculature blood vessels sustaining the forms were visibly red as the thinned shapes separated, for a moment. "I am the three," the shapes merged back into the black woman, "the goddesses of the land; Ériu, Banba and Nemhain."

Dan's eyes widened. "The Morrígan."

She smiled. "You finally recognise us, bard."

Responses like, "What, like a minstrel?" had convinced Dan, for simplicity's sake, to tell people he was a druid instead of a bard. Bard, the first of the three levels to becoming a druid, involved storytelling, poetry and yes, singing. But it was more than that. It was holding the druidic lore in your head to pass down to new initiates. It was learning the words to the rites, and understanding them before you can consider using them for their intended purposes.

You graduated into the next level, that of the ovate. Divining and prophesying were used to give insights to yourself and the world and those around you, allowing healing to take place and facilitating that healing through tinctures and natural medicines.

Once held in the highest place in Celtic societies, druids were equal to those of the rulers. Their wisdom was used to pass judgements, overcome hardships within a community and to be the guide in all aspects of Celtic life. Harnessing all that one learned would culminate in this final stage as the druid emerged.

"We've knocked many times on your window at night, but you just shoo us away. It takes a visit here," she indicated their surroundings, "to open your eyes and see us. The phantom queen, the crow, the seer."

"Pleasantries completed?" Haiseb aimed his sneer at the Morrígan, *"For him to take something from me, he shall have something wrenched from him."*

"Screw you," said Dan sitting back in his seat. Haiseb took a step forward, Dan flinched.

"Enough!"

"I didn't *take* anything from him. What the hell's his problem? And how come he's speaking English with you?"

"Mutual respect, Daniel. Learn it." The Morrígan raised her pale hand to Dan and turned to the boatman. "You shall get what is owed to you for his transgression. That is all."

Haiseb gave a tilt of his head and swiveled around, back to his position at the bow. They felt the boat move once again. Mlilo reached down and picked up a slick, black feather lying on the floor.

"A keepsake from your ancestors."

Mlilo glanced up at the woman, looking blankly back at him. He turned and held it up to the setting sunlight. Focusing his eyes closer he saw the tiny tendrils growing out from the central shaft, like a leaf with blood vessels woven finely together.

Lifting his leopard-print vest up at the waist, he tucked the unusually firm object in his belt, alongside the porcupine quills, and covered them once again.

"Can someone please stop the whistling sound," said Dan, back to wiggling his finger in his ear.

The Morrígan shook her head. "You play with your trinkets. You dabble with your mythology. But do you ever listen, bard?"

"Ha!" remarked Mlilo, and looked from the woman to his friend and back to the woman. "His Amadlozi. Like an abalozi?"

"Precisely." She nodded at him.

"Aba-what?" asked Dan.

"Abalozi hear their ancestors in a whistling."

"I get tinnitus all the time."

"No," said the Morrígan. "You hear your ancestors all the time, but do not listen."

Dan thought about this for a moment. "It's been getting worse since I've been here," he said to Mlilo.

"There's nothing filtering them out. Nothing distracting you from their messages."

"How the hell do I know what they want? I don't exactly know Morse code."

"It's about knowing when they are talking to you," said Mlilo, "thinking about what is going on in that moment, and figuring it out."

"Trusting," said the Morrígan.

Mlilo nodded back at her.

The sound of a word, audible only to Mlilo, pulsed in his head: *Amathambo*.

The memory of the bone in his ancestor's hand, as she lay bloody and broken on the ground, shook up through his spine.

"My family always assumed it was just a regular hyena that had attacked her. A heroic tale nevertheless, but she took even more power from *the* Hyena than we, I, ever imagined." He held up his empty hand remembering the white shard she had held.

"That beast, *uNosithwalangcengce*," the woman spat, "had been ravaging her people for decades. She had had enough. She was about to do something before the fear her people had for the hyena, the very fear the hyena fed off and increased in potency, gave uNosithwalangcengce enough power to obliterate them all. Reverence and worship are not the only things that keep a god alive. Fear is a force like no other."

Mlilo thought for a moment, then said, "Her name was Zandile. Fitting for someone who saved her descendants. The multiplied."

"That bone," began the Morrígan, "has been unused and therefore dormant for the past few lifetimes, until a short while ago when you were directed to it by your ancestor. Zandile." Mlilo looked up at the woman, imagining his ancestor looking back at him. "Your grandparents and parents didn't use it."

"They were not izangoma."

"Not all in a bloodline follow the path," she looked at Dan. "And so, the bone was left alone, never forgotten by uNosithwalangcengce, until it was –"

"Activated, by me," whispered Mlilo.

A moment passed, then the woman said, "For now, we journey onward." Her body shimmered and shattered into a thousand black shards of wings and beaks and feathers. The mass spread out and up, engulfing the back end of the boat, away from Haiseb at the bow, in an undulating cloud of crows obscuring the outside world.

CHAPTER 7

Time was meaningless. Even the glimpses of the unchanging sunset and pale light of the underworld, through gaps in the silent mass of birds, gave Dan less to go on when trying to sense how long they had been traveling. The boat moved steadily; the gentle motion and lapping of the waves became like a heartbeat in the otherwise quiet surroundings. The occasional squawks of a crow, and the subsequent shifting of the mass hanging in midair, were the only signs of the living being protecting them. Ever-present.

Dan was transfixed, mulling over the world he found himself in and this being he knew from his studies, when a voice emanating from the entire flock said, "We are about to make landfall."

Dan and Mlilo both sat upright, watching as the Morrígan rematerialised in the middle of the boat. Keeping herself between the two men and Haiseb, the dark figure was focused on the far horizon. Mlilo stood, holding onto the side of the boat despite its sturdiness in the water, trying to find the Morrígan's focal point in the distance. A faint line the only indication of something between the river and the deep blue-black sky.

Dan cleared his throat and asked, "If you are here, does that mean this," he gestured around them, "*Abaphansi*, is Tír na nÓg?"

Her head turned slightly as she replied, "Tír nAil. Tír na nÓg lies in another direction," her hand gestured to the right, "along with Tír Tairngire, and Tír inna mBan."

Dan looked over the side of the boat and whispered, "And Tír fo Thuinn."

Haiseb shivered at the mention of his watery world below the vessel, then gave a single pound of his staff on the deck.

"Mfowethu," Mlilo scolded Dan.

Feeling self-conscious, Dan stopped alongside his friend, fidgeting hands hidden among the folds of his coat. The Morrígan stood a few feet away, within arm's length of Dan.

41

"Morrígan," asked Dan. "How am I allowed here if, as I understand it, I require an invitation to enter Tír nAil?"

The body of the woman rippled. Dan and Mlilo froze, wide-eyed, as her face pushed through the hair on the back of her head, hands fisted then reopened in the other direction, and her feet shifted to the back, now facing them. Her eyes were fixed on Dan's.

"Firstly, we were never happy about you coming here. But secondly, and alas, your friend brought you through from Tír na mBeo. An invitation, so to speak. You needed your friend with fire here to bring you to this place." She looked from Dan to Mlilo. "There are rules for a reason, you know."

Mlilo shrugged. "I don't subscribe to your rules."

"Rules come from centuries of experience. Mortals must be invited in or use specific talismans to enter, and only in specific entry points. It's you mortals who have caused these to be put in place over time."

"What," asked Dan, "we can't have nice things because some human was an arsehole back in the day?"

"Those are not the words we would use, but yes."

"You gods are the reason us mortals don't invite you into our world."

"I think I see the other side," Dan tried to distract his companion, and stood on tiptoes. "Yep, definitely land ahead."

"Oh but you do," the Morrígan ignored Dan. "Mortals practically beg us every waking moment to come into their world. But if they were actually faced with us, they would run to the hills."

"Or call a nuclear strike," Dan chuckled nervously. He could now make out the natural topography of the riverbanks ahead, stretching up and down for miles in either direction. Everything seemed to morph to the left and right from the lush green area they were heading towards; the deep green reeds flowed down the bank and into the waters that he estimated they would disembark into in fifteen-minutes. The reeds thinned out to the right, dotted with large boulders both on the bank and in the river, almost camouflaging a domed temple structure of similar materials overgrown with greenery and vines a few hundred metres downriver; low red-brown cliffs topped with tall dry grasses spanned at least two kilometres to their left.

"There is a common rule that is said to be the most important in all humanity."

"Love thy neighbour?" offered the Morrígan.

"Close. Don't be an a-hole. But if you look at the world you will see that most don't practice this rule. Why? Because rules are there when it suits the ruler. You say we must come into your world only when invited or given a key, or permission slip or a hall pass," Mlilo took a step towards the Morrígan, "and yet when one of you enters our world, never mind steal from us, me, and return to your world, we,

I, must ask permission first? I think not, crow-women. And when evil creeps into my world, I will do everything in my power to send it back to where it came from. From your world."

The Morrígan smiled at the extended finger pointing accusingly in her direction.

"We are standing before you, not as an obstacle in your path, fire-bringer, but as a protector. Protection as much from yourselves as from the powers you will find yourselves up against. We give you warning. We show you what is to come. We provide aid, when we deem it necessary. We cannot help every puppy in a well. Now," the Morrígan continued scornfully, her body appearing to expand, "either you put down your hand or you point it at your adversary, who we are not."

"Bru," Dan scolded Mlilo with a slap on his shoulder.

Approaching the reed-lined riverbank, Dan was certain he felt the boat shiver. A moment later, a few of the vessel's reed strands had unraveled from their intricate weave, and like mesmerised snakes, they wavered and dipped into the water in unison. Dan felt the vessel slow. Mlilo, meanwhile, had nothing to hold onto. By the time the boat was in knee deep water, the entire outer wall of the boat had unraveled into the river and held the slender deck in place, its closest edge a mere foot above the marshy shore. Haiseb made his way to the rear, indicating to the others to disembark.

The Morrígan was first to step off and wait for the two men to follow.

Dan and Mlilo were relieved to be back on semi-solid ground. The soggy soil absorbed their feet as they took the few paces to a more solid footing alongside the statuesque woman. The riverbank stretched back and up, covered by thick reeds that became a low blackened woodland, as if charred by fire, that disappeared over a rise. In the far distance they could make out a line of hazy hills, the air thick with a pale mist. The two men smiled nervously at one another and turned to acknowledge their ferryman. The last reed stems of the vessel had merged with those covering the shore; Haiseb stepped backward into the water. The exposed deck lowered and vanished into the waters.

Dan pointed his forefinger and middle finger first at his own eyes, then his forefinger at the last ripples made by Haiseb on the water surface. "Keeping my eyes out for you, freaky ferry man."

Winding their way through the thick reeds up the embankment, the two men followed single file behind the woman. Mlilo noticed the reeds thinning out but rather than the thick lush green stems making way for grass or rocks beyond, he passed the black wood protrusions standing at odd angles a few feet apart. And rather than giving way to their passing, they stood firm and unwavering to the extent that they had to shimmy past each object. These were no fire burnt trees.

"Spears," said Mlilo and stopped in his tracks.

"Whoa," said Dan a few paces behind him. "That's cool."

The rise of the embankment was covered in the black, waist high spears, each topped with what looked like chipped and weathered obsidian blades.

Mlilo gripped one between his fist and pulled. Apart from the give of the wooden shaft, it did not budge. He placed another hand further down the wood, bent his knees and attempted to yank with all his strength. Nothing.

"The forest of spears is not a weapon for wielding. You will never dislodge that which was placed here by a god. Even a young god." The Morrígan kept her pace until she reached a small open patch free of the black spikes, turned and waited.

Mlilo took a moment to feel the smooth yet uneven surface of the blade before carrying on through the dark stems.

Dan followed close behind and asked, "Where to now?"

Mlilo looked at the woman, her expressionless face gave no acknowledgement of the question. He took the items from his side and squatted down. Holding the quills and the feather in his hand, remembering handing over the shinbone to Mamlambo at the riverside, he closed his eyes, breathed deeply, and released them to fall on the sand.

Dan approached his friend and pulled out his small sack of runes. Going down onto both knees, he emptied the wooden pieces into his open palm, funnelled them back into the sack and gently upended it again a few centimetres from the ground, spreading out the pieces as he moved.

"You play with your incantations and spells and formulas but you never look further for help," the Morrígan sneered at them. "You never actually ask your gods or your people – your ancestors – for help and guidance. You have access to this extra power, right in front of you, through the veil, that would aid you in being the best version of yourself. But instead, you bash your heads against the same walls. You look at the same paper cards. All they tell you are interesting stories about yesterday, today and tomorrow. Anyone can figure that out."

Mlilo stood, grabbed Dan by the coat and pulled him up. "Steady yourself, mfowethu."

"For–?"

"Anyone can shift the stars," the woman raised a pointed finger to the inky sky.

Lightning fast the Morrígan flicked her wrist and the once static stars blurred across the heavens. Ghostlike images pulsed towards and through the two men reeling at the dizzying sensation.

A snap of her fingers and everything froze around them.

Instead of everything turning back to normal, Mlilo could make out shapes and figures in the dusty shroud surrounding them.

"What the hell is that?" asked Dan with his now recognisable ill demeanour.

The Morrígan, finger raised, moved her hand almost imperceptibly. The frozen images came alive, their murky translucent scenes playing out in real-time like a first-person RPG.

"The porcupine," whispered Mlilo as he made out the spiked form amid the dust of battle.

Another flick of her wrist and the world spun. Dan recoiled as the images set him off balance and he doubled over. He retched and grabbed at the ground, fumbling his runes back into the bag clutched in his other hand. "Can you not –" he attempted before being interrupted by the woman.

"Over the next few days, you will need to find those tools, those weapons, needed to fight for and beside one another. You both have a lot to learn and the lessons are plentiful."

"What's the first lesson?" Mlilo had already replaced his items in his belt.

"Revenge." The Morrígan's form wavered and split into three. Three different faces stared back at the two men, shimmered and rejoined in the centre.

"Yes, I've come for revenge," said Mlilo wide-eyed.

"That's no good," she continued as her face flickered from one aspect to the next, cycling through her selves. "Seeking revenge finds revenge. Using rage to settle a score means rage will be pushed right back at you. Fire against fire builds a bigger fire. A fist against another fist makes two broken hands."

The slender hand pointed at Mlilo's waist. "You used that which your friend brought you to ask where *they* went rather than asking 'what should I do?'. You chased rather than thinking strategically." She brought her hands out, as if presenting an open book, closed her eyes and continued, "You will be defeated in the underworld, by your own rage and anger and revenge.

"You will have to reach over the boundaries of the gods to get help from others. Your gods cannot always help you in this land.

"Later, you will need to do things alone, separately, in order to find your individual paths and skills that will, once again, conjoin in a potent alliance.

"When on your true paths, the fire, ignited from within, will harness the full might of his ancestors; and the bard will become the ovate, on his way to becoming the druid his ancestors know him to be.

"And just when you feel you are alone, others will join you." She opened her eyes and looked around the landscape. "From all worlds. Also, beware the demon hunter," she raised her finger, "for he sees demons in everything. Watch where you walk."

"Must I do nothing then?" asked Mlilo. "I am here now. I will not turn back."

"You must rather learn *how* to do something before rushing into it. You don't leap from a mountaintop before you have learned to fly."

"Tell us how then," Mlilo folded his arms, "if you are so wise."

"That, right there, is the beginning of your first lesson. Attitude. Entitlement.

We are not your teachers. We have better things to do, like guarding these lands from fools trying their luck. We give our warnings. We tell them what we see for them."

A flick of her wrist and her dark shape compressed into her centre, the top of where her head was burst upward in a stream of flapping birds pouring upward and outward into the sky.

"What?!" shouted Dan, "you're not helping us?"

"No," echoed the Morrígan's voice from all directions. "We're here in our capacity as seer."

"But this will be a fight," Mlilo hissed through his clenched jaw, fists tight in irritation, the body of the woman now gone from where she originally stood; the black flecks flitted further and further away.

"We're a war goddess. We handle wars, not mild skirmishes. And as the goddess of the battle, we appear on the battlefield in crow form to feed on the dying and the dead. The injured, in your fracas with the porcupine, will not give us a meal today."

"Let me refer to my trinkets," Mlilo scowled at the sky and picked his amathambo up from the floor.

"The same direction?" asked Dan.

"Yes, we are going to meet the porcupine woman and battle it out, just as the crow lady said. But amathambo ami indicated something more, something sooner. Something about fighting many."

Both men stared at each other, then Dan offered, "Let's get out of this forest of spears and get a look. See if we can see what's coming."

Winding once again through the rigid spikes, after some metres, they finally came to its end, the ground looked like a smooth, paved area stretching up and downriver, but leading away from them in a cartoonish red bricked road disappearing into the hills. Mlilo looked down at the pattern they were now standing on. Uneven oval shapes, like squashed hearts, about two to three centimetres apart and the size of an open palm; deep redness blended from the centre outwards to a bright orange-yellow edge.

"This isn't Oz, bru." Dan reached into his rune pouch and withdrew a random oval piece. The even, burnt zigzag symbol of Eihwaz, without a positive or negative reversed direction, represented defence. He retied his pouch and gripped the rune in his hand left hand, feeling it warm.

"We have to go that way anyway," Mlilo pointed a thumb.

Apart from the occasional tree and bush, the near distance seemed clear of any threats. Dan did a three-sixty around them. "I can't see any problems. And we aren't about to go down that way," he pointed towards the river dipping over the southern horizon.

Unsure of themselves, the two men started walking along the wide road.

They had taken a few paces when Mlilo held a hand out to Dan's shoulder. Both men focused on a subtle movement on the road in the distance. As it neared, they realised it was a low surge of the bricks, a subtle wave pulsing towards them. Almost synchronized, they both placed their feet wide apart and readied for whatever it was that was heading their way.

Within a few second the feeble wave clattered beneath their feet and petered out at the start of the road.

Silence.

Dan, losing his balance on the churning, uneven ground, toppled backwards.

"Damnit," he stopped his fall with a hand and an elbow, feet flailing in the air.

The unstable floor did not allow Dan a quick recovery as he fumbled to get a firm grip on the bricks to steady himself.

"What the hell is going on here?"

"Need a hand?" Mlilo said with a hint of sarcasm.

The red shapes beneath them surged under and away from the men, causing them to stumble into the exposing soil. Trying to figure out what was happening, Mlilo pulled his friend up and alongside himself, keeping their arms interlinked. They found themselves in a low, rough ditch of rich brown soil a few feet around them. What framed the edge of the gnarled earth took both men by surprise.

Red capped, crablike creatures.

"Not you okes again," said Dan.

Now that they were closer to the crabs, they could make out their features. Eyes like crabs, black and protruding from just below the creased red cap, angled to give an expression of anger. The rounded and smooth surface surrounding the eyes and red mouth gave them an almost cherub-like face. Their front pincers, chunky and strong, sat at the ready for anything coming within their grasp. Mlilo could make out eight other legs on each. The four behind the pincers seemed to hold the creatures firmly in place, not as large as the pincers but equally sturdy; the back four, leaner than the others, gave the impression of a stumpy version of a grasshopper leg. They could jump.

The oval red of the mouth split into a jigsaw of tiny shapes moving independently of one another. At first, small bubbles were secreted, soon becoming a froth that quickly turned brown. The sloppy mud substance oozed from their mouths, flowing towards them and into the low ditch.

Movement a few feet inside the gathering caught Mlilo's eye. The creatures in the front line parted to allow one of their own through. It stopped then shivered and convulsed for a moment. Rather than excreting the same mud and slime that the others were continuing to do, a white pointed object, almost like a single fang, grew from the creature's mouth. After half an inch was exposed, it gave a guttural cough, dislodging what was clearly a mollusc shell. The object tumbled down the soggy ditch and came to a stop a few feet from Dan. The broken outer edge of the spiral shell was familiar to both men, remembering when Dan had tossed it at the imposing crowd of crabs earlier before their journey across the river. The sodden earth slowly sucked the pale shell into itself and disappeared.

"Oh shit," whispered Dan.

The mucky vomiting continued and they soon found themselves caked, ankle deep in it. The creature who had extruded the shell hunkered down, signally a stop to the mud processing. In unison, the surrounding creatures flattened themselves in the dirt.

That was when the world erupted in a muddy explosion as the creatures launched themselves at the two men. The hind-legs of each creature sent them flying four to five feet through the air, pincers grabbing hold of all parts of both men. Feeling overcome and exposed, pain seared from Dan's fingertips and scalp as the creatures systematically began pinning both men to the ground. Soon, he found himself face down in the mucus mud grabbing at anything on his head and shoulders.

Mlilo writhed about on his back, kicking and throwing but with each creature removed a new wave bombarded them from all sides. He felt his rage rise, his adrenalin pump.

Dan could barely breathe with his head sideways blowing piles of seeping gunk away from his mouth and nostrils. He was unable to see his friend clearly; Mlilo's head was finally fastened into the dirt by three creatures, pincers on his hair and other legs buried deep into the mud holding onto something unseen beneath.

Quiet descended over the mayhem; both men continued their futile struggle. Two larger crabs climbed onto each of them, one stopping on the side of Dan's head, while the other paused around Mlilo's collarbone.

They froze.

The midsection of each crab split vertically down the middle. A shimmering pink substance, like salt grains in water, glopped out onto their bodies. Rather than trickling down and into the dirt, the pink came alive.

Baby crabs the size of ants spread out over both men.

Dan wailed in the dirt while the mass poured around his ear and down to his eyes and nostrils.

Mlilo stifled a scream, screwing his mouth tightly closed while the babies crested his chin towards his mouth. A pink crescent shape of tiny crabs moved around his mouth and streamed at and into his nostrils. Tears welled in Mlilo's eyes.

A fire and a scream pulsed outward, Mlilo unable to control his pain and rage, blasting Dan and some of the creatures sideways through the dirt. Taking the opportunity of the stunned enemy, Mlilo wrenched his head and shoulders forward, revealing the link upon link of crabs buried deep inside the earth, having anchored both men down.

Dan took a moment to realise his freedom, then jumped to his feet dusting and slapping at his face and head to rid himself of the tiny threat.

Mlilo was at full roar, but now he directed a fireball pulse from each hand, scattering crabs and soil further and further away with each hit. Lumpy blood dribbled and blew from his nostrils, hitting his sneering mouth and spraying outward.

One more blast and Mlilo doubled over on the ground, taking deep breaths and snotting out his nose desperate to rid himself of the baby crabs.

The damp earth surrounding them steamed and crackled from Mlilo's blaze. Carcasses lay strewn around while the remaining crabs scuttled away and under the ground.

Dan was left standing, panting and dumbstruck, with the aftermath; a miniature apocalyptic landscape.

"Holy shit, bru," was all he could muster, and slumped down onto his backside.

"I need to get the hell out of here," Mlilo with halting breath and crawled a few paces, wiping at his face and spitting, then stood and fumbled his way back through the forest of spears. At the top of the bank leading down to the river, he finally sat, his gaze focusing on nothing but the distant horizon.

"What the hell just happened, Mlilo," asked Dan, coming up behind him. He flinched as he bent to sit down beside his friend and looked at the intact rune in his left palm. Dan rubbed his thumb over the black etching. *Defence*, sure. He put it back in his rune pouch.

Mlilo took a few deep breaths, spat, then said, "Everything's trying to fuck us up."

"No shit there. But how about we get some more help rather than bumbling our way through the underworld. I'm pretty sure Amira can–"

"We have to do it now!" Mlilo slammed his fists into the ground beside him. "Before amathambo ami disappear and are lost forever."

"So, you would rather run headlong into this kind of kak without a thought? Without a strategy. Just fok voort?"

"I'm not wasting time. I'm doing what needs doing, now. Not screwing around with Daniel-time."

"What the hell is Daniel-time?"

"Oh, you know," Mlilo gave a sing-song tone to his words, "when Dan feels like it."

"I'll give you a moment to shut the hell up. You've been through an ordeal so you aren't yourself. Neither of us is."

"Whatever."

"While we're nitpicking, at least I'm able to control my magic, focus it rather than blasting everything around it. Including your allies."

"That's just a heat wave. Like an EMP, used to stun. You don't get burned but it gives enough of a kick to get someone, or something, off you. Doesn't it?"

Dan shook his head and lay on his back, hands interlinked behind his head looking up at the starry sky. They remained in silence for a while, staring off into their respective horizons.

Although he would never openly admit as much, Dan had regretted getting involved with Amira almost two years earlier. Their friendship had been close, sharing ideas about magic, rites and rituals, and he had been daft enough to make it something else. That something else became just that, something else. He had quickly realised their true friendship and, when it was too late, tried to backtrack. He was never going to make that mistake again.

Since then, Amira was understandably withdrawn and generally hostile. Understandable for the person who had pushed back in the beginning. She had been the one who had taken the break up the hardest. The wall of his lounge held the scar of the black, palm-sized marking left by her wand's magic. Like a spindly underwater brittle star, it stuck to the paint and plaster, immovable to any scrubbing or painting.

He was very sure of where Amira stood with him, but nevertheless, he trusted her with his life. Maybe she would take pleasure in a slight gaining here and there, but she would have his back, especially when it came to situations like the one he found Mlilo and himself in.

The familiar crackling sound caused Dan to sit bolt upright. Both men jumped to their feet, fixing their eyes on the whirlpool on the surface of the river moving towards them. A few feet from the water's edge, the shape stopped and the glassy form of the lizard shimmered into sight.

"I thought you were allowing us safe passage, Intulo?"

"Passage is all I allowed. Your safety is not my concern."

"It would help us immensely if you didn't send your lackeys to drown us in mud, Intulo."

"If you threaten those of Abaphansi, I cannot aid in any way."

Mlilo looked accusingly at Dan, who shrugged an apology.

"Do you wish for me to deliver some guidance, knowledge, to your past selves?"

"Don't follow the red-bricked road," both men blurted out and laughed.

"Your guidance was offered to your selves."

"Oh shit," Mlilo snapped as they both stopped laughing.

"What a waste," Dan slapped his forehead. "Oblivious idiots."

"You are from the other world. You do not belong here. Not yet."

"You've said this before, glass lizard," said Dan raising his voice. "We will show respect and we will depart your world without any trouble, other than those my friend has cause to return what is rightfully his. Death doesn't need to shadow nor threaten us. We do not wish to die by your hand."

"I consume, not because I am evil, but because it is necessary. I devour you in one world and you are reborn in another. Your rebirth will always be by my hand."

Dan stood, his face turning bright red. Mlilo pulled at his friend's hand and got to his feet, taking a step in front of Dan. "We will find our way out soon enough."

"You were granted permission to pass through, to utilize the portals. And yet here you still are."

Mlilo extended his arm, pushing against Dan's heaving chest. He tilted his head, gesturing for them to back away. "We will leave Abaphansi when my mission is complete," he said to Intulo as they retreated cautiously into the forest of spears.

"I delivered the first death message to man. I'll gladly do it again. Your escort through Abaphansi, I am not! You will leave."

They weaved through the dark wood spikes; Mlilo glanced back. The bank of the river now obscured the eerie form of Intulo he knew would still be hovering above the water surface. He picked up his pace.

CHAPTER 8

Amira jolted awake, finding herself sitting up in her bed, hand gripped around the cool, bone-like wood of her khaṭvāṅga, surveying the dim room. For some reason she could still feel the sound of a voice reverberating around the room. "Dan?" she whispered, more to her disbelieving self than to anyone she assumed was physically with her in the room.

Her thumb worked along the face of one of the three skulls carved into the white sandalwood wand ending in the flat trident at the hilt; her other hand nervously twirled the frayed ends of the rainbow-coloured sash tied midway at the base of the skulls and leading to the rest of the half foot of engraved shaft topped with the five-pronged vajra at its upper tip.

Taking a few deep breaths, she talked herself into the possibility of a vivid dream having been the cause of her startle awake.

Directly above her, the ceiling fan whirred the humid city air around the room, billowing the curtains of her third-floor apartment windows and giving her a moment to confirm no one lurked in their undulating mass.

She could feel her heart beginning to slow from the adrenaline-induced panic a moment earlier and leaned on her elbow to gently return the pale wand to her bedside table, the flat trident hilt. Her mobile device lay dormant alongside. Knowing it was on sleep mode, she picked it up, with the hope it would answer her question.

She narrowed her eyes with the expected blinding glare of the screen. 4:03 AM.

The only message below the time on the lock screen was a brief, "You up?" from Dan received at 3:05 AM. She rolled her eyes and slumped back into her pillow, becoming aware of the faint itch of her tattoo on her hand holding her phone.

The fact that Dan had messaged and Amira had awoken, even an hour later, nagged at her. She loathed opening a message, particularly stalker ex-boyfriends who needed to move on, giving the sender confirmation she had read it, but she had to check.

"Last seen: 3:41 AM".

"I am now," she punched her phone screen. Send.

She waited a few beats. Sent but not received, let alone read. Dan was permanently connected. Rarely did he venture anywhere without signal unless it was one of his druid training getaways in the Midlands, and even those were well broadcast to his close circle in case he was to miss a social gathering.

Amira tossed her phone to the empty side of her bed, slapped her hands together at her waist and stared up at the blur of the ceiling fan.

"Thanks, Dan," she said with a huff as her mind came alive with her own distractions and the easing sensation of massaging her niggling hand. "Wide awake, bro."

CHAPTER 9

"Are you over yourself?"

"Bru, do we really need to be doing this? Do we really need to be here?" Dan trailed behind Mlilo, the ground sloping upward the further they walked; hills were dotted with more exposed boulders, and clusters of trees and vines gathered around crevasses cut into low cliffs.

"What the hell are you talking about?"

"You need your bones. I get it. Our muddied clothes and bruised egos are all neat and tidy, for now. But does no part of you think that we are out of our depth here." Dan flailed his arms about. "I feel like a damn novice fumbling in the dark. That's no strategy. Let's go back, to our world, regroup, get some help, and come back and kick some ass."

"What help do we need? If you want to hightail it out of here because you're scared of that lizard–"

"Screw you. That lizard means business, but he's not my concern. My concern is not dying down here just because we are unprepared."

"We all end up down here."

"Are you not listening?" Dan wrenched at Mlilo's elbow, spinning him around to face him, noses inches away from one another. "We, you, do not belong down here. And I don't care if my clothes self-clean, or if where we're going, we don't need roads, but we cannot permanently remain here to rejuvenate or live in a protected bubble." Mlilo shrugged off Dan's trembling grip.

"Giving up and succumbing to this world is not how it works. That's not the circle of life, you chop."

"Pfft, life." Mlilo rolled his eyes. "I sit and stare out the window, at the ceiling, at the walls, the things we stare at when life gives you no reason to stare at anything else, anything significant. Everything stays the same as it all changes around us. The only things that change, for me, are my bones. The amathambo shift and become something different every time. They tell me things, but I don't know what to do with the information. If it's for another, they rarely listen. Amathambo ami are the

54

only things that bind me to the real word, and yet here we are in Abaphansi. Is that a sign I should acquiesce and give in to the situation and just resign myself to this world that I desire above all else? Or am I meant to take them and myself back to the real? Tell me, Brother. Where do I belong?"

"Opting out. There's a word for that."

"Say it."

"Stuff you, Bru."

"Suicide."

"Shut up."

"Say it."

"Fine. This is suicide. You've willing taken me on a suicide mission."

"You stepped through willingly."

"To help my friend."

"Then leave. Check your wooden stones for directions, and walk the hell out of here."

"The problem is–"

"There is no problem."

"The problem is that I'm here for you and to leave would go against that. I assume then, my runes and my magic will tell me to follow, to protect and aid. I have to assume that you wouldn't knowingly put me in an unwinnable situation."

"Then help me, mfowethu." Mlilo stepped closer to Dan and gripped both his shoulders. "We can do this." He gave his friend's tense shoulders a squeeze.

"But, do we need to be doing this now? Can't we sail back across the river or find a portal nearby that we can slip through?"

"We cannot recross the river."

Dan took a deep breath, eyes scanning the dark speckled sky, the cloud of the Morrígan wavering in the distance. "The sparkly thing has lost its lustre, Mlilo. The novelty wore off the moment my face was in that crap back there."

"We are so close. You," he patted a clenched fist on Dan's chest, then hit his own chest at the point where his beads crisscrossed, the plastic rattling, "and me."

"Fine," said Dan. Mlilo felt Dan's muscles relax in his grasp. "What is close?"

Mlilo pointed towards the rising landscape. "The trail is heading deep into those forests and gorges. We must keep to this ravine. We will no longer be out in the open. Good and bad. If needed, a portal can be found within."

"A portal is definitely required," he patted both of Mlilo's forearms and took a step back. "Maybe our murder of crows," he pointed up with his thumb, "can give us some advice, though."

"Proceed, as you must," said the Morrígan in a blast of wind and feathers, already materializing alongside the two stunned men. "But prepare for your next lesson."

"We need advice not another lesson," moaned Dan. "Those crabs were a lesson: don't throw shells at the locals. Where's the revenge lesson? We need guidance not telling off."

The Morrígan's form shimmered with irritation, pacing a circle around them. "Words. Ideas. Warnings. Finger wagging. Omens. These are not lessons. They are empty. They are a preview. They are a children's fable meant to hinder you. They hinder you from learning. Learning happens in the experience, not the experience or the tales of others. My words are a weapon; something you can have to better understand the situation you will find yourself in. My words will not stop that which is about to happen. What is about to happen is what needs to happen. You can let that defeat you or be your strength. Allow a warning to stop you and you will never learn who you are.

"Remember, you came here together. *uDaniel uletha usizo.*"

"He brought the shinbone," nodded Mlilo. "Allowing me to gain access to Abaphansi."

"Incorrect," said the Morrígan. "Daniel *is* the aid."

Mlilo frowned. "But, how else did I cross into Abaphansi?"

She pointed a gnarly finger at Mlilo's waist.

Reflexively, he patted at the quills in his pants belt. His quizzical look transformed as he realised what the woman meant.

"They were at the portal entrance," he said staring into the distance. "Remnants of nGungumbane, a being from the other side, are substantial as amathambo and as keys to enter."

He blinked himself back to the present.

"So it wasn't the bone I gave you?" asked Dan.

Mlilo shook his head. "I assumed the bone was what they meant. They wanted you with me. Huh." Mlilo looked at Dan and acknowledged his friend with a nod.

"As I say, you came here together. This is not nothing. But you have come here full of rage and revenge."

"I have passed through Abaphansi many times, Morrígan," Mlilo folded his arms.

"Yes, fire wielder. But never across and never under these circumstances. Never in this frame of mind.

"As I say, you have come here full of rage and revenge. Rage and revenge are what you will face. You," she pointed a black finger at Dan, "have respect to learn." Her finger tracked across to Mlilo. "While, even as I speak these words, revenge continues to flow through you, despite lying face down in the earth. Rather be driven by the need to recover that which was stolen and not to inflict punishment or retribution. You have never crossed into this world with something this important to you and your people. Never for war."

With that she splintered up into the sky.

CHAPTER 10

The two men weaved their way through the growing number of rocks and boulders scattered along the dry river sand. The sides of the ravine obscured any sign of a horizon; the sheer orange cliff faces of iron-oxide-stained sandstone a stark contrast to the deep greens and blacks of the lush forests hiding their bases within the damp leaves below. The occasional ivory coloured trunk of a tree stretched upward, topped by a canopy casting a wide shadow over the bushes beneath, thick vines draped elegantly from their branches.

Dan reached out and touched the hairy frond of a fern, part of a large flat-topped patch creating an open area of bright green among the pale rocks. Mlilo, a few paces ahead, seemed cut off at the midriff, his upper body gliding through the mass, hands held flat above the leaves as if stroking them.

Rounding a towering oval boulder in the path, Dan worked his jaw, wiggling a finger in his ear. "The cicada whistles are getting hectic here." He placed a hand on the cool mass to steady his footing, and found Mlilo standing looking at the clearing ahead of them.

"There are no cicadas here, umnganam."

Like a giant had stamped a foot in the forest, a flat rock, at least five metres by ten metres, extended at a low angle from the edge of the forest to a third of the way into the clearing and disappeared under the pale sand. The occasional rock and stone dotted the remaining surface, a beach waiting for the tide to roll in, the dry riverbed's sand was undisturbed.

"And the whistling?"

"I keep telling you. Your amadlozi are probably screaming in your earholes for you to listen to them." He flapped a hand at Dan. "Shh, now." The distant sound of two male vervet monkeys calling, bounced around the valley. "That's a warning." Mlilo crouched down, focusing on the ground ahead.

Dan followed Mlilo's gaze as he tracked along the exposed sand, tracing a neat pattern he saw for the first time, leading through the centre of the clearing and ending abruptly at a dry, black bush about a metre high and wide. A ghostly smoke or dust hung in the air around it.

He heard Mlilo's sudden intake of breath.

As if in echo, a grunt emanated from what Dan could only guess was behind the bush. A fresh puff of rising dust around its base reaffirmed this.

"It's her," whispered Mlilo.

"Behind the bush?"

"Shh," said Mlilo standing and taking two slow paces forward. "She's digging."

The bush shivered; dry spike-like branches rustled and crackled against one another, then stopped. Dan realised the bush *was* the porcupine.

Crab-walking to the left, in a wide arc, Mlilo indicated to Dan to mirror his position to the right. Dan mouthed the word '*small*' and held his thumb and forefinger slightly apart.

Mlilo slowly shook his head from side to side. '*Khulu; big*', he mimed back at Dan. A good space apart, Mlilo stepped closer, Dan doing the same, both locking their eyes on motionless mass ahead of them.

Dan felt his muscles tense at Mlilo's unexpected shout, "nGungumbane!"

Within closer proximity to the mass, Dan made out pale bands along the spines. At the call, the black and white needles, previously reaching upward, began to collapse and streamline against the form beneath. Beneath the layer of quills, a dusty black coat covered the pair of thick legs, hind legs, revealed as the body raised and edged backward. More and more emerged from what appeared to be a shallow pit in the earth. Dust and sand spilled off the bristling black and white form.

Dan frantically fumbled inside his rune pouch and withdrew the odd shaped N or H of Hagalaz engraved on the wooden piece: disruption and events beyond your control. "Oh, great," Dan said to himself and gripped the piece of wood in his left hand. He took a step back, and a breath in.

Mlilo held his ground.

"I see I am now the one coming up behind *you*, nGungumbane. And yet, I still announce myself rather than attacking like a coward."

One of the hind legs stamped a black-clawed foot hard in the dirt; the vibrations heard and felt in the soles of Dan's feet.

"Should I start by holding your arms behind you and pushing a sharp object at your throat? Where is a rock I can smash across your head as I retreat into the shadows like the snivelling familiar that you are. Errand-girl to whom?"

A deep grunt blew up dust and the porcupine, pivoting on her haunches to face the two men, raised herself to a solid, wide stance.

Dan took in the immovable looking adversary: acknowledging to himself that she wasn't standing fully erect, she was at least seven feet of brown-black fur-covered muscle. Unable to make out her face clearly, but pinpricks of white gave away the two tiny black eyes trained on them. The coat at her shoulders smoothly turned into black and white spines, thickening as they extended down her back, stopping at the buttocks and hanging down to the ground like a splayed tail. A shimmer of quills hung from her shoulders, ending abruptly where he assumed her deltoid muscles would be under the fur extending down her arms and blending into the inky, leathery skin of her hands. He noticed the dull shine of her black claws protruding from four of her tensed fingers of her right hand; the thumbs a clawless chunky stub meant for gripping and holding. Her left hand balled into a mallet-like fist.

Another stamp. And like a dog shaking off water, in a blink of an eye, she violently shook her head. The sound of a thousand rattlesnakes from the back of her head, ran down her shoulders, back and into the thicker quills hanging at her waist and skimming the dirt.

The last of the dust and grime fell away from her front, leaving an eerie atmosphere around her.

"All I want are amathambo ami. If you'll just step away from the hole, I can retrieve them and go home."

nGungumbane hunched down further, grabbed a handful of sand and threw it into the gaping hole behind her.

"Goddamnit," said Mlilo through clenched teeth.

"What's that ab–," a low rumble pulsed through the earth, stopping Dan mid-sentence.

"Your friend's bones," the porcupine's low, raspy voice reverberated as she returned to her original stance, "have been sent to those that ordered them." She blew the dust from her hand in Mlilo's direction.

Dan could have sworn he saw her smile at his friend; a smile or a snarl. She shuffled two paces backwards, scraping rather than stepping her large wide feet through the dirt, always on a firm footing.

Almost crossing his arms, Dan reached into his left cowl sleeve, gripping the cool wood of his wand Fagus, and in a smooth movement pulled it from the leather sheath, arms open and ready for what came next.

Turning at her waist, neck and head immovable on her wide shoulders, nGungumbane aimed at Dan, her fists tightly clenched; then pivoted towards Mlilo and snorted. Belying her bulky frame, the spiky black figure sidestepped to her right, paws scraping through the fine sand. Her focus was firmly on Mlilo. As if performing a dance, nGungumbane twirled and rattled, rose up then crouched, clearly drawing a circle around the two men poised for any attack she may deliver.

And her attack came. She leapt at Mlilo, left arm driving forward at his chest but a burst of dull orange from his hands hit the solid fist, stopping nGungumbane like a wall.

No surprise. No hesitation, she stepped back into her crazed path, arcing around toward Dan. Dust permeated the battleground, the surroundings almost obscured, but Dan tracked the dark figure as she approached.

"Her stomach, Dan."

"I got this," he responded, adrenalin hitting his vocal cords. He knew what was coming. He could feel the energy pushing up from the earth below his feet, through his knees, building in his stomach and chest.

Expecting an upper attack like Mlilo, Dan misread the feign; nGungumbane ducked and struck out her one leg, swiping Dan off his feet; his zap of energy barely singed the fur on her head as he slammed into the ground. A dull pain ran through his shoulder and head, followed by panic, realising he no longer held his wand. Before she could reverse her quill-laden back against him, a blaze of red light filled his vision. Mlilo's fire crackled over the porcupine who rolled through the sand and back onto her haunches.

Dan choked on the dust and dirt filling his lungs trying to find the white wood he knew was somewhere.

With a snort and a stamp, nGungumbane stood at her original position, eyes darting between the two men.

Closing his eyes, Dan forced himself to calm down, took a deep breath and got to his knees. The sand around him was in disarray. No Fagus. He looked from Mlilo to the ground to the porcupine. He had to stay alert but he had to find his wand.

"Where the hell is Amira when you need her," he said. "She'd kick the shit out of this pincushion monster."

Ignoring Dan, nGungumbane fixed her beady eyes on Mlilo, turned over her right fist, and opened it.

The whiteness of the bone seemed to glow in the black of her thick-skinned palm.

Mlilo's sudden intake of breath caused Dan to watch his friend's eyes widen; he noticed Mlilo mentally restrain himself from automatically stepping forward to retrieve the bone, just as nGungumbane brought it up to her mouth. As bright white as the object in her palm, her freakishly large upper and lower incisors glinted through the blackness of her face.

"No!" shouted Mlilo.

"What the hell is happening, Mlilo?" Dan rested an arm on his knee, getting the strength to stand.

She eased her fist, and the bone, into the side of her jaw and what sounded like cracking rock broke the quiet.

"She's," hesitated Mlilo, "she's grinding my great grandmother's jawbone." A wave of heat from Mlilo pummeled Dan, almost knocking him off his feet.

"Bru!"

Holding her position, and gaze at Mlilo, after a few more crunches, the porcupine tossed the now reduced bone into the sand a few paces in front of her; a mere three metres from Mlilo and Dan. Her tongue protruded for a moment, sliding over her rodent teeth, savouring the meal.

Dan spotted his wand a few feet away, barely exposed in the sand. "I assume she can literally grind our bones to dust," he said, feeling his confidence well up inside.

"Her belly is her weakness, mfowethu. Do what you like but that's where we have to hit, and hit hard."

"If we can get there, and if you don't take me out in the process, bru."

Mlilo shot Dan a look.

Eyes on nGungumbane, knowing where Fagus lay, Dan took one ape-like stride along the ground and stopped. The porcupine's small eyes darted to Dan, then back at Mlilo. A deep growl began to rumble from within her chest as she tensed her shoulders and back muscles, lowering her head further; the attached quills rose up in a crowning display of shining black and white spikes, fanning out like the collar of a cloak. The two men took in the spectacle of this regal looking monster, her cloak of quills making her appear even larger than before. The lower hanging spines quivered, giving off the distinct rattling sound heard earlier. But this time it was ceaseless, like the switch on a motor had been flipped; overpowering all other sounds and penetrating their skulls.

"uMlilo. Shisa, umlilo," murmured Mlilo, almost inaudible to Dan under the din of the crackling quills. His left hand was turning back and forth over his cupped right palm to the reverse, like turning a ball in a hand. "Bashise phansi. Bashise othulini." A dull vortex of orange light grew around both hands, the occasional spark spat outward.

Another stamp of her leg and she reached a hand back into her quills, removing a clump of spines at least a metre in length.

Dan gulped.

In five swift movements, her free hand speared individual spines into the ground at her feet, forming an arc protruding at odd angles.

"A barrier?" Dan mocked. "Really?"

"That's her armoury, mfowethu."

Dan felt his face flush and focused his attention on the two remaining quills firmly gripped in either of her fists, javelins at the ready.

Dan forced himself to slide over to the wand, grabbed it and waited. The cool of the wood felt solid in his grip. The energy at his feet, and left hand in the soil, revitalised his muscles.

Three slow stamps pounded into the ground, bringing his attention back to the threat of nGungumbane. A moment passed and he notice movement in the sand behind the porcupine. Two distinct areas of the ground bulged and quaked; dust rose as bristling, black quills emerged.

"Her children, her offspring," said Mlilo. "Like her hole, they dig their own portals."

Shaking the sand from their backs, two porcupines three-quarters the size of their mother, stepped out, seething and growling on all fours. nGungumbane responded with a snort and stamp of her foot.

"Hold on a sec," getting to his feet, Dan felt the colour drain from his face. "You knew they would come to help her, didn't you?"

Mlilo glanced and Dan, then back at the dark creatures.

Quills swaying from side to side, they edged closer to their mother; the one on the left followed the disturbed path made by its parent earlier. The rattling sound escalated.

"You knew we'd be outnumbered, you–"

"Bones are gone, little one," said nGungumbane and casually lifted her arm using the spine to point at the exposed bone in the dirt. "Last one left."

"That's three against two, Mlilo!"

"Wait, that means–," Dan watched Mlilo spin around towards him. "Dan!"

The recognisable rattle was on Dan before he could react. All he could do was take the brunt of the force on his left side, arm raised uselessly to shield. His wand hand swung around but not in time. A crackle of energy snapped, followed by a piercing pain through his clenched fist. The black dagger-like quill protruded from the back of Dan's hand, blood sliding down his pale arm. The weight of the fourth porcupine bore down on him, pummelling him into the ground. He could feel the splintered remains of Fagus gripped in his bloodied hand pinned into the dirt. Tinnitus rang in his ears.

Something rumbled nearby, like a charging animal. Pulses of heat filled the air around him. Vision blurred, unaware of what was happening to his friend, Dan's mind raced. Shock dulled any pain that would have seared through his winded, immobile body, pinned down by the porcupine. His eyes welled with tears as he tugged his hand from the ground, leaving the quill firmly pegged in the red mud. He watched helplessly as the spiny figure straddling him brought up its arms, readying another black dagger above him.

Through the throb in his wounded palm, he could feel his tight grip on the remaining bottom shaft of his wand.

Before he could react, a blast of fire ripped the porcupine off him. Without hesitating, Dan took a heaving deep breath of muggy air, catching his breath and rolling onto his side, away from the porcupine recovering a few feet from him.

Amidst the pandemonium and his spluttered coughs, Dan made out snatches of Mlilo's own conflict. His friend stood, defiant, two long quills, one snapped in two, lay metres away from him in the pitted dirt.

"Was it uNosithwalangcengce who sent you?" shouted Mlilo, brandishing the jawbone now in his grasp. The far-left porcupine, on all fours, growled threateningly at him, waiting for any sign to attack.

"Who sent me is irrelevant," sneered nGungumbane, standing panting behind two remaining speared quills, a third in her grip. "While you waste time talking, your precious amathambo are being scattered among those that covet their powers. Powers you no longer wield as you posture before me. You are weak with rage and revenge. I will take that bone and I will grind it to powder along with your own."

Two legs stepped into Dan's line of sight between himself and Mlilo. The middle porcupine, bent onto its forelegs, head tilted like a dog inspecting a curiosity. The white grin of teeth was not friendly. Dan carefully got to his feet, realising the other had recovered. Two porcupines were circling him.

He delicately switched the broken Fagus to his left hand, cradling his right at his stomach, and gave his head a violent shake, trying to quell the rising noise in his ears. Or was it in his head? The ringing had escalated in volume. He could've sworn it was a rising tide of a thousand voices screaming.

A spray of dirt clouded the crouched porcupine snarling in his direction, bringing him back to the small patch of earth in the ravine. He stabbed at the air, a warning crackle of light from his damaged wand giving the porcupine a warning. He switched his hand to point at the other, keeping both adversaries on either side of him at bay; one sliding and scraping along on all fours, mock charging, testing; the other on its haunches, short quills in either fist like a street fighter.

"You can hunt me," shouted Mlilo at the sky. "You can chase me down like a dog. But you will never take this away from me. It is mine, in my blood, a part of me, and although the physical object can be wretched from my bloodied hands, it will never leave me."

"Mlilo!" Dan growled through gritted teeth.

"You will never have full control over it. Even when you use it, your mind will drift to me now and the words I speak. It will trip you up. It will slow you down. A moment's hesitation is all it will take to weaken the power you wish to draw from it. At that moment I will know. I will feel that hiccup, that glitch in the flow, and add to that the knowledge that it will please me beyond measure."

"Can you focus on the threat at hand, bru, and leave the rants for later."

nGungumbane stepped past the remaining quills in the ground, the porcupine alongside its mother crab-walked to Mlilo's left. Dan saw the perfect line: porcupine, Mlilo, porcupine, himself, and the third porcupine. They were perfectly separated from one another. nGungumbane was honed in on Mlilo.

Silence hit Dan like a blow to the face. The piercing sound in his ears had stopped and the rattling quills fallen still.

On cue, a long spine javelined through the air, narrowly missing Mlilo's head; nGungumbane's grunt of frustration gave the signal to the three others.

Before his attention turned solely on his two adversaries, Dan managed to glimpse Mlilo hit the ground on one knee and thrust out his open hands; blue then orange heat fanned out, swiping the porcupine mid-leap, giving Mlilo only a moment to turn onto his side, narrowly missed by the impact.

Dan tracked his porcupines closing in on him.

"Screw this," he said and stabbed the crackling stub of Fagus into the ground at his feet. Blue-white sparks of electric energy branched up through the air, like an electric tree, hitting both animals back a few feet.

No hesitation, no recoil, they lunged in his direction.

Dan chose the stabbing porcupine and sent a bolt of light directly at its clenched fist and quill just as a wave of heat knocked the other across the sandy battlefield. The injured animal clutched its smouldering hand, looked at Dan, and was on him with all its might, like a boulder slamming into his gut.

Finding himself once again pinned, Dan winced at the blows to his sides landed by the raging monster on top of him, spittle muddying the dust on his face. Its fur was course and prickly, like a thousand pins in his abdomen. He turned to the side, avoiding the mucus but feeling his ribs take the blows.

Mlilo had pivoted, locking eyes with nGungumbane.

Dan swiped his wand across, arcing the crackling light into the shoulder of the third porcupine, but not in time to stop the weight like a boulder slamming into his gut. The impact lifted him off his feet and pinned him, winded and gasping, to the ground.

nGungumbane roared, stepped forward into the dusty mayhem and lashed out her quill like a sword. Dan watched helplessly as Mlilo ducked, but a moment later nGungumbane's progeny tackled Mlilo into the dirt.

Barely in time, Mlilo pulsed blue heat, and rolled away as nGungumbane's leg pounded the dirt where he was moments before, the force felt through Dan's body.

The beast pounding Dan began to fatigue. He had to free himself. Straining, blood rushing to his scrunched-up face, he pushed and wriggled, hardly budging. Hoping for aid from his friend he looked back at Mlilo, backtracking in the sand, scrabbling away from the behemoth of nGungumbane bearing down on him. Mlilo sent a burst of fire into nGungumbane's abdomen, staggering her footing. The sound and smell of crackling fur filled the dusty air.

She lifted her lance-like quill and stabbed it into the dirt at Mlilo's shoulder and neck stopping his retreat. Swift movements from the monster porcupine landed the final two quills from the ground between Mlilo's legs and one at his side. Unless he contorted his body, he was stuck.

In two strides, nGungumbane moved on him, pounding her heavy foot onto the side of Mlilo's head, into the sand.

Dan screamed and brought Fagus up, but not in time to lose his power. The animal on him swatted his hand away. Pain shot up his injured arm.

nGungumbane growled and shoved harder on the coughing and spluttering Mlilo, despite the pulses of flame he emitted upward, barely unsteadying her. The younger porcupine, snarling close by to its mother, leapt up and landed squarely on Mlilo's rump, billowing a cloud of dust and spittle from Mlilo's sandy mouth.

Dan watched as it reached down and snatched the jawbone he knew was held readily in Mlilo's waning grip.

nGungumbane let out an elated roar to the sky, followed immediately by her offspring.

Despite the commotion, all a breathless Dan could manage was a whispered, "Morrígan."

The ringing in his ears returned with a vengeance. Black flecks obscured his vision and a scream filled the air like no other he had ever heard.

"I am Badhba!" *Crow, raven*.

The birds of the Morrígan surrounded everything in a chaotic murky haze, startling the four beasts.

"I bring Nemhain," continued the scream of the Morrígan. *Wrath, frenzy*.

It was enough for Dan to kick and thrust the porcupine off him, roll over and up onto his feet, trying not to let the mayhem distract him from getting to Mlilo. He slammed a foot into the quill pinned at his friend's shoulder, grabbed under Mlilo's arm and wretched the stunned figure to his feet.

"Asshole! We get the hell out of here now."

CHAPTER 11

"For God's sake, Daniel," spluttered Amira.

After lying awake in bed for ten minutes, mind jumping from one hurdle to the next, the stuffy morning air had prompted Amira to take a lukewarm shower and get ready for the day rather than stare at the ceiling any longer.

She wiped away the foam of the shampoo stinging her eyes, trying to get a clear view of the room around her.

Alone.

"What the hell?" She looked a moment longer at the fluorescent lit room, door slightly ajar looking into the warm light of the hallway, and doused her head in the steady stream of water. She cranked the tap one turn to increase the flow and get the hell out.

Tap off, swishing her hands down the length of her black hair, she pushed the glass shower door open and stepped dripping onto the white plush bathmat. Rather than picking up her khaṭvāṅga from the shelf above the towel rail, that would be a tad bit overreacting, she moved the bathroom door slightly and peered down the hallway into the entrance to the small, gloomy lounge.

Nothing.

With a snort she grabbed the white towel from the steel rail and stepped through the doorway, looked both ways, and padded moist footprints down the hallway. No stirrings from Anathi's room. Her roommate's door to the left, directly opposite Amira's, was closed and no light leaked through the space between the floorboards. Into her room she picked up her mobile from her bedside table.

Her recent ex in the next room and her other ex, or whatever Dan was, on the other end of the phone. This situation was exactly what frustrated Amira. Distractions. She had assumed it probably be a bad idea asking Anathi to move in with her, but she gelled with them and that was rare for Amira. And with Anathi wielding their own power, they could at least talk magic. Now they were technically broken up.

Still no reply from Dan.

The dark city visible through her windows seemed to be stirring.

Back at her screen, she swiped to her browser displaying an intricate painting of a battle scene. She pinch-zoomed in on a long, curved blade held by Ravana, the multi-headed demon king of Lanka. *'The laughter of the moon'* was the literal meaning behind the smile-shaped blade rather than the power and destruction it contained. As if feeling its energy through her device, the hairs on her warm arms prickled.

Soon.

The divine sword, Chandrahas, was the personal weapon of Lord Shiva who, won over by the intense outpouring of devotion displayed by Ravana, gave him the indestructible talisman said to protect he that wielded it, but only under certain conditions. After much military success, it was inevitable that Ravana would misuse it. As demon gods tend to do, he attempted to abduct and molest Sita, Lord Rama's consort. The vulture-king Jatayu attempted to intervene, but their short battle ended in tragedy. Both Jataya's wings were severed by Ravana brandishing Chandrahas and making his getaway with Sita.

Rumours had circulated for eons about the whereabouts of the infamous sword. Did it automatically return to Lord Shiva? Was it simply wrenched from Ravana's grasp, and left in the wilderness among the blood and feathers of Jatayu's remains?

Having spent the past three years scouring ancient texts and swapping gossip with Parvati's network of gods, demigods and allies, Amira thought she knew.

Movement from the curtains caused her to lift her other hand to the centre of her forehead. Despite her physical nakedness, she felt more exposed without her black bindi in its place.

She tossed the phone on the bed, picked up her tiny vial of kajal paste and turned to head back to the bathroom for what would be a distracted post-bathing ritual.

CHAPTER 12

The sound of monsters filled the air. Mlilo leapt over rocks and roots, making his way towards the portal he knew was a short distance ahead. The heavy breathing of Dan close behind reassured him. While the oddity of Abaphansi meant the snarls and snaps of the porcupine's offspring a distance behind them, aimed directly at him and Dan, seemed as if they were right on top of them.

The forest on both sides of the dry riverbed felt like it was closing in on him the further into the shadows he ran. He had to duck beneath the thickening canopy of towering ferns and arm-width vines hanging in his path. The sound of Dan stumbling and swearing made him look over his shoulder.

"Don't slow down on my account," snapped Dan, hand cradled across his chest. He regained his footing and hopped awkwardly over a clump of loose rocks.

Mlilo's stomach lurched at the anger in his friend's voice metres behind him. Understandable under the circumstances. Circumstances he had put them in. Movement of shadow on the boulders, they had only moments before scrambled over, caught Mlilo's breath and propelled him onwards in the direction of their destination.

He could barely make out the edge of a flat rock stretching across their path, the riverbed now climbing upward. The split seconds searching for and failing to find a lower gap for Dan to get up. He came up to the three-foot high stone and deftly flicked himself up, pivoting in the crouch position to offer his trailing companion a hand.

"Piss off," came Dan's breathless response, throwing himself bodily forward, turning onto his side away from his injured arm and sliding awkwardly onto the sill of old granite.

Dan got to his feet, giving Mlilo a moment to survey their pursuers.

The dark bristling forms of the three agile beasts leapt easily over and around the obstructions in their paths, yelping and moving like hyenas, hunched and hysterical.

The even bigger form of nGungumbane brought up the rear, moving through the rising dust in the air, the sound of her quills crackling the nightmarish echo Mlilo remembered from what felt like a lifetime ago.

Through the gaps in the canopy above, Mlilo made out the reforming mass of the Morrígan against the starry sky.

"Where are we going?" shouted Dan. Mlilo hadn't noticed his friend continue in the direction they were headed and quickly resumed his charge.

"Waterfall," was all he mumbled as he passed Dan to lead the way once again.

A cool wave of air hit his face, a refreshing change from the usual soupy atmosphere of Abaphansi, giving him the much-needed boost to hurry to the water source nearby.

The rise in terrain leveled off and both men emerged in a bowl of densely packed sand and sparse rocks. A cliff of at least thirty feet rose up from the dim forest floor into the air. Mlilo heard Dan's surprise as they stood side by side, panting.

A light spray of water cresting the ledge caught the orange sunlight, a small rainbow arcing outward, sparkling as it fell towards them. The sliver of a waterfall made a perfect line down until it hit the water-blackened rocks at the base, dispersing into nothing but the damp sand surrounding it.

"uNomkhubulwane," whispered Mlilo, eyes moving from the clifftop rainbow to a larger one, no visible light source to create it, at their eyeline bending around the water stream and obscuring the black cave Mlilo knew was hidden within the overhanging granite wall.

"nGiyabonga, uNomkhubulwane," he said more loudly and yanked Dan by his good arm through the cool waters and into the black.

CHAPTER 13

Pitch-black turned to dim light. Dan tripped over his feet and stumbled face forward onto cool, wet grass. The fresh smell filled his lungs as he took deep gulping breaths from the real world.

Even through the ringing in his ears he could hear Mlilo panting nearby.

The front of Dan's chest and stomach were soaking through with the early morning dew. He turned onto his back, taking the sharp icy cold sensation running up his spine. The water or his rage?

The pain in his right palm had subsided to a subtle ache. To his astonishment, raising it up to the pale light of the sky, he realised there was no wound. Caked in blood and mud, his hand was no longer pierced through. The memory of the attack sent a surge of adrenaline through him, and surprising himself, got to his feet and whirled on Mlilo resting on his knees a few metres away.

The dizzying height of the mountaintop was disarming. Dan took a sharp breath and steadied his footing. Although the edge of the narrow plateau he found himself on was at least ten metres away, the sight of a cavernous canyon below a ridge of sharp rocky spires in the distance was the last environment he expected to find himself in.

He turned to see where they had emerged. A squat, square entrance with stone walls rounded outwards onto an almost flat, grassed surface. Seen from the outside, the small rocks were placed without mortar but looked sturdy, as if placed within the quartzite rock-face rather than around it. Dense grasses and shrubs covered the steeply rising hill above; the growing morning mist obscured its peak. Dan was unable to gauge any distance to the top or what lay beyond.

He patted his coat, feeling the reassuring weight of his mobile. He pulled it out, swiped and checked the screen. No signal. But it was only 4:13AM on the same day they had entered the underworld. "We were in Abaphansi for at least a day," he said to himself. "Less than an hour has passed!"

A gust of icy mountain wind hit him like a slap, turning him back to face his friend. He planted his feet firmly on the ground and aimed his frustration at Mlilo who was removing his thin, short-sleeved black button-up shirt from his pants pocket.

"Just sit the hell down!" Dan shook a clenched fist at a startled Mlilo, attempting to get to his feet.

"You knew we might not survive that ordeal, didn't you? You willingly put someone who trusted you, not only in an unknown world, but with an unknown enemy, on a path to die."

Dan threw up his arms, towering over Mlilo.

"You are shit at asking for help. You don't need to kill a friend, *umnganam*, to get there yourself. That's not how you make friends, asshole."

He turned to look around. "Where the hell are we, anyway?"

Standing up, Mlilo gestured to the right of the mountain they were on. "The three rondavels."

Dan noticed for the first time three nearly symmetrical mountains, one in particular with a conical top like a rondavel.

"Blyde River Canyon?"

"Motlatse Canyon," corrected Mlilo. "We're nearly a kay up here."

One of the world's largest canyons, third after the Grand Canyon, Dan knew about the Blyde River area, the northern most part of the Drakensberg. Some of the shale and quartzite massifs dropped more than a kilometre to the meeting point of the Blyde and the Treur Rivers below, the river of joy and the river of sorrow, snaking their way through the lowveld. But admiring the scenery was the last thing on his mind. "Durban would've been better, bru. Hell, I'd flipping take Pinetown."

"We weren't exactly going to go through the porcupines to get to the one near the river, so I took what I could get under the circumstances."

"And what circumstances were those? The one where you convinced me to help you out and then knowingly pitted us against a rage monster and her kids, outnumbering us from the outset? And–" he paused. "Back the hell up a second."

Mlilo frowned at his friend, and muttered, "Eish."

"Let's talk about '*eish*', buddy." Dan stepped within inches of Mlilo's nose. "What the actual hell do you mean '*the one at the river*'?"

"Psh," blew Mlilo and waved a dismissive hand at Dan, turning to the view over the mountainous valley. He placed his fisted left hand through his shirtsleeve just as Dan grabbed his shoulder and wrenched him around.

"What do you want from me," roared Mlilo, tears welling in his eyes. "What was I supposed to do? What am I supposed to do?"

"You were supposed to include me, rely on me, not keep me in the dark. The crone and the Morrígan were right. You were out for revenge and you got your – our – asses handed to us."

"So what," he shook his shirt over his shoulders and waved his arms around. "We survived. And I have some amathambo to forge ahead."

"Yasas, bru," Dan slapped his own forehead in frustration. "You can underestimate an adversary. You can have useless plans that fall apart, and you can even end up in harm's way. But what is utter bullshit, is going into a fight, a goddamn battle, against beings twice our size, hiding the facts and as an extra bonus, being okay to die and taking your friends with you."

"The stakes are high and you have to be willing to die."

Dan grabbed Mlilo by both shoulders and shook. "Tell me that at the beginning! But if you want to put yourself in harm's way, how about letting the rest of us know it's do or die and not some minor spat with a little porcupine who stole your toys."

Dan pushed Mlilo away.

"You are supposed to work with me and not run headlong into kak you know you may not survive, and while you are at it keep in mind those who have your back, even if you don't have theirs."

"I have your back."

"Really?"

"Really."

"Only when you've had the kak kicked out of you and you need to hightail it out of there. Then you have my back."

Dan's frustration overcame him and he fell to his knees clutching at his temples. "Shut up!"

His scream echoed through the mountains. The silence replaced by the whistle of the wind over the grass around them.

Bewildered, he looked up at a stunned Mlilo. "It stopped."

"What stopped?"

"The thousands of voices screaming in my head."

Mlilo walked over to him and bent down on one knee, his right hand taking Dan's from the side of his sweaty face.

"Sorry, mfowethu," he whispered.

After a moment, Dan squeezed his friend's hand and Mlilo stood, bracing himself to pull Dan to his feet.

Hands clutched at their chests they embraced, the cold or the adrenaline vibrating in a shiver through their muscles.

"Wasn't your shirt screwed up?"

They stood back from one another to asses Mlilo's clothing.

Where the porcupine's claws had left the black material in tatters, matted in Mlilo's blood, on the street in Durban what seemed like a lifetime ago, was clean and intact.

Lifted his healed palm and pointed at it with his other hand. "A bit stiff, but otherwise nothing."

"Abaphansi, umnganam."

"What happens in Abaphansi stays in Abaphansi?"

"Not quite. More that it regenerates and heals."

"But if you die, it's over?"

"Exactly."

Dan slid his hands over his torso, feeling for any aches or bruises, settling them into his coat pockets for the slightest bit of warmth.

He brought out the splintered remains of Fagus, turning his wand around to take in the reality of it. Only the tail end of the black ogham script engraving remained visible. "I guess Abaphansi is selective with what it puts right."

"You're here in Africa, mfowethu. Use the things that come from this land; its soil. Use its rocks, and bones, plants and waters. Your ancestors pushed you to this place."

"I use the things that amplify and focus my energy. I can't pick up some random piece of driftwood from North Beach and start pointing and clicking. Fagus was that focus for me."

"Fagus," Mlilo said quizzically. "What does that mean, by the way?"

"Beech."

"As in beech tree?"

"Yes."

"In other words, you named your beech stick, *Beech*." Mlilo threw up his hands. "Decolonize your mind, Dan. Step aside and allow yourself to find other ways, other means, that just may work better."

Dan shoved the piece of wood back in his pocket with a sigh. "What the–" he began, and removed a rune.

"What?" asked Mlilo. "One of your runes. So?"

"Bru, it's *the* rune. The one we gave–"

"Mamlambo," said Mlilo checking his own pockets and pausing. From his front pocket he pulled out the shinbone he had taken from Dan, holding it up. "I guess she was satisfied with our crossing."

Dan was thumbing the engraved 'ᚱ'. "Raido. I will to will thy will," he said with a smirk and looked at Mlilo. "Journey. Indeed."

"Huh," said Mlilo.

"What?"

"Considering where this shinbone has been, it's not some mistaken talisman anymore. It's got its own power."

"And it's a reminder of when we both came together," said Dan, folding his arms with irritation. "And a reminder of the hell you put us through."

Mlilo had no words to assuage his friend's frustration.

"What exactly was that poem Mamlambo recited?"

"*Kunengxabano*. There is a fight," Mlilo added the translation.

"*Umhlobo uhlangana nomunye*. One friend meets another."

"*Abahlobo bayaxabana*. The friends are fighting."

"*Nabaphansi bona bayaxabana. And the spirits below, they too are quarrelling.*"

"*Abahlobo ababili bahlangana nomunye*. Two friends meet another."

"*Bese badelana bonke, omunye nomunye ahambe ngokwakhe*," he paused at the thought and continued. "Then they abandon each other, each one going on their own."

"*Ukuhamba wedwa ngukubona*. To travel alone is to see."

"*Omunye unikezwa umhwebo olingayo*. Someone is given a tempting trade."

"*Uwela wedwa ukufika phesheya, omunye nomunye ngokwakhe*. You cross alone to that side, each one on their own."

"*Abahlobo ababili bahamba bayofuna umhlobo wabo*. Two friends go to find the third friend."

"*Abahlobo abathathu baphuma kude babonke*. The three friends come from a long way together. *Kube ukuthi babe munye*. Such that they became one."

"*Bangene babonke empini*. They entered all together into the war."

"What's our next move?" asked Dan.

"Ask for guidance," Mlilo lifted his recent amathambo acquisitions: shinbone, porcupine quills and the crow feather. Somehow, they felt substantial in his hand. "We have to get the rest of the bones and most importantly, we cannot allow uNosithwalangcengce to gain any more power than she already has. nGungumbane may have sent the rib back to her, but I'm assuming she either still has to receive it or hasn't performed the reintegration ceremony. Otherwise, I'm sure we wouldn't be here right now."

"Will you at least agree that we need to get to Amira and have a little more backup in order to confront uNosiThwal-, the Hyena?"

Mlilo sighed and crouched down on a patch of short grass. "All I need to do is get back to Durban and get some supplies from Sydney Road market."

"Bru," Dan took a step backwards and produced his wand remains from his coat pocket. "Am I talking to a brick wall? We need help. If it wasn't for the Morrìgan, we'd be toast."

"I thought she wasn't fighting with us?"

"You'll notice she didn't. She caused a distraction so that we could haul ass out of there! Supplies are all well and good but we need to regroup and have an actual plan."

Mlilo gave the objects in his hand a gentle blow, recited his mantra asking for guidance, and let the bones tumble onto the grass.

Dan immediately held his breath and bottled his frustration while his friend looked silently on.

"We need to climb," Mlilo said gathering up his items and standing, looking at the distant clouds over their imposing peak. A gust of wind pushed against both men, reminding them just how high they really were.

"Ah shit," huffed Dan. "Can we not just go back through the doorway?" he said pointing to the dark hollow in the rock.

"You know where that goes, umnganam."

"So, no ride-share from here, I guess. Fine, but we are going to Amira directly," Dan stabbed a finger at the ground.

"You can. I'm–" Mlilo doubled over, retching. A sharp pain seared through his stomach and up his chest and throat. Dan rushed at him as he collapsed forward onto the grass, quills and feather and bones scattered around him.

"What the hell," said Dan at his friend's side, holding him under the arm.

Another wave pushed up from Mlilo's gut, this time it felt like his skin was crawling over someone else's body. The hair on his body bristled, a light sweat bubbled out his pores.

His airways were constricting. Or, something was coming up. He sneeze-coughed.

A pea-sized, grey ball dropped from Mlilo's nose, bounced and stopped, wedged in a stalk of grass. He could make out a dot of red on its top. He coughed again. Four or five more spilled from his nose and mouth and settled in the space between his fists clenching the grass. He could feel Dan's presence peering closer to get a look. He did the same.

Water welled in his eyes, his vision blurred. The next wave was building in his gut. That was when he and Dan simultaneously took in a breath, the grey balls moved.

Blood-fattened ticks.

Mlilo gurgled and groaned a splurge of ticks coated in mucus and clotted blood. The green of the grass was immediately covered in an undulating mass of red and black.

Dan had let go of Mlilo's arm and was himself throwing up a metre away.

Two more surges and Mlilo was exhausted, bloodied and gasping for air. He backed away from the pile of ooze spitting any last remnants in his mouth. The coppery taste continued his retching. Nothing more came except his spittle and snot.

Dan crawled over to him and they both collapsed on their backs looking up at the misty skies.

Mlilo's body was weaker. Adrenaline and shock began to vibrate through his muscles. A groan grew within him like a frenetic chant.

Dan swung himself over and grabbed Mlilo by the shoulder.

"Mlilo," he said.

Blackness inked its way across Mlilo's vision. The sound of Dan shouting echoed in the background.

"What's happening?"

A pinprick of light remained in the darkness engulfing him. The sound of water rushing filled his ears. He focused all his concentration on the dot of light blinking in and out, and coolness filled his body.

Crack.

The point of light became a starburst. Then black.

A crackle of what seemed to be lightning across a night sky, spider-webbed in the void.

Another. *Crack.*

The dim mountaintop returned, along with a standing Dan, straddling Mlilo. The final sparks of light faded from his friend's fingertips; Dan's face said it all.

"Mlilo, you ok?"

Mlilo sucked in gulps of air, heaving and coughing, contracting into a fetal position. Dan's warm hands grabbed his cheeks, holding firmly with a pulse of charge tingling his skin. His body warmed down to his extremities.

"Tokoloshe," he wheezed and pointed a trembling hand at the pile.

"The goddamn red crabs?"

"Infected me. This is the real-world incarnation of that infection."

"Ticks. That must be at least two pints of blood."

Mlilo wheezed weakly. "It's still in me; in my blood."

"We need to get you home," Dan strained at Mlilo's arm, manoeuvering him into a sitting position.

Mlilo shook his whole body in disagreement.

"uMayime," he groaned. "uMthsanelo."

"English, bru."

"*'Let it stop'*. uMayime plant!" he growled a pungent breath in Dan's face. "Learn your Zulu herbs, mlungu. Clivia, bastard."

Getting to his feet, he nearly dropped Mlilo scanning the grassy area.

"Or umthsanelo," Mlilo steadied himself with one hand on the ground, the other clutching his chest. "Bushman's tea."

"Athrixia, sure."

Mlilo watched Dan zigzag around their terraced outlook. Finally, he knew what they had to do.

"Climb," he said as loudly as he could muster.

Dan froze, turned and gazed up at the mountain, his coat whipping at his thighs and hair plastered to one side. Mlilo wasn't sure if the druid-to-be was drawing energy from the earth but against the dull morning sky, his pale features stood out as if glowing.

CHAPTER 14

"There," Mlilo pointed to a clump of shrubs, purple daisy-like flowers bright against the grey green leaves.

Making sure he was sturdy, Dan let go of Mlilo and dashed to the plant, looking back expectantly.

"Grab a stem of leaves, a good bunch, and a couple of the flowers."

Dan's lithe form had made it easier to spider his way up the two-metre-high ledge near the portal entrance, before hoisting Mlilo up alongside him. Catching their breath, they had only gone a few paces when Mlilo spotted what he needed.

Now, like a sports commentator, Dan rattled off the mental request to be allowed to take from the earth; to take from the plant, and to promise to use it to give energy back to the earth.

Dan yanked. Soil and roots splayed out the bottom of the fragrant plant's stems. Clods of dirt spattered Dan's pants and coat. He gave the bunch a brisk shake.

"Keep everything. Roots, everything," Mlilo said and seated himself on a small rocky mound. "Bring," he motioned with his hand.

Dan leaped up and put it in front of his friend.

Mlilo stripped off pieces of the soft, dark green foliage and pushed it into the back of his jaw and chewed. Subtle scents of vanilla or caramel wafted through the air. Dan gave the plants in his hand a sniff, gently folded them in half, tugged a tall piece of grass from its base in the earth and used it to tie them securely in a bundle. Into his coat pocket with a pat.

After a minute Mlilo said, "This will ease the symptoms, but we need to get to water." He thumbed his hand up the mountain behind him. "Tea is the best way to eliminate it completely, to cleanse and purify."

"Oh, let's make some tea on a mountaintop, shall we?"

Leaning forward, Mlilo touched Dan's cheek with the back of his hand. "Some say it is also an aphrodisiac."

Dan clicked his tongue. "A sense of humour. It's obviously working. Does it eliminate stubborn bastards?"

Dan stood squarely in front of Mlilo, hand outstretched. "We have a mountain to climb and," Dan gave his best posh British accent, "a warm cuppa tea for the young lad."

Mlilo slapped his hand into his friend's. His grip was stronger than earlier but Dan was aware of the clamminess in the palm. *A temporary respite,* he thought and edged the hunched figure ahead of him, making sure his footing was solid considering the visibility was becoming poor.

Mlilo could feel his strength waning again. The air had chilled to intermittent icy blasts with the coming sunrise, its promise of warmth at least an hour away. Breathless, he stopped and turned back at Dan a metre or two bringing up the rear, his safety net in case he was to tumble backwards. The clouding air around him disoriented him for a moment; vertigo pulled him off his feet. In a second hands were under his arms as his body slumped over Dan's shoulder.

"I'm ok," he managed to wheeze. "Just dizzy." He held himself away from Dan, and got his bearings.

"We can sit for a second," Dan held himself, shivering. "Yasas, where's the sun already?"

"Na, the mist caught me off guard," he turned and proceeded with some tentative steps upward. It would be manageable despite his heaving chest and rubbery legs from the climb so far.

One hand clutching at his chest, he wiped his brow. He wasn't sure if it was the fever or the mist coating his face and clothes in a light dew.

"When we get back, umnganam," he spoke as loudly as he could for Dan to hear above the building wind and spat out the now tasteless mush in his mouth, "I will sort out my mess."

He could hear Dan's footfalls stop. "Say what?" his tone irritated.

"I put you in enough danger," between breathes and shivers he turned and gestured a hand at Dan's pocket.

"Stop talking crap." His friend fiddled in his coat and slapped a few fragrant leaves in his open palm.

Mlilo balled them up and into his mouth and turned back to face the incline. Before he could take another step, firm fingers pushed at his buttocks. "Climb," came the firm command from Dan.

He shook his head and moved around a small clump of shrubs.

Unseen in the pale air, Mlilo heard a distinctive squeak and chuck, followed by the rustle of grass and loose stones.

Rock hyraxes. Rodent rock dassies being the few mammals to make this extreme environment their home.

They carried on.

The recognizable warmth was moving down his throat into the rest of his body. He could feel words rising out of his chest despite his wobbly legs and breathlessness.

"You seem to think I'm part of something," he began. "What? I have skills? To what end? To maybe get my bones back? Then what? What's the use of the bones? I'm not saving the world. I can barely stay alive let alone save anyone else. Must I be a sideshow gimmick when someone wants to be amused or amazed? Must I amass clients who barely listen to me and just want to know they are going to be ok? I don't even know if *I'm* going to be ok."

"We have these skills," Dan replied, crunching his way behind Mlilo. "It is our obligation to nurture them. It's not about the power or the magic. It is about growing ourselves. Knowing ourselves and our capabilities. Screw impressing anyone else or making someone else feel good."

"And then what? They say life is made up of nothings connecting significant moments. But the nothings are most of the time. Nothing is ninety-nine percent of your life. Doing stuff, that on the surface, doesn't mean much. So instead of sitting waiting for the one percent I decided to focus on the ninety-nine. I decided to make the ninety-nine percent special. Important. And holy kak it's boring."

"Living at what you call the ninety-nine percent would be goddamn exhausting, bru. Things wouldn't be special if ninety-nine percent of the time things were exciting, flashy and cool. How tired are we when we've spent the day, and night, checking our devices for that fix of sparkle-high. Buggered deluxe. No one can tell you how to live or enjoy the one percent. That's on you. Surviving is all we can do. We were put here to live otherwise we wouldn't have been incarnated here. We find ways to adapt and survive."

"There you go, the sage advice for those in trouble: *You'll find a way. You'll survive.* Easy for you to say when *you're* alive, or while I'm still alive. When I'm not, then what's the answer? *I guess he didn't find a way?* Thanks so much." Mlilo gave the air a thumbs-up. "As someone who has considered suicide a few times at key points in my life, it may seem like I overcame those moments. But in reality, I didn't. Life just moves on. Those problems morphed and reshaped themselves into others. We wait for the next moment to come."

"I'm not giving you any more of your bullshit drug until you climb out of your deep dark pit, dug with spades full of self-pity, and resign yourself to something constructive. Say for example, the task of finding your bones, and yourself." Mlilo was wrenched to a standstill, Dan yanking on his pants belt. "Because it would seem that something bigger than us," Dan was now in his face, pointing at the ground, "something bigger than our personal problems is growing underneath our feet, and gaining power that soon may be too strong to defeat. I am here," he slapped his chest. "And there are many more, who barely know you, who are and will be willing to fight alongside you. No matter who you are or who you think you aren't."

The wind whistled through the grass; a patch of mist wafted over Dan's reddened features, obscuring his wild eyes, flashing at Mlilo, for a brief moment.

Dan breathed in through his teeth. "And just know, if you find yourself drawn to that other world before it's your time, I am personally going to walk in here, invited or not, and pull you the hell out by your bollocks."

An eerie quiet descended on the hillside. The wind had stopped.

Both men turned to look up at a faint glow emanating inside the cloud above. Like receding tendrils, the mist began to dissipate.

"Sunrise?" asks Dan and took out his mobile. "4:41."

"We've only been going for like fifteen minutes." Mlilo shrugged. "Maybe."

Side by side they proceeded towards the light.

Like a giant hand reaching into the mist, a wave of air blew their way clear.

Stunned, they now stood in a clear, almost moonlit landscape stretching in all directions; a lake, at least half a kilometre wide, like glass between undulating hills, but no moon was visible in the starry sky above, nor any light source Mlilo could pin point. He turned back. No mountain dropped off into a misty, black void behind them. Just an open field of low hills rolling into the dark horizon.

Dan pulled Mlilo's shoulder, turning him back to the sight before them.

Mlilo squinted. He could make out sparkles of lights hovering in the air. He took a step closer. A shimmer of colour arced across the lake. Mlilo stopped.

"uNomkhubulwane," his whisper perfectly clear to Dan in the dead silence.

"What's that?"

Mlilo lifted a finger for Dan to wait.

The sparkling lights moved, rising, emanating from the calm waters of the lake itself. Like inverted rain, it was water falling upwards.

"What–" began Dan.

In areas where the water condensed, Mlilo could make out a form. Beginning with the edge of the lake, rising towards the centre, a waist narrowed upward and widened again becoming breasts; from the shimmering shoulders, arms outstretched and hands raised to the sky, water poured up from the palms in two streams of white, watery light.

"uThingo lwenkosazana," whispered Mlilo, witness to the most vibrant rainbow he had ever seen, arcing between the rising water columns.

The neck supported a head at least thirty feet above, tilted back, with the face of a woman subtly smiling. It was a smile that reminded Mlilo of Queen Nefertiti's bust, or the Mona Lisa, in that even though the facial muscles were engaged, it said "you are wasting my time mortal, prepare to die".

The head tilted down, eyes of water opened to look on the two men, standing dumbstruck far below.

"This is the second time you have helped us, uNomkhubulwane," said Mlilo and lowered his head. "nGiyabonga, Lwenkosazana."

uNomkhubulwane's hands gently closed, shutting off the streams of water and light, but her body and droplets remained iridescent. She lowered her arms, keeping them a distance from her sides, palms parallel with the lake water, droplets continued to rain upwards from the backs of her hands.

"The two boys who fight side by side, but not together." A voice like wind through organ pipes, an even tone that was neither mocking nor friendly.

A chill ran down Mlilo's spine.

"I told you," Dan flicked Mlilo's shoulder.

"Boy!" uNomkhubulwane's voice rumbled through the ground and Mlilo's body. Water sprayed outward as the giant of a woman sank into the lake, drops stinging their faces and waves crashed over the shores, saturating their clothes.

Stunned, both men were frozen to the muddied earth, facing the head now disarmingly close to them.

"There are the old gods who were here long before this world was made," the rain goddess said firmly to Dan, "who are shared by many in your world. Then there are the new gods, the young gods who flourished in the golden age of the world and the emergence of man. Like their human sustainers, they bicker," her head shimmered as it turned to Mlilo, "they are jealous. And yet it was they who fought for this world's survival when the old gods wished to obliterate it, knowing full well what it would become. Just as you," she turned to Dan, "and Mlilo must find common ground, to stand side by side," her hands cupped together in front of both men, "and fight together, so too must the gods whom you summon to help you."

"I cannot live in that world," said Mlilo, thumbing over his shoulder. "Why must I when no one wants to learn anything, grow, or change? Like a two-bit psychic in a caravan looking into her crystal ball, I tell people what I see in the bones, I listen to what the ancestors say. But they want the sugarcoated love life and money for nothing, and even better, a curse on someone who slighted them. Becoming a better person seems at the bottom of the list. A list topped with surviving no matter what. I can't say that all men are evil but it's as if it's right there for the taking. The option is always on the table to choose the easy path. I am here for my bones, not to save mankind."

A rush of wind and water blew against Mlilo, the shoulders and arms of uNomkhubulwane lifted from the water.

"If we told you that man is evil, would you lock yourself in a cell, away from the harm that man may inflict on you? Are you not inflicting harm on yourself thereby proving how evil man is? Or do you believe man is so evil he is beyond help or guidance? Man's belief in evil is self-fulfilling. The world around him, in nature, is not evil. Yet he looks around and needs to have evil be incarnate to prove it exists, and so he looks for it in himself and his fellow man, becoming evil incarnate. He destroys the other. He points at the other, himself, as the evil. This creates his demon gods.

"When faced with an infant with cancer, it is not which benevolent God allowed this but rather which malevolent god did this and what we can do to counter it? Balance it.

"When a god, or man, becomes more powerful, whether for good or for ill, the worlds have to right themselves. Just as each being has opportunities for good and evil, they have to maintain their own balance. That is how it is with the universe."

"So, no utopias then?" asked Dan.

"The universe is made up of the chaos of good and bad. Birth and death. Stars are born and stars are dying constantly. Do you mourn the dying star? Its gasses will transform and become something else. The balance of the universe is all about the transferal of energy.

"You have to pay your way, go into the land of your gods and ancestors ready or not for what awaits. You may not get there, and if you do you may not survive or you may be ejected. But you do what you can to give them notice."

Droplets from either hand of uNomkhubulwane drifted towards Mlilo. Unsure of what was happening he instinctively took a step back, realising the mud at their feet was no longer saturated but dry earth once again.

"I am trying my best to get back what is mine," he gestured meekly with his hands, watching the water coalesce into a single undulating sphere the size of a football a metre from his face.

"No, you run without listening," uNomkhubulwane said angrily. Bubbles were forming inside the ball of water and a faint steam rose into the night air. "You are standing here because your ancestors made plans. Not because they stumbled through their lives accidentally surviving. An individual survives by being part of the land. Families survive with support. Communities unite with common purpose. Cultures thrive through sharing and trade. Nations are built by design. Battles are won on strategies. Enemies are overcome by foresight."

The sphere was seething and rumbling, the water boiling angrily in midair.

"You will face your own destroyer here. Each will be a rage-monster of your own people's making. Unlike me, common to both of you, your monsters will want to destroy each of you in their world before they carry on their battle for the land you both call your home. This land you were born in, Dan, is not *yours*. It is not your god's. We know you. We've seen you. But here, you are the tourist. Your gods are the tourists. You may see where some of us came from, and we are strong here because this is the land of our making, but your gods are new here. Like the people who worshipped them, they migrated throughout the lands. They dispersed from this land of all origins and their powers weakened. And to this land, with the decedents of those people, they return like prodigal children reconnecting with the true source. Like you, they may think they are here to stay but they have to fight for a seat at the table once more. And that fight has been waging for the past millennia. Some have taken root, some have nearly destroyed others, but they have become complacent to what gods lie under their feet. The people may have absconded from the ancient gods, but the gods have not died. We are here. And you, and those like you," she pointed a large hand at Dan's waist, startling him out of his trance, "will raise them up to help him. He can have all the bones and talismans that he likes, but he still needs his gods and his ancestors."

"uMthsanelo, umnganam," Mlilo pointed at Dan's coat pocket.

Dan removed the drying bundle, stepped forward and offered it to the giant hand.

"In that," said Mlilo with the tilt of his head at the bubbling water.

Dan walked over and twisted the plants, breaking leaves and stems in his hand. He crunched and sprinkled the herbs over the steaming mass, almost subconsciously sounding off his memorized incantation of healing and rejuvenation.

"You do not see it yet, but there are forces gathering that wish to destroy you, destroy your ancestors and what you stand for. Word of your amathambo being stolen has made its way around to the ears of the enemy of truth and magic. You need to be aware of everything around you. Yes, retrieving your bones is important to you on a personal level, but most importantly, they hold power that others covet. In the end, they add to your power, and though not having them does not take away from you, you can replace and move on, it is in the power gained by the enemy that you need to be concerned."

"Can our gods not simply intervene and fight their counterparts?" asked Dan, pocketing the remains of the plant. "Who are we to take on the underworld?"

"Your gods fight their own fights, unseen by you in your world. And so too do your demon gods of your own people's making, those who you believe are set to destroy you. They will hunt you down and kill you, just as they hunt down and destroy your enemy's gods and demons. They will be on your doorstep," uNomkhubulwane faced Mlilo and nodded at the watery brew, the bubbles having subsided. "They have already broken down your door."

Mlilo stepped forward, unsure of what to do next, so he opened his mouth and tilted back his head. He could feel the warmth as the murky mass hovered a few centimeters above him. Starting one at a time, drips fell into his open mouth, and he swallowed. Opening again, a steady flow poured and stopped. He swallowed again. The scent filled his nostrils and his body felt as though the liquid were moving rapidly through his blood stream, warming him to his fingers and toes. Two more gulps and the remaining mass of water drifted three or four metres off to the side and lowered into the ground at the shore.

"Your gods are always at war with one another, not just the demons, just as you are at war with yourselves in your world. To succeed you have to find your common gods, your different gods, your unique gods, just as you must find your own powers, your unique powers, and together be the single power in all the worlds, to overcome."

Mlilo looked over at his friend transfixed by the form before them. Whether it was the tea or guilt, emotions welled up inside him, realising what he had willingly put his friend through. His revenge had clouded his desire for his amathambo. Mlilo wiped the sweat forming on his brow; a buzz of energy ran through his muscles. He crouched down to a squat and held himself tight.

"My power comes from the earth," said Dan. "I use what is underneath me and I use this," he fumbled in his pockets and brought out his broken wand. "Fagus is what hones it. *Honed* it. I no longer have that."

Mlilo snorted at the name.

"It may be a simple name, but it's what I named it. What's in a name, anyway? All that matter is that it served me well in *battle*." The final word punctuated his frustration.

"What's in a name? A name is what connects you with it. The moment it was named is when you connected with it. Connect with its new name and that's as far as you can go. Yes, there was a time before it was named, when it just was, without any identity. It was an idea, it was that which was seen before it was talked about. That is why you have to connect with the gods for that. They were here before it existed and when it first existed. Before man came and gave it a name. We have to connect with them to go right back to when this was just light and dark. Before matter."

uNomkhubulwane cupped her hands together, water filled and poured over her fingers into the lake water below.

"Standing on a dampened precipice," she said above the deafening sound of the falling water, clouds of moisture filled the air around them, "witnessing Mosi-oa-Tunya, the Smoke that Thunders, do you stand in awe of Victoria Falls or do you feel its true name rumble through your body like a thundering force of nature?"

Her hands parted and the waterfall ceased.

"The name is felt before it is thought of," she looked to Dan. "You will feel it and then you will name it. A name that does not limit its life force but enhances it, and enhances what you can do with it."

Mlilo's body ached. He didn't bother about the sting of the salty sweat running into his eyes.

"You can try and take this all on from your point of view, your skill set, your beliefs and your gods. But this is Africa, Daniel. There are African gods and their ways are like nothing you have ever experienced. You cannot treat this like a one of your myths, where the hero is offered a challenge, refuses, takes it on, defies death and, against all odds, prevails. Here, there are no structures, preset paths, say this incantation to unlock a gateway, solve the riddle to drink of the cup of life. No. Here we have to take everything one step at a time, without any prescribed ideas. Look around and listen and learn from *all* the gods around you."

The giant, watery mass of the woman above them gestured to the shivering Mlilo. "You point to your friend for being isolated, and alone. But as is typical of your people, you insulate yourself from those peoples around you, holding to your ways and your own people's ways instead of seeing what's right in front of you, or beneath your feet, and using that to your advantage. Tap into the power around you in this land rather than diminishing yourself by yearning for gods across the sea with little power here. You try to bring your people's customs here, but like their hold on the land, it has diminished. The land didn't want them here. It chewed them up and spat them out."

Her right arm swung violently through the air, palm and fingers splayed, raining down a torrent of water on the shore a hundred metres from them. By the time uNomkhubulwane lowered her hand, the soil had muddied into a small cavity filled with black brown water. Stunned by the display, warmth washed over Mlilo having witnessed the might of the rain goddess. A tingle seeped into his muscles and bones, energizing his limbs.

"Either leave or embrace that which is around you and which has become part of you without you even realising it. You were born here. You are a child of Africa. This ground is your soil, and you were made from this. The gods that brought your people here are diminishing, they are going back where they came from, but they did what was needed. The sum of your ancestors leads to you standing here. You feel you need an external mechanism to channel the power you draw from the earth? If you're relying on a piece of wood, indeed a powerful part of the earth, then we're all in trouble because it is you that is wielding that power. You are the one responsible for what it does, not the stick. You trust the tool more than the one wielding it. Trusting in yourself is what will channel that power. Until then," uNomkhubulwane nodded her head at the spot where, moments earlier, the muddy pond had been created, but now the thick, grey trunk and dense green leaves of a tree grew fifteen feet into the starry sky, "so be it."

"uMathunzini," said Mlilo. *Shadow.* He stood and made his way over to the tree. Dan stopped next to him and stretched out a hand to touch the shiny, rounded leaves. "Natal Mahogany, umnganam." He felt the same awe he could see on his friend's face, as Dan circled the mass of leaves. Living up to its name, it cast a solid black shadow on the drying soil at their feet.

"You have a companion who you can learn from, Mlilo," said uNomkhubulwane. "And it is nearly time for you to start your journey, together."

Dan ducked under some leaves, his hand glided along the rough bark, tracing a branch as it thickened into the bough and finally the trunk. He stopped and placed both hands around the solid wood. He closed his eyes and knelt down at the roots.

One hand on the tree and the other on the ground, Mlilo couldn't make out the words Dan was using but he knew he was asking permission, reaffirming his intentions and drawing on the earth for guidance.

Another wave of warmth washed over Mlilo. Bending down, he rolled back his pant leg and unsheathed his palm-sized knife. The tear-drop shape of the blade caught the light, its rounded belly of the cutting edge, though perfect for skinning, was ideal for chopping herbs and roots. The smooth wooden handle soon warmed in his hand.

He waited for Dan to select a branch and offered the blade. A clean cut was always preferred to ripping at a bush or tree.

Dan took the knife, lightly sliced a circle around the branch's bark at the knot, then did the same again about five millimetres up from the first line. Pressing harder on this second line Dan retraced the marking. Mlilo could hear the squeak of the blade running through the damp wood beneath. One final, firm slide round of the branch and Dan passed the knife back to Mlilo. He wiped the moisture from the blade on his pants and resheathed the knife in his boot.

Dan stood for a moment, one hand gripped around the branch and the other pressed against the main bough from the trunk. One sudden jerk was that was needed to crack it away.

Dan inspected the branch end, swiping away any debris, and then with his free hand he peeled away the narrow strip of bark he had scored. The pale, pinky wood exposed a nearly perfect circle. He pocketed the bark and stepped out into the light alongside Mlilo with a satisfied smile and his three feet of foliage.

Mlilo gave a nod and asked, "May I?"

Mlilo was certain his fingers tingled as Dan handed him the leafy branch. He turned it over and rested the ball of a seedpod in his hand. Inside the three segments of thick, rough outer shell, he knew, were the edible dark seeds, covered in the thin, though striking red and black, poisonous skin. He pulled and snapped it off at the stem, followed by three of the leaves. Balled up together, he shoved them into his pant pocket.

With a wry smile and the twitch of an eyebrow he said to Dan, "For later."

His friend took back the branch and proceeded to snap off the remaining dozen or so leaves and placed them carefully in his coat pocket. Slimmed down, it now looked about two feet in length.

"We all right, Dan?" Mlilo asked Dan hopefully.

"Not yet," Dan tucked the branch under his arm, slipped his hands into his pants pockets and turned to face uNomkhubulwane.

"Gather yourselves, together," said uNomkhubulwane, as if on cue and returned to her original stance, hands raised and illuminating the hillsides with her watery light.

Mlilo watched as a ripple broke the glasslike surface of the lake. The waters swelled over the shoreline, pulsing waves welled up, pushing outward and flooding the landscape all around them. It lapped over their feet, tickled past their knees and around their waists. Rather than feeling cool waters, the sensation for Mlilo was neither bracing nor warm, but rather like a thin veil passing up his body.

The inky blackness, of what Dan assumed was the depths of the lake, was penetrated by shafts of light slicing down at an angle. Shimmering in and out, he could barely make out the shapes clearly coming towards him.

He took a moment to look around. Just where he was before being engulfed by the waters of the lake, Mlilo stood firmly and surprisingly calmly alongside, staring straight ahead. Sensing Dan's panic he turned and gave a friendly smile. Dan didn't feel any better.

Rather than choking on water, he realised he was neither breathing nor gasping for air. The one underwater sensation he could identify was the dull pressure in his ears. No longer the tinnitus or blood pulsing through his head, there was a low hum accompanied by the occasional swish of water movement.

The shapes were now more distinct than before. If he had breath, it would have been taken away as he realised he and Mlilo were surrounded by figures walking steadily towards them, on all sides. In his mind, he pictured a ring of people from the top, encircling the two of them. At that moment the image was shattered. The gaps between the figures showed even more people following behind. It was crowds closing in on them, reaching further and further into the murky distance than he could comprehend.

He noticed the sensation in his ears had changed. Like rising from the deep end of a pool, the dull pressure had alleviated to become a single monotone. The open mouths of the people closest to him were sounding with an *Aah,* overwhelming him like a rising tide.

His natural instinct was to step back, knowing full well he was moving closer to the masses behind him. Another step and he felt the world shift around him.

CHAPTER 15

Heading towards the two squares of light, Dan, followed closely by Mlilo, hit the dense wood of the double doors, bursting through and into the cool chill of the Durban morning.

Momentarily stunned by the white figure standing, arms outstretched, with its back to them in a circular garden, Dan managed a, "Jesus Christ," between gulps of air and pointing his branch reflexively in self-defense. The ringing in his ears was back and the overwhelming sensation from earlier was stuck as a lump in his throat.

"What the hell was that?"

Mlilo casually sidled up to him and took a deep breath.

"Amadlozi, umnganam." He rubbed his hands together and set off down the gentle slope of the red brick entrance. "What a rush."

Dan stood dumbfounded watching his friend amble around the neat garden and statue onto the black tar driveway. The vibration and chime of his mobile in his pocket made him leap into motion to follow Mlilo, grabbing at his pocket to look at his device. "Finally, signal." He shoved the stick under his arm and swiped his phone open.

A light came on in a room in the nearby, multistoried building. "Shh, Mr. Popular," Mlilo turned on Dan. "You'll wake up the patients in the psychiatric block."

Topped by a stark white Celtic cross against the grey sky, the church-like building was strangely familiar to Dan. "An Odin's cross," whispered Dan with a wry smile. His gaze was drawn a few metres down by the two redbrick columns framing a St Joseph's blissful statue, blessing the morning air. "Are we–."

"Nazareth House, mfowethu," Mlilo rounded a hedge and paused to waved Dan to follow into a small parking area. "Shesha." *Hurry*.

"We're around the corner from Amira's work, then," said Dan. He scanned and swiped on his device, "Past the hospital along the Ridge," he said while punching in some characters and hit send. He looked up to see Mlilo scrambling up the side of a squat electric substation with a concrete slab roof. He looked around and saw the perimeter fence covered with razor wire curling around metal spiked fencing. "That'll do it."

He stopped at the brick wall. Mlilo bent down from above and offered his hand. Gripping his friend's forearm firmly, he used his free hand to leverage himself up onto the roof.

"Is your phone even on, bru?"

"Who the hell would be messaging me at," he retrieved his mobile from his pants pocket, "nearly five in the morning?"

"Pft," Dan blew and watched Mlilo drop down to a grass bank and onto the sidewalk. "I get calls at three in the morning and I answer them."

"Will you stop checking the harbour view and get down here? I need food."

Dan sat on the edge of the concrete slab and looked out over the lights of the harbour in the distance. The buzz of the city coming alive filtered up to them on a salty breeze. "I need a good scrubbing," he wriggled his finger in his ear, "and some coffee."

He pushed off the edge of the substation roof and landed on the soft grass just as his mobile pinged.

CHAPTER 16

On only a handful of occasions had Amira been in the eerily empty and cavernous mandapam, the 'outside' pavilion, before anyone else. Seated in a plush sofa at the rear, west end of the almost hectare square hall did not feel like she was in an open space without walls enclosing it. Rather it was like she was within a mountainside cave system.

As a designer she could appreciate the neat binary number of pillars, spread across the smooth marble slab floor, supporting the vast granite roof. One thousand and twenty-four ornately carved and striated rectangular columns, all currently topped with stylised lions engraved into the corbels jutting out from the pillar shafts, adding more support to the weight of the fresco-adorned ceiling ten metres above. Charged with the perpetual redesign of all ornamentation, this week the lions were secondary to Amira revamping the hundreds of frescoes within each set of four columns. Using her tablet device along with her khaṭvāṅga as her stylus, manipulating the lion corbels, or even the column designs, was a matter of designing one and clicking 'iterate', spreading a wave of duplicates throughout the pavilion.

But for the intricate paintings, Parvati insisted each be unique, depicting the many lives, dramas and battles of the various Hindu deities. Or least those she liked, while those she despised being shown in their humiliating or crushing defeats.

Despite the entire sixty-four-hectare temple complex plans being readily available on the tablet in her hands, after three years of being mentored by Parvati, Amira could clearly picture the image of this open pavilion in her mind. Emerging from the dark chasm of the gigantic gopuram at her back – the seventy-metre-high tower with its hollowed-out levels like concentric mandala shapes narrowing into the highest reaches of the vaulted roof above – the open pavilion consisted of thirty-two rows down and across, with the columns three metres apart, intersected by a six-metre-wide central passage running west to east, and north to south. While one thousand and eight columns were rectangular, twelve, spread around the outer edge, and four at the central intersection, were a more robust and square shape.

Amira rarely updated the carved horses and elephants rearing out from these two-metre-wide rock supports, and in her tenure in Parvati's employ, she had only done so once before.

Her device pinged and a message slid in from the side of her screen.

Dan. "You wouldn't happen to be at work right now, would you?"

She tapped her response into the on-screen keyboard, "Why the hell would I be at work at five in the morning, Daniel?" And hit send.

Then quickly added, "And why have you been texting me so damn early in the morning?"

The khaṭvāṅga held in her tattooed left hand swiped the message panel away and continued scrolling through the reference images. Bloodied and impaled figures writhed mid-battle, faces contorted in screams of rage and pain. Amira dragged one into a folder and continued down the page.

Ping. "We're on the Ridge and need to meet with you."

Ping. "Urgent."

Amira sighed. Dan's requests to meet were usually important. To him.

"Who is 'we'?" she replied.

"I'm with Mlilo. You've met."

She swiped the panel away again, irritated with it intruding on her research window.

She remembered the first and only occasion meeting Mlilo. He had been standing alone on the balcony encircling the penthouse perimeter of Dan's father's compound apartment block in the central city. She had wanted to get some fresh air after a discussion between Dan and Anathi had become exhausting. She could only roll her eyes so much at the two competing egos, and so had taken her wine, bottle and glass, outside.

A handful of people were scattered around in their various close-knit pockets, while a broad-shouldered guy in a leopard-print vest, black leather pants and snakeskin boots caught Amira's eye standing alone, cradling a whiskey glass at his chest and taking in the city lights.

She had kept a good two metres between them, grateful for the unconscious agreement not to acknowledge the other person. Until Dan, clearly sounding as though he thought he had won an argument, burst out into the space between them excited that his two besties had finally met one another.

Anathi had ambled sullenly up to Amira, visibly irritated with how their earlier conversation had ended, and put their arm around her.

Frustrated with both Anathi and Dan, Amira hadn't absorbed much of what Dan had waffled on about his friend, Mlilo.

Dan was winding down his biographical summation when an eye roll from Mlilo had brought a smile to her face. Though Anathi had insisted they both leave without anyone having the chance to carry on any degree of conversation, that one gesture had endeared Mlilo to her.

Ping. "And?"

"Fine. I'm at work," she sent off.

"Why are you sitting in the dark, Amira?" Parvati's soft but firm voice from behind caused Amira to drop her khaṭvāṅga, clattering to the marble floor. The bases of the four pillars surrounding the sofa gradually illuminated. Parvati stepped around the chair into the low, warm light and eyed the wand warily as Amira picked it up. "Still using that," Parvati paused, with disgust on her face, "poisonous *magic*."

Amira always admired Parvati's elegant poise, this morning in her regal, red sari draped around her tall form down to her delicately sandaled feet. A thin, brass headband, with the decorative crescent moon Amira had recently designed in the centre, kept her long black hair away from her iridescent eyes, eyes that never missed a flourish or detail added to a new piece of Amira's work.

In the warm light of the pillars, she wasn't able to clearly make out Parvati's true skin colour. Her layer of matte oil gave off a soft glow, one moment appearing a deep blue-purple, the next a warm henna tone. Black meant Parvati was getting annoyed or worse, angry. Her embodiment of Kali was not a pleasant experience.

"I didn't realise you would be around this early, Parvati," Amira attempted to change the subject. Her benefactor had never been comfortable with her recent acquisition of the halāhala, now flowing through her wand. Despite being proud of Amira's ordeal in finding it, it was that exact ordeal, showing Amira's true mettle, that Parvati tolerated the toxic, black mass. Amira made a point of not engaging it when she knew Parvati was around the great mandapam. Although it brought out some of her best work, Parvati's personal history with it and the fact that, in essence, it was a poison meant Amira used it only when necessary.

Striving for immortality, the recently defeated Devas had formed an unlikely alliance with the demon victors, the Asuras, and all set about churning the Ocean of Milk hoping to create the nectar Amrita. Whether released by the frothing sea itself or spewed forth from the serpent king Vasuki, the fumes of the halāhala began to poison the Devas and Asuras to the point where they called on Shiva to protect them.

By ingesting the black mass himself, Shiva was overcome with piercing pain, and although not capable of killing him, Parvati could no longer stand by as her love suffered. She gripped her hands around his throat, and with all the power she could muster, halted the venom's flow from infecting Shiva's lower body. His resulting blue throat was a constant reminder for Parvati, a scar representing

Shiva's willingness to aid those with desires for immortality, at his own expense. She detested the halāhala, but admired Amira's accomplishment.

"You do not need that poison flowing through your khaṭvāṅga, Amira. You have your own power within you."

"It is what I have to use for now," Amira attempted a defiant look.

Ping.

Amira glanced, self-consciously, at her tablet, tapped in a reply and hit send. She brought her attention back to the tall woman staring expressionless at her.

"I do sometimes question my decision to build in the Bhuvaloka. Ganesha always maintains it was the most conducive plane to connecting with Bhuloka, that *earthly* realm. But these devices," she pointed to Amira's tablet, "are most intrusive for me, let alone distractions for my staff. I'd rather we were in Svarloka, apart from having to put up with Indra and the other Devas. Don't make me reconsider, Amira. I'm sure Ganesha would be most put out, what with his selves flitting in and out of realms so frequently."

As one of the many gods brought to the land in southern Africa, Parvati had grown in power and renown. Those brought against their will or with few prospects in their native India needed hope. They needed purpose and they needed a sense of a grand plan for their lives as indentured slaves. Their gods and goddesses gave them this. Their despair fed the beings brought to protect them.

A tumultuous marriage, Parvati and Shiva's relationship ebbed and flowed like monsoon season. Today, Shiva resided at his sanctuary atop Mount Kailash, while the past few decades saw Parvati take over and expand their shipping empire across the globe, reaching all the way back to the lands of their origin. Parvati was in her element in this land and she was not about to abandon the people who willed her into power.

Parvati placed her hands behind her back and looked away into the distance with a sigh. "I'll get Pushan to send a vehicle to pick up your friends," she said and glided off into the shadows of the hall as silently as she had appeared, leaving Amira speechless.

A black Dodge SUV, door emblazoned with a gold decal depicting a flaming cartwheel and vertical golden lance, pulled up alongside and startled the two men. The back door popped open while the front passenger window lowered to reveal a dark-suited, ashen-faced man. "Get in," he said deadpan, his blackened glasses giving even less of a hint of the intent behind the words.

"Cool," chirped Dan and skipped lithely into the vehicle, clearly happy with the offer of transport.

"The hell you are," Mlilo tried to stop his friend.

"It's fine," Dan patted the empty black leather seat next to him, already reclining with his branch cradled in his lap looking at his mobile. "It's Parvati's guys. I've seen them drop Amira off a couple of times."

"Leave the canine," said the man up front.

Confused, Mlilo turned to see a scrawny dog sniffing around the pavement a couple of paces from him. Sensing the eyes on him, the dog froze, looked up and turned, tail down, and skittered off down the hill.

Mlilo took moment to bring himself back to the car and reluctantly got inside.

"Go," said the passenger to no one driving the car.

Mlilo had no chance to object when the SUV immediately pulled off.

In the muted interior of the vehicle, Mlilo fidgeted awkwardly, trying to think of a friendly topic to bring up with his companion. Although Dan seemed okay, heading to Amira's having given him some distraction from their ordeal that now felt like a lifetime ago, Mlilo knew his friend hid his irritations well and wasn't a hundred percent.

"Abalozi. How often do you get the ringing in your ears?" Dan's ancestors' talking to him was something they hadn't quite covered properly. "Like when you're stressed or what?"

"No," Dan looked up from his phone and stared out the tinted window at the passing view of Entabeni hospital, already alive with activity at the crest of the hill. "Pretty random. Maybe it's stress but it's mostly when I'm going through something and trying to figure out my life." He shrugged and returned to his device. "But stress is maybe a strong word. It's not like my blood pressure is hectically elevated."

"Isithutha". *Idiot*. Mlilo sniffed out a laugh and shook his head, as the car dipped down the steep hill. "You need to stop and learn to listen rather than sticking your finger in your earhole. You are abalozi who can hear but does not listen. You are in a cocoon of sound right now. You could pause and hear." Mlilo held up a finger, waiting.

The car hit the bottom of the hill, and the sinking feeling Mlilo knew they both felt, goose bumped through his stomach as it sharply ascends once again.

"Right in the gut," he smiled at his friend.

"I take my cues from what I see, what my runes and cards say. How can I listen *better* to a ringing sound, bru? It's not like it's Morse code. And I'm not always scaling the Ridge every day at eighty k's an hour."

"Unlike your wooden stones, or amathambo ami for that matter, which all involve us quieting our minds and surroundings and asking a specific question for ourselves or the person who is asking for our guidance, we have to listen in those other everyday moments. Our ancestors do not sleep. They do not get tired. They are there constantly, and they want to constantly help us."

"How can I understand what is being told, then?"

"Only you know what is happening in any given moment in your life. If you are actively doing something, what is the ringing telling you? If you are at a crossroads, is it there nudging you in one direction? Only you can learn their language. Trial and error. But go with what feels right, from deep within yourself, mfowethu."

"And when all I want to do is sleep, how can I tell them politely to shut the hell up?"

"There are ways of turning them off," Mlilo sighed, remembering the ordeals leading up to his initiation, his ukuthwasa in the cool mountain rivers near his family's homestead. "But," he turned to Dan with a wry smile, "they find a way to wake you up. They will use force if necessary."

At the crest of the next hill, Mlilo felt the car slow. A line of palm trees dotted his side of the road to the left, rustling in the morning breeze, leading to a white concrete wall covered with razorwire. The SUV turned into a bricked driveway, wrought-iron electric gate already sliding open, and slipped inside the property.

Barely at a stop, the front passenger hopped out and opened Mlilo's door, bending stiffly at the hip to welcome them both. Imagining he hadn't quite acclimatized to the real world yet, another man he was sure looked identical to the one at his door, pushed through two ornately carved wooden doors at the entrance to the single story, white building spanning at least three house-sized plots.

He slowly stepped out the SUV, his gaze momentarily drawn to the gold covered, ten-metre high, odd shaped dome above the entrance, similar to ones Mlilo had seen on many Hindu temples around the city. The man that now stopped alongside the other was definitely identical. "Are you two," Mlilo began; his eyes flitted suspiciously from one man to the other while he pointed at each of them.

"Ganesha," they both said simultaneously, each with a hand gesturing to the other. The hint of a smirk was the first real expression on their otherwise dull faces.

"As in Ganesha, I have four arms and a trunk?" asked Dan stepping onto the driveway.

"In this day and age," replied the man holding the car door, "it's apparently frowned upon to walk around in polite society with more than two arms."

"So, there are two of you?" asked Mlilo.

"I am no Devi-Lalitha," said the greeting Ganesha scornfully. "I have four bodies. Eight when *really* necessary. Now, if you'll follow me this way," he indicated the open doors. "Amira is expecting you."

"Nice threads, guys," said Dan waving his branch up and down the two men.

Not normally one to stop and appreciate a person's outfit like Dan, Mlilo continued to admire the mirror image spectacle in front of him. Mid-thirties with the same pasty grey faces, close-cropped shiny black hair and sunglasses, the tailoring of their black silk sherwani now caught Mlilo's eye: the neat collarless, frock-coat style generally kept for special occasions, had a fine gold thread, dotted with red jewels, embroidered around the cuffs and Chinese collar – barely hiding identical scars on both men's necks – spilling down the gold buttoned chest seam to end at their midriffs. Snug fitting black silk churidar pants rumpled around bare ankles with slip on, black leather mojari shoes to finish off the look.

Arched over and waiting patiently, each man's black pearl-layered kanthimala swayed from their necks, its four strings of iridescent purple-black gems a rare sight for Mlilo. He searched his mind for their true meaning and powers. From healing, to protecting the wearer from malevolent forces, they also brought with them clarity. Clarity that eliminated any confusion brought with incorrect information, helping to better achieve one's goals.

Trailing behind Dan, Mlilo entered through the decorative doors and the immediate atmosphere change was startling but familiar, thickening against his cool skin. *Abaphansi?* He looked over his shoulder. As the Ganesha closed the weighty doors behind them, he caught a glimpse of a misty air obscuring the driveway and departing SUV outside.

"What the–" he heard Dan whisper ahead of him, his voice dissipated into a vast space above them. Following Dan's gaze, he could barely make out the design, but as his eyes adjusted to the low light, he realised they were in another dimension altogether, and not the small dome they had entered in the real world. Although the squat passageway was oblong, Mlilo noted that the walls on either side were in fact six broad pillars, five or six metres wide, with two metres of space between; and the dome above, more like a tower, formed by geometric stories tapering to an unseen point in the darkness.

Dan was stopped, wide grin plastered across his face, waiting for Mlilo to catch up to him.

"Pretty cool, or what?" he asked Mlilo.

"Sure," he shrugged and they walked side by side towards the approaching arch leading out. "I thought you'd been here before?"

"Nope. Amira's pretty cagey about her work life. All I know is she's an interior performance designer for Parvati."

"A what?"

"Hopefully you'll get to see. She's done few exhibitions that were impressive. She's got some magic skills."

Ahead of them, Ganesha rounded the corner of the archway, and Mlilo took Dan's elbow.

"Danny, you do realise we are not in Durban anymore?"

"How do you mean?"

"You keep mentioning *Parvati*," Mlilo raised a palm in expectation of a penny to drop for Dan.

"Yes, Parvati," replied Dan with nod and followed after Ganesha. "She runs that big, global shipping empire."

Mlilo sighed with exasperation, but before he chased after his unwitting companion, he noticed the expanse of pillars in the room they were entering. Directly in front of him, the wide dim passage carried on to a faint light in the distance he assumed was an exit outside. Rows of decorative pillars lead off on either side to smaller passageways, creating a mind-bending pattern of columns no matter what angle you looked at them.

"Parvati," he carried on, and trailed behind Dan, "as in Shiva's wife. You know, Shiva the Supreme Destroyer, Lord of the Devas."

Ganesha had stopped ahead, waiting expectantly for the two men to arrive at the only area lit in the gloomy surroundings. Dan stepped into the warm light, immediately transfixed by something.

Looking through the nearby pillars as he moved closer, Mlilo caught sight of a woman focused intently on a tablet in her right hand. Bathed in golden light, the rich purple silk of Amira's sleeveless, foil patterned midi tunic and embroidered hem cigarette pants glistened. Her feet, in simple flat, black sandals were planted firmly on the marble floor, while her one hand gracefully twirled a wand millimetres above the device's glass surface, seemingly unaware of their presence.

He moved to stand by the other two men, watching as Amira, with a flourish, brought her wand down and gave a flick, like an artist splashing paint on a canvas.

Like an octopus, an inky substance bloomed and expanded outward in a dozen arms, bleeding along the marble floor.

Everyone, except Ganesha and Amira, jumped. Rather than spilling onto their feet, it slid around the three men and made its way to the four pillars around Amira.

As it hit the base of each column, Mlilo noticed that it was not a three-dimensional substance like water or ink, but rather it moved as if below a transparent surface. Literally moving art. The only indication that he wasn't seeing things was a faint ash smoke rising off the blackened surface.

He stood, slack-jawed, as it ran up the columns, all four points reaching the ceiling simultaneously. Like a clouding vision, the lush fresco battle scene made up of greens, golds, purples and bloody reds, was engulfed by the black.

Dan and Mlilo were momentarily startled by the clack of Amira's wand hitting the marble floor. They watched her, in a crouch position, wand held in a firm stab on the ground, focus on the ceiling. Mlilo turned back to the mass above them.

As if running backward in time, the ink retracted to reveal an unaffected painting beneath, but this time a regal figure, multiple arms outstretched, with a stylized glow about them. The ink slithered down the columns, and quicker than it had appeared, seemed to suck up into Amira's wand.

She stood, tapped her tablet off and turned to her captive audience. Mlilo noticed, for the first time, the single piece of ornate jewellery on her right ear, in the shape of a fishlike creature. With the fish tale at the top, the intricate gold design encasing scales of red gems curled down to end with what seemed to be an elephant's head at the lobe.

"Thank you, Ganesha," she said to the patiently waiting man. He responded with a nod, turned on his heel and left them. "There is a certain stench in the air and it's not my halāhala either."

"Coffee and a shower would be great," said Dan with a cheesy grin.

CHAPTER 17

Amira could sense Dan's irritation boiling to the surface the more he spoke of his ordeal with Mlilo in the underworld.

She could not remember another time her ex was this rattled by an experience. The usually happy-go-lucky and optimistic man that she knew was replaced with a pale and hand-wringing boy seated alongside her. Dan had wolfed down two shots of steaming coffee, but hadn't touched the array of sweetmeats laid out on a silver tray on the low table in front of him. Realising the reason for him holding on to a trimmed tree branch, Amira was aware of the weight of her own wand in her hand. She couldn't imagine going about her day without it within reach. Although she understood Dan's frustrations, particularly when hearing about Mlilo's inclination of charging headstrong into a dangerous realm, it was something Amira could relate to. Doing whatever necessary to get what is rightfully yours, even wresting it from the clutches of evil.

She didn't always like to rely on others but she did prefer a well-planned strategy going in.

Dan's posture immediately changed. He sat back and folded his arms with his rough branch across his lap, eyes on the approaching Mlilo.

"Hey. Thanks for that, Amira." He rubbed his arms together. "Feeling a bit more human."

Amira smiled back and gestured to the food.

Mlilo picked up one of Amira's favorites, a burfee, the dense, fudge-like square packed with almonds and pistachios. He took a bite, crumbs sticking to the corner of his mouth.

"Dan was just finishing the tale of Abaphansi," said Amira, breaking the silence.

"Right," said Mlilo finishing the first burfee and picking up a second. "I still don't think we need to involve you, but Dan had other ideas. So here we are." He took a bite.

Amira could hear Dan take a deep breath.

"It's no problem, really," she turned her tablet on and swiped. "I've asked to speak with Parvati. I'm sure she won't mind giving us some resources to help out."

Mlilo stopped chewing and faced Dan. "Mfowethu?"

"What, bru?" Dan's eyes narrowed.

"We don't need to go involving the whole world in problems that I have under control."

With that, Dan abruptly leaned forward. "Mfowethu!" he brandished his stick at Mlilo, his other hand waving in the direction Mlilo had emerged from moments before. "Everything you've ever abluted, ejaculated, exfoliated, spat out, shat out, sneezed out, squeezed out, prised out, tweezered, razored, clipped, cut and sniffed, is going to bubble up out of that shower drain, sink and toilet and bury you in your own faeces of bullshit you've inflicted on your life and the world around you."

"Well, bugger you then," said a nonchalant Mlilo and picked up two sweetmeats. "I don't need your help. Never did. I just followed an instruction and look where that got me."

Dan's pale face flushed a peachy pink. Amira hopped up off the chair before he had a chance to lunge at his friend, or throw a stick.

"Children, children," she said holding her tablet like a barrier between them. "Firstly," she looked at Dan, "you bastards come to my place of work and bring your bickering soap opera; and secondly," she turned to Mlilo standing defiantly with his arms crossed, "you need to wake up to the fact that we are all now involved."

Amira slipped her tablet under her arm and approached Mlilo while she twirled her khaṭvāṅga between the fingers of her left hand. "Mlilo, we don't know each other that well, but from what I can see you have a problem. Something of yours has been taken. A porcupine and her kids got the upper hand and you almost managed to get one bone, an actual bone, back."

"Arrogance," said Dan and picked up a crescent shaped poli pastry, his stick safely on the arm of the chair.

"The two of you," Amira raised her wand to silence Dan, "barely survived. Were it not for the rain goddess, uNomkhubulwane, you would probably be man-sized pincushions. It is therefore apparent that you need feminine assistance. Would you like to do this together or, when you are dismembered and bleeding, give us a shout? Up to you," she shrugged and stood alongside Mlilo looking at Dan.

"Amira," Mlilo dusted his hands on the exposed leopard-print vest showing through his unbuttoned black shirt. "I don't see why this needs to be anyone else's problem but mine. I appreciate the offer but–"

"But you think you can go up against forces you know nothing about, in a world you barely understand, wielding magic you assume is your God-given right to burn."

Dan was on his feet, while Amira watched Mlilo spin around to face Parvati behind them. The startling voice had done the opposite to Amira than the two men.

Momentarily frozen, she turned with a wry smile on her face to find Parvati, red and gold sari iridescent in the light, flanked by two Ganeshas.

"Ma'am," said Mlilo with a head nod.

"Hi there," Dan made his way next to Amira with his hand extended. "Dan."

Parvati eyed his hand suspiciously and turned to the Ganesha on her right. "Whom do you suspect?"

"We have narrowed it down to five individuals, mother," Ganesha replied.

Amira looked to the Ganesha on Parvati's left, patiently waiting for the other two to finish their discussion that was obviously underway before they arrived.

Far from the multi-limbed *elephas maximus* of mythology, Ganesha worked in the background, silently going about his business with his multiple bodies, currently four, operating independently and at the behest of his mother, Parvati.

Estranged from his legend of a father, Shiva, Ganesha immersed himself in the machinations of the family business while creating his own network of operations suited to his needs and clandestine activities. Amira had yet to work out Ganesha's true motivations or agenda, if he actually had one, but having a parent decapitate you, justified or not, tended to fester bitterness.

"Asteya is one of the five yamas," Parvati was saying. "Find the deviants responsible."

Mlilo leaned over to Amira and whispered, "What are yamas?"

Parvati stopped and gazed intently at Mlilo before saying, "Restraints, is a pleasant name for the sacred vows. Do not deceive. *Satya*. Do not be violent. *Ahimsa*. Do not steal. *Asteya*. Do not succumb to sexual desires. *Brahmacharya*. Do not covet. *Aparigraha*."

Mlilo simply nodded his understanding.

"The slave trade continues. And if someone is trafficking in human lives, they have managed to break all five of the great vows. They have lied, used force, stolen freedom, preyed on sexual desires, and coveted another being. They have broken the yamas while utilising my ships." She turned back to the Ganesha, her skin a slick, purple-black sheen. "Find out who they are and as Kali, they will feel my wrath for eternity."

Parvati looked at the three friends standing wide-eyed in a row and gave a faint smile.

"Three individuals," she cupped her palms and gestured to the group. "Three quests. Many outcomes."

Amira was glad to see her benefactor's rage subsiding and thought it the ideal opportunity to inform Parvati of Mlilo and Dan's reason for visiting her at work.

"May I introduce my friends Dan and Mlilo."

Parvati nodded at each of them.

"They've–," she began before Parvati raised a hand.

"Ganesha," she gestured to her left, "has brought me up to date."

Of course, thought Amira.

"You know what happened?" asked Mlilo suspiciously.

"Items of yours were stolen. At the behest of your ancestors, you enlisted the help of your friend. You attempted to retrieve them. You failed. Here you are."

"My *'quest'*, as you call it, is not over. I may have failed in acquiring all amathambo ami, but I have not failed yet."

Looking Mlilo up and down, Parvati's eyes narrowed. "Your words contain many *I*'s and few *we*'s. Yet, your ancestors saw fit to pair you up with Daniel. Your journey then brought you here, to Amira. Those who guide us take a broad view of what is happening in the worlds around you, even if your own view is narrow. Why not trust that you are here for a reason."

"I do trust that. But I also believe this is a trial I need to endure, to prove myself, and I certainly don't need anyone stepping in harm's way on my behalf."

"Fair enough," Parvati acquiesced with a shrug and turned to leave. "Ganesha will see you out."

"Thank you," Mlilo replied with a glance at Dan. "uNosithwalangcengce is my problem to sort out."

"Sarama?" Parvati turned on a stunned Ganesha, the name seethed from her tightened lips. "You did not tell me it is she."

"I felt it was the boy's quarrel, not ours, mother."

Parvati took a deep breath, composed herself and said, "*uNosithwalangcengce*, as you call her." She faced Mlilo once again. "Ever since that bitch of the gods rescued Indra's sacred herd from those demons, she has felt entitled. Deva-shuni may be fair-footed, my dear, and fortunate so far, but the fetus snatching dog needs to be brought to heel. I feel this is beyond your capabilities alone."

Amira watched Mlilo bristle at the implication. "As I said," he folded his arms, "I will get amathambo ami back."

Parvati stepped closer to Mlilo, her eye line matching his. "Sarama more than likely has what she wanted from you. If she hasn't already invoked its power by now, doubtful, she will be even stronger than before. This then implies something more concerning. Something that your narrow view has not taken into account."

"What is that?" Mlilo gulped.

"She will be gathering strength. She will be seeking out more talismans and mobilize her forces to do who knows what. But the inevitable is that the power she gains will free her from this world."

"How do you mean?"

"Some entities can move between worlds. Some may only reside in one, while select beings can travel between multiple worlds. Incarnating into the real world, your world, usually takes an outside force or additional power."

"Like Shiva granting it," interrupted Amira. She noticed Parvati's irritation at the name. "Sorry."

"But," continued Parvati, "this ability is either granted to them or taken away from them. And Sarama has long been confined, unable to move into your world."

"Your ancestor," whispered Dan.

"Partly," replied Parvati, "but also having more power removed over time."

"May we talk in private?" Mlilo asked her. "Your office?"

Taking a moment, Parvati looked around the pillared hall and lifted her arms. "This is all my *office*, Mlilo. We are private here."

With irritation building at his suggestion, Amira noticed Mlilo's subtle head-tilts at her and Dan.

"Walk with me," said Parvati and strode towards the central passageway, followed by the two Ganeshas at a respectable distance to their mother.

Mlilo took the cue and fell into step with her.

"Don't embarrass yourself," Dan said to the back of his friend and shook his head. "That guy."

"He's," Amira considered a moment, "interesting."

Dan looked at her and said, "There are other words I could think of to describe that chop right now." Amira turned and watched him walk back to the sofa and slump into its soft cushions.

"Sorry about all this, Amira," he slapped his knees. "I told him early on that we should come and get your help."

"I know," she said, arms behind her, tablet and wand clasped in either hand and looking thoughtfully at the floor s she paced. "When you were telling me everything earlier, something kept nagging at me."

"Mlilo is stubborn?"

"You both are stubborn bastards. But no, not that. Twice you mentioned me by name to Mlilo while you were in the underworld, right?"

Dan mused for a moment. "Could have been. And?"

"And, twice I heard you."

"How do you mean?"

"I actually heard your voice," she stopped her pacing and stuck out a thumb with her wand-holding hand. "Firstly, like a bad nightmare you woke me up at four in the morning. And secondly, you interrupted my shower and morning ritual."

"I wish I could hear that clearly the other side. But hey," the sullen look on Dan's face was replaced with a smirk. "Any time I can wake you up or interrupt your dreams," he winked at her.

Amira rolled her eyes. "Let the wild things out, Daniel."

"Say what?"

"You complain about Mlilo being insular and independent to the point of self-harm but here you sit, and twice you've begun to tell me what's going on for you but you don't actually allow the feelings to come out."

"I told you how I felt about everything. Mlilo knows how I feel."

"You told me facts, Dan. You have not once told me how angry you are. You have not screamed your adrenalin at the world for nearly dying. And you haven't come to the realisation that no matter what Mlilo decides, you will help him, despite the cost."

"I cannot help him if he doesn't want me to."

"Crap."

"You cannot pull someone up if they will not take your hand, Amira."

"If they will not take your hand then you need to put out the fires around them."

"Fires that they started?"

She shrugged. "Come," she indicated he should follow her. "We need to be there for Mlilo, no matter what he decides to do."

Strolling through a wider central hallway towards a bright opening at least a hundred metres away, Mlilo realised Parvati's presence was illuminating the surrounding pillars as they passed by. Looking over his shoulder, beyond the two Ganeshas following them, he imagined a lit trail mazing through the pillared expanse. Before turning his attention back to the regal woman at his side, he saw Amira and Dan step into the hallway, talking in low voices.

"Speak your mind, Mlilo," said Parvati.

"I appreciate everyone's help, but after what Dan and I experienced in Abaphansi, I cannot involve any more people to get what is rightfully mine. I know everyone means well but I can handle this."

"Your ancestors see things differently."

"And how did their guidance turn out? A friend is now pissed off with me."

"Because of your approach, not for involving him."

"Regardless. I will have to find a way. Alone."

"I understand."

They walked on in silence for some paces, and then Parvati said, "You proceed with your undertaking. Gather your bones as you will. But I will not stand by while Sarama breeds resources and gains strength. She must be stopped."

"Agreed. Then all I ask is for a lift to my destination within the city and we are done."

"Very well. I will ask Pushan. Ganesha will accompany you."

"To the market. That is all."

Parvati nodded.

"One final point regarding Amira. She has her own journey to follow, and I will not allow anyone to hinder her progress. Helping a friend is important, but never, never at the cost of your own wellbeing."

"As I say, I don't want their help."

"Good. Now, let me show you something," she said as they emerged from the pavilion out onto a patio stretching the width of the building and, rather than enclosed by a balustrade, leading down hundreds of stairs to the complex below.

Mlilo stood in awe of the scale of the seven concentric courtyards covering what must have been dozens of hectares of hillside. Beyond, and growing over the walls, were lush trees and bushes, thick vines and banana trees making up a dense forest of green blanketing the undulating hills down to a wide river and coastal inlet to the turquoise sea turning inky black towards the eastern horizon. With the recognisable sunset tinge far behind them, the clarity of the star speckled sky caused him to take in a breath of the atmosphere he knew so well.

Looking to the left and then the right of the pristine view, Mlilo stepped closer to the edge of the top step, overcome with unease.

"What the hell?" he heard Dan whisper behind him. Rather than take his eyes off the sight to acknowledge his friend and Amira standing alongside him, he stared at what he assumed were fields of green sugar cane on either side of the river mouth, stretching up and down the coastline as far as he could see. But, rather than the resplendent picture of a potentially abundant harvest, the fields were ablaze. Vibrant orange flames flicked wildly tens of metres into the sky. A thick black smoke trailed upward and bent suddenly out over the ocean, creating a wall of black on either side of the paradise that were the temple grounds and forest.

"When you look at your land, the city where you reside, you see a delicate veneer of sparkling lights and crashing waves, while a thin layer of grime crusts the alleys and doorways, giving you the impression of minor flaws. This," she gestured outward with both hands, "is what I see. The world, as it really is. My people, as they really are. It is not the scholars and theologians that keep us alive," said Parvati, "or the versions of ourselves, the selves we used to be. Who we think we are changes as our people change. It is the everyday person, even with their limited understanding of us, that keeps us going."

She raised her hand to the flames in the distance.

"There burns my people's suffering. My people's rage. It burns so that they no longer need to carry the burden of decades of suffering. It is my people that brought me here, to this land."

She turned to face the three companions. "This is your land. You are the people that give it power; the people that give us power. People put their faith and the purpose of their lives in gods. When they overcome adversity, their pride eliminates the need for gods, but rather than replacing them with a belief in themselves they succumb to circumstance once more. And the cycle continues. If only they would believe in themselves as much as they do us gods, they would themselves become gods. Or at the least godlike.

"Three Ganeshas will be at your disposal. Use them within reason," she said as she reentered the hall, adding, "Amira?"

"Parvati?" asked Amira expectantly.

"Come to me when you are ready. I would like to speak with you before you all depart."

The two Ganeshas gave a discreet bow to the three and turned to follow their mother.

"I didn't think we were helping," Amira called after her.

"You're not," Mlilo responded.

The pit of his stomach lurched as Dan watched the graceful woman disappear into the hall. He had felt a glimmer of hope rise inside him when he assumed Parvati would get involved. Now, it seemed, even Amira was not going to enter the fray. He looked down at the stick in his hand and suppressed the urge to scream and snap it in two.

Mlilo had turned back to view the immense landscape surrounding the temple.

"So that's it then?" Dan asked him.

"You are not happy with me, mfowethu. How can I ask you to keep helping me when you're so pissed?"

Dan noticed Amira deliberately moving away from the two of them, keeping a respectful distance.

He lowered his voice. "As long as you understand where I'm coming from. I just want to be prepared."

Mlilo stood silently for a moment, hands in his pockets.

"I am sorry for what happened," he finally said. He turned and pointed at the stick in Dan's hand. "You lost something over there. But I now have to do this myself. And I don't need to be worrying about someone else." He lifted a finger to stop Dan. "Even if you think I'm stubborn. We obviously have different ways of dealing with our crap."

CHAPTER 18

Amira left the two silent men and headed directly through the centre of the mandapam, towards the towering gopuram where she knew Parvati would be waiting for her. More of Parvati's aids, attendants and staff were moving about the temple main, the pillared hallway bright with light and activity.

She gave polite nods to passing beings; some she recognised and others that held auras from other worlds she had little experience with. She slowed to allow a Ganesha, rounding the corner from the wide archway leading from the tower hallway, past and go about his business. From the hallway, she turned left at the first gap between the gigantic squat pillars.

Identical to the other space to the right of the hallway, the gopuram tower loomed across the entire expanse. What would have been a cold and echoing chamber, was instead a muted and warm space; intricate tapestries were spread evenly along the walls, lit occasionally by brass oil lamps mounted into the granite, while a single rug of plush reds, purples and golds fell only a few feet short of the near fifty metre square marble floor.

Hands behind her back, motionless, Parvati stood looking up at the overpowering red tapestry depicting a violent battle scene. Krishna and Satyabhama, frozen in time, fighting the armies of the once benevolent Naraka, the now power-hungry demon Narakasura, finely embroidered into a four metre wide by eight-metre-high stretch of draped fabric.

Amira approached her mentor, unable to take a reading of Parvati's hidden face or posture. Staring at her exposed back, sari draped delicately from both shoulders, she knew she didn't need to announce herself.

"The quest for power, and yet more power," Parvati said more to herself than Amira, "leads to a drunken fool's belief in invincibility."

Unsure of whether Paravti meant the battle before her, Sarama the hyena or Amira's own desire for the sword Chandrahas from the fallen Ravana, Amira's thoughts drifted to her next steps in acquiring the powerful sword.

Some of the rumors and tales assumed Chandrahas had been destroyed by

Rama or lost in the wilderness. But the more Amira had delved into Sita's own history and character, the more she realised the one possibility that no one else had considered, or hadn't put to paper in the legends.

She knew that Sita had not been incarnated again, and so resided somewhere in the underworld. And as the embodiment of prosperity, success, and happiness, she could easily have walked away from her abduction by Ravana with the one symbol of triumph. The sword that had once threatened her.

Amira had followed the many trails left in ancient parchments, utilised Ganesha's network of informants and aides, and had narrowed Sita's location down to one of the realms.

Parvati finally shook her head and turned to face Amira.

"I noticed the painting you did earlier. A stunning likeness of my husband," Parvati paused a moment. "Thank you, Amira. But I do hope you don't use halāhala too often around here. Maybe this morning's representation of dear Shiva, ironically oozed from the substance that brought him harm, was your way of making a statement, a contradiction to my wishes."

She waved a dismissive hand and changed her tone. "Albeit in bad taste, I do encourage independent thinking in my organisation. But its negative presence is not the only thing that is a cause for my concern, my dear Amira."

"What is that, Parvati?"

"You wield it as if you are in control."

"I do have it under control," Amira presented her khaṭvāṅga with her left hand.

Parvati released a throaty growl, her skin taking on a purple tone and then subsiding. "Your hand says otherwise. That is not some henna that will fade over time, my child. That poison sits within you."

The intricate ink on her skin was something to behold. Each time she looked at it the design would be different. Since she had first noticed it as a small spiral on her middle knuckle, it had expanded up past her left wrist. It seemed to grow every time she used it. The sensation was mostly like pins and needles, but sometimes it itched.

"When I am done," said Amira, "I will release it."

Parvati raised a firm palm to Amira and said, "Infusing your khaṭvāṅga with that poison goes against everything it represents. You epitomise the wanderer, Amira, seeking out the world with nothing tying you down to a single place. The khaṭvāṅga symbolises that spirit. Everything you possess is merely a tool to do what you need to do. Yet the filth you willingly assimilated is a fine representation of your hunger to seek out, even at the cost of it restricting you. Constricting you. Do not be overcome by that desire."

"I understand."

"Speaking of being beholden to something," Parvati cupped her hands behind her back and walked along the path of exposed stone flooring. "Mlilo has his own quest to pursue."

"A quest we are not going to help him with, apparently."

Parvati eyed Amira now walking beside her. "If someone does not wish to be helped, they very rarely accept help, especially when their lives are not in immediate danger. No, I will work with Ganesha on our part of the problem. But you, Amira, have your own quest."

"I–," she began.

"As long as someone else's journey does not divert you from your own destiny, you must do what you will to fulfill that desire within yourself. I may disagree with your need for these," Parvati rolled a hand in thought, "things, but I know how single-minded you can be. It will also be your first venture out into this world, alone. This is significant."

Amira held her gaze at the passing granite under her feet.

"The fact that we have agreed to not assist your friend does not mean you will not find a way to be drawn in, to interfere, or take control. As long as it does not come at a cost to you."

Beneath the layers of insinuations Amira realised Parvati's underlying message to be true to herself. Her relationship with her own mother was always on edge, taking words and turning them over and over in her mind for their real meaning and never feeling accomplished in her eyes. Her clenched jaw slackened with the frankness of her mentor's feedback.

When she had first encountered her, Parvati's abrupt approach had taken Amira by surprise. Now, after the initial irritation, Amira understood her need to be open in order to get things done. No matter what she did when she spoke with her mother, she couldn't navigate the emotional mine field without blowing up and leaving her parent's bewildered.

She knew her desire to seek out and gather *things*, as Parvati called them, was Amira's way of proving she was someone. If not to her parents, then to the world.

"You will be departing when your friends depart," said Parvati and came to a stop. "Is your reciting of the Shiva-Kavacha improving?"

The mantra was said by anyone wishing to gain protection by Shiva, Parvati's husband. While many used it as a symbolic gesture at the beginning of the day, Amira was determined to call its true power into being, physically. The divine armour of Lord Shiva was said to make the wearer invincible and immune to harm.

"Listen, Oh Goddess," Amira effortlessly began, "as I elucidate the armour of all perfection, the name which protects the three worlds, restraining all negativity. Not even hundreds or thousands of mouths, nor the Gods, nor even Mahe[]vara himself, the Great Seer of All, possess the capacity to proclaim the qualities of this armour," the rest of the chant flowed automatically from her mouth. With each stanza the ball of energy expanded within her stomach, rising upward and growing outward. Gazing at her chest, the first signs of the translucent gold breastplate began pushing through the delicate cloth of her tunic like a porous liquid. Her right hand showed signs of a jewel-encrusted glove pushing through her knuckles. The final line came, but Amira felt the energy waver as she uttered, "he will be released from the bonds of all sin, of this there is no doubt."

Anger and frustration blushed her face. She took a deep breath and said, "I keep practicing."

"Hardly in full effect," Parvati said and resumed her walking. "You obviously have those boys on your mind."

They walked on in silence around the perimeter of the hall, then Parvati said, "On the one hand you are about to embark on a journey to retake the sword Chandrahas, and yet you do not simply go and take *his* actual armour, the kavacha. Rather you attempt reciting something you truly do not believe within yourself. Besides, what does that old man need it for? No one cares about him, not enough to attempt to kill him. I certainly do not. But, do what you must to get my ex-husband's sacred sword."

"All prepared, mother," Ganesha's voice echoed from the pillared hallway of the gopuram.

Mlilo could feel the daggers from Dan's stare in his back, but he was clear about his way forward. He stood, arms folded, looking out over Parvati's domain.

"Despite everything, despite ancestors and gods telling you otherwise, you are adamant that we are not going to come with you?"

He allowed Dan's question to hang in the air for a moment.

Mlilo turned slightly to look at Dan over his shoulder. "Their advice didn't exactly amount to getting even one of amathambo ami back, now did it?"

"Yasas," Dan said with exasperation. "The journey is only just beginning and you weren't exactly being honest with everyone."

"While we are messing around here," Mlilo faced Dan fully, "I could be out there getting my bones back."

Both men paused when Amira appeared from inside the hall.

"Chaps," she said wearily. "Ganesha has made arrangements for our separate transports with Pushan."

"Fantastic," blurted out Mlilo and stormed past them.

"One day you will open your eyes," shouted Dan, "and everyone in your life will have disappeared."

The fact that the sun was rising a rich red behind him was of no interest to Dan. He needed to get away from Mlilo and sort his own stuff out, starting with his wand. The wood in his hand was warm and the bark already smoothing under his constant grip. He took out his rune pouch from his pocket, opened the drawstring and picked up one of the pieces of wood.

The ribbon-like symbol of Othila, for separation and retreat, gave Dan pause and confirmed his next action.

He took out his mobile, the time on the screen read 5:31AM, swiped into his messaging app and typed: *Len. Need to come to you ASAP.*

Len Herbst had been Dan's mentor for the past three, nearly four, years. Tracking down a druid in South Africa had been harder than he had expected.

The work he had done overseas, the circles he had attended, all at the expense of his father, had stipulated he have a mentor with whom physical contact was essential. No screen chats, text messages or emails. All had to be done face-to-face. Dan had found a few in Cape Town and Johannesburg, and even in remote areas of the Eastern Cape. But those were impractical.

Despite being nearly two hundred and fifty kilometres away, Len was the closest. And it turned out, the best. For Dan, anyway.

Knowing Len would have been awake before sunrise, performing his morning rites, he wasn't surprised by the quick reply: *Come, boy.*

After some weeks of emails, text messages and a handful of phone calls, Len had suggested they initially meet at one of the local spiritual and psychic fares that was being held on Durban's Golden Mile, the beachfront.

The antithesis of the image of a druid, Dan had nearly laughed out loud when he turned around from the tap on his shoulder. The tranquility of the scented, tented hall had been shattered by the, "Daniel! Boy!" from Len, with his arms wide. After Dan's initial shock, Len's sweaty hands had enveloped his own in a warm shake.

At around five foot eight, the round-faced, balding man in his early sixties wore a rumpled grey suit at least two sizes too big for him. In the Durban humidity, he wiped away the sweat with a limp, but flamboyant, patterned handkerchief, which matched the wide tie over the pale yellow-buttoned shirt. The smile, and rosy cheeks, that beamed at Dan as they talked over Len's purple satin table, various tarot decks spread out faced down, had begun to set him at ease. Len's distinct Afrikaans lilt, the rolling r's in certain words, and the occasional over the top pronunciation of English words soon became the calming sing-song tone Dan would long for on the other end of the line.

Becoming a druid was never a sure-fire path to success or personal improvement. Len had told Dan as much. It was also evident in the turmoil that was Len's life.

Assuming Dan was oblivious to the fact, the council of druids that had convened in Johannesburg to acknowledge and endorse Dan's choice of mentor, had seemed too pleased when they informed him that Leonard Herbst was no longer considered a druid of the order they presided over.

Warlock.

Dan had remained unmoved at the utterance of the word.

A quiet had filled the room as the six individuals in the semicircle of dark, high-back wooden chairs realised their assumption.

Their first encounter at his satin covered table, Len had been frank about his status within the druidic community. He had wanted the face-to-face meeting with Dan to be the opportunity to lay it out in the open. It was one of the many reasons Dan had continued with Len as his mentor and teacher. The imperfect druid appealed to him. The harsh realities of what can go wrong, no matter who you think you are, were something Len and Dan openly discussed. No shame. Just lessons.

Even the spells cast by six of the top druids in South Africa, and the world, were nothing to prevent Len from listening in to the deliberations, the back and forth as Dan had held his own before the council.

He had never admitted as such to Dan, but Dan knew the love and doting Len had showered on him a day later was from Daniel having stood up to the council, putting his druidic path on the line, to vouch for the teachings even a fallen druid could continue to provide.

Dan had agreed to report to them, and he assumed they would keep their own tabs on their relationship and its developments, despite their vehement reservations.

Dan would often reflect to himself that he had a better relationship with a warlock than his own father.

He pocketed his mobile and flexed the fingers of his aching right hand. No scar. No visible evidence of a quill having pieced through his palm, just the occasional ache he now wondered was imagined.

Amira said some words and stepped back from the closing passenger window of the lead vehicle, the other two black SUVs lined up behind on the bricked driveway. She approached Dan.

"Your ride is ready, Dan," her head tilted at the vehicle as it started up.

"Thanks," he attempted a smile. "Sorry about all this."

"Oh please," she rolled her eyes. "You were about to drag me into all sorts of drama. Now I get to see the back of you."

Dan screwed up his mouth and looked at the ground.

Amira took a deep breath, then said, "I know you mean well, Dan. It's good to see you bring about someone else other than yourself."

"Thanks," he said dryly.

"Seriously."

Dan looked up at the subtle smile on her face, and smiled back.

"Give me a shout sometime," he said and leaned over and gave Amira a hug. He turned to face Mlilo a few meters to his right, leaning against the end car mesmerised by the warm sunrise. "Bye, choppy."

Mlilo jerked out his jaw in acknowledgement and turned his attention back to the view.

Dan shrugged at Amira and walked over and climbed into the idling vehicle.

"Home first?" Ganesha asked from the front passenger seat.

"Thanks," said Dan as the SUV rumbled out the front gate.

Mlilo was battling to read Amira. The composed figure seemed to glide over to him. He pushed off the side of the car and stood to face her.

"nGiyabonga, sisi," he said and gestured to the car.

"I'll send you the bill," she replied with a wry smile.

Mlilo snorted and opened the back door.

Amira's eyes narrowed as she put a hand on the doorframe and said, "You need to be careful, Mlilo."

He raised his eyebrows and nodded. "I will be."

"You know where to find me."

"Sharp," he said and got inside. Amira gave the door a gentle shove and lifted her hand as the vehicle reversed, then drove off.

"Congella market?" said the matter-of-fact voice from the front.

"Khangela," Mlilo corrected the man. "Yebo."

He preferred the isiZulu word, both for its original naming by kaShaka and its literal meaning from *kwaKangela amaNkengane*, place of watching over the vagabonds. Or as he'd once told Dan, keeping tabs on those dodgy white settlers.

Amira stepped up into the front passenger seat of the last SUV, and asked the Ganesha pressing the ignition, "What's the lay of the land?"

The vehicle glided forward with a rumble.

"Our interim destination is the Royal Hotel in town. Mlilo will go to the market for supplies," Ganesha paused and looked for oncoming traffic before pulling out and heading north. He continued, "Dan is going home first to gather some personal belongings. My selves that have dropped off Mlilo and Dan, respectively, will be meeting us at the hotel to assist with the pick-up of two suspects who work in the harbour. Mlilo will also follow a lead I receive when we are at the hotel. He is unaware at this time, but Mlilo will then be picked up again and taken to his sister's village in the dragon mountains. After a brief drop off with Parvati, Dan will travel to a Len Herbst in Ladysmith."

Over the double arches of Tollgate Bridge, the vehicle turned right at the traffic lights, barreling down King Dinuzulu road, east into the city ahead.

"And me?"

"Our hotel visit requires only three of us, efficiently synchronised, and we prefer not to involve you. You will remain in the vehicle in the hotel parking until we have secured our 'leads'," he removed both hands from the steering wheel and finger-hooked the last word. "Then you and the single I can proceed, unencumbered, on your quest."

CHAPTER 19

The dark SUV rumbled off into the morning traffic of Sydney Road, heading southwest away from the city for a hundred metres before turning right, up Canberra, and disappearing from Mlilo's view. A moment later, Amira's identical vehicle passed by, the tinted windows obscuring her and the Ganesha behind the wheel. He gave a feeble wave anyway.

The main arterial road through Durban's Umbilo and Congella industrial areas was congesting with vehicles. He checked the oncoming flow of one-way traffic from his left, then hurried across the six-lanes to the already bustling, squat market complex spanning the length of the block between Dalton and Canberra roads. Each adjoining building featured the same mud-red brick walls, grimy corrugated asbestos roofs, and all visible windows were frosted over by grease and time.

Every time Mlilo visited Congella he half expected it to have been raised to the ground, obliterated and wiped clean by the municipality. But it survived. It lived like an ancient malformed parasitic beast, ingrained in the landscape.

The epitome of a city with its festering wounds of the past, the stench of the long-closed city abattoir from a hundred years ago seemed to ooze from a distant realm to hang over the squalid block. Once teaming with the activity of death, flies and commerce, where livestock were corralled across the road, brought to butcher, packed for wholesaler deliveries or sold on the outside pavement, either raw or cooked, little had changed. Unlike its counterpart at Warwick triangle, which had been revamped for the tourists and taxi and bus conglomerates, Congella market was only frequented by those either seeking authentic, traditional materials, or sneaking to the beer hall on the corner. The latter were not patrons as the beer hall, barely remaining upright due to neglect, now served as a roof for dozens of dwellings within – an overflow from the once-white painted public hostel complex diagonally across the intersection. Once, Mlilo had found himself navigating the crammed living conditions of the dingy, three-storey buildings for a specific herb. No plug points meant residents would draw on the power supply from the light fittings in the ceilings. His skin had crawled at the sight of the cephalopoda-like array of cords spindling from his dealer's ceiling, mere centimetres from a brown leaking crack, feeding various appliances, mobile charges and state-of-the-art entertainment systems.

Never again. He would only ever use one trusted supplier.

A man, knitted white topi and white thobe covered by a faded and peeling black faux-leather jacket, offloaded bails of rolled and tied animal hides from a white bakkie. He gave quick nods to the recognisable vendors setting up outside the first section of building, their new batch of hides being draped alongside handcrafted traditional weapons leaning against the brick wall, while rows of neatly arranged drums, varying in sizes lined the pavement. Where the first building ended, the next stretch opened its dim, undercover shopfronts to Mlilo's right, receding further from the road in the early darkness. A variety of traditional, hard skin shields decorated the walls on either side of half a dozen opened doors, leading to small stores supplying a plethora of traditional crafts, herbs and tinctures Mlilo knew too well.

A man Mlilo knew to steer clear of, emerged from the one dark space. Wearing a suit jacket and once-white button-up shirt, his skirt of animal skins, furs and tails swayed as he moved, while his beaded anklets the only adornment around his shoeless feet. Their eyes meet, and a flicker of recognition passed over the other man's scowl. Mlilo bristled at the knowledge of who the man was, what he claimed to be and how he conducted his business in the shadows of the market and the world. He quickened his pace along the block. He only trusted one supplier for the items he required, and she was deeper in the maze complex of the market.

Mlilo made his way towards the end of the block, keeping close to the barbed wire wall of the Dalton Beer Hall parking lot as it curved to his right leading into the quieter Dalton road. The stench of noxious industry was already filling the air, leaking from the small, multi-storey buildings of the neighbourhood, hanging inside and around the warehouses to mingle with the oily, on-shore harbour breeze lifting from Maydon Wharf only a few hundred metres further south across the rail yards.

Sitting perpendicular to the market frontage of Sydney Road, the double-pitched roof of the warehouse-like Dalton Beer Hall ran half the length of its block and housing not a beer hall but a makeshift hostel. Or rather an indoor squatter camp.

Mlilo could picture the central gravel area behind the beer hall, littered with debris of all kinds, and a lone structure inhabited by more vendors and a handful of squatters. Further behind that, taking up more than a quarter of the block, was the taxi rank backed by a seven-metre-high perimeter wall enclosing a scrap metal lot.

The once vibrant stick-on designs of the Durban Solid Waste public trash drums sat inundated and overflowing with foul smelling garbage, surrounded by piles of bags spilling over with plastics, liquids and patches of maggots, seemingly holding up the lopsided streetlamp. An emaciated dog nuzzled its head into the mass, slopping and chewing with the occasional growl and sneeze. Its fur was matted wet and cruddy.

Spaced evenly along its window-lined outer wall were twelve formally built vending stations. Each on a raised concrete slab, a green steel frame held up a tin roof decorated with rows of thin gumtree splitpoles and the occasional tarpaulin roughly rolled back, while an inch-thick concrete slab of a table top on two thick steel poles, and a mini version to the back as a bench for the vendors.

At the end of the row of vendor stalls, Mlilo turned right into the passageway leading into the beer hall courtyard, running the length of the building attached to the beer hall. Paved with square concrete slabs, but rather than a clear open area, makeshift roofing and walls made of sheets and blankets, or strips of cardboard and pallets created dingy living spaces for the desperate. He crossed the litter-strewn area and stepped up into the doorway.

Passed a leaking tap, its exposed pipe leading down from the web of steel beams of the roof structure above and bracketed two metres from the ground to the remains of a rough, broken concrete column in the damp ground. Pieces of paper lay strewn around the worn concrete floor, puddles of other liquids leaked from a variety of unseen sources, most with a translucent, oily film.

He stopped at an intersection of walls. His destination the one featuring haphazard doors as makeshift walls, making it difficult to know which was the actual entrance.

A hunched passerby looked up from their mobile phone, glanced from Mlilo to the door Mlilo was about to knock on, and picked up their pace away from the scene as quick as possible.

Mlilo knocked.

He heard the sound of a heavy lock being turned behind a peeling turquoise painted door, and a click. That was his cue to enter.

He had felt the next sensation on many occasions with his visits, but it never failed to give him a ripple of goosebumps throughout his body. The moment the door moved away from the doorframe, the air thickened and his ears gave the distinct muffle of being underwater.

He stepped into the darkness beyond and took a deep breath. He was back in Abaphansi.

"That will be all. Thank you, Chef Abeer," Ganesha said and pressed a button on the steering wheel to end the call.

The SUV headed north up Simelane Street and slowed to a stop a few metres from the main intersection with Lembede Street.

Holding the long branch inside his coat, Dan stiffly stepped out the vehicle into the morning city air and took a deep breath. He turned to Ganesha and said, "Give me half an hour, forty-five minutes".

"Let's make it forty-five minutes," said Ganesha and without waiting for Dan to close the door, gently pulled off allowing the door to thud closed.

"Enjoy breakfast," said Dan and gave a wry smile to the disappearing car. He looked up at the apartment block on the corner. His apartment. His father's anyway.

The two construction company signboards were bolted to the north and east facing sides of the half painted exterior walls stretching up the six storeys. No visible signs of construction activity. Not for another hour at least. The newly painted white ended abruptly at the fourth floor, leaving the last two storeys in the previous peeling dirty pink hue.

The bottom floor consisted of the "One Stop" supermarket and take away, the lone holdover tenant since his father purchased the building over five years ago. One that Dan had argued to keep. Convenience at all times of the day or night was not a lease you canceled lightly. Rotis and bunnys were a valuable commodity and the mutton biryani special legendary.

Smells of spices and boiling food preparations greeted him as he rounded the corner past the wrought-iron gated store entrance, and saw the familiar face of the homeless man slouched near the entrance to the apartments. Two green wheelie bins, roughly painted with the building numbers sat alongside the taxi stop on the roadside.

"Howzit, Sanele," said Dan.

Hearing Dan's voice, the man perked up from beneath his thick woollen coat, despite the weather.

"Hey brada, Dan," said Sanele and pulled two ragged dreads away from his face. "The all-devourer is hungry. We must be ready."

Seeing Dan properly through puffy morning eyes he raised his eyebrows and said, "Looking a bit rough, ne, mister Wild?"

Dan waved off the observation and said, "Mister Chunilall smells like he's going to have a good one to kick off your day." Dan bleeped in the security door passcode on the wall and with the sound of the buzz, pushed the door ajar.

The man clapped two hands together and gave a wink to Dan. "Appreciate the breakfasts on your tab, Daniel."

"Keep safe on the streets, Sanele," Dan hollered as he headed towards the stairwell. "You'd think the elevator would be the first thing to be repaired." Dan rolled his eyes.

By the time he reached the third-floor landing, having taken the stairs two at a time as he usually did with ease, Dan was out of breath and his hand ached.

The branch at his side was warm to the touch. Though rough-edged and knotted he could feel its energy humming. He took a deep breath and carried on his climb to the top floor.

The impenetrable steel-paneled door was as secured as he had left it what now felt like days ago rather than the early hours of that morning after receiving Mlilo's message. He pressed the keypad and it clicked a centimetre away from the frame. Everything was an effort. The hinged door seemed to be heavier and bulkier than he remembered.

He was grateful he had left some of his lights on. The homely warmth of the lounge welcomed him back to his quiet space.

Instead of collapsing on the wide three-seater couch, he dragged his heels along the polished concrete floor, headed where his stomach demanded. The Kitchen.

"Ganesha's breakfast menu sounded fantastic. No idea what the hell it all was but some almonds will have to suffice."

He gently placed the branch on the countertop, picked up a glass jar and popped the bail lid. Dan recalled a reprimand from his friend a year ago. Dan had been decrying his father's decision to totally remove his allowance. "I've got bugger-all food or money."

Mlilo had picked up the near-full jar of almonds and given a posed display of the produce.

"Most people who have no idea what "no money or no food" actually means." He had stepped into the kitchen and swung open a random door. It happened to be the pantry door. "Mfowethu," Mlilo had gestured to the cupboard.

"That's like only a third stocked!" Dan had wailed.

Mlilo had held up a hand and walked back into the lounge.

"How much money have you got in your bank account or wallet right now?"

A shocked Dan had ummed and ahed and finally said five hundred bucks in all.

"Roof over your head?"

"Yes."

"Power and utilities paid?"

"Yes, but I don't have food–"

Dan now looked at the pile of deep orange-brown nuts in the palm of his hand. He closed his hand and funnelled a few into his mouth and chewed. He walked over to the small round breakfast table and opened the French doors to the side of the kitchen to reveal the Juliet balcony overlooking the quad created by the square building. With a glance up at the blue morning sky, he peered down below.

Where the ground floor used to be, a water-stained, pigeon-crapped slab of concrete was now opening right down into the parking lot to an excavated sandy square beneath. Having asked his father to make the clearing within months of securing the property deal, he had watched the earth-mover vehicle, barely fitting under the parking ceiling, drop the rich KwaZulu-Natal soil over the sea sand bottom. Waiting less than a month to coincide with Beltane at the end of October Dan used the ceremonial date to perform the tree planting rite. The carefully selected Ash seedling, at under a metre high, was placed in the centre. His sacred grove was started.

Now over twelve metres high, roots firmly in the rich, dark earth, the lush green leaves reached up into the unobstructed space provided by the building.

Grateful for the piece of tranquility beneath his feet, Dan whispered, "Awen."

Following the network of pipes and gutters spidering up the sides of the walls, his attention was brought back to the top floor. His floor.

Though all accessible through the single steel door, the area through the opposite windows were starkly empty, pillared spaces for open plan studios or living. What it gave Dan was a three-hundred-and-sixty-degree view of the surrounding neighbourhood and side road below.

His living quarters made up half of the floor, taking the full corner of the building facing north-east and overlooking the busy intersection. He could take in the monstrosity of the education building diagonally opposite, or the skulkings of the sex shop clientele directly opposite. The east facing windows were three metres back from the outer-wall, providing a vast patio running the length of the building. Sunrises were killer.

His thoughts turned back to his friend and their ordeal. He threw the last remaining almonds in his hand into his mouth and awkwardly jimmied the lid closed.

He needed to get some lavender oil on his injured hand.

Dan flexed his hand, the solid weight of his silver and obsidian ring a welcome relief after missing it in Abaphansi. Passing by the bathroom he retrieved a small brown bottle of essential oil and dropped himself on the couch. He watched the clear liquid drip three drops onto the back of his palm, closed the lid and proceeded to gently rub and knead his hands together. The tingling sensation ran from his fingertips up his arms and through his spine.

He cupped his hands together and took a deep breath of the fragrance, and sighed.

Moved his left hand from his injured right and felt the weight of the torc bracelet.

He knew he had been hard on his friend. You don't always know what someone is going through, but it had enraged Dan to know the dangers they had been in after the fact.

He could feel himself softening to the friend he loved and admired. Abaphansi had been the first time he'd seen the true power Mlilo could wield. He knew he needed Len to tell him what to do. He had to help Mlilo even if he didn't want helping. And even if Dan was reluctant to put himself in harm's way.

He ran through a checklist of items he needed to pack. And to pack light. His glass bottle of water, a snack, his full Golden Tarot deck and heavier stone rune set, the lavender oil would be needed daily, and two crystals. The smooth oval amethyst, for connecting and protection; and the odd-shaped tiger's eye, for grounding. And his mobile charger and battery pack. He had felt unprepared against the porcupine and her kin, despite always having his essentials even for a trip to the store, or to help a friend.

What he most felt at a loss about was his wand. He looked over at the branch lying on the kitchen counter.

"I need to put you in the grove for a bit."

Bumping onto the flat surface from the ramp down into the hotel parking lot, the Dodge SUV tyres squealed and squeaked their arrival on the shiny concrete. The vehicle ahead of them turned into a parking bay. Two spaces down from it its duplicate was already parked.

Ganesha would have already dropped Dan at his apartment and arrived here a few minutes before them.

Amira's transport rolled in between the other two vehicles and came to a stop. The other Ganesha was already at her driver's side nodding at her Ganesha.

"Back in a whiz," he said to her.

The rich, spicy scents of his meal hung in the muted air of the empty hotel restaurant as Ganesha relished the food on his plate and surrounding dishes.

He lifted his glass, filled with fresh, green-yellow aam panna, and tipped it to his second self now approaching from the lobby. He took a sip, allowing the flavours of ripe mango, jeera powder, mint leaves and a hint of sea salt to stimulate his senses and reach his other selves. He proceeded to eat as the other pulled up a chair and sat at the round dining table.

"We may have to eat in this world in order to survive but by god it is no torture."

The second Ganesha removed his mobile from his jacket pocket and glanced at the time, 6AM, and replaced the device and waited.

"Ready?" he finally asked the first, knowing full well the answer.

Number One shook his head and took a sip of his drink. "If we feel the urge to start eating the tableware," he paused and looked up at the decorative light hanging a metre from the low, dark wood-beamed ceiling, "and this chandelier, we'll have to order the roasted rice balls."

"Ah," sighed Number Two, "at least this real-world humidity of this city is countered rather smashingly by that beverage." He pointed at a remaining modak, looking like a garlic bulb rather than a steamed rice dough dumpling packed with fresh coconut and sugar, sitting in the aftermath of the four previous plates.

Number One lifted a finger and nodded while emitting a growl of a burp, picked up the final item and tossed it into his mouth. The second Ganesha took out his mobile again while the first proceeded to wipe his face with the white cloth napkin.

Number Two pressed some buttons, waiting for the device to ping, then nodded to the other.

Number One dropped his crumpled napkin in his plate and took one last pull on his juice to empty the glass.

They both turned in unison as the third Ganesha, looking sullen with his hands in pockets, stepped into the dining room.

Through his final chews, Number One said, "I don't understand the air of entitlement certain 'professional'," he spat the word, "gatekeepers seem to possess in this world. I understand not giving out information about your clientele or room numbers willy-nilly to randoms, but even when we say who we are–"

"No respect for local gods." The other remained standing, shoulders slumped. He took a deep breath, and folded his arms. "Or any gods, for that matter."

Number One placed his empty glass on the table. "Well, at least Chef Abeer knows who we are."

"He doesn't have long to go."

"Faiza, his daughter, is coming on nicely with her training in Paris."

"Along with her yearning for her home."

"And her gods. A silver lining, I suppose."

Number Three brought out a small tablet and said, "I'll be doing some admin from the lobby lounge."

The other two got up and made their way to the lobby elevators.

Amira swiped through the virtual map app on her mobile, a rapid walk-through to the spot she knew she would be going through later this morning into the other world. She was nervous. She was unsure of her research, as thorough as it had been over the past year or more. She knew her walk through the other realm would not be simple. Sita would not shrug her shoulders and hand over Lord Shiva's sword, Chandrahas.

Amira's other hand gripped her khaṭvāṅga, its weight reassuring. She placed a virtual pin in the location and exited the app to look at her photos.

The sight of the crescent shaped sword automatically caused her to recite the Shiva Tandava Stotra.

The elevator pinged and the mirrored doors opened onto a long hallway lined with numerous doors to both public and long-term residence suites. Its width meant the two Ganeshas were able to exit the elevator and, walking side by side, make their way down the stretch of plush carpeting and warm lighting.

"The aam panna was fresh," said Number Two.

"Just the right amount of mint to not overpower."

"The puran poli were light."

"So light, with the right amount of sweetness. The pistachios were a delightful change to the rather bland almonds."

"We do prefer the almonds, though."

"We do."

They walked on in silence for a few more doors.

"What time do you have?"

The other flicked his wrist to reveal a silver wristwatch. "6.10AM," he said and lowered his arm and readjusted his shirt and jacket sleeves.

Two apartments ahead a door opened and a man in his late fifties, dressed in an all-white kurta and hat, stepped into the hallway followed closely by a medium sized leashed dog.

Both Ganesha's stopped.

"That's convenient."

"It may be awkward, though," said Number One as they both nodded at one another.

The older man had noticed the two inert Ganeshas gazing at him, causing him to reflexively pull the eagerly panting bulldog closer to himself as he edged slowly passed them.

"Hi, Winston," said Number Two to the dog. The man recoiled at the sound while the dog gave a friendly gruff at the two Ganeshas.

"Can I help you?" stammered Winston's owner. "Do I know you?"

"Saleh," said Number One, "We've eaten in the best restaurants from Lagos, to Cape Town, New Delhi to Maymyo, dined in the vast banquet halls of the second and third realms with some of the most venerated and reviled devas. But nothing comes close to a breakfast of puran poli and sliced bananas with a tall glass of ice cold aam panna to wash it down in your fine dining hall downstairs."

"We're vegetarian," added Number Two.

"He didn't ask," said Number One. "And a side of modaks."

The weary man made to pull his animal closer to himself, away from the two strangers but Winston's stocky form held fast.

"We don't drink either, Saleh," Number Two added to the man. "Not for religious reasons, mind you."

"He didn't ask," said Number One, emphatically.

"Can I ask what I can do for you two gentlemen and how do you know my dog's name?" The man blinked and continued, "Or my name for that matter."

Number One reached into his jacket pocket and pulled out his mobile. He tapped the screen and turned it to show Saleh.

The illuminated image was of a familiar bulldog, tongue lolling from his happy jaws, seated in a lush green public park lawn surrounded by a dozen pigeons.

"This is your dog, yes?" asked Number One.

"Winston the bulldog," added Number Two.

"Yes, when–" Saleh began, squinting his eyes for a closer look at the image.

"That was two years ago," interrupted Number Two and finger-hooked the air, "when he went 'missing'."

"Is this some kind of joke?" asked Saleh.

One and Two looked at each other.

"He did have a sense of humour," said Number One.

"He did," agreed Number Two.

"He had needed to run wild for a few weeks. Nothing personal," Number One nodded at the confused man. "It's really no surprise he came back to you."

"He had told us how you had been so kind to him, and loving him for the past ten, now twelve years." Number One tucked the mobile back in his jacket.

Winston emitted a low moan.

"Really? Feeding him fillet instead of the rib-eyes since he got back?" said an astonished Number One with a smile.

"He appreciates that," mused Number Two.

"Are you guys for real?"

"That time, two years ago, that he went missing?"

"Yes?" Saleh squinted.

"He was out reconnecting with old friends," said Number One.

"Acquaintances," Number Two said to Number One.

"Friends," Number One stated firmly. "While defeating certain demons–"

"Who," interrupted Number Two, "shall remain nameless under these circumstances."

"We kept Winston up to date," said Number Two. "We kept tabs on you."

"Thoughtful," nodded Number One.

"How the hell did he stay in touch?" Saleh asked, visibly confused.

Number One and Number Two exchanged puzzled looks, and turned to the other man.

"The pigeons, obviously," Number One stated as Number Two bent down on one knee and took one of Winston's paws.

"The pigeons," Saleh considered for a moment. "Wait. Tabs on me?"

Number One waved away the question. "Winston appreciates the morning and evening walks around the neighbourhood, by the way."

Number Two mumbled as the dog growled and yipped responses.

"The pigeons!" Saleh's eyes lit up.

"Do calm down, old chap," Number One looked around the empty hallway.

"All the other peoples' dogs run barking into the flocks of pigeons in the park," said Saleh. "But never Winston. I always thought it strange. I would trail behind his leash with the birds cooing around him, some even on his back."

"Ah, yes," mused Number One. "Catching up and relaying gossip."

"Now that you mentioned it, there was always a pigeon pecking at the window near his sleep basket."

"Bob."

"Bob?"

"Bob. Winston and Bob are pretty good mates."

"Best mates, actually. Winston managed to get Bob out one of those feral cat's jaws. I think that was how it all started."

"Quite right. That's how it all started."

"Excuse me," interrupted Saleh. "How do you two know all this?"

"Not important," said Number Two standing to his feet.

"No. Not important in the greater scheme of things."

"What scheme of things?"

Winston gave a low howl with a final gruff.

"Oh. Right," said Number One. "We'll leave you to your morning walk."

The two Ganeshas gave a wave and turned, leaving the stunned man holding the leash being eagerly tugged by Winston.

"He said it smells like three doors down," said Number Two as he typed into his mobile.

Amira's mobile bleeped.

A message from Ganesha read: "Tell Mlilo: confront the dog."

She knew better than to ask what the ever-cryptic Ganesha meant. She simply copied the phrase, pasted it into a message and sent it to Mlilo.

The mingling smells of sweat, smoke and fragrant incense oozed through the gap in the apartment doorway.

"We don't need any room service, charna," said a shorter, leaner man, neck and shoulder muscles visibly tense beneath numerous blue-black tattoos as he feigned casual irritation. His right hand was noticeably held behind his back as he peered around the door.

"If I had known you had a private suite in this establishment I would have come directly here, mister Lourens," said Number One.

"But, Eben, as fate would have it," Number Two said and tilted his head to the hallway, "my queries weren't too far from the mark."

"My visit with Winston proved informative," Number One agreed with a nod.

"What you chops want," the man asked with a scowl. "I'm busy."

"Don't you mean 'we're' busy," said Number One.

"You and Charan."

Eben's eyes widened and he readjusted his hidden hand. "Who the fu–"

"Please!" Number Two held up a hand. "Language."

"It has come to my attention–" began Number One.

"And the attention of your employer," added Number Two.

"That you may be involved in activities–"

"Which are not only illicit–"

"But are being conducted within your employer's infrastructure–

"Systems, networks, personnel, facilities notwithstanding–"

"As already mentioned, 'illicit' but also gravely harmful to others–

"Others whom you seem to have no regard for–

"Other than for personal gain."

They shook their heads. "Considering the fleeting duration of this life in this world, you would think that personal gain here would be of little concern."

"If anything, not pissing off my mother–

"In this or any life for that matter–"

"Should really be of prime importance."

"Therefore, your employer–

"My mother–"

"Requires an immediate audience with your good selves."

"And I would advise against using your–"

"Weapon–

"In any way."

Infuriatingly, the message to Mlilo remained unread. Amira turned her mobile off and tapped her thumb-ring on the car door handle with irritation. Her device came to life with a vibration.

Another message from Ganesha: "I'll be down momentarily."

Before she could send a thumbs up, a second message appeared.

"We ALL will be down momentarily."

Seated straight-backed in a plush patterned couch, Ganesha had subconsciously blocked out the growing bustle of the lobby coming to life with the morning shift of staff and patrons. Moments earlier he had given a wave to Saleh and Winston as they headed out the double doors, happily opened by the concierge, into the morning air. Number Three paused his finger mid-swiped on his tablet screen, looked up at the ceiling and gave a deep sigh.

"Looks like I'll need a third set of hands for this situation."

He slipped his tablet into his jacket and headed for the elevators.

Amira watched as two men, black cloth bags over their heads and hands tied in front of them, were trundled into the back seat of her SUV by the three Ganeshas.

A Ganesha approached her driver door, took a moment to smooth down his jacket front and got into the vehicle.

"I seriously need to work on referring to my selves as we in human company. 'I this' and 'I that' always confuses them when I'm more than one around them."

Multiple car doors slammed and all three engines came to life. The SUVs on either side of them reversed and rumbled through the underground parking.

CHAPTER 20

Head still spinning from uNocabu's potent tea concoction, Mlilo stumbled out into the noxious, guttural stench of Sanusi, the older isangoma, clearly skulking around the beer hall and uNocacbu's domain in wait for Mlilo.

"Yebo, insizwa," the man blurted out, smoothing his jacket and shirt collar while Mlilo regained his footing.

"Qaphela, ixhegu," said Mlilo and instinctively held his new bag of herbs and concoctions away from the other man, feeling with his hands that all was intact.

The man's eyes narrowed and he clicked his tongue with irritation. "What, no respect? No ubaba, ubabamkhulu, umnumzana?"

"Sorry, inkosi," Mlilo spat the last word, keeping himself focused on the light of the doorway outside the beer hall while he tied the cord of the small leather bag around his belt and one of the pants belt-loops at his side.

"You know very well it is Sanusi, umfana."

"You have not earned that title," Mlilo said over his shoulder. "Only one was worthy enough to call himself that, umthakathi."

Mlilo could hear the shuffling of Sanusi's bare feet on the dusty concrete keeping pace with him as he rounded the corner into fresh air. His mobile vibrated and bleeped in his pocket, but Mlilo suppressed the urge to check it. Hand held up to the blinding morning light he once again found himself stumbling, this time over a scrawny mongrel of a dog who yelped and scuttled off into the shadows of a nearby doorway of filth.

He needed a moment to gather himself, but he knew the old man would be relentless. He had to get out the complex and to the street corner to hail a taxi and get home to his apartment in the city. Taking a deep breath, he telekinetically pushed the earlier sight of the maggot bins and refuse on the pavement directly to Sanusi's mind hoping the man would move off.

"Bastard boy," came the old man's response a few paces behind him.

Mlilo wheeled around to face him.

"Not today, ubaba," Mlilo said defiantly holding up his free hand.

"Your mind tricks will only get you so far, umfana."

"What are you sniffing around here for, like one of those dogs," Mlilo pushed out his jaw as he paced backwards. "I know you don't frequent inkosikazi uNocabu's establishment for your supplies."

The old man stretched out a crooked finger, pointing at Mlilo's waist. "I can take those for you. I can make better use of those porcupine quills rather than them getting in your way and pricking you, boy."

Mlilo stopped where he was and touched his hand on the three quills in his belt, reassuring himself they were secure.

Sanusi pulled out a bundle of ragged herbs, roots and dirt clinging to them, and forced a grin. "I can trade."

"I don't want your tainted hoard, scavenged by your minions from the wild lands, sacred resources torn without permission or regard for replenishing that which you consume. They, you, pull and tug and take but give nothing in return other than your stinking piles of crap you excrete when you've digested. Every day, slowly but surely, your body turns into a festering blob of faeces. You think your power grows every time you feed, feed on that which is not yours. And so, your soul rots and fades into nothingness until there is nothing to pass on to Abaphansi, and nothing for anyone to remember that was you, Sanusi. I may be umfana to you, but you are nothing in this or any world."

Mlilo approached the other man, voice lowered spoken through clenched teeth. "uBaba, I know you will know that these are no ordinary porcupine quills. You will also know that nGungumbane's quills are not some bushveld rodent's whose powers can be extinguished with boiling water. These have survived Abaphansi and nGungumbane herself. If I pricked you now with them," Mlilo swiftly pulled out the quills like a three-pronged dagger and jabbed it at the air in front of Sanusi who recoiled, and continued, "will the evil, the sickness, in you ooze out with your blackened blood? Come," he taunted him to approach, "we should try, old man."

Sanusi scowled at Mlilo, his rage visible in his milky old eyes.

Turning back to his path out of the complex, with the old man motionless at his back, Mlilo carefully replaced the quills in his belt and headed out onto Dalton Road.

The vendors were already trading with the commuters heading to their places of work. Mlilo, head down, ignored the brightly coloured local crafts and merchandise sitting side by side with cheaper imported gimmick paraphernalia, packets of unheard-of chips and sweets brands, and the occasional stack of fresh fruit.

He weaved through the people and came to a stop at the corner of the busy main road. Without having to bother lifting a finger, a minibus taxi came to a squeaking halt, side door sliding open, and he hopped inside.

The only sounds in the bare stairwell were Dan leaving a voicemail message for his father, somewhere in the world, and the occasional squeal of his takkies on the concrete. He stopped on the landing, which opened out into the pillared expanse of the underground parking.

Though he was focused on his mobile screen, his mother's social media page, the scents from the tree out of sight wafting past him and up the stairs stirred him. He paused his finger mid-swipe on a family photo, some local game farm as the backdrop. His mother stood behind two young children, his half-brother and sister, each of her hands on either of them. They looked just like her. But then again, so did Dan.

He stepped around the corner heading to his grove and swiped one screen back on his mobile, allowing the pang of guilt run its course at the "accept", "decline" friend request buttons, and closed his phone.

The weight of his Mark Seven, green canvas shoulder bag at his hip, leather strap slung over his shoulder, was a reassuring warmth against the chill tingling up his spine. The tree was always impressive. His tree.

The space was also a jarring juxtaposition: the raw concrete gloominess of the parking area surrounding the entire square; the stark, linear walls rising from the level above upward to the sky; and the bright green, almond shaped tree solidly holding centre stage.

Nearing the rich brown, soiled square, he used the moment to empty his mind of distractions by tracing his movements around the apartment earlier, ticking off the items he had packed.

He had taken a quiet few minutes to do a five-card reading with his Golden Tarot deck, and then put that Visconti-Sforza pack in his bag.

His wooden runes – and his small, dog-eared, thirty-two deck of Petit Etteilla tarot – remained in their places in his coat but he added the heavier, white stone rune set to his bag. He knew he would want these while at Len's. He dripped three drops of lavender on his hand and put the bottle in one of the bag's inner pockets.

He double-checked he had his silver and obsidian ring on, for solid protection.

As he had headed to the emergency exit, to the parking stairwell, he had made a quick detour to the kitchen. He took a small cream leather pouch and poured a good two handfuls of almonds into it. He filled one of his many glass drinking bottles with filtered water, emptied the milk from the fridge he knew wouldn't last the week down the kitchen sink, rinsed and tossed the carton into the recycling.

Legs set shoulder width apart, Dan felt his shoes settle into the soft earth.

The cool of the tree's shade, was invigorating and the sound of the leaves rustling just above his head like a soft whisper welcoming him in. He bent down and placed his tree branch gently on the ground, a foot from the stone he had engraved himself with the ogham symbol for Ash tree: ⊓⊓⊓

The horizontal line with 5 vertical lines below represented *Nion* or *Nin*, in Old Irish, meaning "fork" or "loft".

He took a deep breath, soaking in the sounds and scents around him, and prepared for his bardic meditation.

The fourfold breath came easily, unconsciously. In for a three-count, holding for another, out for a three-count and holding again, and over and over, rhythmically moving through his entire body.

"Awen," he said and repeated it a few more times. His voice resonated in the grove, a lilt to his voice that deepened by the time he uttered the final one.

His skin felt like it was connecting to everything in the air, the light, the humid damp, and the tree itself. He watched as the two dozen or more leaves on the ground, and one or two from the branches above him, lifted and landed on his skin, his clothes and his hair, attracted to the static lightning energy of his body. Small blue sparks clicked and crackled in the space between him and the leaves until they were part of him.

He closed his eyes, seeing the blue light behind his eyelids, pulsing and shimmering in another world. He brought his breathing back to the rhythmic beat of before.

"Ganesha says: confront the dog," read the text message from Amira on Mlilo's mobile. He thought he was reading things through a hazy funk because the message made no sense to him.

His chest was tightening and the bass thump from the taxi sound system was aching through his bones every half second.

Not even five minutes into the ride and barely over the bridge toward Maydon Wharf, he had to call it. He tapped the passenger in the row in front of him, sending the silent message to the driver in mere seconds; the taxi came to a stop.

Mlilo squeezed himself past the other passengers and onto the sidewalk, dizzy and disorientated. Getting his bearings, he headed for the direction of the park on the other side of the highway overpass.

Dan opened his eyes to the sight of his branch a foot off the ground, silver-blue lightening from the earth holding it up like spindly legs, while spreading upward and out to connect it with his body.

He stretched out his left hand and took the branch as it glided up to his grasp.

The energy subsided. The leaves on Dan's body zigzagged gently down to the ground. He noticed a single leaf stuck to the back of his right palm, his wound aching as if the leaf were a heavy weight on it.

He peeled it off, emitting a quick spark, and placed it in his side bag. He knew the rite had just gifted him with this sacred item.

Though one would expect it, Dan would never take a branch from this tree for a wand. Leaves were always offered, but a branch for a wand needed to be firm, not a brittle drop-off, and not at the cost of *taking* from the Ash.

The squeak of tyres entering the underground parking signified the arrival of Ganesha.

Dan checked the time on his mobile: 6:30AM. Exactly on time.

The vehicle stopped at Dan's back.

He nodded his appreciation to the tree and the space containing it, unsure of when he would be back, and got in the back seat of the car. He placed the branch on the back window ledge to absorb the sunlight for the duration of their journey to Ladysmith two hundred- and fifty-kilometres northwest from the coast.

Cupping his hands, he took a deep breath of the fading scent of the lavender oil, hoping its effects would drift him off to sleep.

Fortunately, another Ganesha was waiting on their arrival as Ganesha pulled into the driveway at Parvati's compound. Amira wouldn't be required to handle any suspects, so without waiting for them, she headed straight through the heavy doors, into the squat-pillared passageway, with the muffled protesting men following shortly behind her.

Through the final archway, Amira found Parvati, iridescent as ever in her sari, waiting for her. The regal woman turned gracefully on her heal as Amira came up alongside her and they headed left to the wide staircase Amira knew would lead down to the next level.

"Your friends seem to be embarking on their individual journeys in good order."

"I hope so," said Amira. At the first landing on the staircase, the main mandapam floor just above head height, they turned perpendicular to the right and started down into the darker space below.

Austere compared with the columned temple space above, the labyrinth of passages lined with flaming torchlights led to numerous "rooms", only a handful seen by Amira. She had never explored the extent of the passageways or what lay deeper than this level.

Parvati stopped at the bottom and waited expectantly for the Ganeshas. Their captives' angry tones and struggling shadows preceded them down the stairs. Both

Ganeshas, clearly flustered with all the bother, brought them to a stop on the final level and waited for instructions.

"Charan. Eben," said Parvati coolly. "Hello."

The sound of Parvati speaking seemed to have the effect of a mute button being pressed. The two blindfold men held their collective breaths and stood frozen. Amira could've counted off the five seconds it took for both to attempt their excuses through taped mouths, their tones slightly higher pitched than the bolshie arrogance moments earlier.

"I am aware one of you may not be familiar with the five yamas. One of you, on the other hand, seems to be in need of a reminder of the meaning of the sacred vows: satya, ahimsa, asteya, rahmacharya, aparigraha. We have just the facilities for this purpose.

"You may have other accomplices in your deviant activities. I know you will be forthcoming with those individuals and their whereabouts. Ganesha will see to it that you are made comfortable in one of the many rooms we have available. As you make your way, please give some thought to what it is you will be sharing with us very shortly. We have a variety of refreshments that can loosen the lips, stimulate the mind, jog memories. The facilities will also provide the ideal setting for this stimulation, without unwarranted distractions.

CHAPTER 21

He was grateful his city was now alive in the growing light of the morning with the activity of commuters and polluters, making it moderately safer to cut through Albert Park.

The feel of the grass and soil under his feet had managed to calm him, feeling fresh since departing Abaphansi and uNocabu. And that dog Sanusi.

He slowed his pace at the thought, remembering his message from Amira, or Ganesha.

He took out his mobile from his pants pocket, checked the time – 6:35AM – and looked at the open message.

"What the hell does "confront the dog" mean," he asked out loud. Ganesha was an odd character at the best of times. This was extremely cryptic. Did he mean the dodgy old man at the market? He could handle him. A chill crept up Mlilo's spine.

Without changing his pace, he looked over both shoulders, scanning his surroundings.

Just the usual movement of people, clusters of vagrants, and leftovers from the night before.

And a familiar looking dog at least ten metres behind him.

The dog.

He reached the far pavement of the park, trotted across Diakonia avenue to the apartment buildings and storefronts overlooking the tree-lined park, wracking his brain.

In a flash it all came back to him: the dog on the roadside when he and Mlilo were picked up by a Ganesha and taken to Amira; and the dog outside and inside the Congella market. The same one now trailing him, nose to the ground, weaving along inconspicuously.

He crossed the Nduli Street intersection knowing he could duck into Lellos Passage, an alleyway that would be secluded, and out onto Mfusi Street. And just two minutes from there to his apartment, a city block up.

Mlilo skipped aside for two guys pulling their trolleys overloaded with huge weaved plastic bags - supplies for the local street vendors in the area, and caught a glimpse of the dog, closer than before.

Fifty metres ahead sat a woman surrounded by charts of weaves and hairstyle options on the sidewalk, marking the entrance to the alley he would often cut through. Mlilo picked up his pace.

His senses were heightened. He was noticing everything happening around him: two well dressed women, heels clacking as they made their way along the opposite pavement, laughed and shouted their conversation at one another; two kids ambled along in their school uniforms, engrossed in their mobile phones; the aunty leaning out the third storey window of an apartment further down the street yelled something inaudible at the kids who turned and waved in confusion; cars passed by in either direction.

The hairdresser noticed Mlilo hastily approaching and hunkered down lower in her plastic chair, favouring one side. Her valuables or tools or money.

He nodded and said, "Qapela inja," and headed into the narrow alley.

The sounds of the city muffled the further in he went. The hairdresser's MO was to obviously pre-empt the alley's salons and nail bars that would be opening later in the morning. The copy and print shop owner placed his signboard outside his doorway, eyes tracking Mlilo's movements and slipped back inside.

Halfway into the alley, Mlilo stopped and turned around. Five metres back the dog was making its way along one of the bare walls, nose to the ground but gazing through lidded eyes at Mlilo.

Mlilo sneered, "uHlakanyana".

The dog recoiled and yelped, tongue lolling out of its grinning jaws.

It darted to the other side of the alley, as if to find cover that wasn't there. A metre or two closer to Mlilo, like a form catching sunlight, the dog shimmered. In that moment it was as if Mlilo's world wobbled. The line from the alley down to the street wavered, then whipped back to normal.

The hairy creature than crouched on their hands and knees in front of Mlilo, unfurled themselves to their full, lithe metre-and-a-half height. The rough, pointed features were more canine than human. And though sleight looking, Mlilo knew they were nimble and cunning, their muscles lean and ready to strike at any given opportunity or sign of weakness. Mlilo always thought of a teenage werewolf, but with more attitude.

"Chakide," Mlilo said.

The shapeshifter gave a canine-like snort.

"It has been a while, fire boy."

Mlilo had first encountered Chakide soon after his ukuthwasa, his initiation, when becoming isangoma, in the form of unogwaja. The unassuming rabbit form had come across as intended and had enticed Mlilo into a conversation. The sacred bones he had been acquiring over the months became a constant source of enquiry from the being. A bat-eared fox, a mongoose, a meerkat and a genet were all used as their approachable form. But they were always mangy and emaciated. Never the cute and cuddly kind.

"Must we play these games again, Chakide. If it is not Sanusi, then it is you trying your luck."

"I like uSanusi," the animal sniffed the air. "He knows the value of a good deal or a partnership."

"Well, I'm not interested. And you probably are aware I no longer have my bones you have spent the last few years trying to steal from me."

"Yes, yes, yes," the creature said, sounding more like laughs than agreements. "And so, I come to offer a partnership." They presented a closed fist of course, matted hair spiking from the knuckles.

Mlilo couldn't contain the revulsion that exploded from his spitting lips. "Get the fu–"

Chakide opened their fist to reveal two beads that took Mlilo's breath away. _His_ beads.

"Before you do anything stupid, please do not insult me with the parlour tricks you use on our colleague, Sanusi." They closed their fist and reopened it with a conjurer's flourish. The beads had disappeared. "We have never needed to fight, young fire bringer. Let that not change today in your haste of emotions that I see brimming up from within your being."

"How–"

Chakide clapped their hands together, relishing the moment, "Oh, I offered my services to uNosithwalangcengce. I have always kept an eye on your comings and goings and the knowledge of your whereabouts was something I could trade with her."

"I will never understand your motives and methods, Chakide. Jackals have always been the nemesis of the Hyena."

"Folktales, fire boy. You must instead listen more closely to the myths and legends of your people. There are more truths in those than the tales spun by parents and grandparents to placate and quieten brats in the crib. You have listened to your insipid children's tales, watered down and made palatable for the young to grow drowsy to by the elders weary of provoking outrage in their communities. Oh, how parents have allowed their children to grow up complacent to the true might of the creatures and monsters made into quirky caricatures of their true selves – when in reality they should be terrified rather than the petulant boy standing arrogantly before me. No, we do deals with those willing, when it suits us."

"And those knowing full well you will double-cross them."

The creature looked around the quiet alley. "I'm glad we are finally alone, umlilo mfana. If you are willing to listen to my terms rather than castigate?"

"The size of the balls on you, weasel," Mlilo said shaking his head in disbelief. "Khuluma."

Visibly excited, Chakide paced in a narrow arc in front of Mlilo, mind racing, thinking of the words. Mlilo knew this was the creature controlling their urge to spit out the truth, their real motives, but taking the time to craft the offering like a finely tuned contract. They stopped and faced Mlilo, hands and fingers working and rubbing together in anticipation.

"For a small fee," Chakide began, "be it a share of the spoils, for example."

"You mean a share of *my* bones that we recover," Mlilo said and gave an exasperated sigh. "You gamble with your life, uchakide. You hold that which is mine in the hopes of tempting me, even though you run the risk of being defeated and having nothing. Spit it out. What is your actual offer? Why must I bother with you when I can do it on my own?"

"Oh, I have plenty more than your trinkets for my power. Unlike yourself, Mlilo, who has nothing. Your new bones have yet to grow in potency. Your companions have left you. Your ancestors have abandoned you."

Mlilo's irritation grew.

"Or," the creature resumed their pacing, unfazed, "be it the quills of nGungumbane as collateral, for me to hold until we both are satisfied, or should things not turn out in your favour, or *you* double-cross *me*. In simple terms, I can share the whereabouts of uNosithwalangcengce. You do see my need for security," they nodded knowingly, "if I am to pass on this information before our deal is complete and we have your bones returned."

"How about you give me my beads and we be on our separate ways."

"And then you will be in my debt."

"I will owe nothing to the likes of you, impungushe. You helped to steal what was mine to begin with and can willingly give them back. I am not your friend the baboon who is easily tricked into self-destruction, you jackal! I may be desperate but I know of your ways. You can play-act at nursemaid, but the weasel in you comes out, lazy and tired of the act."

Without warning, Chakide gave an explosive cry followed by their distinct short, high-pitched yelps, which echoed in the confines of the alley. "I led nGungumbane to you. I was on the street last night watching her wrench your amathambo from your hands."

"Skulking in the shadows," sneered Mlilo. "You won't find me so easily again, uchakide."

"You are weak without them, umfana," the creature said and zigzagged from one wall to the other and in a flash of teeth and fur, they leaped against the wall, and in two bounding strides made an arc to come back down and behind Mlilo. A claw-like hand shot out, attempting a swipe at Mlilo's exposed kidney area, but Mlilo's already burning hand and arm buffeted the blow away. Chakide let out a cackle, the jackal in them pleased with themselves, and quickly attempted the same manoeuvre, this time darting low and successfully cutting a slit in Mlilo's pants at the knee. The surface wound burned almost immediately, Mlilo breathed in a sharp hiss of air through his teeth.

A volley burst of fire, his left hand immediately followed by his right hand, connected with the canine's hindquarters, the latter trailing behind the wiry tail down the alley and dissipated. Chakide was momentarily thrown off balance but quickly recovered, and like an eel, slithered low and leapt at Mlilo.

It took him a split second to realise the creature had grabbed either shoulder, with unusually firm claws, somersaulted overhead and used the momentum to rip Mlilo, in turn, bodily over their head and slammed into the concrete almost two metres away.

Mlilo tumbled and rolled, each impact searing through his bones, until he came to a clanging stop against a rusted dumpster. Flies buzzed and bumped into his face. A yellow plastic bucket, faded black print indicating the greasy contents was spent oil from the takeaway up the alley.

Not wasting a moment, or allowing the creature an opening to pounce, Mlilo used the bucket as elbow leverage to get to his knees and burst flames in all directions toward the skittering, cackling animal.

While Mlilo's breathing was already laboured, Chakide seemed to be thriving on the fight, energised at every move.

Mlilo pulled out the two intact porcupine quills from his belt, for the first time aware of the punctures they had made to his side during his manoeuverings.

"Time to fight like a dog," he said and grinned as he placed the spikes protruding from his right fist. Positioning himself into a crouch he used his left hand to remove his small blade from his ankle sheath, and held the hilt firmly with the blade facing downward. The rounded pommel felt solid and warm in his soft palm.

In the taxi he had slipped the circular shinbone onto his right forefinger for safekeeping, and now tapped it with a ting on the knife blade. "Would you make a whistle out of my bones, or this shinbone, impungushe?" He wiggled his finger at the animal. "Or would you lose your whistle yet again to the lizard?"

"I have no need of whistles. But that which should be mine I will soon enough retrieve." Chakide edged forward, their gnarly feet scraping on the ground. "If you are not up for a fight," they taunted Mlilo, "give me meat first, and I will go away."

Mlilo burned a rumbling blue flame around both hands and leaped at Chakide. A twirl to the left, brought the quills whistling through the air, drawing two darkening lines across Chakide's chest; Mlilo's back shielded him momentarily from any deflection as he brought his left hand slicing backward, inches from the animal's snout.

Even his low centre of gravity didn't help Mlilo counter the swift swipe of Chakide's leg, taking him off his feet onto the hard ground. He crab-legged backwards, finding himself once again against the dumpster.

More jackal-like cackles filled the air.

Think!

He replaced the quills and knife in their respective places and stared down at the yellow bucket. Normally carrying twenty-five litres, the morning light cast an oily silhouette of what he estimated was half full. Something he could heft into the air.

Confidently, Mlilo stood and grabbed the metal handle and gave the bucket a drag, edging his way to the middle of the alley.

This act seemed to get the creature into a frenzy of excitement and more pacing.

Mlilo bent down and removed the sticky lid, and threw it like a Frisbee at Chakide who easily dodged the projectile. Standing side on to his adversary, feet firmly planted, like a shot-putter he brought the container around and up, sending the black-brown liquid into the air above Chakide. Mlilo released the bucket to clatter to the side, and to Chakide's visibly stunned surprise, the oily mass wavered, suspended two metres above them. Mlilo held his hands outward, heat markers pulsating and distorting the air around them.

The animal sneered, realising the oil was beginning to boil.

Mlilo flicked a finger, causing half a cup's worth of the bubbling mass to drop inches away from Chakide with a sizzle.

The threat was acknowledged by their wide eyes fixed on Mlilo.

"I could leap the distance to your throat with ease, Mlilo."

At that, Mlilo swiftly twisted both hands. The waterfall of boiling oil hitting the concrete sent pungent steam up into the morning air, momentarily misting and obscuring the two beings.

Visibly shaken, Chakide was encircled by the sizzling grime. Yet a half metre underfoot was free of the harmful mass. A glance up, the animal's fur shivered at the sight of what remained hovering above them. Their mind was racing, calculating. To Mlilo he slyly began, "In one bound I could–"

"I'm well aware of your deft skills, weasel," said Mlilo feeling his powers waning. "But can you perform your acrobatics like this?"

Without exerting himself with a fireball, Mlilo simply flicked a spark from his forefinger. The tiny blue lightening crackled and spat in a slow arc into the fatty muck.

The spluttering explosion that followed was almost muffled by the hiss and howl of rage emitted by Chakide through clenched teeth.

Trapped by huge flames.

Mlilo shrugged his shoulders, enraging the creature even further, and pointed above their head.

The remaining slimy film above shimmered with flame and sparking liquid.

Chakide cowered down with rapid yelps, making sure to keep all parts of themselves away from the licking flames at their knees.

"Don't beat me," they pleaded over the sound of fire, "and I will let you have them."

"Throw them to me, dog!"

Through the heat haze, Mlilo could see the animal forcing themselves to reluctantly conjure forth the precious items and toss them over the flames. Mlilo snatched them up safely mid-air and held them close.

"You can take all the hounds of hell, umpungushe, uchakide," he yelled, his right hand holding fast. "Go back to where you came from. I know this will not be the last time that you show your true self to me but I wish that it were."

Chakide's form flickered and faded along with a high-pitched howl, and they were gone.

Mlilo calmed the flames and brought the oily slime to a cool on the ground, leaving a dark patch nearly three metres in circumference.

He finally had one of his amathambo in his hands. Catching his breath, he opened his palm to reveal the two beads. Just over two centimeters long, they were pieces of acacia twigs rather than your usual rounded beads. Each wedge-shaped end was burned and pierced through the sides with a hole for tying through with a leather strap as a necklace. Dinizulu's necklace design was renowned, even coveted and used by Baden-Powell as a symbol of the international Scout movement.

Mlilo closed his hand and shoved it into his pocket, keeping it there as he headed toward the end of the alley.

Past the takeaway restaurant, the bible correspondence and the laundry service, he nodded acknowledgement to the lady bringing out two mannequins for her fashion store, and stopped on the pavement, allowing the sun to warm his face and body. The shivers of adrenalin pulsed through his muscles, his skin clammy with sweat, and he felt weak but strong at the same time.

The recognisable shape of the black SUV, stylised gold, flame decal on the side, rumbled to a halt in an open parking at the pavement edge. On cue, Mlilo's mobile bleeped. He took out the device and looked at the message on the screen.

"You must come home to your family and your ancestors, umfowethu omncane."

Ulwazi, his sister.

The front passenger seat occupied by Ganesha, and not a soul driving, Mlilo made his way to the back of the vehicle and opened the door.

With a nonchalant tone Ganesha said, "I see you handled the canine situation without needing any assistance."

The sweat growing on Amira's brow had nothing to do with coming out into Durban's summer air. Distracting herself, she checked her mobile for any messages as she stepped into the SUV. What took an hour in Parvati's world, took a mere ten minutes in the real world.

Parvati had brimmed with the might and fury of her Kali power. Amira would do everything she could to never get on that side of the goddess she had witnessed in the room that had held her wayward employees. "I have used my power for more noble foes than the likes of you." Parvati's voice had rumbled through the entire temple structure. "But rage, I shall."

Her skin had turned the blackened purple of her alter ego, morphing like a Jekyll and Hyde monster, eyes terrifying and burning into your soul. The spectacle was not for the effect of drawing out the information she needed – that all came within seconds of having hoods removed, gags torn off, and seated, arms and legs restrained against sturdy wooden furniture. Rather, the rage that poured forth from the goddess beat down on body and soul alike. The two men would never walk in the world of man again, and their path into the beyond would be made, for all eternity, in a pale sliver of a shadow – their souls forever stripped of all light and matter. A consciousness without substance.

"Always a pleasure to watch my mother in action," said Ganesha getting in the driver's seat next to Amira.

He turned to Amira and asked, "Where we are headed?"

Speechless, Amira simply presented her mobile screen to him.

Recognising the map location he nodded and said, "The First River Temple."

Mlilo watched Ganesha smoothly navigating the morning traffic and feed onto the highway heading out of the city. He had untied his bag from his belt and was laying out the variety of contents on the soft leather seat next to him.

Despite his altercation with Chakide, everything was intact. Only the umhlonishwa bundle was slightly misshapen; some of the needle-shaped leaves stuck to the rough inside of the leather. He picked one off and, removing the shinbone that was constricting his finger, rolled the leaf firmly between his forefinger and thumb.

He brought it to his nose and took a deep breath. The aromatic scent of the psoralea plant's resin filled his nose, and in an instant was transported back to his meeting with uNocabu.

Stepping through the makeshift doorway from the beer hall, the thick air and muffled sound of Abaphansi had soon enveloped Mlilo along with a plethora of fragrances filling the dimness. Initially overpowering to his senses, he managed to steady his breathing to fully absorb the properties of each scent while through the milky haze of smoke his eyes adjusted to the noticeable dim light filtering through the draped fabrics, and milky haze, that made up uNocabu's abode. The pungent and sublime mphepho, hints of the dried lavender hanging from the fabric draped ceiling, and the cleansing and rejuvenating sage, among so many others he could not name.

He moved through the labyrinth of richly patterned and embroidered materials, never knowing how vast the woman's domain truly extended.

The smells grew stronger as Mlilo parted the rich purple and gold fabric he remembered was the entrance to the meeting space.

Plush carpets lined a room of about five metres wide and seven or eight metres deep, while low overhead draped materials, ropes and cords from which dozens of bundles of dried plants, brass oil burners and lamps hung from chains.

Along the sides and among huge cushions and squat wooden chairs and hexagonal tables, various jars, crates, bundles and boxes filled the remaining space, creating narrow footpaths. His sniffed a thick scent that permeated the room from a brass dish on a small lounge table, flame flickering beneath, emitting the grey-black oil of frankincense.

Three-quarters of the way to the back of the room, an ornately carved, ebony wooden desk spanned the width of the room. Lamplight through the fabric wall leading to the room two metres behind the desk showed the silhouetted movement, and with a flourish of smoke and clatter of gold bracelets, the nearly seven-foot figure of uNocabu emerged with a bright white grin at Mlilo. Her stunningly black skin, seemingly permanent moist lips, contrasted with her gold jewellery of bangles, rings and necklaces, echoing the shimmering thread running through her embroidered, flowing garments and headscarf. Her lithe hands fanned out in welcome, her fingernails a matching glossy, black sheen coming to narrow points, accentuating her elongated fingers.

Like a blinding light in the dark, the sight of uNocabu always took Mlilo a moment to recover from. He attempted an aloof casual air, which only resulted in him fumbling her name, causing her grin to grow even more.

"My love," she said smoothly and gestured to the plush cushions and seating at Mlilo's knees, "I know you are rushed, but sit, relax."

Mlilo felt the urgency of his journey dissipate and he slipped down onto a cushioned chair. Taking his lead, she too prepared herself, flourishing out her garment and gracefully descending into her own chair. "You look like you could do with some tea," she said and stretched out her hand and pinged a brass a musical chime that filled the muted room.

"I could do with a dose of my usual kanna."

A moment later the shorter, five-foot figure of the man Mlilo recognized as Msizi, uNocabu's husband or mate or partner or concubine – he was never quite sure – emerged, looking flustered from whatever activity they may have been engaged in prior to Mlilo's arrival. He and Mlilo exchanged nods.

uNocabu gave it some thought before turning to Msizi and whispering, "uMhlonishwa, my love."

She could offer him the blood of his enemies and he would take it with enthusiasm. She was the expert. uNocabu never contradicted you or shook her head at your requests, but she would offer a suggestion or an addition.

Attention back to Mlilo, with a smile, uNocabu said, "Something a bit more potent to catch up over, my love." She tented her long fingers to her lips and said, "The parasites remaining inside you will need the continued consumption of umthsanelo for the next few days. I'll also give you a bundle of umhlabelo. The dried leaves from the Nidorella plant will help heal your muscles and bones–"

"And healing an ego?"

uNocabu let out a deep laugh. "This is why I have always liked you, Mlilo. Always forthcoming. No hidden agendas. So very much like your strong-willed ancestor Zandile."

On the occasion of his first visit to uNocabu, after his ukuthwasa, he had been seated where he was now, and only after what seemed like hours had uNocabu softened to him. Her questions and the conversation she commanded turned out to have been an interview. Inexplicably, he had opened up to this stranger, answered her questions and as it turned out, showed his true self to her.

uNocabu had survived eons through her cunning, her business dealings and acumen. She knew who to trust and who to hurry out of her sight.

Once she had warmed to him in that first meeting, she had revealed her relationship with Zandile all those lifetimes ago.

Mlilo looked across the vast desk to the intricate device among other smaller gadgets and implements uNocabu had created. Lenses, cogs, cylinders and wire made things Mlilo could never imagine their purposes. His ancestor, uNocabu had related to him, was an enquiring mind and had respectfully demanded to know the world uNocabu resided in, what Abaphansi was to Zandile and her people.

Better at using her hands and her creations to bring forth an idea, uNocabu had meticulously constructed what Zandile, in setting her eyes on it at their second meeting, had aptly named and uNocabu always relished to speak: the oBungapheliyo uMhlaba Amazulu". The model of Abaphansi. Like the astrolabes Mlilo had seen used by astronomers, philosophers and scientists of old, the model depicted the structure and workings of the other world beyond.

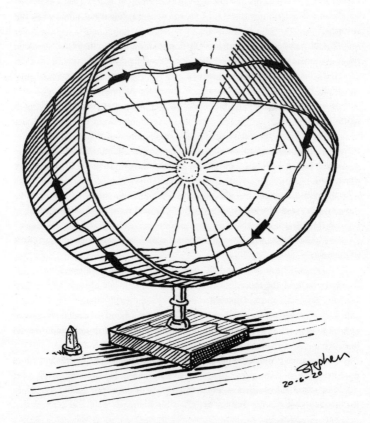

A flat plane had been joined, end-to-end, in a twisted loop like a contorted orbital in space. The two flattest surfaces opposite and perpendicular to one another served two purposed. The first surface at the base, flat to the tabletop, provided the supporting brass rod connected down into a block of black and white marble. In contrast, a perfect brass ring was hinged on the top and bottom outer axis, and could be swivelled when needed. Over five centimetres in width, it featured detailed engravings and script, illustrating various star formations of the universe.

In the middle of the entire structure, suspended down from the upper surface point, hung a thin cord with a light representing the sun, the pure energy of the universe, the source. uNocabu had taken a stumpy brass figurine, the size of a chess piece, and placed it below the light and had Mlilo imagine he was this person standing on the bottom surface. If he looked up it was like midday, bathed in full sunlight.

"A soul, new and old, is born here. Walking clockwise along the plane, 'upward', the soul moves through life, and as they do so, the light source changes." uNocabu moved the piece through the first curve.

"Like the sun moving towards the horizon, the life begins to age." uNocabu shifted the brass piece to the top surface, directly above and perpendicular to the light.

"To you, Mlilo, the sun is setting, split by the horizon, and it is time for you to leave your world. And so, the soul re-enters Abaphansi here. Its journey back to wholeness begins." uNocabu moved the figurine, gently following the next curve downward.

"It moves onward into the darkness." Mlilo had realised it was twisting outward away from the source of any light. "The soul is required to leave its life in your world. It has to let go of its physical experiences, its body, and move through."

She had slid the piece along and stopped it directly underneath the start point of the base.

"It is now in complete shadow. The soul is devoid of its physical. Now it is drawn to the light, the source."

She began the journey upward.

"The first light of the soul's dawn fills the space around it." As the piece came around to the top, Mlilo could imagine the first light of the sun peaking over the horizon.

"The source is pulling it onward, the soul is regenerating." Along and down the final curve, the brass piece glinted in the light suspended from the centre.

The sound of Msizi bringing in a clinking tray of steaming cups brought Mlilo back to the room, eyes fixed on the brass figurine where uNocabu had left it, all that time ago, directly below the light.

"I see you are remembering." The woman smiled at him.

Mlilo realised uNocabu had allowed him to get lost in his thoughts.

Msizi set down each of their glass cups, with gold handles in front of them.

As she had the habit of doing whenever they talked, uNocabu had found a ball of golden thread on her desk and had unconsciously weaved a weblike pattern, like a cat's cradle but even more intricate and delicate. In a few swift motions, her fingers unravelled from the knitted mass, dropped it to the side of her workspace and picked up her tea.

Msizi placed the tray on the desk, smoothed under his wrap-around garment and sat himself and his drink down, and gives the surface of his cup a gently blow.

"We have much to discuss. Your provisions will be sorted out by the time you need to depart," she said and exchanged nods with Msizi, clearly enjoying his beverage. "And I realise you are eager to continue on your journey to retrieve your amathambo, my love."

Mlilo reached for his and took a sip. The flavours hit his senses and he could immediately feel its effects taking hold.

"But, since your battle with nGungumbane, much has happened. Yes, uNosithwalangcengce retrieved the piece of herself that would make her whole and powerful once again." She raised her eyebrows at Msizi. "We all felt the rumbles which shook Abaphansi at the moment the Hyena realised her two fatal errors."

Mlilo sat forward, cradling his hot drink, allowing the steam to rise up into his face.

"The first change of circumstance was realising you," she said and pointed a long finger nail at Mlilo, "were now the entitled holder of the bone, rather than the bone simply being released on the death of Zandile; the second, her underlings had passed up two opportunities to kill you." uNocabu seemed to relish relaying the information to Mlilo. "Her furious rage had roared through Abaphansi and her anger grows every moment she cannot become whole."

The bigger picture was emerging for Mlilo. He had remembered being told how Zandile had cast a spell over the bone, effectively cloaking it from uNosithwalangcengce, even after she died. But on Mlilo receiving it during his ukuthwasa, all holds over it or spells would fall away. For that brief time, like a beacon, uNosithwalangcengce would have felt the ripples through every world as the bone was reactivated just as the Morrígan had said. And despite Mlilo performing his own cloaking rite, uNosithwalangcengce had used her resources, like Chakide, to track Mlilo down and take his amathambo. In her frenzy, she would have ignored the obvious situation that Mlilo was not merely holding some trinkets passed down through the family, but that Zandile had specifically handed them on to the next true isangoma in her family line.

"Since I got that bone, since my ukuthwasa, my life has been hell."

"Yes, it was the Hyena causing havoc to get it away from you. To wrest it from your hands."

Mlilo slouched back. "This morning was the first time it was a direct assault."

"uNosithwalangcengce," uNocabu continued, "cannot integrate her breast bone until the one who has a hold over it, the one to whom it belongs, is dead or gives it freely back to her. She will be even more furious that she has this in her grasp but remains unable to enter your world to do the deed herself. So, in here," she gestured to the world around them that was Abaphansi, "you must tread extra carefully, my love, as that dog tries all she can to return to her full power and endangering all our worlds."

She allowed that final thought to hang in the air like her thick incense fragrances.

"You are after the bone that was rightfully taken by your ancestor, but uNosithwalangcengce will not let it go without a fight. Do what you can to cloak your whereabouts. This may not be completely effective, so be on your guard and reveal nothing about where you are going. I would advise you to get away from your city. Don't underestimate the power of joined forces. Your friends bring their own gifts to your aid. It's not just about power in numbers but power in collective support."

Mlilo suddenly felt overwhelmed. Another sip of tea pushed those feelings down.

"This is a weight for you to bear, even after your recent ordeal. But you have one thing in your favour, so do not underestimate yourself, fire-bringer. "The Hyena's weakness is fire."

Mlilo placed his cup on uNocabu's desk and sat with his head in his hands. "What would *she* have done?"

Considering the boy before her, uNocabu's fingernails tapped the table surface. Msizi stood, quietly placed each cup on the tray and withdrew behind the curtain.

"Zandile is her own person. You are your own person. Imparting knowledge to another is like casting a spell: it will either hold them, constrict them, to its will or if they choose to finally let it go, discard it, or absorb it or overcome the restriction, they will discover their true selves. Taking on knowledge from others is like casting spells over yourself. You become beholden to these mantras and truisms of others instead of conjuring and creating your own."

"Go where you are called. Regenerate the inner strength that burns within you, my love. You will know when you are ready to take back your amathambo."

The SUV shuddered over the Paradise Valley bridge

Mlilo remembered how they had sat a long while with more tea, his urgency to leave long passed.

He laid out his provisions on one side, and the seemingly random amathambo he was amassing, on the other. He knew they all had their purpose, and the purpose was driven by his amadlozi behind the scenes.

Taking stock, he checked them:

Aside from the small bundle of umhlonishwa he had asked her for, for when he needed something stronger than his regular kanna tea, from uNocabu he had purchased the leather bag, along with an extra half metre of black leather cord – always handy – along with a roll of mphepho for burning, bundled tightly in copper wire. Remembering his lighter, he shifted his weight and retrieved the small black *Bic* and placed it next to the herb; then there was the small dose in a tea-bag sized packet, three days' worth, of umthsanelo, sturdier in potency than the weatherworn one picked on the mountaintop, for his parasites; uNocabu's recommended bundle of umhlabelo for his aching muscles and ego; and finally, she had given him a small umlomomnandi root, saying, "Your friend is a bard, a druid, is he not?" Having not spoken about his friends, Mlilo had been taken aback that she knew about Dan. "He will soon be needing this. When you chew on it, it blesses you with quick wit, a poetic voice and a silver tongue."

"Oh great. Like he really needs to be encouraged to use his silver tongue." But he didn't argue.

uNocabu had picked up the discarded mess of golden thread, and in a flash of nails and rings, had wound it neatly into the size of a large marble, like a miniature ball of twine. "You may be needing this." He had accepted it without question.

Part amathambo, part provision, were the red seeds from the branch uNomkhubulwane had allowed Dan to remove for his future wand. The natal ebony was a good protective war charm, and if necessary, good for stomach issues. The rough pod was now splitting open, the red of the three beans-shaped seeds like flames within; and the three limping leaves going a darker green that would soon turn a hard, brittle brown.

His real amathambo included the three porcupine quills, one bent and nearly in two, lying neatly parallel to the inky-black feather from the Morrígan; and the ring-shaped shinbone. The two beads he had taken back from the sly Chakide lay untethered, so Mlilo reached down and unsheathed his knife, looped the leather cord around his wrist, and sliced enough for a knot. He gently picked up the oblong wooden pieces and fed the cord through them and tied a neat, firm knot around his wrist, alongside his right hand isiphandla skin.

He started to place his items into the leather bag, feeling each one's weight, touch and scent as he did so.

"I was told you would need something else for your journey home, Mlilo."

He was shocked at the sound of Ganesha's voice from the front seat. He had grown used to the calming drone of the vehicle and little else.

"I filled two plastic canteens with sea water and sea sand for you. They are in the boot."

Bringing the much-prized commodity back to his home, his sister's home, was something he always made sure he did. Important in so many ways in a home and community, from cleansing the body to connecting with the amadlozi, he hadn't given it a thought when he saw Ulwazi's message, her call, for him to come home.

"Who told you this," he asked, knowing the answer.

"Zandile."

CHAPTER 22

The car had turned off Sarnia Road into Oliver Lea Drive and driven a short distance, parallel to the canal, and parked on the pavement under the overpass.

They stood facing a bland and innocuous concrete block, grimy and graffitied, with no significant markers to indicate the location's power or purpose.

Ganesha folded his arms with a sigh and looked around their surroundings. The low concrete sides of the canal to the slow-moving river, as far as you could see, were almost hidden beneath the overgrowing, lush green paraffin weed. In stark contrast, towering pylons and bland blocks of offices and factories reflected the oppressive industrial area.

"I assume you know what happened here, what was built here?" he asked Amira.

She nodded.

"The first Hindu temple built on this vast continent," he said.

Amira knew the basics but didn't stop or interrupt Ganesha. Minutes earlier, on their drive through the Cato Manor area, they had both automatically turned their heads as they had passed the current structure to their right: the Umbilo Shree Ambalavaanar Alayam Temple. Also known as the Second River Temple for a reason.

"It was 1869 when two young boys, born in the old country, dived in the river here," he pointed to the canal waters trickling along under the bridge. "They were unaware that they had crossed over. But what they were very sure about was that the spear, the vel, that they had retrieved from the bottom, was that of the war god Subramaniar." Ganesha paused, and added, "My brother. With this auspicious sign, it was his namesake that the first temple, Shree Subramaniar Alayam, was dedicated to when it was completed six years later."

Amira imagined the thundering sound of the freeway above, with its full force of morning traffic, like the raging Umbilo River over the decades at full flood, washing through the first temple structures and the subsequent rebuilds until the land was finally expropriated. Banning Hindus from further temple building or property ownership at the turn of the previous century, they did everything in their power to keep the sacred site intact. But the river of oppression was stronger. The harbour and railways expanded their workshops and marshalling yards further inland.

"When we intervened on numerous occasions in 1965, to halt its outright destruction," Ganesha continued right on cue, "the news reverberated around the world. Strange occurrences caused demolition machinery to be destroyed, workers and those in charge were injured." He gave Amira a wry smile. "We did what we could but we knew we would not prevail against pure hate, but they were unable to fully demolish the structure, and like cowards, resorted to filling it in with soil and building this monstrosity over it. It remains in there."

"Bastards," Amira muttered.

"Indeed," Ganesha agreed and stepped closer to the concrete and extended an open palm to the cool wall. "But a sacred place is about the intent behind it, and the new structure we passed earlier stands today as a beacon for our people. Though some may have forgotten this first one, this space has retained its power. It is its own beacon, drawing us back once again."

He pushed his hand into the bridge wall, turned to Amira and said, "As you and I part ways on the other side, I have reluctantly taken this as a sign that I must visit with *Sigidi*. Mother will be pleased," and stepped inside.

Dan checked his GPS on his mobile. The vehicle had slowed as it navigated the main road through the busy market town of Ladysmith. Only a short distance left to Len's home on the outskirts of the residential area, he noted.

Moments earlier, Ganesha had pressed a button to adjust his front passenger seat back to the upright position, waking Dan from his quiet rest. His body, and right hand, ached.

Superstores and wholesalers, informal traders and pedestrians drifted past the tinted windows Dan was grateful for dulling the impact of the morning sunlight. The only things to penetrate the cocoon of the SUV were the noises of the morning commute of minibus taxis and objecting trucks and cars.

"I do like the small towns of our country," said Dan. "They have the habit of bringing you back down to earth from our superiority complexes in the big city."

"Hmm," grumbled Ganesha.

"You disagree?" Dan asked, surprised at the tone from the usually even-toned Ganesha.

"Small towns and their people are probably the most ardent worshippers of any god worth their salt. I would throw out a completely anecdotal stat and say that the majority of our strength, from said worship and veneration, comes from these pockets of devotees. And yes, the cities are where that veneration tends to be weakest."

"I feel like there is a but coming," said Dan.

"We gods walk among the people. Can you imagine if I stood on a soapbox in the middle of this town and proclaimed who I am? I'd be crucified, or the equivalent in this day and age. In the city, you'd maybe get a second glance before they returned to their mobile devices and carried on their way."

The SUV turned left, heading west. Dan watched the other man with amusement, staring at people crossing the busy road and weaving randomly between vehicles.

"The second coming's already happened," he continued, "and no one even noticed. And so, we live our lives, hiding our true identities in a closet while we feed and thrive on the worship of our people. They don't wish to see their gods to believe that they exist. Hope is what keeps them going.

"I suppose it is a mutual understanding: I will pray to you, pay homage, bow and scrape at your likeness as long as I get what I want, or the hope that I will get what I want, eventually. As long as you never show your terrifyingly beautiful face or your physical manifestations. If you do choose to show yourself, I will faint, scream and tear at your false image.

"We are the pies in the sky. To the people, the gods may have, at some point in history or legend or fantasy, walked the earth. That is gone. That is not the real world. Their world is the fantasy. We are there when times are tough or tradition dictates, we materialise as an inert and impotent gold statue to be set at a non-threatening distance.

"And yet, a time is coming that we are going to be called to show ourselves. And that time too, will fall into legend and holy texts, to be prayed upon, unpacked by the scholar and reinterpreted to the benefit of the sly.

"No, gods no longer walk the lands as they once did. We walk them in anonymity; not unrecognised but rather unacknowledged.

"The second coming came, as prophesied, and went, burnt at the stake. Will they recognise us next time around?"

"Yasas," said Dan. "That's a bit heavy for this time of the morning.

"Besides, most of these small towns are stuck in the past. Show me the good old days and I'll show you the boils and plagues you so easily forget."

Five minutes later the vehicle wound its way into Bungalow Road, and a short distance to the dusty panhandle driveway leading to Len's house.

The 1960s and 1970s corrugated roof house, typical of the area and the times it was built, revealed itself along with a number of outbuildings and the fenced area housing Len's pigs and chickens.

Abhorred by many, Len kept pigs as a throwback to the ancient myths of

Europe, an aspect of the goddess and the cycles of the earth and moon. One Welsh legend had it that sacred pigs were given as a gift from Annwn, the underworld, to Pwyll. His son, Pryderi, was considered one of the three powerful swineherds of the British Isles. Swineherds were considered to be magical men, unable to be swayed or deceived.

The latter, Dan remembered with a pang in his stomach, Len had succumbed to, earning the manacle of warlock and subsequently spurned by his fellow druids around the world.

The vehicle came to a stop, dust billowing around Dan and Ganesha as they exited. Dan stretched and creaked his joints while Ganesha smoothed and dusted down his immaculate, black silk coat and centred his black pearl necklace.

Side by side they stood at the front door under the low patio roof and Dan knocked.

Through the mottled glass in the top half of the door, a figure approached and opened it with a flourish.

"Oh hi, sugar lips," said the shirtless, lean man in his mid-thirties. His only garment was the pair of loose, colourful shorts and thin blue slops on his feet.

"Hey, Conrad," Dan said and gave Len's boyfriend of over ten years a broad smile. "Is Len in?"

"Where else would the man be, bokkie?" He shook his head dramatically and waved them in. "If he's not at one of those bloody spiritual fares, he's here."

Conrad Ahrens' bright blue eyes, never missing a thing, locked on the smart figure of Ganesha entering behind Dan.

"I'm wanting to meet the esteemed Leonard Herbst," Ganesha said to Conrad as he walked inside, hands behind his back.

Dan could see Conrad looking the well-dressed Ganesha up and down and clicked his tongue. "He is spoken for, honey."

"Spoken for?" He turned to Dan. "What does that mean?" he asked Dan, who shrugged his shoulders.

The man sidled up to Dan and, lifting his hand to Dan's ear, loudly whispered, "Don't say anything about it to Leonard, but some religious nuts paid a visit the other night and left a sheep's head at the top of the driveway." He sighed. "Obviously too bang to come down to the house." And with a wave of his fingers, Conrad headed down the hallway back to the kitchen, casually scraping his slops along the wooden floors.

Their attention turned to the thudding of feet from the lounge to their left, as the large, just under six-foot frame of Len in his unkempt and oversized grey suit jacket and baggy pants rolling over his well-worn shoes, walked through the archway. During the summer months especially, Len always seemed to have a layer of sweat on his face and balding head.

The man gave a phlegmy cough and wheezed out an excited greeting in his characteristic thick Afrikaans accent. "Paroxysms of mirth," Len exclaimed, using one of his favourite English phrases, and grabbed a willing Dan in a tight embrace. "There he is."

The additional person standing at his door momentarily startled Len. "Oh my God, up and down! Who is this?" Dan's mentor sussed Ganesha out and finally decided to offer his hand to shake. "Can you spell 'chrysanthemum'"?

"I can, but I'm not staying, mister Herbst. I'm Ganesha." Ganesha reached out a hand. "I just wanted to make your acquaintance. I have heard a lot about you."

"Lovely," Len said and clapped his hands together and gave the other man the same enveloping hug. "Call me Len."

A wide-eyed Ganesha accepted the gesture and patted Len on the back, before the two parted. He nodded to Len. "Len," and turned to Dan. "Keep safe, Daniel."

Dan and Len watched Ganesha leave, closing the front door behind him.

"Daniel. You look like a herd of wild boar ran over you. Have you performed your morning rites?"

Dan shook his head and rolled his eyes. "I have not, Len."

"Out you go to the Tighthe nan Druidhneach," the man jostled him toward the back of the house. The structure they were headed to was the sacred space Len would share with other druids, students and guests, but in recent years Dan had been the only one visiting or learning from him.

Through the lounge and past the delectable smells emanating from Conrad's kitchen, Len caught sight of the branch gripped in Dan's hand.

"And this," said Len trailing behind Dan and giving the stick a prod.

Dan gave the man a moment to figure it out. And he did.

"Hells bells and buckets of blood," his firm hands stopped Dan in his tracks before he could make it through the open kitchen door and into the garden. Dan was pivoted around to face a clearly red and flustered Len. "Hells bells, boy!"

Dan gave a sheepish smile and raised his eyebrows. "Shit happened, Len."

Len was already pushing away Dan's left sleeve to look at the empty sheath where his dear wand should have been safely tucked away. Len pulled the sleeve back, his other hand warmly holding Dan's.

"Right," he moved past Dan, continuing to hold onto him, and led the way into the garden along the gravel pathway that wound through the patchwork foliage to the building nestled at the back of the property. Everything grown for a purpose and a use.

The buzzing sound of the bees could be heard even before he could see them.

True to form, Len's Druid house was somewhat unique in its design as well as its co-occupants. Similar to the local rondavels – round, mud-packed, thatched buildings – Len's had an almost wizard-hat-shaped straw roof whose sides looked like they flopped to the ground, leaving a low archway over the carved, pale blue door. The rope engravings along the edges and the triskele symbol in the centre gave it a unique look.

But it was the beehive that always stunned Dan. The shimmering mass of hive took over the left side of the thatching and ended only a foot from the ground. The bees always kept to that side of the structure, whether coming or going, and Dan was safe in the knowledge that no one had been stung on the property. Not always something you trusted when faced with this phenomenon on this scale.

Len had trusted that they had made their home here for a reason. What that was he couldn't be sure, but they helped his herbs and plants grow in abundance.

"We gave it a bit of a clean, fresh linen, but it's pretty much the same as you left it from last year's visit."

Dan could hear a sadness in his mentor's voice.

"Still no new trainees?" Or friends popping down for the weekend.

Len finally let go of Dan's hand and opened the door, leading the way inside. The sounds from outside, the bees, the birds, cars in the distance, all faded as the coolness of the single room abode enveloped them.

About three metres in diameter, it housed a sink with running water to the right, in the middle back was a neatly covered double bed opposite the entrance, along with a small lamp on a matching blue side table and shelf, and a three-drawer chest-of-drawers for clothes against the left wall under a tiny window opening on to the view of the overhanging thatch. The ablutions were outside: an outdoor shower which was a horrendous ordeal in Ladysmith winters, and a separate toilet.

The vertical space made by the thatch was surprisingly deceptive from the outside, and gave fair headroom to the likes of Dan and Len. Support beams rose upward, tied to the grass, and through its centre was a steel chimney pipe for ventilation.

"Right, my boy," said Len, "I'll let you get settled, do your connecting with your what whats, and we can catch up just now over a cup of rooibos tea on the patio." He took in a deep breath and looked out the door. "And we'll see what Con has prepared for brunch."

Len's face was flustered with emotion. Dan removed his side bag, and along with his branch, placed them on the end of the bed. He turned back to Len and gave him a tight hug.

"Oh hemel."

"Good to be back, my friend."

Amira had been walking for a while, weary of the world she found herself in, far away from the protection of Parvati and her temple complex.

Passing through from the concrete bridge in Durban, she and Ganesha had emerged on the bank of a vast river flowing to their left, the sun sitting warmly on the horizon before them. They were surrounded by huge brown and grey granite boulders sitting immobile like giant creatures emerging from the river and onto the bank. Away from the river the rocks were engulfed in trees and vines, creating a small hill that tapered off on either side up and down river. What immediately struck Amira, was the central rock formation that peaked out through the lush canopy of foliage. It was then that she realised many of the boulders were arranged in ascending size on either side to create a short pathway, the inside of the rocks carved with horizontal lines and patterns leading into the structure. At the end was something similar to what she had seen in photos, and reminding her of Al-Khazneh temple in Petra, sculpted out of the cliff-face. A three-metre-high entrance archway was hollowed out, while two ornately carved columns on either side displayed various scenes of battle wrapped around them. The top of the structure, at first glance part of the rock formations around it, Amira realised was perfectly symmetrical and more like a dome, and came to a slight point at the pinnacle.

Ganesha had left her to visit his brother, while she made her way upriver, past a stretch thick with reeds and turned inland.

She had wound her way through a huge expanse of a forest of what appeared to be stone spears, reminding her of Ganesha's brother, Subramaniar. She also couldn't help thinking of the two boys in the Umbilo river and the spear they pulled out possibly belonging to a Zulu impi passing through the ancient landscape eons before.

Amira held her khaṭvāṅga firmly at her chest, like the hilt of a sword, aware of everything around her. She walked along what appeared to be a long, rough trench going on for over four hundred metres, but it was as if an earthquake had ripped up the earth. Long since behind her, the start of the trench a messy crater of mud and dirt, like a small battle had taken place. Small smooth rocks covered the remaining area like an untidy Roman road, and the further edges becoming larger rocks and into small bush and low trees. Nothing that would camouflage any large beasts or predators. Ahead in the distance she could see the beginnings of a valley, mountain ranges in the farther distance and to the left.

Amira recalled one of her many conversations with Parvati regarding war, conflict, and hand-to-hand encounters. "A champion is triumphant in a conflict not because they are the most experienced, the strongest or most brutal, they succeed through their use of weapons, their inherent powers, their cunning and their knowledge of themselves. It's how they use these powers, their magic, against their enemy that matters.

The most powerful goddess, magician or army in the worlds can still be defeated by someone less experienced. Their magic within determines the outcome. Determines who is defeated.

You have to learn how to best use what you have. And you can defeat anyone. You can overcome anything. Your neighbours can have all the bells, whistles and fire-breathing dragons they like, but if they don't know how best to use them it may as well be a knobkerrie.

Something stirred in the air around her and she stopped, holding her breath to listen. Oddly, her left hand tickled. She looked down to see the halāhala design under her skin shifting in brief pulses of movement. That only happened when she was actively wielding its power.

She carried on walking, eyes peeled for movement. Her shoe caught on one of the smooth rocks, protruding more than she expected but kept her footing and her pace. Her adrenaline was pumping. She had to relax. Spooking yourself was no way to go through life.

Amira realised she was weaving her way around and over many of the rocks, sitting out of the ground more than before.

In that moment the ground began to vibrate and the rocks appeared to push out of the earth.

They were no inanimate stones. They were crablike creatures, multiple legs and pincers spreading out from their sides and pushing themselves above ground. And they were not friendly.

Amira stepped into the low trench, free of obstructions and the growing throng of animals around her. Their slow, steady movements were not lethargic, rather measured and calculating of her in their domain. She wasn't sure what to make of them, but they were definitely hostile, and one thing she had learned about fighting was to avoid conflict. Not cowardice, but to de-escalate a situation or to remove yourself from something that appears to be becoming hostile.

This was one of those moments.

Rather than pointing her wand threateningly at the mass of beings, she held it upright with both hands and inward, tight like a vice, and cautiously stepped backwards.

A clatter of exoskeletons, like seashells, filled the air as the horde moved with her, some climbing into the low trench.

She picked up her pace as much as she could without stumbling, glancing behind her to keep aware of the topography and any obstacles, or shelter nearby. No substantial trees or boulders to climb. And those may not be reliable against these spider-crabs.

The cacophony following her increased like the building of a rain storm.

With no other options, Amira muttered, "Assholes," and turned and broke into a bounding run.

Nothing was clear to her, rock or crab, she hopped, weaved and dodged everything that sprung up in her path. Soon she was ploughing through the bodies of the crab creatures, fully out of their earthly burrows, but hope was in sight five metres ahead. In three strides she leaped up, pulling her legs sideways and planted a firm hand on the head of one of the startled animals, sliding along the top of the last two rows of beings and into an open stretch, finally free of the blockade. She sprinted, unhindered, with all she had.

First as a whisper, Amira began reciting the Shiva-Kavacha chant, trying to focus her mind. She could feel the energy building, and could imagine the breastplate and glove forming around her body, without looking down. But the distraction around her was too much.

Louder, she shouted the words. But her ears filled with the sound of the swarm gaining on her. She could not keep the distance between them and she could not summon the sacred armour. A glance behind her took her breath away. The entire horizon seemed covered in a swarm of creatures honing in on her like a massive triangle moving across the landscape in her wake.

The ground had lost its muddy surface and become sandy, making Amira slide to a stop when she decided to whirl around, tunic swirling in the air, to face the onslaught head on. "Back off!"

To her surprise, rather than clatter to a stop like a cartoon train piling up on itself, and without hesitation, the mass of creatures kept moving like liquid in an engulfing arc around Amira.

Finally, the noise and movement died down, the creatures sitting at least ten metres deep all around her. Having some idea of many of the creatures that roamed this world, she was at a loss with these. And not knowing meant she didn't know what to expect. She only knew what she could do to fend them off.

Amira gave a firm snap of her khaṭvāṅga at the ground, an ink black pool of halāhala bloomed out from under her feet, as she had imagined it, tendrils moving out to create a circular space nearly three metres in diameter with her in the middle.

There was a noticeable withdrawal by the frontline creatures, giving Amira a momentary breather, which soon faded as one of them edged forward.

Amira's eyes darted between the advancing animal and a single tendril of halāhala closing the gap between them.

It wasn't afraid of the black poison.

She gave another flick of her wand and the black ink splashed outward and over the creatures, three or four rows deep, saturating them in halāhala. Stunned, it took Amira a moment to realise it hadn't spread as far as it should have, at least the outer edges of the swarm. But another wave of them was coming, pushing over the fallen towards Amira.

She lifted the wand to head height, drawing the fluid back in to herself, and dropped to her knees waiting for the wave to overwhelm her.

Using all her energy she could summon, she pushed outward with all she had inside herself. Her khaṭvāṅga felt like an opposing magnet in her hand, being simultaneously drawn in by one force and repelled by another.

Keeping it constant, with nothing more to give, she realised she had created a shimmering bubble of energy around herself, made apparent by the spectacle of the creatures unable to breach it, piling up around her on the invisible balloon-like force. Poking, stabbing and slicing at the field around her, Amira was aware of them engulfing her, the pale light from outside getting blocked out, bit by bit.

One final shove of energy sent a burst into the throng that scattered them off and away from her. There was still no exit. She had to choose: stand and use her own power or summon the armour for protection. Right now, she could not do both.

Though she didn't feel drained, from the expulsion of energy, it wasn't going to hold them off for long, let alone kill anything. She held her khaṭvāṅga firmly and gave all she could as she flicked it downward again. The black mass moved over everything in sight, an unnatural gloom spreading. Her fingertips were being pulled by the liquid rapidly seeping out of her, until it could reach no further.

She gazed wide-eyed as the crab-like animals slowed their frenzied attack, the creatures closest to Amira dead still in their tracks while the others clamouring up behind reached the halāhala. Rather than staying back or retreating they came within its reach. Amira couldn't understand it.

The bedlam of approaching bodies subsided, taking only a few seconds for every animal to be immersed, the dark ring around Amira finally falling silent. Nothing moved.

But it didn't feel right.

It was as if a giant elastic tied her hand, her arm, to the ground. Using her other hand, gripping the metal wand, she struggled to pull it upward. She got it to shoulder height but could go no further. Amira collapsed to the ground, a wave of nausea moving up from her stomach. She was exhausted. An unusual sensation for Amira in this world.

Unable to retract the halāhala into herself, she had to get out of the surrounding bodies. There may have been some alive beneath and she needed to get far away from them. The first step was awkward, wobbly and uncertain. Her hands gave her support as she crawled up and over the hard creatures, and part of the black poison clung to her palms. Reabsorbing.

Getting herself as steady as she could she noticed one of the beings she was passing over and thought for a moment that it was slightly different to the earlier attacking swarm. She stopped and looked around her. They were all different than before. Although the halāhala had blackened everything, smearing away the inky substance from what appeared to be a breastplate, revealed a dull metal rather than the bright red and white of the crab forms. She looked down at where the pincers would have been and saw a hybrid sword-scissors, jointed at the forearm to something like armour.

The crablike features, multiple arms, and exoskeleton had become more humanoid, and clad head to toe in formfitting armour. Amira looked closely at the mud and ink splattered face beneath the helmet. The segments of the crab features had pulled together like a jigsaw, to form an angular pixie face. She narrowed her eyes further, focusing on the closed eyes. The surface of the body was moving, morphing millimetre by millimetre. It was changing before her eyes.

A sense of unease pulsed blood through her ears, her adrenaline rising once again. She carried on her clambering over the last two metres of bodies. She could hear stirring sounds beneath her.

One metre to go.

Then pandemonium.

Amira pushed off whatever was underneath her feet and leaped as far forward as she could, tucked and rolled onto her knees in a defensive position, khaṭvāṅga pointing at whatever might come her way.

No longer short and squat, the creatures were more like three-foot spidery elves, and they were even more menacing with faces she could relate to. She took a hunched step backward, planning to ease away from them and break into a run, but her left arm holding the wand wouldn't move. She could push it forward but not back. She knew the halāhala was stopping her, but she was not ready to let go of the one magic she had attained and could wield. Parvati would be pleased right now.

Damnit. She had to think.

Every moment she wasted allowed the creatures to spread out around her. Déja vu. She couldn't get surrounded again.

It struck her. Were these small monsters the yakshas?

They had to be. Her mind raced, figuring out what it meant, what she was up against.

Female yakshinis and male yakshas were deadly nature spirits hellbent on protecting anything and everything coming from their lands from those wanting to steal from it. Amira realised she was here specifically to take from this world. The sword. But she could not figure out why the halāhala had not worked on them.

Who was their leader? Their king? Kubera. Queen?

"Bhadra–" she whispered.

"You've brought me back my precious halāhala, princess."

A murmur rippled through the yaksha army, forming neat ranks around her.

The centre mass parted and a female, half a foot taller than the others, ambled through and stopped two metres from Amira.

Amira took a breath and began to stand.

"No, no," the figure waved a dismissive sword at her, "as you were on your knees."

Amira complied, but kept her attack stance. Now at the same head height, her eyes locked on the inky black orbs of Bhadra, a glint giving away their position in the sharp features of green-grey skin clearly absorbing the poison.

"My blood runs with halāhala, girl. You think you can use it against me?" The queen took a sharp breath, tensing her whole body from her multiple legs planted in the ground to all the arms spread out and flexed.

In that moment, it was as if the halāhala was being wrenched from within Amira. The nausea welled up again.

It was known that Bhadra, goddess of the hunt and queen consort to the king of the yakshas, had halala coursing through her like blood, giving her unnatural power and the ability to imbue her armies with it.

Attaining it was something Amira was proud of. But she had not realised, until now, where she had drawn it from, where her summoning rites and incantations had extracted it.

"I can finally return to my king, in my true form, with honour," she said, "and a little gift." She wrenched her arm, an invisible force yanking Amira onto her stomach in the dirt. Bhadra was tied to Amira with the halāhala like a chain.

Amira turned onto her back, exhausted, holding onto the warm metal of her khatvāṅga at her chest.

The clash of metal blades and a high-pitched cacophony of cries and yelps erupted as the horde of yakshas engulfed her.

The SUV continued its final leg west, the road rising up ahead with the Maloti mountains spanning the entire backdrop, their sandstone cliffs a deep blue in the distance. The border between the Kingdom of Lesotho and South Africa was even more impressive from their peaks overlooking the vast valleys and rivers feeding the countryside he loved.

They pulled up to a driveway on the right, a few hundred metres away from the top of the hill and the local school Ulwazi worked at.

Mlilo hopped out the car, took a deep breath of the familiar fresh air, and unhooked the rusted chain from the splitpole to open the wide farm gate surrounded by large trees and bushes.

The long grass slithered along the underside of the vehicle as they wound their way up to the homestead. Mlilo caught sight of the isigodlo, his sister's sacred rondavel to the left, nestled among two lush green trees. The distinctive scraggly, grey-green air-plants could be seen hanging in abundance from underneath the contrasting greenery – an eerie sight during the dry winter months, and firebreak burning throughout the valley, when the wind would blow through the blackened bark of the skeletal branches.

In her trademark pleated and beaded, black skirt and white golf shirt with the school's crest on the pocket, Ulwazi stepped down the short flight of stairs from the front porch, between the two sturdy lion statues placed at the bottom. The car came to a stop and she spread out her arms, waving her hands enthusiastically.

Mlilo got out the right side of the vehicle and walked up to the beaming woman, while Ganesha made his way from the passenger side.

"uDadewethu omkhulu," he said as they embraced. A warmth grew between their two bodies, moving over Mlilo's chest and down his arms. Along with it came a welling up of emotion he had not felt in a long time.

"uMfowethu omncane," she said, then whispered, "uKhanyisa." Chills ran along his neck and head. His big sister always held him a bit longer than he wanted to, but right now it felt good.

"Ganesha," the other man extended his hand with a short bow. "You must be Ulwazi. Sawubona, nkosazana."

She frowned and cocked her head, and instead gave him a hug.

Formalities done, Ganesha turned to Mlilo and said, "I'll get your canteens." He made his way to the back of the vehicle and opened the boot.

Mlilo felt the arm of his sister around his waist pull him closer to her. "Interesting friend. Akahlalwa mpukane."

"You have no idea," he said.

Belying his frame, Ganesha hefted the two containers out the car, and headed to the stairs. He gave a nod to the two lion statues and stepped into the house.

A young girl in school uniform, carrying a cardboard box, came down the stairs and stopped alongside Mlilo and Ulwazi.

"uSulungile, nkosazana Qwabe," she said.

"uMsizi wami." Ulwazi touched the girl on her shoulder. "nGiyabonga, Zamaswazi. This is my brother, Mlilo."

"Hi," the girl said and smiled at him.

"Off to class. I'll be up now," she said to the girl, then to Mlilo, "I'll be back around lunch break. I know you will need a moment to soak in your home."

She gave him one more hug and left him with a wave to Ganesha standing at the edge of the patio. "Thank you for the seawater, umnumzana."

CHAPTER 23

Dan sipped his red wine as he watched the synchronicity of Len and Conrad moving about the kitchen. Full from the meal earlier in the day, Dan was overwhelmed but not surprised by the amount of food being prepared for dinner.

It was obvious that Conrad was the chef, throwing together ingredients Dan could not image their combinations, while Len was the assistant, knowing what utensils, ingredients and work surfaces were needed by his partner. The occasional gesture, flourish of a spatula, a touch or a nudge, their process was something to behold and savour.

The meal in the oven and on the stove was well underway, Len putting things back in their original places, wiping off countertops and getting the sink ready for rinsing. Dan took his cue alongside the dishwasher.

Conrad patted his brow and raised his glass to them and said, "Gesondheid," and took a long sip.

The other two men raised their glasses and repeated the toast. Len returned his attention to the used cookware in the sink, lightly rinsing them off and passing them to Dan as he stacked them in the dishwasher.

The domestic bliss of the man he called his mentor was something in stark contrast to the training he had imparted to Dan over the years, and the drama of the warlock Len was now called.

Before Dan had met him, and before Conrad had come along and reignited the spark of life and hope within Len, the then fifty-year-old druid had been driven by loss to make errors of judgement he would never be able to shake, even over a decade later. The damage had been done. The oath, the pact, made with an entity was an oath broken with the druid council.

It had taken Len nearly two years with Dan to feel safe enough to give his account of it in vivid and emotional detail.

Len had vowed that if he were ever faced with the same circumstances, maybe he wouldn't summon an entity to help him, but he would certainly do everything in his power or along with that of another to save the one he loved.

He had sat helpless at Deon's bedside, the cancer in his pancreas, having gone undetected and overlooked as a symptom of his picky eating habits and sensitive digestive system, had seeped into the rest of his body. Len had tried for months to eradicate, cure and finally ease his husband's pain.

Deon's passing over was inevitable but Len was angry. He would not let the man he loved go without a fight. He researched. He studied. He tested his abilities and his limits. Len knew he would not have the skills to bring Deon back.

In the early hours of a Friday morning, the rays of the sun filtering into their bedroom, Len had watched as the life force within the man he loved faded and moved on. With Deon's warm hand firmly in his he had initiated the words he had found in the dark reaches of the internet, the beginnings of an incantation.

The room, though light and brightening with the dawning day, had lost its vivid colour. The warm, golden sunrays had turned cool in both colour and atmosphere. Deon's body seemed pallid and waxy.

Len had continued saying the words, over and over on repeat.

He had looked outside, startled at the sight of the landscape rapidly being covered by an inky blackness, not darkness but as if a liquid was being poured out over everything, saturating and blotting out his world. It moved towards him and over him.

The window, the room, the bed, everything was there, but as shapes covered in shadow. Len's mind had played on him; a sense of claustrophobia hit his chest. He stopped the incantation, coughing and spluttering and doing all he could to convince himself it was just an illusion.

A sooty cloud coalesced in the air above Deon's blackened body and bedding. Len had imagined his shocked expression, the whiteness of his eyes glossed over with black, staring terrified at the being forming before him. But no distinct feature ever came.

Len tried to speak, but his throat allowed nothing to be uttered. Instead, he concentrated, focused his mind into the single thought: bring Deon back from the other side.

The cloud became more animated, rumblings filled the air.

Len recoiled at the sensation of Deon's hand gripping his tighter. He had felt a moment of relief, utter joy, which soon faded.

Deon's blackened form sat upright in the bed, images, and thoughts flooded Len's mind. Deon was showing him that he could not come back. His time was now on the other side.

Len had refused; trying what he could to summon images of love and hope. It was no use.

The cloud entity began dissipating and as the last whiff vanished into the air, the room and Len's world shivered. The sooty darkness shook to the core and in a thud, puffed out of existence, leaving Len alone in the bright morning room.

A week later, Len had been summoned to appear in front of the Druid council in Johannesburg. It was a trial.

"Oath-breaker. Warlock." When that happened in druidic circles it reverberated around the world.

As it had done many times before, whenever they were together, and more than likely after dinner tonight, conversation would inevitably land on the Druid council. And that was Conrad's exit cue to bed.

"I tick all the boxes for them. I like and share their social media posts. And yet, they do this. Since when did we need certificates? They have their embossed, gold filigree business cards and letterheads and sit in their bland building in central Johannesburg. They stripped me of my qualifications." He had laughed one evening with drinks in hand. "What the hell is that supposed to mean? They can't take my skills away. Are we not meant to use everything at our disposal? All our skills?"

"But not the summoning of entities, Len," Dan had replied smugly. "You were expelled for that, remember?" He had immediately felt bad, seeing Len slump further down in the couch.

"I don't need to join a group, a religion, a sect, a cult in order to be able to cope with adulting. If you need some moral compass, other than simple decency, to guide you through life, to give you the coping mechanisms and direction and meaning not to blow someone's brain out, or your own, then maybe this life is not for you. They don't know either. You have to seek your own truth. There is no book of the ancient druids to follow. That COUNCIL is built around rules and ego. No matter what happens with your training, never expect them to guide you or teach you anything. They are the red-tapers, the stampers. They take their imaginary rubber stamps and put their mark of passed or failed on your certificate of achievement as if it means anything to the Earth that you draw your true power from. They cannot grant or deny that connection. Everyone has it. Just to varying degrees of efficacy."

The clink of crockery brought Dan back to Len's kitchen, just as Conrad shouted, "Aandete," and dished up the last ladleful of food onto the dinner plates.

"Fire is going," exclaimed Len in the kitchen, "Wine is flowing."

"There's no wine for you, chap," laughed Conrad.

"Figure of speech, skattie," Len lifted his whiskey glass and gave a rosey-cheeked grin.

The late afternoon sounds of the insects and birds were a welcome change to the sounds of the city Mlilo was used to.

Ulwazi placed two small, engraved clay pots, creamy froth almost spilling over their edges, on the table next to Mlilo.

He picked one of the ukhamba up with both hands and took a long pull on the umqombothi, freshly brewed over the past four days by his sister. The traditional beer made from sorghum was like nothing he could get in the bottle stores near his apartment or roadside brewers. Though full from the food his sister had brought to him on her lunch break, prepared at her school, there was always room for umqombothi.

It took only a moment for the tingle to pass through his body.

"Maybe this will sort out my gut," he said, attempting to keep it light. "Still not a hundred percent after the tokoloshe things."

Their catching up and pleasantries had been done over their earlier meal, and in this quiet moment, Mlilo knew his sister would have a whole host of things to say to him. Including why she had sent her message when she did.

Ulwazi was well known to be clairvoyant and clairsentient since an early age: having visions, whether premonitions or guidance presented as visions, had meant she was earmarked to become an isangoma. Something their parents had not been happy about. Like their parents before them, they had tried what they could to dissuade Ulwazi and play down her abilities. Mlilo on the other hand had grown up with no interest or inclination, and he had kept his own magic between himself and his big sister.

The age that his grandparents and mother and father had grown up in was dark times of disinformation and indoctrination, aimed at shaking the bedrocks of their communities and portraying their long-held traditions as black magic and witchcraft. uSangoma became witchdoctor. An herbal remedy became a potion. Muthi became sinister spells. Many of their people would permanently turn away from those traditional beliefs passed down for generations from their ancestors. True magic was suppressed, never spoken about in the wider world for decades. The things that held them together for centuries were tossed aside for the promise of a new and improved life, which never came. Unlike their father and mother, Ulwazi pushed Mlilo to test himself and grow his abilities. Most of all, encouraging him to believe he could do it. The time was gathering momentum, with Mlilo's generation, to burst forth into the world and acknowledging their place in it.

But rather than becoming isangoma, Ulwazi was drawn to the properties of the world around her, beginning with the plants many of the people in the area used in their everyday lives. This expanded into the animals and insects and the earth under her feet.

It was her final year of school that almost derailed her getting her matric when she experienced her ukuthwasa. But, within two days she was rearing to go. She had seen what she needed to do and began her studies to become a teacher of biology and chemistry. From her perspective, this gave her the ability to delve into the areas she loved, while sharing the knowledge with the young minds of the nearby towns. Without relying solely on the textbooks, she visited the older izinyanga close by and eventually further afield, to record and share their knowledge.

Mlilo wondered what it would be like as a student in her class, because of how Ulwazi would hone in on a problem he was having and lay it out for him before he himself even knew what was going on. His big sister had the uncanny ability to sense what someone was thinking. Mlilo first thought it was him projecting his thoughts to her, but as he got older, controlling and restricting the pushing out of ideas and images to people's minds, he realised she sensed things. His late teenage years brought out the stubbornness, but he always knew his sister meant well. And with her experience with her students, she knew when to give her guidance and when the big sister needed to back off.

It was this time of his life that he needed her most. When their mother and father had died.

"*Home is never far away when you believe in it,*" she said softly.

A warm flush washed over Mlilo. He held the clay pot tight against his chest. "We loved that book."

"I always tell my students to read '*The Hidden Star*'. You must read it while you are here, mfowethu."

"Or you can read it to me like you used to, udadewethu." Mlilo said as his eyes blurred with tears. They looked at one another and smiled.

He took another gulp of the drink, and said, "This place is strange yet familiar to me. When I am in the city, I feel like I am home, and this place is a distant dream. Sometimes a dark dream, sometimes pleasant. A part of me feels like it is not mine anymore. It is becoming more your place than ours."

"This will always be part of you, Mlilo."

"And there are other places I need to be than in the past. And some places I must go alone."

His sister clucked her tongue loudly, a habit he found her doing randomly even with no one around, or directed at inanimate objects. A spluttering frying pan could be a recipient, followed some choice words; a random cluck while reading or marking, castigating herself for something she had overlooked or missed; or someone saying something she deemed incorrect.

"The teacher in me wants to remind you of our greeting, umfana." She narrowed her eyes at her brother, waiting for him to acknowledge what she meant.

He rolled his eyes and shook his head. "Not this again."

"Sawubona, young student. Sa-wu-bona," Ulwazi said it slowly.

Mlilo slid down in his chair in response, but couldn't help himself. "We see you," he said and immediately regretted encouraging her.

"And who is *'we'* if it is only I that is speaking with you? Why not just 'I see you'?"

Mlilo bit his tongue.

"It is me, the one greeting, along with those unseen ancestors who are always around you."

"You are never alone, mfowethu.

"And where is it that you need to go alone?"

"You know where. And if I am supposedly 'never alone', where the hell are *they, Ulwazi*? I have searched Abaphansi."

"Mlilo!"

Ulwazi's outburst caught him off guard. He sat upright, eyes wide and full of tears, looking at his flustered sister.

"No, Mlilo."

"They were not there the first time, in that water, among our ancestors. People I had never met and one or two my body recalls, but never our mother and father. Why? Have they nothing to say to me, to us?" He stood up, splashing beer over his hands, and stared into the garden below. He held the clay pot to his face and screamed into it. The liquid turned to steam with the heat flowing through his hands and fingers.

"Ima!"

"I walk Abaphansi in search of them and the only thing I find is a world better than it is here. A world that makes more sense."

"Lalela: ukhasela eziko. That is you, Mlilo. *He crawls to the fire.*"

"More teaching, proverbs, uKhethiwe," he snapped.

"Language is everything, Mlilo. It is how we tell the world who we are."

"Fine, tell me if you've heard this one, nkosazana Qwabe: akuxoxo lingalunguzi esizibeni."

"I have no need to venture into this outside world you look to. It's like looking outside of yourself for the answers when it is here all the time. I have gone where I was needed, and where things needed to be imparted to me for a purpose. I sought out answers away from this place and returned.

"I wasn't kidnapped and brought here against my will. I wasn't taken from the big city or the prospects of an education to be here. I came here myself. Yes, the ancestors led me here, but I came here. Have you seen Ulwazi? I am here."

You've believed that you need to go out into the world to make a difference, to use your powers for a greater good. The greater good is as vast or narrow as you perceive it to be. Maybe we take our abilities for granted and think we are special. But in everyday life there is power in a positive word to a child, that they hold onto for the rest of their lives, that makes them a better person. Something a mother shares with her daughter, empowering her at school and later in life.

That's magic. Can you say you are able to harness that? I'm not sure that I can, but I try every day. I'm not sure I'm cut out to be the magicians that many parents are. Mothers and fathers, grandparents and foster parents, aunts and uncles. Brothers and sisters. Colleagues and bosses. You hold magic in your hands and in the words you use to conjure. You can make or break someone with a turn of phrase - a spell isn't some fancy set of words that invokes the powers from the other side. A spell or a curse can be the words spoken in such a way, or a concept imparted in the ordering of everyday words, into something powerful that can change someone's life immediately or only years later.

"You look at the people here, speak with them. They aren't ignorant of the worlds we know are there. They don't go about their day unaware of the magic, gods and realms beyond their senses and sight. No. They know it's there. In fact, they live in hope that it's there. Otherwise, what else is there to live for in this world that you, Mlilo, find so shitty? They don't know how to reach into it. They can't see it every minute or easily. But they try to find the magic in the small things. They find hope. They are the masses that keep the god and magic alive. Whether they know we are fighting for them or not, we do. We aren't doing it for a ticker tape parade. We are doing it because we are the ones that can, not them. They cannot, so we step up and do it for them."

"You are just speaking words." Mlilo let out a sob. "I know all this, and yet I find myself staring at the walls unable to engage with anything. Everything is uninteresting, to the extent that I can't start something like a book or a movie or some activity that would get my mind off things. And then your mind starts on those *'things'*.

"You have been given life, umfowethu. Your obligation is to live. Not survive. There are millions surviving. You must live."

"Damnit, Ulwazi." Mlilo turned, fist clenched and pounding his chest. "I'd rather be away from the ones I love, dealing with my sulky self, than the potential of making you feel bad about yourself by taking a dig at you, like just now, to pass on my frustrations or worse, a truth said in a hurtful way. I mean, look at all the well-intentioned social media posts about how everyone cares about suicide and those depressed. I don't even for a second consider responding to that kak."

"What happens to me here in this world is irrelevant. Bring it on. But I'm not going to fake a brave face."

"So reckless." Ulwazi snorted. "Mary Shelley wrote: *'Beware; for I am fearless, and therefore powerful.'*"

"Whatever," Mlilo said with a dismissive wave.

"I have never felt the need to run into danger to prove myself. But you," she gave her irritated cluck. "There's nothing more dangerous than a man who believes there is an afterlife. That man cannot be scared. That man cannot be broken. But that man can wreak havoc in this world, for that belief. On the other hand, the man that does not believe he will live on in another realm will do everything he can to live this life to the fullest. Immortal life is for the gods, not for man and his weak soul, Mlilo."

They each took a drink from their clay pots. The sun low on the horizon brought a chill to Mlilo, despite the warm afternoon.

"I feel a darkness growing somewhere, Ulwazi. I don't know what it is. We all thought the darkness had been broken all those decades ago. Our parents fought for it."

"Mhm," she agreed. "They fought the only way they knew how."

"Without the magic they were called to accept."

"Hmm," his sister gave a questioning murmur.

"Their lives were made harder by the ancestors insisting they follow their calling. Or am I missing something?"

"Remember mother's stories to us? She never read them from a book, right? About two years ago I was told to write down what I remembered of those tales. When I did this, I realised something about our mother, umfowethu. She had the gift, and she used it in a way she was not fully aware of. Yes, she shunned our abilities. She flat out refused any calling by the ancestors. Our father made sure of that. But she would make up stories to tell us at night, to get her children to sleep. I think she was telling us things she was shown, like me, and she took them to be inspirations and simple ideas to embellish her fantastical tales to her children."

"And the darkness?"

Mlilo heard his sister sigh and take another sip of drink. "Gogo was a maid, yes?"

"Domestic worker," Mlilo corrected her.

"No. She was a maid. Domestic workers have rights and laws to protect them. Maids and workers in general back then had nothing. Gogo was given a quaintly named 'khaya' outside the owner's house. A Khaya to you and me is a home, of warmth, not a damn hovel without hot water. When we were born in a free world, they had the televised hearings. Yes, the extreme horrors of apartheid were trundled out in dry courtroom proceedings. But where were the everyday stories? We never got to talk basics. Where was the story of the live-in maid, in her outside room, leaving her white family once a month to return to her real home on 'the farm'? Her own children, motherless most days while her white children imagined her family wandering their huge fields of corn and pasturelands of cattle in a dreamy landscape. Because that was what they knew a farm to be. Not one goat and five chickens, and some mielies at the back. Those stories were never brought out into the open, exposed to dry out and whither. No, they have been pushed down into the depths and forgotten. Move on. That darkness has been fed for all this time.

This is what is seeping back in. The hate and resentments are everywhere, thriving around the world, and they are oozing out onto the streets. Some use it to justify their own hate. The demon hunters of the world are trying to force their will on everyone. The demon hunters see evil in everything that is different to them. The other. Now you have me worked up, Mlilo," she clucked her irritation and took a final gulp of her umqombothi.

"I have no interest in the world's problems. I have one problem right now and that's all I can deal with."

"Things will spill out into your path and you will be forced to put your own selfish needs over others."

"uDadewethu omkhulu," Mlilo raised his voice, "the hyena has my bones, and if I don't get them back one way or another, then that will be everyone's problem. Not whether people get along or not, or if they keep holding grudges."

"Are you admitting that your quest is actually more than just a selfish need, umfowethu omncane?"

"Oh, nicely played."

The tension lifted as they laughed together.

"But let me get to the reason I told you to come home," Ulwazi added emphasis on the last word. "You and your soul need a good cleansing. You need to go to the mountains, speak with the ancestors. Whatever happened to you in Abaphansi needs to teach you something; either about what you need to do or how you need to conduct yourself. You are headstrong and it's as if you rushed in without much thought."

Mlilo huffed. "You cannot tell me not to. You cannot expect me not to."

Ulwazi clucked. She looked up at the handful of small, pink and peach clouds in the sky and said, "The weather is right for you to hike to the mountains tonight." She pointed to the sun above the mountains to their left.

"Why don't you go to the mountains? I've just got here. Give me a moment to acclimatise to my *home*," he added sarcastically.

"It is what I saw this morning that I know you must go tonight."

His sister's advising and big-sistering aside, Mlilo trusted Ulwazi's visions.

"Tell me what you saw, udadewethu," he said.

The first light of morning was showing in the cloudless skies as I made my way to umsamo in the rondavel, the air a refreshing cool in contrast to the stifling heat and restless night before.

I went about my usual preparations in my sacred place. The scent of burning mphepho had barely filled the dark room before I realised the movement in my peripheral vision had nothing to do with the smoke rising from the brass bowl. The candle next to it on the low, cloth-covered table was blown out, the two lines of smoke pulled together at an unnatural angle in the windless space.

Something was in the room with me.

In my mind I asked amadlozi for protection. I stood to face whatever was about to happen.

Again, the ripples of movement to the sides. I glanced left and right and saw nothing but the smoke filling the room. What appeared to be a smokey haze I realised was rather a watery atmosphere. I knew it was getting light outside but the room was getting darker.

The sensation was like being in a tank, like at the aquarium, the walls undulating with waves of blue and black. A sliver of light emerged from my right, and rather than look to find nothing, I held my gaze forward and waiting. An eel-like movement, as if in slow motion, revealed a form encircling me. With each ripple of light and shadow, the form became more distinct.

Inkanyamba.

That malevolent, silent, serpentine creature was threatening. The albino form grew in length until its head and tail met, end-to-end, encircling the room and me.

There was nowhere to go.

Fades into a single wavy line of mercury, bright against the murky watery background. Like the rush of blood in your ears, a sound was building. Rushing water. In a flash, the line of light cracked the room horizontally in two and a blast of water hit me, knocking me off my feet, engulfing me.

And just as quickly the room was dry and calm and brighter. Mphepho filled my lungs, relaxing me, as I gasped for air, kneeling on the hard mud packed floor.

"But Mamlambo showed me she had tamed the serpent," said Mlilo, thinking hard about the meaning of his sister's vision.

"No brother," Ulwazi said, "Inkanyamba is merely the form we are being shown. Something sinister is stalking you. And something is stopping you, barring your way. Whether a crossing, a journey or a task. You will go where it is dark, where you cannot see things clearly – whether your way through or your way back. But that line, that silvery line in the darkness is your way out. You have to go into the darkness to find your way through. Remember, ukhanyisa, you must bring your light to the world."

Ulwazi stood, clearly energised by their conversation, despite the ominous tones.

"Get up," she demanded, with her *what-are-you-waiting-for* attitude. "You must make preparations. You must reconnect with amadlozi and amathongo. You must go to the mountains. Today." She headed inside.

Mlilo rounded his shoulders and rolled his eyes. He carried their clay ukhamba and followed the sounds of his sister stomping into the kitchen.

"You always amaze me, udadewethu omkhulu," he said and placed the pots in the sink, starting the hot tap.

"Of course," she replied with a wry smile and a nudge at his side, adding more dishes to his load.

"No, seriously, Ulwazi," he said and added soap to the rising waterline. "The people in the city, modern society, have locked away their seers as madmen. Mad *women*," he added emphasis on the last word with a snort. "They take the word of people in power as the word of their gods and their amadlozi, and follow them blindly, handing over their own wealth and wellbeing. The ancestors and the gods continue to communicate, not through the preacher on the pulpit, the politician representing their rights, with their shiny new car and palace built by their followers, but the isindhlanya. The ones who hear and see. Like you, my sister."

Ulwazi gave a mischievous grin. "I am not mad, though, umfowethu omncane." And blurted out a high-pitched cackle.

Mlilo could only shake his head and laugh at his sister who lifted one of the large containers of seawater onto the well-worn, wooden kitchen dining table in the centre of the room with a thud.

Mlilo stacked the pots and plates on the dish rack and swirled the foamy water down the drain. Listen." He paused. "There's uNqonqonthwane," Mlilo said pointing a soapy hand out the window. Ulwazi came over and they watched the robust black beetle scuttle along the grass and stones, stop and tap-tap-tap, then proceed towards the driveway.

"That's a good omen for you, Mlilo," said Ulwazi, patting his shoulder and returning to her task of placing an assortment of smaller, empty containers on the table along with a funnel. From larger soda bottles, to old peanut butter jars and Tupperware, anything for storage and sharing out of the water. The second canteen would be stored under the table for a few more days, then decanted in the same way.

Mlilo knew the process so he unscrewed the large white lid and said, "The healer of the road." He hefted the canteen over at an angle while his sister held the funnel over a well-used two-litre cola bottle. As the water poured, the contents of the container became murky with the sand swirling up from the bottom.

"Mhm." She nodded. "Following the stars."

Seven two-litre bottles, a couple of jars and a mix-and-match of plastic containers later, the canteen was almost empty, and to Mlilo's relief, lighter. The final touch was the sea sand at the bottom, in a small amount of seawater. Each vessel would require its own portioning of the sand. Moving steadily around the table he allowed the mixture to gradually ooze into the containers.

One final swish of the contents, making sure to get most of the sand and bits of broken shells, Mlilo poured over a jar.

In his solemn concentration, the clink of a shell against the glass container jarred him, with Ulwazi giving a surprised yelp. A conical shell fell to the wooden tabletop and with a wobble finally came to rest.

The siblings looked at one another, knowing the significance of the gift given to them by the amadlozi.

"Amathambo come to you in many ways," she said.

Mlilo picked it up, moving over to stand against the kitchen counter, and studied the perfect spiral detail, the colours and the texture from a beach hundreds of kilometres away. His hand was already warming.

He gripped it tight and placed it inside his pocket.

"Ooh, soetkoekies," he said, attention drawn to the biscuit jar next to the kettle. "I'll need a bunch of these for my hike." Mlilo opened the container and took a handful of the misshapen homemade treats. A flood of memories and sensations washed over him with the first bite.

"Your favourite aunty," said Ulwazi of their mother's strict sister. "uMamakazi Yibanathi."

"Goddamnit, she makes a good cookie," he said between bites and shaking his head. "Perfect. It's so perfect I can hear her cookie lecturing me about my life. _When are you getting married? Where are the children?_"

"Oh, I know the feeling. But she did take care of you in, I would say, what were your most _difficult years._"

Mlilo snorted. "Punishment for her. Karma."

Ulwazi clucked her tongue at him.

"Hot-head. Let me know when you're available for a demonstration on combustion for my students. The twelve-year-olds would be blown away by my kid brother lighting a Bunsen burner from the other side of the science lab."

"Hell's bells, boy!"

Dan wasn't surprised by Len's reaction to his retelling of his entire ordeal with Mlilo in Abaphansi.

"There's a thing, hey," said Len and slapped his knee, almost spilling his whiskey on the couch. "Who would've thought you would go to Tír nAil."

"That's it? That's your takeaway from all of that, Len?"

Len laughed loudly, trying to catch his breath.

"My seun," he sloshed his drink wildly, "your adventure was astounding in so many ways but let us not overlook the fact that you went there in the first place. I haven't even seen that land in my sixty something years."

A small fire was burning in the stone fireplace, popping and crackling sparks here and there, keeping the late evening chill out of the cozy lounge. More a ritual than a source of heat, Len always lit something, incense, candles or the fire, throwing a mixture of herbs into the kindling at the start.

Conrad had said his good-nights, giving the two friends their much-needed alone time, catching up, and more than likely some mentorship. Dan could hear the murmur of the television from the main bedroom at the end of the hall.

He sipped his wine.

"Sjoe, the Morrígan," said Len shaking his head in disbelief. "Here I've been focusing only on skills and the practice rather than what I assumed was unattainable from this world, Daniel. You need to find out more. I will find out more. It is no small thing for this to have happened to you. It means there will be more to come."

"How do you mean more?" Dan looked over at the man at the other end of the couch.

Len tried to sit himself up but only got himself deeper into the soft couch. He grunted and gave up the attempt, instead turning to face Dan. "Your friend, Mlilo was the one who invited," he finger-hooked the air, more whiskey spilling, "you into the other world. That was the start. Everything that unfolded there is not Mlilo's alone. You were intricately involved. Yes, you two headstrong boys went your separate ways in the heat of the moment. But it is together that you will succeed. And it doesn't sound like it's just about getting something belonging to your friend back again."

"You're saying by me getting roped into his drama I've now got a target on my back."

"Boy!"

Dan nearly spilled his wine at the word ringing through the quiet house.

"I am saying there are bigger things at play here. The Morrígan mentioned demon hunters. There's one right-wing nut-job who comes to mind, and I've kept my eye on him and his growing influence around the country, the world. True evil is the one who, in fighting and wanting to destroy evil, will destroy that which they wish to protect from evil. They willingly destroy their world in order to rid it of all evil. Do not underestimate the situation. You say Mlilo underestimated what he was bringing you both into, a fight with a large porcupine, because he was hellbent on revenge. But you are doing the same. You are not seeing what is beyond the short-term goal of getting Mlilo's sacred bones back."

"What then?"

"For one, you both need to gather your strength. You will be put to the test in ways you never have imagined. And I'm not sure I've prepared you well enough for that," he whispered, concern flooding his face.

"You have taught me plenty, Len."

"Your rites this morning, after you arrived and settled in. What did you do?"

The mentor was back, checking in with the student.

Dan put his wine glass down on the dark wood coffee table and turned sideways to face the stern, flushed face of the older man.

He quickly ran through his process in his mind and said, "I began with Sigrdrifa's prayer."

"Oh lovely, my boy," Len nodded his approval. "Say it now," he waved his hand for Dan to continue.

Dan smiled and slowly stood up from the chair and staggered over to the fire. He took a handful of the dried mphepho in the tray on the stone hearth and tossed it the flames. He turned back to the waiting Len and began:

"Hail Day. Hail Sons of Day." He flopped back into the chair. "Hail Night and her Daughter. Unwrathful eyes look upon us and grant us victory." The smells of the herb were filling the lounge; Len took a deep breath and closed his eyes. Dan did the same, and continued, "Hail Gods. Hail Goddesses. Hail to the abundant fields. Speech and wisdom give to us and healing hands with life."

Dan paused and opened his eyes. "Vigi Vé Thetta," he said the ending in a low whisper, the blessing and protecting of the sacred space.

Len was smiling at Dan and took a sip of whiskey.

"I went through the initiating rite, using your bell and lighting the candle. Purification breathing followed by the honouring of the Earth Mother. My purpose was to heal and be strengthened. The kindred were invited by name and I offered the handful of Jungle Oats you gave me. I thanked the beings–"

"In reverse order," Len interrupted him with a lifted finger.

"In reverse order," Dan said with a nod. "I thanked Earth Mother, and ended the rite."

"Good," said Len and drained the remaining golden liquid from his glass.

Dan picked up his wine glass and added, "I also did the healing galdr using the runes", and took a sip.

"Really?" asked Len. "Opening the Hamr?"

Dan nodded. "Opening the etheric body up," he elaborated, aware that Len was testing him further, "to receive healing from the galdr, the spell, and transmuting it into physical healing. But that is enough from the student and master."

"Oh, please, young man," Len balked. "I'm not going to get a wink of sleep reading up what I can in my study."

"I want to know how my friend is," Dan said. "What is this kak about sheep heads, Len? Small town folk?"

He could see Len's eyes narrowing, staring off into the distance.

"Not everyone in this town, no. Thankfully not." Len waved his glass at Dan. He leaned over and grabbed the pen whiskey bottle and slid over a seating space closer to the outstretched arm and poured a tot. Len took a sip and smacked his lips.

"Many more people and many more beliefs have moved into the area. But it's the old school beliefs that linger."

"Fester," said Dan. "I noticed you've planted more aloe since I was here last. Keeping the bad spirits at bay?"

"You know, Daniel, these conservative people, they don't know their own histories. They look at the teaching passed down to them in isolation, instead of looking back at the ones that passed it down to them. There were real people, skilled individuals, who used those teachings during their lifetimes."

Dan remembered a variation of this talk from Len before.

"The skills you and I have, as druids," said Len.

"Thaumaturgy," Dan added.

"That one exactly," said Len and sipped his drink. "Miracle-workers. Kings, rulers of England and France, were said to have the Royal Touch, able to cure diseases in their people. Right up to the nineteenth century until it was labeled superstition. The litany of ordained saints with the ability is astonishing. Nearly ten individuals credited with various supernatural acts. The first one–"

"Saint Gregory," Dan interrupted him.

"I'm boring you with my history lesson I've obviously told you already, Daniel."

"Tell me again, Len. I can always do with a refresher."

"Who knows how many others, not made saints, for whatever political reasoning. Never mind the Judaic Baal Shem, the Hindu Godmen, and the siddhi powers of Buddhism. Australia, the Americas." Len shook his head.

"Africa," said Dan and finished the last of his wine.

"Africa!" Len echoed, his face brightening. "Imagine the galdr they all would have used, Daniel."

He could see the youthful energy returning to his tired friend.

"Galdr, spells, incantations. All the sacred words in other languages, many forgotten through time. Men and women speaking their words into the heavens. What is another definition of a spell, dear bard, oh Druid-to-be?"

"A meditation. A prayer," said Dan.

"So many recite their incantations, asking, imploring a magical force to aid them in their lives. They close their eyes and go within to bring forth answers. Rituals, hymns and prayers invoking and praising their deities and those they can rely on for help. Druids, vaidyas, and izangoma, use it in speaking to or calling on those that can assist them or their people. Incantare, in Latin, meaning 'to chant upon'."

They sat for a while in silence, watching the small flames, imagining the smoke rising up and out into the night air.

CHAPTER 24

Mlilo's boots were not ideal for climbing through the Drakensberg Mountains on any given day, but his footing was sure and he knew the terrain like it was part of him.

The heat of the day was long behind him, or rather behind the mountains in front of him, while the full moon was rising at his back, providing a faint shadow on the rocks he was skipping between.

His chest was heaving, not as fit as he had assumed the city walking would have made him. It was good though. Irritating when his sister knew better. He smiled to himself.

About four hundred metres from Ulwazi's home, the crunch of the gravel road beneath his feet had turned to soft grass, once he had passed over the cattle grid and entrance to the uKhahlamba Drakensberg Park World Heritage Site.

Three kilometres later he had hit the hiking trail, with the flowing Mooiriver winding its way to the right.

The impressive range of Maloti mountains, the natural border between the Kingdom of Lesotho and South Africa rose steeply, soon pulling on Mlilo's thigh muscles as the sun had turned the sky a deep orange red.

He came to a level area, his usual stopping point to catch his breath, and spied out the river five metres away. The freshest drink he could ever get. The sky in the west, now a dark blue, clearly silhouetted the gigantic peaks and towering buttresses of the mountains. The cliffs and valleys vaguely visibly in their darkness. A dreamlike, fantastical world at night.

Mlilo turned back, trying to make out the path he had taken. The moon shimmered behind a puff of cloud, the landscape growing fuzzy in the muted light. The mismatch of shapes, jagged mountains, flat topped hillsides, and soft, forested crevasses. It was here that Mlilo felt normal. He could gaze out at the earth's creations and see the imperfect lines drawn across the skyline. Nature could be precise, and imprecise. He didn't have to be perfect to feel perfect. Everything nature birthed was just the way it needed to be.

If something as massive and grand as a mountain could be imperfect, then so could he. And in that imperfection, it was perfect.

Time had dragged and Amira's discomfort grew with each step of the dozen or more yakshas hauling her, climbing the rocky hillside.

Like ropes, the halāhala bound her arms and legs firmly; the swirling patterns she had grown accustomed to on her hand were more angular over her entire body. The gold trim of her tunic was stained with the blackness like a thick mud against her waist and thighs while her left arm and hand, pinned to her side, held her khaṭvāṅga covered in the oppressive design.

She could barely turn her head to keep track of the horizontal journey, feet first, in the pricking clutches of the yakshas, over the past day or longer. The sun to her left in the west, in its permanent setting position, and the stars above, were the only constants. The landscape had become rockier and steeper the further on they travelled. She knew of king Kubera residing in a mountain kingdom somewhere.

Attempts to rouse her forcefield, though momentarily energising her aching muscles and bones, had been met with a tightening of the black restraints on her body.

Her stomach lurched, this time not from any poison reacting inside her, but the thought of having lost the halāhala because of her ignorance. She should have been more prepared.

A sharp poke in her ribs brought her back to the moment as the yakshas beneath her scaled a set of red brown boulders. Amira did not like being constrained like this, and she was not looking forward to traversing a mountain pass of any kind, no matter how secure she may seem. She was sure that Gulliver was treated better than this.

The earthy smells of the rondavel's wooden beams, thatch grass and mud walls had their usual calming effect on Dan as he lay in the double bed in the semi-darkness of the evening staring at the roof. Apart from the nighttime sounds outside, the beehive's daytime activities had subsided and so too its hum, now a background murmur, like an air-conditioning unit in the wall.

He could easily stay here with Len for a few weeks. And his friend wouldn't mind. Their conversations earlier in the day and around dinner continued to buzz through his mind. Len had the knack of putting things into perspective. Cynicism with a dash of optimism. Experience may have weighed Len down in the past decade, but he remained a lover of life and magic.

Dan sensed a change in the tone of the hive. Possibly louder than a moment before. Movement in the space above him turned out to be a lone bee coming into the room and flying upward in a gentle spiral. Slowing to a point near the thatching, it changed direction and zipped down at Dan, but half a metre from his face it exploded in a burst of bright light.

Dan sat bolt upright in the bed.

The noise from outside was fever pitch. Dan could hardly think. Instinct kicked in and he went to reach for his wand at his bedside.

The memory of Fagus broken in two was quickly blotted out as rondavel door crashed open. Despite the small size of the doorway, Dan could see the hulk of a man stooping through towards him was well over six feet of muscle.

Dan's hand shot out, blue and silver sparks crackled frenetically at the attacker and surrounding room, only slightly taking the man aback with the burst of energy.

A roar erupted from outside. There was more than one of them.

The man was on Dan as he tried to roll away and off the bed. A knee hit his ribs, pain slammed through his face and chest as he hit the hard concrete floor. An iron grip pinned his hands to his sides and the panting breath of the bearded man was at his ears.

"Moer!" shouted a voice entering the room. More hands grabbed his feet and pulled him along the ground while the first man swivelled in place, twisting Dan's arms above his head and zip-tied in what seemed like a single movement.

Another cry from outside.

"Daai vervlakste insekte," the second man cursed and added zip-ties to Dan's feet. "André is oorgekom. Ons moet gou waai."

A black bag was pulled over his face, cutting out all remaining light and he was hefted up and into the cool night air.

The sound of bees on the attack was all that he could hear surrounding him. The two men carrying him stumbled and waved at the millions of adversaries on the offensive. Though he could feel dozens of taps against his own skin and clothes, nothing stung him.

He could hear the pained groaning, and rasping of a man low on the ground as they passed by. He sensed his two captors were trying to get the other man to his feet while keeping hold of Dan.

"Hey!"

Dan recognised the scream of Len and the sound of the kitchen door slamming open, followed immediately by a strip of light, dull through the dark bag over his head, laser beam into something solid.

Dan's feet were dropped and he heard the sound of a body hitting the ground next to him. The man holding Dan under his shoulders released him to the damp grass with an awkward thud onto his bound hands and wrists. For a couple of seconds, the bag covering his head slipped up, giving Dan a glance at an image he would not soon forget. One moment his eyes were trying to adjust to the gloomy night, the pale moon insufficient for him to discern anything, the next split second another flash of light, Len's magic, lit up the horrific scene of a body on hands and knees rocking back and forth, covered in angry bees.

Another flash of light, this time short-lived, and Dan was grateful the bag slipped back over his eyes. He heard the impact of a fist against flesh, against a gut.

Dan heard the air from Len's lungs woofed out of him, a final fist hit skull and his friend was silent.

"Varke hoeder," growled the man and wheezed with pain from the incessant insect stings. Dan was wrenched to his feet and dragged backwards.

"Kom, Wynand!" he bellowed in Dan's ear. "Kry vir André."

Conrad's scream pierced the dark countryside.

CHAPTER 25

"Smile, princess," growled the guard.

"Smiling is not anything anyone should be doing when faced with the likes of you," Amira sneered through the bars of her low cell door. Dungeon really. The ceiling, and the network of dimly lit passages leading here, were only a foot higher than Amira's head. For the kingdom's subjects smaller than her.

The final destination of the mountain kingdom seemed to have taken the smaller yakshas at least two days journey. The term 'castle' did nothing for the spectacle Amira had witnessed rising before them.

Like the Amphitheatre in the Drakensberg Mountains of KwaZulu-Natal, a crescent shaped expanse over five kilometres wide and nearly the same in height of shear, rugged grey-blue basalt filled her view. Each end of the arc was topped with what could only be described as large-scale lookout structures and battlements, and tapering off into the lower spires of mountains on either side. In contrast to the blue mountain as its backdrop was a giant extruding quartz rock, a monumental complex of buildings carved and shaped out of its dramatic form. Split through the middle was the perfect silver line of a waterfall cascading down and blurring into the billows of clouds below. Amira knew the water's source was from the lush greenery covering the entire stretch of mountaintop. Chaitraratha. Said to be the most beautiful garden in all creation.

Rather than any pomp and ceremony through castle gates, they had made their way into the lower network of passageways and dungeons beneath the impressive natural spires and hand-worked towers above.

Amira was relieved when Bhadra had finally withdrawn the black poison restraints, and fully stripped her of any halāhala in her body, and left her in the gloom.

The routine of the guard's rounds, every two hours, was the only measure Amira had for a sense of time. Nearly a day in the cold room. Fortunately, food, if it were even offered to prisoners, wasn't necessary in this world, and feasts merely a form of pleasure rather than survival.

Roughly the same height as the yakshas Amira had faced off with, the guard was more robust. Their armour-like exoskeleton of their multiple limbs were marked and dull, through a life of warfare or labour. Amira could not tell which. Up close she was able to discern the facets that made up their head, and the features coming together to form their eyes, mouth and face.

"Your trial should commence in the next day, child," the guard said as they headed on their way. "I shall be smiling then."

"Where is your boetie, charna?" asked the man pacing in front of Dan.

At least six foot two, the older man in his mid-fifties, looked fit in dust coloured tactical clothing tight on his muscled, weathered frame. When he had stepped into the room a minute earlier, Dan knew exactly who he was. Maybe not his name or why he recognised his face, but Dan knew who he was in the world: the demon hunter.

Dan sat strapped into a chair, bracing for the inevitable. He may not be ready for what they would do to him to extract the information, but he would go down in flames before he told them where Mlilo was.

He couldn't help himself. "Sjoe, Oom. Die duiwel dra khaki kitte." Dan snorted. "Better than safari suits and kort-korts, hey?"

"Yirra," the man holding Dan's bare right shoulder hissed and tightened his already iron grip.

"Don't worry, Marius. We will be having some fun with this one tonight." The man reeled off his words forcefully, the room filling with the eloquent tone of a deft orator. He took pleasure in his use of words, stroking the middle of his goatee and grinning. "Even if it takes us until morning."

He gestured to a row of car batteries, electrodes and wires along the left wall. "A conniving dog whispered in my ear today. Not only did he tell me that you would know the whereabouts of your mate, but he gave us a heads-up on your abilities. Normally we would enjoy placing electrodes on your nose, or your genitals, but unfortunately for you, these little gadgets of ours will not be utilised tonight. *Unfortunately*, because you won't be able to tap into that extra bit of electricity for more oomph, but also because it means we will be using other methods to loosen your lips. You will also be aware of the room you find yourself in right now."

Dan took the moment to look around. The room had the dimensions of a shipping container but renovated with a floor, walls and electricity. Everything was black. But not painted black. It was wall to ceiling rubber matting. Interlocking squares usually found on tyre fitment foyers and mechanic shops, lined all the surfaces. A double strip of fluorescent globes the only light directly above him.

The chair Dan was sitting on was like an outdoor chair, made from recycled, melted plastic in robust planks to imitate a similar style traditionally in wood. His arms and legs were strapped with thick black rubber belting and secured with plastic buckles. Other than being shirtless, as he had been when he was lying in the rondavel bed, his only other clothing were his pants, rolled up to his knees. He felt exposed and naked, not from the lack of covering but from not having any of his gear on hand.

Apart from Marius gripping his shoulder, a third man, expressionless, stood at the ready at a single door to Dan's right. He could see red blemishes on the man's exposed skin of his forearms, neck and face.

"How's André doing?" Dan cocked his head at the guard. "I hope he's not allergic to bees."

It felt like a brick hit his face. Dan's eyes watered and his whole body rocked in the chair. His adrenaline pulsed through him.

"Moenie, Marius," the man said in a sing-song tone as if to a child.

Dan's pain shifted to rage; his fingers crackled with electric sparks. Without being connected to even concrete under his bare feet, it was useless trying to summon anything more than a jolt.

"As I was saying, Daanie," he stood squarely in front of Dan, hands held formally behind his back. "We are insulated from any unwanted electric charges."

There was a knock at the door.

"Wynand," the man nodded to the man in front of the door.

Wynand pivoted in place and opened the door to let in a fourth man, grubby towel over his shoulder, pushing a trolley with a steel tub of water and a smaller steel bucket sloshing about inside it.

"As soon as I heard of your whereabouts and the possibility of getting my hands on Mlilo and more of his bones, the five of us drove all the way from Potch to pay you a visit. Let us not have wasted our time, seuntjie."

The trolley was positioned in the far-left corner of the room and the man departed with a nod to his leader. "Dankie, Leon."

"Since you raised the issue of our colleague, André," he emphasised the name, "Marius, Wynand and Leon here are going to be adding a little of their own medicine to our activities this evening. André may not have been killed by your hands, but he was nevertheless killed on that swineherd's property. This will not be tolerated." He nodded to Marius.

Dan's stomach lurched as the man released his grip on Dan's shoulder. He heard the sound of rough metal against leather, but refused to look.

"You know, laities like you haven't experience pain in their lives," said Marius and tapped something ice cold on the skin of Dan's shoulder. His reflexes took hold of him and his eyes darted to the red and black rust-covered blade repeatedly tapping his shoulder bone. One side was serrated and clogged with grime, while the blade itself remarkably blunted and chipped. Marius stepped around to face Dan. "And like all of us you will feel pain tonight. It has passed you by for the last twenty years. You've never seen a moment of dread in your life. You've never felt the pain that followed that dread."

Dan's body went ice-cold as Marius slammed the blade down between his legs, the chair vibrating with the impact. The frenzied, wide eyes of Marius, bore into Dan's mere centimetres away. The quiff of his black fringe, touching his right eyebrow, wavered with the tension from the large man's neck and shoulder muscles. A drop of spittle, white against his thick beard.

"And never felt the memory of that pain as it brings a new wave of dread," Marius continued, leaving the blade implanted in the chair, "half expecting that pain to repeat itself. Because why wouldn't it? If it can happen to you once, it can happen again. So, look at me now and know that the feeling you are ever so slightly beginning to feel is dread. My face will be that dread for the rest of your life. A smell, a sound and smirk on someone's self-righteous face - like mine - will trigger the dread. Anticipation with a dash of fear: vrees."

"I fear no one except the sky falling on my head."

"Is it, hey?" Marius moved around and back to his original position, with a pat on Dan's shoulder. Marius' leader stood, arms folded, smiling with appreciation at his man's threats.

"*A little too loud is that cry, for the sky is above, the earth beneath us and the sea all around us, but unless the sky with its showers of stars fall upon the surface of the earth or unless the ground burst open in an earthquake, or unless the fish-abounding, blue-bordered sea come over the surface of the earth, I shall bring back every cow to its byre and enclosure, every woman to her own abode and dwelling, after victory in battle and combat and contest.*"

"I don't like poetry," said the leader. "You can ask for the earth to swallow you up right now, I don't care. No one is coming to save you. I can assure you that the sky is about to moer you stukkend. I also don't like spells, and from where I'm standing, the only things you've got are your evil utterances. But we will sort that out with either duct tape or some pliers if we hear you speak anything other than Mlilo's whereabouts. Besides, I've heard the temptation of summoning demons can get you ousted by those pagans." He laughed. "That *warlock*. Nothing more than a swineherd, shovelling kak and lying in his own filth."

He nodded his head towards the trolley. "You are probably aware of the water. Not meant for drinking. Marius, how do water and electricity mix?"

Marius snorted.

"Our other creative methods include hanging you by handcuffs for a few hours."

"Writhing and howling for it to stop," said Marius. "Breaking your nose and shoving both our thumbs into your nostrils and pulling it until the blood and snot ooze out."

"And then there's the knives, pliers and hammers," said the leader.

"But we'll start," Marius said with a punch to Dan's ribs, "with our fists."

The bright, silver disc of the moon hung in the cloudy night sky above the silhouettes of the mountains surrounding a standing Mlilo, taking in the awesome spectacle. The pale reflection sparkled on the surface of the black river water in the large rock pool. The only sound was the stream upriver and the splashing overflow a few metres away, leading back down into the valley Mlilo had spent the late afternoon and evening climbing.

His hot and tired feet, free of his snakeskin boots and socks, absorbed the coolness from the huge granite boulder. He had removed his leopard-print vest but kept his beads and pants on. His pockets and belt held his new amathambo securely in place.

He sat down and gently slid along the rock into the cold water, easing the waterline up his neck and finally submerging himself.

The watery world engulfed him, his feet and legs pulled close so as not to touch the bottom, allowing a moment to float fully suspended in the body of water.

He poked his head out to take a breath of air and a tingle ran up his spine and his scalp. He kicked his feet and splashed his arms in the water to get himself horizontal. The water settled and his buoyancy held. He could relax and look up at the stars peeking through the clouds.

"Amazulu," he whispered. He kept his breathing shallow for a moment longer, to remain above the surface, but he loved it under the water. Another world. He knew his body and his amathambo would be receiving the much-needed cleansing and rejuvenating from the fresh mountain water.

Mlilo took a deep breath and went under the surface, into the darkness.

At about a metre and a half deep near the edge, he was able to touch the sandy bottom. A couple of strokes took him deeper still.

He swam back up for a quick breath and went under again. He was a kid again.

For a second, he thought he had become accustomed to the chill of the river water, warmer against his skin. Rather than panic, he understood what was happening.

Without flailing about or thinking he would run out of air, Mlilo allowed the sensation to take hold. He relaxed.

He slowly sank to the sandy bottom, crossing his legs as he settled. What should have been a watery world was a gloomy, desert-like landscape, the horizon indistinct against the black sky filled with stars, whose clarity and positions he recognised.

A pool of light shimmered in the space around him, like a spotlight of energy from an unseen source.

Forms began to emerge from all directions from the darkness, like three-dimensional silhouettes, indistinct features shrouded in shadow. At first, he thought they were twenty or thirty metres away because of their size, but soon realised they were small figures. They stopped a metre from him, encircling him.

His amathongo.

The shape directly in front of him moved closer, and as if stepping into the light, her features were revealed. He had never met her in all his journeys to Abaphansi, nor during his ukuthwasa, but he knew her immediately.

Zandile.

"Sawubona, Mlilo," she said in a tone he could only describe as pure love.

His body buzzed with energy and emotion. He was speechless. All he could do was nod.

"uNosithwalangcengce's bone is rightfully yours. I, Zandile, took it from her during her cowardly attack on me, on our line. It is what keeps her from entering your world and doing harm. It was passed on to one who would become isangoma. You. It is you who can get it back. It is you who must take it back, and destroy it, forever preventing the hyena from gaining her full power again."

"But I'm not strong enough to fight that hyena and her minions."

"You are strong enough to fight. That is all. But you need to be strong enough to believe in yourself."

"I will do everything in my power to stop her. I know that."

"Believing in yourself is knowing where your weaknesses are. There is strength in acknowledging weaknesses. And where you are weak, that is where you must bring in those who can fill that void with their strengths. We, amathongo, came before you and prepared you. And amadlozi are guiding you."

He thought of Amira and Dan, his friends he had pushed away.

"You are loved, Mlilo," Zandile said and her diminutive form stepped back, into darkness, and the group of figures started walking to Mlilo's left. As the next figure reached Zandile's original position, it was like the same light was turned on, and he saw another person, another of his family of ancestors, in vivid detail. As each figure passed into the light, so the previous one faded back into the shadows and their voices filled his ears, lots of them, all talking simultaneously. But he found it easy to understand every one of them. Messages from the other side. Messages, knowledge, foretellings. It was like a flood of energy was filling him up. Mlilo brimmed with emotion. He felt supported and loved. He would not have to attempt to remember everything now. It would all come back to him in the real world as insights, vivid memories or dreams. It would all still be there.

CHAPTER 26

"My king, Kubera," Bhadra's voice echoed around the great hall. "Yaksharajan, Dhanadhipati, Vaishravana, I present to you my promised gift."

The halāhala tightened around Amira's wrists, Bhadra's hold on the poison absolute and powerful, as she followed behind her captor into a wide hall with low ceilings. Low to Amira rather than the multitudes of yaksha people milling about the edges. Beyond the king's subjects, beyond the throne platform and the supporting pillars, she could see the curve of this world's landscape. On either side, the crescent mountain range curved outward.

A dwarf of a man on the raised throne turned from his intimate conversation with a mongoose creature at his side.

"Bhadra," he said, throwing his four arms out in welcome, "what monstrosity has my queen of the hunt brought me? You have tantalised me over the past three days. Give it!"

Amira was wrenched down onto the stone floor.

"A mortal attempting to take from your lands, oh king."

"Welcome to my palace, thief, conceived of by the great builder god himself, Vishwakarma." Murmurs of agreement from his subjects.

Close up she could see veins of gold and rust-coloured textures within the milky creams and pinks of the quartz floor. A type of jasper, or agate? But it was one seamless rock rather than individual tiles. The squat pillars rising up around the edges to the ceiling no doubt all part of the intricate stonework of the mountainside.

A sudden pain in her wrists brought her attention back to her circumstances.

If she didn't know better, knowing who the king of the yakshas was, she would have thought he was misshapen dwarf. Milky pink skin like that of the pale floor under her feet, the small man's beard spilled over his lily-white paunch, milky pink skin like that of the floor under her feet, speckled with pomegranate pips and juice. He took a bite of the large fruit in one of his many hands, momentarily exposing his broken and misshapen teeth and two small tusks protruding from his mouth.

"I hear you had my queen and her minions whipped into a fine fury, girl."

189

Amira glared at the woman at the other end of her restraints. "I would relish the opportunity for a more equal combat. One on one." She gritted her teeth, bracing for the response tightening around her hands.

She looked back at the king. His one squinting eye gave Amira an opportunity. In moments like these, when Amira detested talking over action, she imagined Dan's silky tongue working his magic. The only means of inflicting a blow.

"I see your eye is not yet fully healed," she said. "Parvati was gracious to restore it, was she not?"

Coughed and spluttered.

"After she inflicted it on me in the first place!" He rose to his full height, standing on his three legs, and threw the fruit across the room, splattering to the floor.

"Who is this, *girl*," Kubera spat and gestured to the room. Turning, Amira noticed the arched doorways, solid stone doors blocking entry, along the entire back wall with the central hallway she had entered through moments earlier.

Eight doorways.

Immediately she thought of the Nidhis, the treasures said to be closely guarded by Kubera. There were supposed to be nine. Amira scanned the room, but there were no other solid walls in sight. She looked up at the rotund ruler and his platform.

She stood, eye's searching along the floor.

A seem of thin gold ran in a perfect square around Kubera's platform. The ninth door, for the ninth treasure.

"Next time I'm invited here maybe I will bring Ganesha as my plus one. He has an appetite for all things Kubera. He is currently visiting his brother, south of here. Shall we call him? Do you have enough pomegranates?"

The mongoose animal beside the king chuckled at the insinuation.

"This amuses you, trickster?" The king turned on it. "Chakide enjoys suffering?

"My king," the animal whispered, "I only find amusement in the mortal's attempts to deflect from the inevitable wrath of my king Kubera. The hyena queen simply asked me to deliver her request for support and I shall return to her in the cave lands." Chakide sucked in a hiss of air, looking around the room self-consciously, clearly realising their mistake.

The hyena that seeks Mlilo is in the cave lands. Amira feigned a distraction at her feet, pretending not to have heard.

"I am not here for your stuff, King Kubera," said Amira. "I would not dream of stealing from your lands, your riches. I would only wish to have any wealth bestowed on me by your doing, and my deserving."

The king slouched back into his throne, taking a gold tray offered by Chakide and resting it on his stomach. "What is the reason for your being in this world, mortal girl?"

"Chandrahas," she said.

The king stood, clattering the plate full of fruit onto the stairs. "The sword gifted by Lord Shiva to my half-brother Ravana?" His voice bellowed through the hall.

Silence descended. Amira felt like a fool. Of course, Ravana was Kubera's half-brother. She stood her ground and said, "The sword. And then I will leave."

All four of Kubera's fists clenched and he brandished them at the ceiling. "That wretch of an animal did not deserve that treasure from Lord Shiva! Wasted. I warned him."

Amira stood stunned. That had taken an unexpected turn.

"Where is it?" He asked.

"With Sita," said Amira. She turned to see an equally flabbergasted Bhadra, flustered at the notion of what was to happen next.

Kubera waddled down the stairs and over to Amira, taking her hand. He looked to his queen and gestured at the restraints.

The armour covered frame of Bhadra rattled and bristled with irritation, but with the flick of one of her limbs, the black poison released its grip on Amira.

Strangely, the yaksha king was endearing, looking up at Amira with warmth. "The sooner you are out of the world the better," he said with a crooked smile. "The lizard will have my skin if he knew I released you without protest, but this sword deserves to be in the hands of one worthy."

He held onto Amira's elbow as they walking towards the edge of the hall and the precipice below. "You will therefore need to cover ground rapidly. You will take Pushpaka Vimana." With a flourish he turned to the room, "The great Vishwakarma conceived and built my flying chariot, Pushpaka Vimana." He waited for the room to erupt in agreement. "This girl–" he turned to Amira.

"Woman," she said, "Amira."

"This woman Amira, will journey to Sita's lands on the mighty Pushpaka Vimana."

The hall burst into shouts and applause. All but queen Bhadra celebrated the news.

Kubera headed back toward his throne. "Come! More soma," he ordered and gestured to Amira. "But not for the mortal. She is on her way."

CHAPTER 27

Dan's abdomen ached. His breathing was shallow, after heaving from the initial blows from Marius. At least a rib or two cracked. His bum cheeks were numb, and the sensation of pins and needles pricked his skin as he shifted in his seat. A layer of sweat coated his entire body. The rusted knife between his legs remained firmly in place.

"I have been around for centuries. Don't think I'm some wet-behind-the-ears plaasjapie, or potato farmer. I've adapted. Destroying talismans and trinkets. Killing druids and obliterating demons. It all gives me strength. It's how I live on in an immortal body."

"You won't get away with this," Dan wheezed. He took a couple of deep breaths and forced himself upright in the chair.

"But I do. There's the law. And then there's the lord. I am doing God's work."

"Everyone is entitled to revere whichever sky god they choose. And there are many," Dan winced. "I don't care which one you think you're working for, doing the *good* work for, but let's be clear: you are doing this for you. It's people like you that are evil. Putting the fear in people. Sheep heads."

He saw the leader of the group lift a hand for Marius not to intervene, a wry smile of interest on his face.

"And if your sky god created this world, and everything in it," continued Dan, "then he created me as I am. And, if I am possessed by some imagined demon, who allowed that? Who created that demon? Next time you are having your one-sided convo with it, why not ask it about that. But I have a feeling your sky god is a sadistic bastard who likes its followers to jump through hoops like a circus animal. That's what feeds it. That's what gives it power, like most gods. Not destroying demons but feeding off your praise and adoration and fear of it. A god's power is only as strong as its follower's faith in it. Go feed your sky demon. If it created this earth that we stand on then tell it to stop allowing me to draw energy from it. That's where I get my power. It's not from me, as you know. I don't have power, or some demon inside me. It's the earth beneath my feet that gives me everything. Sell your fear and hate somewhere else."

"In this day and age, I don't need a congregation in front of me or a hall filled with people, a couple of thousand at a time, or those rare events filling stadiums with even more. I don't have to pass a basket around asking for donations. No. I press record on a mobile phone and millions upon millions of people from all walks of life, wanting to hear the truth, my message, rack up my views, rack up my ad revenue. And the donations are the bonus."

It finally dawned on Dan.

"You are that conspiracy nut-job on social media," Dan said stunned. "Whassaname Saul or something."

"Oom Sol," Marius growled in Dan's ear, followed by a punch in the ribs.

"It's always been about the money, Lebowski," said Dan as he coughed and heaved. "I don't need to join a group, a religion, a sect, a cult in order to be able to cope with adulting. If you need some moral compass, other than simple decency, to guide you through life, to give you the coping mechanisms and direction and meaning not to blow someone's brain out, or your own, then maybe this life is not for you."

"The sun will soon rise on this great land. Darkness will be left behind."

"You are Prime Evil. Your ignorance of that is stunning. Newsflash: the Earth is no longer flat, choppie."

"The Earth is ours, through and through. As above so below. We reap the harvests; we tunnel into the depths. Vastrap. We make a stand. Ja, I may be vilified, but I am part of everyone. Everyone who hates me hates that side of themselves. I am useful to the world. Now, I think it's time for some blood-letting, Marius."

Marius gripped Dan's jaw in his hand. "This pretty little face is going to bleed."

Dan's gut sank, more from the image Marius' words conjured up than the pain.

"This could all be over with a couple of words uttered by you. The beast that you know of as the Hyena, she has her ways of finding your boetie, eventually, no matter what cloaking spell he has put around himself. He hasn't cloaked his buddy here, now has he?"

"Let's warm up these rosy cheeks, chom," Marius said and slapped Dan squarely across the face. The tingling pain sent more adrenaline through him.

"And when you've achieved your goal of retrieving Mlilo for uNosithwalangcengce," sneered Dan, "I'm sure I know what happens next. Does she know you are going to sell her out to your sky god and attempt to destroy her, the demon that she is? I don't think she does, does she?"

"She has her objectives, and I have mine. One day her and I will clash, but tonight we have a common goal."

All Dan could think of doing was rattling them, angering them. He looked over at the man at the door watching Sol and Marius pacing around Dan. Every now and then his fingers would touch and prod the numerous welts on his forearms. He wanted some of the action.

"How's the scabbing, Wynand?" Dan's words received a glare from the man, his hands flitting back to his sides, at attention. "I hear some species of bees lay their eggs when they sting their victims."

Slap.

"Boetie," Marius said with a toothy sneer in Dan's face, spittle flying, "you are lucky it isn't time to kill you yet." The chair shook with the force the man needed to extract the knife from its position. "Otherwise, I would take this rusty blade and slowly saw through your throat right now. And the pleasure would be mine to watch you splutter in your own warm blood."

"Would that make a welcome human sacrifice to your sky god, I wonder?"

Marius roared and in a swift feline-like movement, he was behind Dan, his head gripped between palm and chest, dull knife blade at his throat. "I'm going to splay you like a chicken and offer you up to your gods!"

For Dan, the room went into slow motion. Sol was shouting, Wynand lunging forward at them.

The excruciating sound, like fingernails on chalkboard, of metal on metal, pierced their ears. The other two men, stunned, covered their own ears. A blinding white light filled the room followed by an inexplicable heat and sparks.

A burning smell filled Dan's nostrils.

His eyes adjusted back to the light of the room and the body of Marius lying spread-eagled on his back.

Both the man's hands were pink and red with blisters.

"Wat die duiwel?" whispered Wynand.

CHAPTER 28

A variety of citrus and thick leafed banana trees peppered the ornate gardens surrounding Amira. If she looked out over the expanse of the mountain range her head felt dizzy, let alone the effects of the warped landscape seen from this height. A low parapet ran the length of the terrace she was standing on, the central area open with deep stairs leading to the final terrace below and the drop down the mountain face. At her back, immense trees, structures and rocks blocked the northern view from the mountain.

From where she stood, she could see sunken areas, steps and seating platforms, encircling fountains and neat gardens. Various birds and insects flittered about among the bright foliage and trees. Columned arches and domed gazebos enveloped by massive trees and overgrown vines provided quiet sanctuaries engraved with decorative scenes and imagery. Pathways wound in and out of bushes and flowering shrubs, past neatly kept flowerbeds and thick green grass, intersecting at open pergolas with large tables lined with platters of foods and drink. Mingling fragrances wafted on the breeze, incense, flowers and spices, and in the distance, the lilt of music.

The sun to her right was in its usual golden red position. She traced the flow of the small stream at her feet, a narrow gutter carved or worn into the basalt rock, disappearing over the edge of the palace. It wound through the valley below and into the silver sliver of the massive, arterial river of this world and its eventual disappearing into the dark void of the distant horizon. She could only imagine the utter gloom that that part of the underworld represented, sending a shiver up her spine.

"Wondrous," a female voice whispered at Amira's right.

Although her body didn't flinch, she hated it when anyone managed to come up next to her, off guard. Her tone carried her irritation. "Excuse me?"

"Our land is wondrous," said the yakshini standing formally with a spear, the same texture and colour as her armour, two feet higher than Amira. She turned to Amira and said, "I have been commanded, by my leader, Queen Bhadra, to accompany you on Pushpaka Vimana."

"And you are?"

"Dhrti. Lieutenant Dhrti."

"So, Lieutenant Dhrti, you are my chaperone," Amira said with a sigh and folded her arms.

"Please," the soldier indicated to Amira to walk with her along the eastern side of the mountain. "This city, Alakapuri, is blessed with all that our King Kubera protects. The chariot, Pushpaka, the gardens alive with abundance like the lands that provide riches beyond belief, and his subjects."

The lieutenant kept them on the stone path on the other edge of the terrace, acknowledging passersby and their stares up at Amira, with a nod.

"You sound like a true follower, Dhrti," said Amira.

"You do not have anyone you follow like this?"

"I have those who I am willing to learn from. Those I look up to. But I do not venerate anyone. All are fallible. God or moral."

They trotted down a curved staircase, Amira noticing how light on her feet the yakshini was, leading to the bottom gardens and into a wider, central pathway. Over her shoulder, Dhrti asked, "Whom do you put your trust in then?"

"Myself." Amira caught up to her.

"And are you trustworthy?"

"I am."

"And you have never let yourself down?"

Amira glared at the soldier walking beside her. She noticed the music had become louder, clearer.

"You are not trustworthy, yet you have no one else to put your trust in."

Amira had to bend under an area of low hanging trees as the soldier led her through and onto the paved rim of one of the sunken gardens below. Amira saw the source of the music she had heard earlier. A group of strange folk Amira couldn't quite figure out their true forms, were relaxing on cushions, mats and the soft grass playing intricate instruments. Unlike the yakshas or yakshinis, they looked more human but at the same time feathers or a wing confused her.

"Kinnaras," said Dhrti.

The celestial musicians.

With the music drifting away behind them, the path curved to the right, opening up from the trees of the gardens and leading them along the eastern end of the crescent mountain.

They passed through a flock of about twenty pale grey and white geese with two distinct black stripes on their heads pecking at the grass and pathways, gaggling their response to the intrusion, and stepped up onto the battlement structure of the mountaintop. Amira could see its duplicate at the opposite end of the stretch of basalt in the distance, and how reinforcing from beneath allowed the platform to extend past the outer edge by at least five metres. The parapet, thicker than the garden balustrades, at least a metre deep and just below the chin of the yakshini, had gaps every two metres for discharging weapons or firing projectiles through.

"Here we are," said Dhrti stopping in the centre of the open courtyard.

After the sheltered calm of the gardens, Amira felt exposed, the wind whipping her hair and tunic. She looked around, then asked, "Where is this fabulous chariot?"

"You are standing on it."

With that the entire fifty metre square building rumbled beneath Amira's feet. The vines attached from nearby trees and pillars tore away. In a raucous response, the flock of geese took off and disappeared below the rising platform, squawking their discontent into the valley.

Dan could not find an explanation for the scene earlier. He hadn't had the strength to exert the kind of energy that was emitted. His neck was tingling from the sensation of whatever had deflected the attack from Marius. But it was clear that his kidnappers would have to find another way to hurt him. Or kill him.

"We can keep this up until morning, sunshine."

Dan couldn't tell how long they had been at it. For his body, it felt like a lifetime. Apart from the bandaged Marius, having been given door duty, they were not waning. They thrived on this.

"My father told me about okes like you. Wars on the border gave you an excuse to grow your power with the blood of the so-called enemy."

"Boetie, war is war. I've seen them all from the frontlines. And that war you speak of – it feels like yesterday – was a true crusade. I had them all eating from the palm of my hand."

"You whispered in the ears of the self-righteous, you fed them lies, they fed our boys lies. All for another holy war. No, war is a battle between adversaries in combat, not a bloodlust involving innocents using a warped ideology."

"Innocents?" Ha!"

"You thrived under the dodgy science, warped interpretations of sacred texts and outright lies for the powers of darkness. Darkness you assumed was the light the world needed to make it better. But at the expense of multitudes. Boys younger than me forced to defend something that should never have been defended."

"Yirra, now you are making me nostalgic. Yearning for the good old days. All that blood, that screaming and the icy adrenaline. Blood in soil. I can tell you this for free, the screams of soldiers are different to the sounds of women and children, who shouldn't be there. The weight of an R1 rifle gripped in your trembling hands is not a source of comfort when the ground around you is exploding with anti-aircraft rounds, or your friend's life is running into the white-hot sands. No, it is the power that you put your faith in that comforts you."

"One idiot's 'good old days' is someone else's hell. Even when the brainwashing tactics were exposed–"

"Telling it like it is isn't brainwashing, child," Sol interrupted Dan. "Over the past two millennia I've put a lot of effort into my words. I craft them like an engineer crafts a well-designed weapon."

"Even when the lies that had been told to young boys, and the rest of the country, were exposed for the manipulations they were, some – like these muppets," Dan jerked his head to the other men in the room, "continue to believe it, continue to use it to justify your hate of others."

Wynand landed a fist on the back of Dan's head, sparkles of light filling his vision.

"There is right and there is wrong in the world. If you cannot see that I am right, then you are wrong," the leader stepped up to Dan and slapped him hard across the right side of his face and ear. The ringing and pain took his breath away. Tears welled up in his eyes and he choked back the emotion brought on by the adrenaline and fright.

But Dan forced himself to continue. "The light will prevail. You and your followers are literally a dying breed and by god your ageing out and dying off couldn't come sooner. And with those deaths, less energy and idol worship of you. You too will fade. Your black light will flicker and fade and puff out in a stream of sooty sulphuric stench. Little do they know your light is that of the one angel of light himself, cast down and leading you by the nose, broken and bleeding with two thumbs stuck up it."

"Your father has fed you a load of kak, boytjie," he slapped Dan's other cheek squarely, and thankfully not the other ear. "He sounds like a coward, one of the ones that probably broke under the stress of too many pushups in the first week of basics. I bet he never served his country."

"Like most of the boys, _laities,_" Dan emphasised the last word, "he believed in his country. But it became clear to him what the motivations were to send innocent kids into someone else's hate-filled fight. And that's where your own power comes from, doesn't it? Your hate. Hate will get you so far, and then it will collapse in on itself. That's why you soak up the powers of others, to survive. But your power is waning."

"I am here to destroy evil, boy." Sol's face reddened and he pounded his fist in his palm. "We put our faith in that."

Dan snorted. "Some people believe we need evil in the world just so they have something to show how righteous they are. Once evil is destroyed, what use is there for a warmonger? Look at the world today. The person in need is the one on their knees. People continually put their faith and the purpose of their lives in their gods, and not themselves. When they overcome adversity, they thank their gods, but they give themselves credit as well. They feel emboldened and so their pride eliminates the need for their god's help. But rather than replacing it with a belief in themselves they succumb to circumstance once more. They've been punished, or they have been given a lesson. And the cycle continues. If only they would believe in themselves as much as they do in their gods, they would themselves become gods or at the least godlike."

Sol's fist hit Dan's cheekbone and jaw, flicking his head back with a crick in his spine. Icy pain shot through his head and shoulders. Throbbing filled his skull and he tasted the blood seeping from inside his pulpy cheek and gums.

It took Dan a moment to focus himself. "The irony is your followers look to you like a god."

This time Wynand punched him from the side, Dan's jaw popping in his ear.

"They worship you," Dan slurred, saliva and blood oozing over his lips. He sprayed out spit onto the floor. "Should we, or Marius over there, destroy you? Leadership becomes worship. But your power wanes and gods who are forgotten have to steal their power to survive."

Two rapid fire blows landed on either side of Dan's ribs.

He wheezed, his lungs searching for air. He ignored the taste of the blood in his mouth, the pain everywhere, keeping his thoughts and words focused.

"I can't remember now if it was a god, a dream or a flash of inspiration, but what if man was made mortal in order for racists and bigots and outdated ideologies to eventually die along with them. Like evolution. Survival of the smartest. Progress. Marching towards civilisation means culling the dead ideas like dead, rotting meat."

The laugh from Sol took Dan by surprise when he had been expecting another punch.

"My video views say different. My followers are there, maybe not waiting in plain sight, but they are there. And they are there for me when the time is right."

"Talk all you want." Dan forced a pained sneer. "Spread your hate all you want. But we are the bards; the storytellers. We are the gatekeepers of your ilk and your stories. We keep you alive. We feed you. We feed the myths of you. We have the ability to let you die; to have you fade away and die out. Because those that worship you, through their reverence, they die off or forget or grow weary of the same fairytales told badly by the controlling. If we decide to never speak of you and never tell them about you, you will truly fall away like the myths that you are and be forgotten. Our words or the lack thereof can kill you slowly, off into obscurity."

Dan's world shook in a flurry of blows to the head and abdomen.

The massive structure continued its trajectory south. Solid beneath her, Amira remained unsure on her feet, imagining it being like a ship on an ocean. The wind came in waves, sometimes blowing along with the chariot and other times a gust buffeting from the side.

Dhrti stood squarely at the rear, long spear placed firmly at her side, like she was part of the rock itself.

Amira ran through her objective and destination – Sita's forest abode of Sitamarhi – and what she anticipated would occur when she was given an audience with her. Amira hoped she had what it would take to convince Sita of her worthiness to wield the sacred, crescent sword Chandrahas. Using it justly.

Taking advantage of the quiet time of this aerial journey, Amira had attempted two full recitings of the Shiva-Kavacha, summoning Lord Shiva's divine armour for protection. Each attempt had materialised more and more of the breastplate and jewelled glove. On the third and final attempt she had ignored the side-glances from the yakshini, closed her eyes and proceeded with the incantation again. But the iridescent form wavered. She would have to keep at it but, for now, it had worked.

From this vantage point, Amira could see the mountainous cave lands rising from the lush valleys in the distance to the southeast, and blending into the lower hills of Parvati's coastal domain overlooking the Eastern Sea. A familiar sight that felt so far away now.

"We have a visitor," said Dhrti dryly.

Confused, Amira looked around. The starry sky had large clouds obscuring them, the rays of the sun casting a muted pink on their dull forms. Nothing was coming at them from any side that she could see. She looked back at the yakshini who was looking at a spot a metre or two away from her feet. A section of the rock floor was swirling like liquid.

Startled, Amira jumped back a pace at the sight of the same in front of where she was standing.

"Do not engage."

Over the breeze flicking her hair, Amira could discern the sound like gravel or glass crunching. The liquified circle of rock, half a metre wide pulled downward into a dark void. Sunlight caught a tiny sliver of dust, snaking upward and finally settling into a perfect line. Solid. The cracking sound intensified, becoming more like a scraping noise. Amira stood ready, her khaṭvāṅga held firm in her left hand.

Expanding from the line, a form like glass turned outward to reveal an ornate design that took Amira a moment to realise was a lizard, head facing down and tail curving upward and back in on itself.

"Intulo," said Dhrti.

Amira was now equally astonished by the duplicate form suspended in front of the yakshini looking relaxed and unfazed by their guest.

"You are from the other world," said the voice whispering from the creature's barely open jaws. "You do not belong here."

Apart from the hypnotic stare of the reptilian eye, Amira was drawn to the intricate design of the creature's scales. Like minuscule mosaics, the iridescent blues shimmered like liquid.

"We will complete her mission in short time," said Dhrti. "King Kubera has granted her passage."

"Your king grants no being passage. He grants transport and protection. Passage is mine to allow."

"I am on my way to Sita," Amira offered.

The single visible eye, the black vertical slit of its pupil looked up at Amira, unblinking.

"One way or another, you will soon leave this world – by my hand or by the approaching storm bird."

Amira watched as the two-dimensional form of the lizard, and its marble-like vortex, moved around her and disappeared.

"What?" she said to herself.

"He is allowing us through," said Dhrti.

"And the storm–" Amira cut herself off as she caught sight of the black horizon to the east.

An undulating squall had come out of nowhere. As if in response, a violent gust blasted them, nearly lifting Amira off her feet.

She heard Dhrti curse and add, "ǂKagara."

A metallic screech filled the air around them, vibrating through the solid stone Pushpaka. At first Amira thought it may be the wind blasting through the battlements, but a second scream confirmed it was a short distance from them.

Lightening lit up the clouds, now closer than before and moving at a rapid pace at the platform. Amira could've sworn she saw a silhouette inside the mass of brewing grey, black, like a bird many stadiums wide, with its wings outstretched.

"Storm bird," said Amira, more to herself than her companion.

"Usually, we do not speak its name, but it is upon us. Stand firm. Hold your ground. Do not go over the edge."

"Oh, thanks for that." Amira scowled at the soldier standing ready for what was heading their way.

The wind was growing, buffeting them, as they braced at an angle against the insubstantial force they could not fight.

Dhrti's spear was held out, secured under her arm and elbow, pointing and ready.

Finally, she had the time to focus, unobstructed by any enemy. "Listen, Oh Goddess," Amira initiated her chant to materialise the sacred armour.

As far as she could see, the east was covered in clouds and mayhem. Dozens of twisters reached down to the earth, writhing like angry animals wreaking havoc across the landscape.

Amira kept the words flowing, the beat of the rite natural and soothing. She could feel a weight to her chest and right hand. The energy did not waver.

"If one wears such an armour at the base of the throat or on the right arm, she will be released from the bonds of all sin, of this there is no doubt," she ended firmly.

Amira moved closer to the yakshini soldier, eyes scanning the mass of storm and mayhem directly above them. Amira was ready as ready as she could be.

Metal on metal sounds squealed through the air. Everything grew dim and muted. The sun was a pale light through the haze engulfing them. Spindly forks of electricity licked the edges of the platform's walls, over the floor and quickly dissipated. It was surveying their territory.

She could not clearly make out the form within the writhing clouds. Glimpses of layered, rusty iron, maybe feathers or a wing. Sharp edges and spines, talons or a beak. Amira was unsure where to focus on, but it was huge. Where would the threat come from? This antagonist was everywhere.

A giant wing, like an axe, swiped inches away from Amira, landing a blow to Dhrti and sending her sliding across the rock floor and into the battlement with a clatter of armour.

But the yakshini was on her feet and by Amira's side once again. Preempting another strike, Amira built up her energy, immediately feeling a shift in the blasts of air around her. Dhrti saw what she was doing and stepped closer to Amira.

As if in response, a hurricane of wind pushed down on them, forcing the two warriors into a crouch and unable to move an inch. Amira used every ounce of her willpower to sustain the ball of energy around her and Dhrti.

"When I say now," shouted Dhrti above the rushing turbulence, "push up. Stand with everything you have."

Amira nodded and waited for the yakshini lieutenant to give the signal.

"Now!"

Legs straining under the downward force, Amira stood, giving Dhrti the opportunity to slide to the side and stab her spear upward.

Amira recognised the sight of the halāhala poison rising like a black shaft into the pandemonium of cloud, lightening and wind.

The screech of the giant metal bird pierced the air but did not diminish the force of the storm raging around them.

Electricity crackled. A roar built to a crescendo. In a flash, a bolt of lightning struck Amira's golden breastplate, blasting her up against the outer wall and bending her backward. Her muscles strained to get herself upright and ready to push back, but another blast of light and electricity lifted her feet. She reacted with quick reflexes, shooting her free hand out and grabbing the inside edge of the wall as her legs pivoted over the side of the Pushpaka.

The shaft of Dhrti's spear darted into Amira's view. The warrior gave a quick tilt of her head and Amira grabbed hold.

She had no time to appreciate the strength with which the smaller woman pulled her back onto the platform, as she rolled down and back onto her feet.

Amira's divine armour had vanished.

As if in response, a bolt of lightning blasted Dhrti onto her back, spear clanging to the side. Realising the pattern of double hits of lightening, Amira anticipated the secondary blast that was coming. She screamed above the cacophony of the storm creature and stepped between the lieutenant and the incoming lightening.

Unaware of Amira's intentions, Dhrti, spear already in her grasp, had aimed and sent a volley of halāhala in ǂKagara's direction.

Amira could never have imagined what occurred next. The building kinetic force from within herself erupted in a magnitude ten times stronger than she had ever released before. The halāhala seemed to pass right through her and out in a prism of black and blue waves.

Quicker than it had materialised, the storm abated, moving off to the east. Electric currents subsided and the sky began to clear.

"Back to your mountain cave!" Shouted Dhrti.

Amira's body shook from the energy. "Ha!" was all she could muster. Her muscles tingled. Her eyes and mind were hyperaware.

Dhrti turned to Amira. "Did you just–"

"Amplify your power?"

"I can only reason that my blast was not intended for you but for," she hesitated at the name, then said, "the storm bird. It passed through you unharmed.

Amira didn't know what it meant, but they had survived.

CHAPTER 29

The figures had now faded into the black landscape. Buoyancy returned to Mlilo's body and the starry sky blurred into shimmering water above.

He kicked off the ground, arms pulling him upward. The urge for air compelled him to the surface.

Soon he realised he was not making progress, the surface still out of reach. There was a current holding him, then pulling him back down. He could see nothing around him besides bubbles and water.

Panic rose. He flailed and kicked.

He looked up at the surface, and rather than the moon or stars, he could make out a silhouette of a person seated in a chair, surrounded by light and other figures.

Mlilo struggled with all he had to get closer. Centimetre by centimetre he edged closer. The fingers of his right hand broke the surface while he maintained his kicking and strokes. The person in the chair was half a metre from his grasp. He was sure it was Dan, back to him, slumped over and motionless.

Heat rose from Mlilo's body. Rage. Frustration boiled. His hand got closer.

He kicked. Closer.

With one final lunged he pushed up and managed to place his palm on Dan's boney shoulder blade. The energy surged from his hand into his friend and Mlilo's world collapsed in a tsunami of waves.

"Mlilo," he heard Dan whisper as the chaos pulled him under.

The familiar solid feel of the bottom of the pool gave him the leverage to push upward and a moment later burst from the water in the moonlit night.

He spluttered and swam limply over to the rock and pulled himself out of the water. He was out of breath, panting, more from anxiety than exhaustion.

"What the hell was that all about?" He muttered to himself. He pushed his vest and shirt aside, grabbing for his phone.

Useless. No signal to call his friend and find out if he was ok. He slumped backward onto the cool rock, his mind racing.

"Mlilo," Dan whispered as a surge of energy filled his ice cold and aching body. Through the puffy haze he looked around, disoriented, looking for his friend. His torturers were all in his field of vision and yet he could still feel the warmth on his shoulder he knew was from Mlilo. He blinked, imagining a hand reaching from the void behind him to touch and comfort him.

"Yes, Mlilo," said Sol in the corner of the room, pissing into the metal tub of water. He pivoted his right leg at the hip, toes turning inward, to loosen his cheeks and emit a fart and a grunt of satisfaction. "Tell us where he is."

Dan forced a deep breath, using the energy to summon the words. "He's going to stick a cracker up your arse, chop."

Icy water hit him, like a slap, waking his lethargic muscles. A twinge ran through his injured jaw as his teeth clenched instinctively at the fright.

All three of his captors roared with laughter, Sol standing with the empty metal bucket swinging from his hand.

"Can we get this over with, for gods' sakes, bru."

Slap.

"Blasphemy," shouted Wynand.

"Saying god isn't using the lord's name in vain. I mean, god isn't a name it is a designation. Maybe it's Bob and we're using it wrong."

Punch.

"I can save you, you know," said Sol. "I can get you a ticket to heaven."

"Apparently I am saved," Dan interrupted the other man, and flexed his hand. "Been there, done that, got the other-worldly wound."

"Renounce all your powers. Hand them over and be released. Or I can take them from you by blunt force."

"No, thanks. It's not all white fluffy clouds and harps," Dan turned to Marius. "You know that? Right, Marius? Your faithful leader has told you what's really on the other side, hey? If I had a ticket to your afterlife, I'd burn it to hell. We are all going to the same place. It's our own demons that will determine whether it's a hell or not. Maybe that will be your eternal torment – living in a hell of your preconceived ideas of heaven."

A punch landed on his brow and forehead.

Dan heard the squeak of trolley wheels. He managed to lift his heavy, swollen eyelids to see Marius awkwardly manoeuvering the water tub around and behind Dan.

Dan shook off the haze, black spots finally fading from his vision. "Your people will cross over and be stunned into purgatory. Like cattle, you will walk around for eternity waiting for St Peter to arrive and hold your hand through some gates that never existed, but only in your minds, to keep the unworthy out."

At first, he thought his world was collapsing, then realised the chair he was fastened to was being tilted backward, coming to a clanging stop on the bath rim. Voices murmured. His straps were tightened.

"*Beware the demon hunter*," he whispered the Morrígan's words to the blurry shadows moving about him, the fluorescent light hurting his eyes, "*for he sees demons in everything*."

Dan's body was draining of all energy. He pictured his tree, his grove, the smell of the rich soil nourishing through the roots, up into the thickening trunk and the bark; the dozens of branches growing up and outward, and the leaves like open palms reaching for the light, the sun in the pale blue sky above. The sound of rustling leaves.

The smell of grease and oil filled his snotty nose as a dirty rag was placed over his face. Water sloshed in a bucket next to him and the heaviness of the cold liquid hit him. His instinct to breathe took over, his mouth and nose sucking in watery air. It was as if the supply was endless, pouring slowly over him.

He hacked up water and blood and bile.

The chair was elevated and hit the foam-covered floor with a thud, his restraints pulling, tearing at his skin.

Dan gasped and sucked in as much air as he could. His ribs protested as he choked and coughed up water.

"Where's Mlilo," said the sing-song voice.

Dan's muscles shivered uncontrollably. His vision was blurred, his eyes barely open to any light from the room.

"Magic cannot be destroyed," he stammered. The image of his tree turned into the shadowy form of the Morrígan, but no longer encircled by his apartment building, rather bathed in a column of sunlight in pitch darkness, arms held out from her sides, fingers and clothing like wings and feathers, blowing in a breeze he could not feel. "Evil cannot be destroyed. Everything is energy. Energy cannot be destroyed, only shifted, redirected."

"Nog 'n keer."

The room whirled as he was pulled backward. The soggy cloth slapped onto his head and the water poured. It felt like minutes. Every inch of his mind was focused away from the suffocating, focused on the cool column of light growing around the Morrígan's splintering form.

Air. Water. Light. His mind raced.

Upright once again, he gasped, his lungs bubbling and aching.

An iron grip wrenched Dan's jaw, face to face with the whites of Sol's frenzied eyes. "Tell me where the devil your friend is," the man hissed through grinning white teeth.

Dan allowed his head to lol in Sol's hand. "One thing I am coming to realise, something my friend has been trying to tell me for a long time. We've got no time for the devil here."

Irritated, Sol released his hold on Dan's jaw, his head flopping to his chest.

"Here, in this land," Dan continued, trying to look up at anything, "this rock of a continent, we've got so many aspects of evil that one being isn't capable of holding all the evil of the world. Maybe in your western world, where everything is black and white, where you've created one evil scapegoat to hurl your hatred at. But this is Africa, baby. Here the good can be bad and good at the same time. You have to figure it out. Play their game. Your rulebook was made because of you, not before you were brought into existence. They have no rules here."

Pain. Jostling. Water.

He could no longer hear his heartbeat in his ears, just a constant ringing. Whistling.

Choking.

Warm breath against his face. Someone trying to listen, to hear him. "Like our ancestors coming to this land," he whispered to the darkness surrounding him, "in order to survive and flourish you have to learn the environment, learn the local knowledge, traditions, ways to heal and the ways to connect with the land under your feet. You cannot pick and choose. You cannot use their herbs without acknowledging their beliefs – their gods – otherwise you'll get chewed up and spat out. The magical powers inherent in this land are what kept them alive. But you spit on that." Dan dribbled whatever he could out of his mouth.

"Magic?" Sol's voice reverberated through Dan's body. "Magic is what has made this continent suffer."

"Nope," Dan shook his head. A pale light was wavering in the distance, in the deep blackness behind his eyes. "It's what's finally bringing it back to balance, to equilibrium. Rather than accepting the kak forced down throats for generations, we get to stand out in the open and shine our magic for the greater good. For someone who doesn't want to accept magic, you are doing your damnedest to obliterate it for your own power."

The whistle in his ears grew louder, the light brighter.

Disoriented, he murmured, "Mlilo."

CHAPTER 30

"Mlilo," came Dan's whisper like it was right next to him.

Mlilo sat upright on the moonlit rock, his clothes already drying against his skin.

"Dan?" he shouted. "Where are you?"

"Water," said Dan's voice. "Confused."

He scrambled his belongings together, shoved on his socks and boots and headed for the nearest portal: near the overhanging rock and caves housing the sacred cave paintings a kilometre away.

He shouted into the night sky, "My druid. My brother. My blood. I am coming."

He bounded over boulders and rocks, ignoring any bumps and scrapes, finally winding up along the well-worn pathway and stepped over the rope cordon.

He glanced at the faint lines and shapes of the ancient images on the rock surface, acknowledging them and asking for guidance as he leaped into the dark space ahead.

He pictured his destination, a sacred place he had read about, the closest to Dan's friend Len's home. He would have only a moment, suspended between worlds, to call out to Amira to help him get to Dan.

Pushpaka Vimana glided low and steadily over the vast swathe of forest below. Tributaries from the Great River broke off and weaved in and out the greenery, and the occasional red stone structures, domes, peaked out of the canopy.

The forest of Sitamarhi was immense.

"You are a brave warrior, Amira." Dhrti used her name for the first time. "I am proud to have fought beside you."

Amira smiled at the yakshini lieutenant at her side standing behind the battlements at the head of the chariot platform. "And I you, Lieutenant Dhrti."

She could feel the slow descent of the chariot, barely metres above the trees, making its way toward a clearing of about two hundred metres square. In the centre were a stepped pyramid temple complex and carefully plotted gardens and ponds.

"The halāhala you wield through your spear," said Amira.

"It is what allows the yakshas to take multiple forms. Our shapeshifting relies on it."

"I understand," said Amira with a pang in her gut.

"I would gladly impart it to one like yourself. But it is not mine to do so. Bhadra is the keeper of this magic."

The platform came to a gentle rest on the open lawn, scattering a herd of small antelope, like duiker, skipping into the forest surroundings. Both women turned and walked to the open stairs at the rear.

Dhrti stopped and waited for Amira to step onto the grass, then said, "I must leave you now, Amira."

"I hope we shall meet again, Dhrti," she said and gave the warrior a wave.

The yakshini remained in place, spear held firm, as the great chariot lifted into the air and away north, disappearing behind the huge forest trees.

Amira took a moment to listen to the quiet, the sounds of the forest and insects, birdcalls and shadows moving in the dense bush at the edges of the great lawn.

From her aerial vantage point moments before, Amira knew there were four entrances to the temple so she walked toward the closest set of stairs, a handful of beings moving in and out, and climbed to the second terrace and headed into the square doorway.

Amira had encountered strange creatures and mythical beings within Parvati's temple complex, but these were what you would expect from the southern forest creatures and sprites. Nature spirits the size of tiny flying insects, to tall, elegant, dryads bending through the low passage ahead of her. She slowed her pace to take in the intricate details of the murals on both sides of the passage. Fine brushwork and details, gold inlay. Creatures depicted that she had never seen in any books, scrolls or buildings in the real world.

The cool interior, muted sounds, and scents of spices and other aromas welcomed Amira in. A warm, hazy light permeated the wide passageway that opened out onto a huge square hall, a central angular ceiling rising high above. Light filtered in through various vents and gaps in the masonry.

It reminded her of Parvati and her domain. People, beings, of all shapes wandered about performing their duties and errands, while reclining on a large bed sofa sat the elegant figure Sita. In the same way that Parvati glowed, she had an iridescent warmth about her, but in contrast to Amira's benefactor, Sita was soft and her manner reflected this. Delicate fabric fell lightly over her body while her hair, stunningly long and shiny black, lay draped along the bed next to her.

Sita was finishing a conversation with a gold mantid-like creature bending low to hear her words. Transluscent purple-pink wings extended from its thicker outer wings of leathery gold, and with a rattling flutter it flew up and out through an opening in the ceiling twenty metres above.

Amira's gut churned with anticipation.

"I was just informed of your recent exploits, Amira."

The statement should not have surprised her but Amira could not hide the emotion on her face.

Sita smiled and gestured for her to take a seat in a lush cushioned chair alongside her.

"I have a suspicion about your reason for visiting me." She waited.

"Ah," Amira said, realising she was expected to formally tell her. "I have come to ask your permission, or shall I say, if you would be so kind as to–."

"Spit it out."

"I feel I am worthy to wield Chandrahas."

Sita narrowed her eyes at Amira. "And?"

"I would, let's say, if you would see it in your power to grant me permission to take–"

"Take?"

"If you would bestow upon me the privilege of being the bearer of Chandrahas."

'You see," said Sita matter-of-factly, "that wasn't so hard for an accomplished warrior as yourself, now was it, Amira?"

Amira shook her head.

"But I am afraid not," said Sita.

Amira's heart sank, and her skin went cold.

"Pardon, Sita?"

"You have come a long way. You have experienced much in your world and this world. But I cannot pass on the sacred sword to you."

Rage or sadness, she could not decide which, welled up inside Amira.

"Why?" was all she could whisper.

"Oh, the number of so-called worthy warriors, knights and skilled fighters who have passed through the very same door you just did to ask for me to hand them Chandrahas. Mostly men with less decorum than yourself. Seeking for themselves. You cannot expect me to hand over the sword to every being, every god, every mortal who comes into our world and asks for it. It doesn't work like that. Look beyond your own wants. The one who is deserving is the one who shall wield it."

Amira slumped back in her soft chair.

"I can sense your frustration. You are strong. You are needed. Use your own strength, Amira. And use it wisely. Within is where you should be looking rather than outside of yourself. External tools are useless to those who do not know themselves. A sculptor does not pick up a hammer for the first time and start pounding the marble, expecting a masterpiece to emerge. No. A pile of rubble is what he shall have."

All just words. Amira was one for action not platitudes and placations.

"For a time you wielded a power that was parasitic. It gave you a false sense of power. That has been stripped from you. Ask yourself why and you shall finally begin your journey. How did you feel when the queen of the hunt wrenched that poison from your body?"

"Weak."

Sita nodded gently.

"And how did you feel, moments after your immense battle with the creature in the sky?"

Amira thought for a moment. She remembered the exhilaration and how her body, though pounded and beaten, had felt as the storm bird had retreated.

"Alive."

"You had Shiva's armour for protection but you stood up and looked within. You are a force, Amira."

Amira sat upright, thinking about the fight alongside Dhrti.

"The woman, beaten and weak at the knees of the king in the mountains, is not the same woman who sits beside me now." Sita paused, and lifted a finger. "Listen."

"Amira," said Mlilo's voice as if he were inside her ear. Startled, she looked around the hall.

"You are needed, Amira," said Sita.

"Dan needs us," said Mlilo.

Sita stood and pointed to one of the exit doorways. "Through there. It will take you to your friend."

"Thank you," was all she could think of saying and hurried across the room.

"Please send my regards to Parvati," Sita shouted after her.

CHAPTER 31

"I am coming."

Mlilo's faint words lingered in Dan's head, like the subtle ringing in his ears. Low but distinct. After his initial confusion and the swirl of light and sounds, Dan recognised the landscape he now found himself in.

Shit.

A familiar figure, sitting atop her giant bull, ambled languidly through the mass of grazing Nguni cattle in the long grass and stopped short of Dan. He could've sworn her immense structure, her abode, had grown threefold, both up into the starry sky and across the stretch of river for two kilometres or more.

"You return," Mamlambo said, looking down at him. "You have no reason to cross my river and you have nothing to trade for passage to be granted."

Dan looked down at himself: empty handed, shirtless, with only his pants as covering.

"Your beliefs will keep you here, hold you here. Your soul knows the path it can take." The woman turned on the animal's back and pointed to Dan's right, down river, past the rising green hills and low mountains, in the distance toward the ominous shadow over the horizon.

Mamlambo reached forward, placing a hand gently on the top of her bull's head, between the giant, curved horns. In response, it lifted its massive head and gave a thunderous bellow, reverberating around and through Dan and the landscape.

The animals surrounding them stopped there feeding and began gravitating in the same direction, right. Dan watched as Mamlambo and her bull made their way back to the river's edge.

He felt helpless, alone.

"Have you called a taxi?"

Mlilo pivoted around where he sat on the temple stairs. "Yasas," he blurted out at Amira.

She looked out over the nighttime scene, the air cool and refreshing. Her irritation from her ordeal, leading up to the anticlimax with Sita, lingered like a bad taste in her mouth.

Now she was being called to help Daniel.

"Where are we?"

"Hello to you too. We're in Ladysmith. The Lord Vishnu Temple. And that over there," he said and pointed to the nearly three-metre-high statue to the left of the garden, reflecting the moonlight on its static form, "is Mohandas Gandhi, stretcher bearer to the troops. Our ride will be here momentarily." Mlilo stood and stepped down onto the grass.

Amira followed behind him as they made their way out the gate and onto the quiet street under the light of a lamppost. He shoved his hands in his pockets and leaned against the pole with a sigh.

"What's the emergency, Mlilo?"

"Something's definitely wrong with Dan. And from the brief conversation I had with Len, that warlock oke who tutors him or whatever, something hectic's happened."

"Right," Amira said, "he was staying with him for a while."

"I popped out here, like you, and immediately phoned Dan's mobile. Len answered and I couldn't make head or tale of what he was saying, other than _abducted_."

"Abducted? Who would've–"

The sound of tyres squealing, and the sight of car headlights up the road stopped her.

"That'll be Conrad. Len's boyfriend. Our ride."

Almost moving as one mind, Dan and the large animals were coming up on the rise of one of the hills. He had not realised until now, the rocks having been part of the landscape, but they were moving through a wide channel created by low stone walls on either side of them. Looking back at least a kilometre, they had started inconspicuously as a line of rocks and stones, gradually building up to around Dan's waist in height.

At the top of the hill, Dan took the opportunity to climb up onto the river-facing wall, over a metre high now, for a better vantage point. The three-hundred-and-sixty-degree view provided Dan with an aerial view he could never have imagined.

Apart from the stunning landscape itself, the hills turning rocky and impressive the higher they went, it was the structures that seemed to be oozing out of the ground like a colossal maze.

The network of walls, like circular channels branching off in spirals, hugged the hills in an endless pattern. Some lead down to the river as inlets for water, or platforms, jetties and slipways into the water itself. Herds of animals gathered around those to drink. Others wound their way through the hills and into the distant mountains. While on the nearby hillsides, cows and bulls grazed on the rich green grass, using the channels to move about.

But every land creature seemed to be moving toward the gloomy horizon. Slow but steady.

Dan recalled Mlilo talking about his visit to the Bokoni structures in the high-altitude grasslands of Mpumalanga. The pre-colonial, pastoral society of the Koni had created a marvel. A marvel Dan felt he was now witness to.

The bleat of a passing cow nearly startled Dan off his perch.

"Careful, human," said a small voice.

Dan looked down at the mongoose, upright and alert on its haunches, peering over the wall.

Mlilo barely managed to hit send on the text he had written to Ulwazi, letting her know where he was, from the car wheeling around a corner.

"Mfowethu," he said from the back seat to Conrad who was wide-eyed behind the steering wheel. The man had obviously rushed out the house as is in sleep shorts, a creased and dirty T-shirt and slops.

"Who were they," asked Amira in the front passenger side, gripping the roof handle.

"Some bastards, I don't know," Conrad's voice was fever-pitch. "I think Lennie knows. All I saw was my man on the ground and those bastards carrying Daniel away."

Amira placed a hand on the driver's arm. "Sorry. We'll do what we can to help."

Mlilo thought he could feel the car slow as Conrad forced a smile and nodded at Amira.

"Thanks," Conrad said. "The cops were useless. Came and went like it was another day at the office while I cradled Len on the couch."

Right into another road and a short distance later they turned left into a driveway. "Here we are," said Conrad with a sigh.

Through the rising dust, the headlight beams picked up the shape of a man hunched over in the doorway.

The car pulled to a stop.

"Lennie," Conrad rebuked the other man, "get yourself back in there. Lie down."

"I'm fine, hon," Len waved him past. "Put the kettle on. We have guests."

Conrad clucked his irritation, kissed his boyfriend on the cheek and headed inside.

"Daniel's friend," exclaimed Len with his arms open wide, then flinched and held his side.

"Please," said Amira, and took Len's arm around her.

Mlilo grabbed the older man's other arm and they sidled through the door and hobbled him into the lounge. Len's breathing was laboured, clearly tired and injured.

Len gave them both a tight squeeze before slumping down into the couch.

"I wish we could be meeting under better circumstances," he said.

Amira traced the path of mayhem evident in the kicked-up grass and dead bees. Len was only able to tell them what had happened when he got outside, but it was clear. From the rondavel room, the kicked in door and bedding strewn about, to the spot she and Mlilo were looking at now.

"This is where Len said they had dropped Dan," whispered Mlilo, "after he had woken to the commotion and sounds of shouting."

"I let them have it," said Len from the patio chair outside the kitchen, "but before I knew it, I was down on the ground, right here, from a punch. A punch?!" Tears welled in Len's eyes and he coughed a wheezy cough into a tissue.

"Ssh, it's okay," Conrad consoled him.

The bees were buzzing, with no sign of disturbance or threat to the hive.

Amira imagined the struggle and Dan's confusion. The confusion her and Mlilo felt right now.

She stood up and they made their way back to Len and Conrad.

"You said who might be responsible, Len?" Asked Mlilo.

The old man sighed and rolled his eyes. "From everything Dan told me about what you boys went through yesterday, I have a feeling it's that bastard Sol who's behind this gemors."

"Why is that," asked Amira.

"Because if there's ever anything to do with our magic, he's there trying to wipe it from the face of the earth. His cleansing crap. And if I were to guess." He turned to Mlilo, "He's trying to find you, Mlilo."

"He's going through Dan to get to me?" Mlilo folded his arms and stepped back into the garden to pace.

"I've had a few run-ins with the bastard, and his ilk, and he is powerful. The decades have given him plenty opportunity to hone his techniques, and his cruelty. I don't have a good feeling about this or how Dan will be if we find him?"

"*If* we find him?"

Len just shook his head and looked down.

"Any idea where he would take Dan?"

"Assuming he needs info quickly, rather than driving far, there are two locations. There's the abattoir on the east side of town, but I'm nearly a hundred percent sure he owns or uses the warehouses and vacant land on the outskirts to the north."

"I'll drive you there," said Conrad as he headed inside, followed by the sound of car keys.

"You will not," Len protested.

"Kak, man!" Conrad bellowed from deeper inside the house. "I'm going to put my foot up some white-supremacist arse."

CHAPTER 32

At about the size of a medium sized dog, the large mongoose, or meerkat – Dan wasn't quite sure of species – had peppered Dan with questions for the last stretch before winding their way over the final hill and down into the misty, oppressive murkiness below.

They had both taken a minute to adjust to the dizzying valley dropping into nothingness, water vapour hanging in the air, further obscuring the scene. The herds of cattle hadn't slowed their pace, continuing the endless flow of bodies down the hillside that became steep and ragged with cliffs and sharp rock outcrops that seemed to all converge into gloomy shadow, like something had sucked the earth in on itself.

After some time in stunned silence the creature said, "You can join me in another, less troubling part of this world, Daniel."

He shook his head. "This is the correct path for me. Mamlambo confirmed it."

"Mamlambo, Mamlambo," they uttered her name with irritation. "The old crone does not look out for those who pass through her kingdom. She only sees as far as the river and the mass migration of souls. Individuals mean nothing to her, Daniel."

Dan's increasing unease had shrouded the animal's skittish behaviour, their speech becoming more urgent the deeper they walked. He slowed his pace, weary of them for the first time.

Like him, they were afraid of the prospect of the invisible path ahead. But there was something else.

"I can help you," they said as their wiry clawed hand roughly grabbing Dan's elbow. "But I fear I cannot go on much further."

"This is where I must go." Dan shrugged and carried on walking.

"You must have loved ones, friends who need you."

"They have their own problems. I'm no longer theirs. And if they come for me–"

"They are coming for you?" The creature was a tad bit eager.

"If they come for me, then I will go."

"But you can come with me. Let us go back up. Or, or," they hesitated, "or let us wait for them. Yes."

"No."

"You have powers," they said edging closer to Dan, their fur, course and bristly, caused Dan to pull away. "Use them. Use them now."

Dan stopped. "How do you know I have powers?"

"I hear things," their eyes darted, thinking quickly, "I am told. Not important. You can get yourself out of here."

Dan's eyes narrowed at the animal, irritation building. "Tell me, whatever your name is, tell me what you *think* I can do for myself."

"You know how to speak the words, say the rites, summon that which is more powerful than yourself," they said rapidly, taking the opportunity given to them, "to aid you in your time of need. Do it. Call on *it*," they implored him.

Even in the dim light, Dan could see a look pass across the creature's black eyes, something that found pleasure in the suggestion they had uttered.

Images of Len and his undoing flashed through his mind. It would be so easy to conjure up, to connect to anything he imagined from within this world. But that would be tempting to do so. And would he be further tempted to remain here to retain that ability, that unending power?

"Yes," said the mongoose as if in response to Dan's private thoughts.

Dan recoiled. "What?" he hissed.

"Tap into the powers that are all around you, Daniel," the creature snaked closer to him. "I can show you how. I can–"

"Leave me, you dog," shouted Dan.

They bristled at the rebuke. A growl formed in their throat.

"Know your gods, boy!" The form of the animal shivered and Dan's surroundings shook violently. "Show some respect. Say my name. _Chakide._"

After a moment Dan's world righted itself. He could barely make out the wiry, canine form in darkness in front of him, but it was no longer a friendly mongoose.

"Where is your friend," asked Chakide.

He realised their game, their ploy. "They will come for me," he said through gritted teeth, hope welling up inside his chest.

"He will leave you to rot down here. Where is Mlilo?" Chakide shouted and slammed a fist into the nearby wall, stones and rocks tumbling into the dark world below.

Ragged claws grabbed at Dan but he fended Chakide off with a blast of his electric power, a momentary burst of light in the obscure surroundings, followed by bellows of protests from the cattle. Chakide bobbed in and out of the milling animals, moving back up the path.

"Come back to the light, Daniel, where it is safer. Let us wait for Mlilo together."

Mlilo was grateful Conrad had dressed quickly and knew his way around the dark streets of Ladysmith in the middle of the night. Their angry driver had thrown together a stylish ensemble of blue trainers, zipped navy-blue tracksuit jacket with red trim, and matching tracksuit pants.

The car came to a halt in front of a chained gate.

"I'll sort this out," said Mlilo and got out the vehicle. In the light of the headlights, he could see the substantial lock linking the weighty rusted chain. Not enough to keep anyone from simply jumping over the two-metre-high gate but enough to keep out cars or bakkies. He made swift work of the inside of the lock's workings, the heat from his grip around it focused on melting the mechanisms and popping the loop. He whipped the chain out and gave the gate a shove on its rollers to the right.

Mlilo could hear the grunt of surprise and approval from Conrad behind the wheel. The car revved and lurched into the parking area running the stretch of three huge metal warehouse structures and tarred grounds beyond.

Mlilo followed behind the red brake lights of the car, eyeing the dead and darkened office on his right.

Amira and Conrad were already out the vehicle, closing their doors quietly and scanning the area.

"The end one," whispered Amira and headed in the direction she had pointed.

The two men craned their necks to get a look and nodded when they saw the gap in the immense rolling doors on the last warehouse front.

Barely wide enough for them to sidle through, the three edged into the shadowy expanse. Conrad clicked on a pocket-sized torch and panned the powerful light through the space to get an idea of the lay of the land, while Mlilo and Amira used their mobiles for extra light.

Dozens of neatly stacked wooden crates lined either side of the vast room, at least fifty metres deep, but it was the single shipping container in the centre of the room that drew their attention.

Mlilo hesitated. If this was where Dan was or had been, the extreme quiet was not a good sign.

Mlilo paused at the door.

Amira's hand on his elbow gave him the willpower to reach for the metal handle and turn. It was unlocked.

The stale stench of sweat and damp filled the air. Mlilo coughed and lifted his mobile to light up the room.

Pools of liquid on the black floor and a single solid looking chair in the middle. The three stepped inside and Amira found the light switch, flooding the room with fluorescent light.

Mlilo could now see flecks of dull red blood on the chair and diluted in the puddles on the floor.

"Dan," whispered Amira.

"Animals," shouted Conrad. Mlilo's adrenaline shot through his body at the sound of clanging. Conrad had thrown a metal bucket against the wall.

In the corner lay an almost empty bath of water and car batteries.

His body vibrated at the thought of what had happened in this room.

"He's dead," said Amira alongside him. "Daniel's dead."

Mlilo's rage grew inside his chest. He coughed and choked and fell to the floor in a heap. He could not hold back the roar that rocked the small space, heat and flames licked out of his fists as he slammed them into the rubber flooring.

"Mlilo," said Conrad. "What can we do?"

Mlilo's muscles ached with the tension, on his knees, hunched in a ball.

"You two get to the car, get outside the gate," he whispered. "I'll be there now."

He knew Amira wasn't going to budge that easily.

"It's fine, Amira," he said. "Go."

He waited for the sounds of his companions retreating to fade. Everything was quiet except for the rumbling anger boiling his blood.

Amira jumped in the front passenger seat as Conrad started the car, reversed and headed through the open gate.

Within seconds of coming to a stop, engine idling, a double explosion rattled the windows and reverberated through the still night air.

"Christus!" yelped Conrad.

For a few seconds everything turned a bright yellow-orange and quickly faded into darkness.

A moment later the back door opened and an out of breath Mlilo hopped in.

"Conrad, we need you to drop us at the temple."

A terror was building inside Dan. Darkness was everywhere. Enveloped by bodies up against him it was claustrophobic, yet he felt completely alone.

The ringing in his ears had become like whispers on the wind. Snippets of words he could not discern.

Though the movement of the cattle was steady, there was another sound, more like a feeling, coming up from the depths of the gloom below. The occasional reverberation through the ground told Dan something was approaching with a steady rhythm.

His blood ran cold. He reached his hands out, feeling for the wall, sidling along the way he had come. A sharp horn pushed into his soft, exposed abdomen, hooking under his ribs and dragging him along the stone structure. The pain was excruciating. He grabbed the head of the animal and pushed downward, leveraging himself off and stumbling onto his backside against a rock.

This world was hellbent on keeping him here.

The whistling pitch rose.

"Where are you?" said Mlilo's voice through the din of other sounds around him.

Dan stood up, wobbled and found the wall for support.

"I am in utter darkness," he replied. "I don't know where I am."

"Come back."

"I can't find my way."

Amira sat dejected on the hard deck at the back of the reed boat. No wand. No halāhala. And sure as hell no sword.

Her and Mlilo had dashed into the temple after Conrad had dropped them, loudly protesting his exclusion from their mission.

Amira hadn't quite expected the sight of the structure that stretched up into the starry skies above them as they found themselves in the other world. Mamlambo's kingdom, Mlilo had told her. He had wasted no time in speaking to Dan as if he were right next to them. She was learning more about this world than she ever imagined.

Mlilo had said Dan was beyond the horizon in the south. The shadow lands. Amira had felt the same shiver up her spine she had felt before at the thought of this.

She had reluctantly followed Mlilo to Mamlambo, the ruler of the river, to ask for passage down into the blackness now looming before them.

Amira had argued with Mlilo in hushed tones in front of the woman, with him saying, "I don't know the portals there, and I do not wish to know them. We have to travel by river. It's our quickest option."

Mlilo had tried to give Mamlambo a shinbone, one of his amathambo, for his passage but the river ruler had refused. "I have no use for that which you have already given to me," Mamlambo had told Mlilo. So, he had reluctantly handed her a black crow feather.

And then it had been Amira's turn.

"Give her your wand," Mlilo had said with a far too nonchalant eagerness.

"Will I get it back?"

"You give it without expectation," Mamlambo said.

And here she sat, being ferried by a half man who, along with his boat, had materialised out of the river. And without her tools she needed to protect or defend herself, let alone find Dan and bring him home.

"ǀGaunab," was all the strange half man, Haiseb, had said.

Mlilo had emphasised staying in the boat, not touching the water and doing as he did when spoken to by the half man. But the one word was all that had been uttered.

From the stern of the boat, she could barely make out his form in the darkening atmosphere and the void of a landscape ahead of them. Amira wondered how this being, Haiseb, could constantly remain between worlds, no matter where he was, the option to seamlessly transition at a moment's notice. This world had much for her to learn.

Looking over the side of the vessel, the landscape had become hilly and rocky, but still green with grasses and small shrubs. Herds of animals ambled over and around, following the strange patterns of walls of stones.

Haiseb lifted his punt pole and pointed it to their right.

Mlilo got up from the left side of the boat and walked to the starboard-side. He mumbled a few words to the boatman, receiving a hammer of the pole on the deck in response. All Amira could make out following the direction of Haiseb's pole was a single hill standing out from the rest, and the haze of grey mountains fading into the distance. A steady stream of cattle walked up the hill and disappeared over the other side.

Mlilo walked back to her and said, "We have to go over there. Haiseb's not taking us further than this."

"We have to climb that?"

"Yes. And on the other side is the dark world of the Shadow Lands."

"ǀGaunab," said the boatman with another bang of his pole.

"Can he stop doing that?" Amira huffed. "And who is he talking about, anyway?"

Mlilo lowered himself onto his haunches next to Amira.

"It has all manner of names, superstitions and mystery about it," he said. "ǀGaunab, uPhondo, Milu, the Dagda, or just the Dark One. It takes the souls, from Mamlambo, or from Death, and sends them on through the afterlife. It is guide and shepherd to all souls. Some get reborn. Some return to the source. Eventually. It decides."

"Yama," said Amira. "God of the dead?"

"ǀGaunab," said Haiseb.

Amira sensed the boat slowing. Her and Mlilo stood to see where they were.

The boat was drifting into the nearby shoreline. The hills loomed above them, steeper than Amira imagined from further away. The fading light was now like an early evening in the real world, but for the first time in this world, Amira's skin prickled with a cool breeze coming up river.

"This is where we'll be getting off."

Mlilo followed close behind Amira, nearly at the summit and the increasing sounds of animals herding and lowing along the hillside. He hadn't looked back, focussed intently on the mission ahead, but it was as if the landscape was reading his mind. Dark thoughts. Castigating himself for getting Dan, and now Amira, into this situation all for his own ends. He didn't know how they were going to find Dan, or if they could leave Abaphansi safely, together. His jaw tightened at the thought and he tried to shake it off.

Two metres ahead, Amira jumped onto the outer stone wall and took in the view around them. They had made it to the top.

Her intake of breath was all he needed to know what he was about to see. The terrifying beauty of the world he thought he knew.

Rich, warm colours to the west on their left, the rising world and river up north, and the deep green forests spilling into the blue Eastern Seas fading into the stars in the distance. But, shifting their gaze at their backs, it was the pitch-black void which gave a dizzying sense of reality.

They tracked the flow of animals over the rise and along the zigzagging channel of wall down an almost shear hillside or cliff. Within a hundred-metre drop, the world was utterly dark. Unnaturally so.

Mlilo looked to their left, to the river, and could barely make out the land curving downward before vanishing into the same darkness. He scanned the hillsides to their right.

"There," he said pointing to a complex grouping of stone walls, converging to a point like a star. "If, when, we get back from down there, that's a portal out of Abaphansi."

They glanced at one another and reluctantly got down on the other side of the wall, among the cattle and proceeded.

"You need to tell Dan, wherever he is," said Amira, "to stop walking. If he's down there in that world, he needs to not go any further."

"You can tell him," said Mlilo warmly. "Direct your voice or your thoughts at the person you want to hear it."

Amira looked back at him for a moment, forming the words in her head, and said, "Dan. We are coming. Don't walk any further."

She nearly stumbled when the response came a second later. "Ok, Amira. Hurry."

Mlilo came up next to her.

"One thing I've heard," Mlilo stopped Amira, "because I've never dared come this far into Abaphansi, is that neither of us has ever encountered this type of world, its physics, its utter blackness. We have to rely on our other senses and stick together, Amira."

Jostled against the crammed bodies of the animals surrounding him, it took a couple of paces, feeling his way through the gloom, back to the outer wall before Dan could stop and sit. The creature Chakide had not reared its conniving head again.

Hearing Amira had shocked him. A cool tear fell down his cheek. His hope was growing.

Amira could barely see her hand in front of her face. They had each stumbled at least a dozen times and the going was slow. Mlilo had already given up using his energy, his flames, as a means to see. The darkness was oppressive.

"Stop." Amira grabbed his elbow.

"What?" Mlilo said, surprise or fear in his voice.

"How can we carry on like this?" she whispered helplessly. "How are we ever going to find Dan? How are we going to find our way out of here?"

"I don't know, Amira," Mlilo said through clenched teeth. "But we have to try."

She sensed him slump down onto the rough ground, hands slapping his knees.

"What the–" she cut herself short.

"What?"

A warm glow permeated the ground around Mlilo.

"What the hell's in your pocket, Mlilo?"

"Whoa," he said and jumped up with surprise.

She watched him shove a hand into his pocket and carefully pull out a small, glowing orb-like object.

"uNocabu's thread," said Mlilo, clearly amazed with the find.

"The what?" asked Amira.

Mlilo was already untying the fine golden string. "She said I might be needing it. But I never thought like this."

He ran a few metres back along their path, bumping through the thick stream of cattle, the thread keeping him and at least two metres around him strangely illuminated.

"What are you doing?"

He tied a loop around a large boulder and, pacing backwards, allowed the ball to unravel as he came up alongside her.

She watched him pull the centre end of the ball out, feed it through his belt and tie it to Amira's right wrist.

Amira traced the line all the way back to the boulder. A thin golden sliver ran along the ground, over rocks and tufts of grass like a neon tube in the blackness.

"It's our way back," said Mlilo in the soft glow surrounding them. "uNocabu's string will help, but I don't know. I just don't–"

"We can do this." Amira put a hand on his holding the ball of thread. "Dan is depending on us."

CHAPTER 33

The glow of the thread was barely enough for a metre's visibility ahead of Mlilo. The occasional tug let him know Amira remained attached to him, managing only to walk single file among the throng of cattle.

The sound of the river had faded but the air had become colder the deeper down they went, the sounds of trickling water and gusts of air pushing upward more frequent. And the occasional rumble in the ground beneath them.

A rush of air and spray of water burst out of the cracks in the rocks and ground to their left causing Amira to yank him backward two paces. In the dull light he could make out the wide-eyes of Amira, almost hypnotised by the sight within arm's length of her. She stuck her hand out and they realised it was water, rising into the night air. After the initial blast had subsided, with no more pressure buildup of any kind, the water simply drifted upward.

"It's falling up, Mlilo," Amira said with wonder and confusion.

"We can't succumb to this world, Amira. We have to remain focused."

"On Dan," she whispered.

"On Dan."

A steady, thunderous thud, like the pounding of a massive drum, reverberated through the ground and cliff-faces Dan imagined were surrounding him. His mind was warping, seeing lights that weren't there, landscapes morphing from one imagined setting to another. Anything to latch the sounds and smells and textures he could sense without an ounce of sight. But these pounding sounds he was sure of, and they were edging closer, up from the path below him, step by step.

An unease of bleats and lows murmured through the herding animals around him, some edging backward, others moving to the sides.

Dan could sense a massive presence in the shift of the atmosphere.

All the creatures quietened. Dan stood frozen to the spot.

A gruff grunt and warm breath hit his face followed immediately by the stomp of an immense hoof in the dirt.

An impulse came over Dan and he stretched out his hand, shaking in anticipation of what it would touch.

Wider than his opened palm, his hand came to rest on the warm, moist muzzle of what he could only imagine was a giant ox or buffalo, a beast bigger than those cattle he followed. His fingertips prickled on the course hairs leading up the snout.

Another snort and Dan snatched his hand back.

"Hmm," came a resonant voice in the space beyond the animal's head. "You don't belong here, mortal."

The thumps had ceased. Amira wasn't sure if that was a good thing or not. This world was unbelievable. Even with her weapons, long gone, she wouldn't know how to defend and fight down here.

She had taken to closing her eyes altogether, walking a dozen paces, or until she stumbled and pulled at the cord attached to Mlilo. She had to force her other senses to take over where her sight was failing her. But the constant moving bodies, strange emissions from the landscape, did nothing to inform her senses of what exactly was out there. What foe could be lying in wait for them?

The thread at her waist pulled her forward.

"Something's up ahead," whispered Mlilo and picked up his pace.

"Your companions," boomed the voice followed by a deep snort from the beast.

"What," asked Dan. He looked around, aware the attempt to see was useless.

But then he saw something. An orange glow approaching them.

His face went warm, his eyes blurred with tears.

"Mlilo? Amira?" He whispered into the dark.

"Daniel," came the dual response.

The glow became a string of light, moving, stepping closer until suddenly he was wrapped in an embrace, and another.

Sighs of relief filled the air.

"My friends," whispered Dan.

"uMfowethu," said Mlilo, tightening his hold on Daniel and Amira.

"Companions," said the deep voice.

Amira and Mlilo simultaneously let go of Dan, jumping away, Mlilo's flaming hands barely lighting up the gloom.

"You do not belong here."

Dan was unable to make out the origin of the voice in the dark.

"It's ok, Mlilo," Dan held up a hand to his friend. "This is his realm. I chose to come here, and I have to deal with it."

"Crap. You're here because of me. My fault. I dragged you into this."

"Can we talk about this later, boys," whispered Amira. "Large something or other looming over us."

"One of the Hyena's minions knows I'm here," said Dan.

"They'll assume I will come for you."

The boom of hooves in the ground shut them up.

"Mortals," bellowed the voice. "You are in my shadow realm. You are my charges now, whether you should be here or not."

"We should not be here, dark one," said Amira. "We will leave you now."

"We would very much like to leave this dark place," said Mlilo.

"Hmm," said the voice, "you are afraid?"

"Ya think," said Dan.

"Of what could you possibly be afraid of here?"

"The dark, for one," said Dan. "Your wrath for another."

"Darkness is the natural state of the universe. And you know nothing of my wrath. You do not belong here, so make your way out of the darkness that terrifies you."

The huge animal shifted its weight and the god's voice spoke into the distance. "There is goodness in the shadows. An unseen form cannot be seen as malevolent, or wrathful because you cannot perceive it with your eyes. It exists outside of your interpretation of it. Light brings judgement.

"I live in the dark. I love the dark. It is expansive. You bring in your weak light and it narrows it; limits it; gives it a dimension and so confines it to this here and that there. Darkness is. Darkness is Space with a capital S. It bleeds on into infinity. Light up a room and you are stuck in that reality. Live in the darkness and you live in a realm of potentialities, unlimited possibilities.

"Your kind need everything to be visible, and obvious," the voice came closer. "You lack imagination. You insist on seeing where you are going. Does that really help? Does it help any of these creatures moving towards their destiny? They have been moving in the same direction since they were birthed from the Source. Does it serve you in the long run? Sometimes you clearly see the way forward and yet you continue to flutter and fumble and fall. In the darkness of your minds, you continue to err, bump into things, stub your toes. All because you are blundering forward without imagination of what is or could be there. But in the darkness, I breathe possibilities. I come across something and I shape it into what I want it to be not what it is or should be if I choose to shine a spotlight onto it.

"Darkness is the natural state. Light is an abomination of the senses. You stand now in my shadowy realm with a thread of gold light. That light does not reach the rocky crags towering invisibly above, or the cavernous spaces dropping into nothingness below. All you see is the uneven ground dissipating the further away it leads from the pitiful light. Imagine what is beyond that. You cannot. Imagine it goes off into a meadow, a desert, an unearthly landscape of horror and destruction. Mmmm," the voice sounded ecstatic.

"A shadow contains something obscured, sometimes hidden. Shadows are where anything can be. A being of light loves the dark. A being of light suspended in space can feel the expanse surrounding them. That is freedom. That is aliveness. There is no here or there, just Them. A singular being of light and fire, existing. Why would we want to enter your world of limited light? Why would we enter a world that is rock, and mud, and walls and doors? Enclosing and suffocating."

"We like our world," said Mlilo. "We wish to return to it."

He snorted, echoed by a stamp from the large buffalo. "You desire a memory. I am not cursed with what you mortals call memories. Mlilo," he said thoughtfully. "Amira. Dan."

"Yes?" Said Amira.

"Mlilo. Amira. Dan," he repeated.

"Why do you keep saying our names as if they're statements and not names?" Asked Dan.

"Because Mlilo-Amira-Dan is this state that I sense before me. From now on I can use Mlilo-Amira-Dan when I am faced with these feelings and experiences associated with you. Mlilo-Amira-Dan. When, in the future, you think of me and our time together, in your _memory_," he spat out the last word with scorn, "will you be able to sum it up in a single word? Will _Mlilo-Amira-Dan_ not be the best way to describe it? And so, I have been absorbing these moments and reciting the name that will be associated with it. Much like the word "mother" - does it not have a different connotation depending on the person thinking or experiencing it? And why is that? Because of their experiences with a person named mother in their life. The memories fade, the scenes once played out are forgotten, but the emotions remain.

"I cast my perpetual shadow onto your kind, all kind, that they may forget, that they may journey on to the source unhindered."

"Or to be reborn."

"Mhm," the god agreed. "Here is for the forgetting. Allow me to shut out the light."

"Wait. No," demanded Mlilo. "You may be king of this, this blackness. You're king of your domain. But you can't tell me I need to be okay with my life, wipe my memories as if they didn't exist or shape me, when you have what you want and have control over what you want."

"What is it that you want," asked the voice.

"What we want," said Amira, "is to return to our world."

"Or what?"

"We stand here for eternity."

After a moment the voice said, "You cannot remain here. Your journey is onward."

"No," said Amira as Dan watched her untie the gold thread from her wrist, pulled from the slack at Mlilo's belt, retied it to her and tied the end around Dan's wrist. "We are going back the way this golden thread leads us."

"I do not wish to step into the light of your fragile thread. I do not wish to rip you limb from limb from the bindings you have made with this glowing fabric. My world is perpetually moving. Nothing stays. Move downward or return the way you came."

"Thank you," said Mlilo.

"You will pass through my world eventually."

"But you will not remember us," quipped Dan, receiving a shove from Mlilo.

"Mhm," he agreed. "But I will know the feeling that is Mlilo-Amira-Dan."

"And when we return, we will no longer be the feeling that is Mlilo-Amira-Dan," said Mlilo, guiding Dan away. "We will be forever changed once we leave this world."

The giant animal grunted and slammed a heavy hoof into the ground, shattering rocks and stones in a shower of sparks.

"Go," he growled. "You do not belong here anyway."

Dan strained his eyes, tracing the thread from himself and along the ground upward. He could faintly see where they had all come down into this world, the thin thread, a squiggling line drawn over an invisible landscape, weaving its way up through the gloom.

"We need to get to that portal on the hillside, Amira," said Mlilo from behind Dan, "and get the hell out of here before the Hyena finds out where we are."

A gust of wind from below startled Mlilo. He whirled around to see the fading gloom behind him. The journey up to the light had been slower than their decent, having to weave between the oncoming flow of cattle through the dark.

"What is it," asked Amira a couple of paces ahead of him. They had removed the golden thread linking the trio, Mlilo meticulously winding it back into a ball as they climbed back toward the light above.

"It's like voices, whispers," he said glancing around.

Dan stepped down to them and said, "I heard it too. That whistling you told me about?"

Mlilo nodded.

"Down there it became whispers, indiscernible words. Amadlozi?"

"I can hear my amadlozi just fine," said Mlilo shaking his head. "These were something else."

"These?" Asked Amira.

"I think my parents," Mlilo gave a deep sigh and looked back into the shadowy depths. "They are far away. Wandering."

He shook it off and carried on to the preaching rise of the hill.

Amira felt relieved as the trio stumbled out into the familiar temple gardens, the full moon an hour or two from setting over the dark hills. But was really odd was the weight in her left hand.

"My khaṭvāṅga," she said, stunned by the object in her grasp.

She turned to Mlilo who was holding the feather he had passed to Mamlambo a lifetime ago.

"We got them back," said Mlilo with a sigh of relief.

"Well, thank god for Abaphansi giving me my strength back," said Dan. "Hey, isn't that Len's car?"

"Conrad," said Amira who, tucking her wand under her arm, took out her mobile, swiped the screen and pressed call.

They all watched the car, the red of the brake lights flashed as it came to a stop.

"We're back," Amira said into her device. She hung up and looked at the time on the screen. "For Conrad, we've only been gone a minute or two."

The car wheel-spun off, took a wide arc of a turn and headed back towards them. Dan gave a wave.

"Mhm," agreed Mlilo. "We were so deep in Abaphansi, time slows even more. I've never actually done that."

"Let's not do that again in a hurry," said Dan shivering. "Wait. I'm confused." What," asked Mlilo.

"If I died, where's my body? How am I standing here?"

Amira and Mlilo shared a confused glance. "We assumed your body was disposed of," said Amira, "because we didn't find it at the warehouse."

"You. Didn't. Die," said a stunned Mlilo.

"That means," said Amira, "in your utter desperation, you were able to move into the other world. You went beyond your own belief systems, Daniel."

"I what?"

Conrad swung the car around and screeched to a stop alongside them and they all jumped in, Dan in the front passenger seat.

"Daniel," Conrad squealed in the confined space.

"Conrad," Dan winced and pointed to the road ahead.

"mFowethu, you've been taught that you can travel into the other realm by invitation only. I brought you in the first time. That was fine. But firstly, if you know the right places, like the portals I use, you can go back and forth freely. And secondly, if you trust enough, believe enough and know enough about yourself, you can do it wherever and whenever."

"So, I just need to be kidnapped and tortured to unlock my ability to transport between realms?" Dan shivered at the thought of the rubber-lined room. "Imagine the looks in Oom Sol's face when I vanished in front of him. One day I'll meet up with the demon hunter and give him a piece of my mind."

"Is that why the god of the dead let us off so lightly," asked Amira.

"His last words to us were that we didn't belong there."

"I didn't die," whispered Dan.

"A belief that held you back died, Dan," Mlilo tapped his friend on the shoulder.

"When I was on trial before King Kubera–" Amira was cut short.

"Say what?"

"When was this?"

She shrugged at the men staring at her. "After my defeat at the hands of the yakshas and yakshinis. Not important. When I was in front of King Kubera there was this animal that was talking with him and they said something about the Hyena being in the cave lands?"

"uMgede," said Mlilo as they pulled into Len's driveway. "I know how to get there."

The car stopped and they all jumped out.

"Hurry," Mlilo said to them. "Get your things, Dan. uNosithwalangcengce will not be expecting us to take the fight to her, in her domain."

"And, um," said Dan opening the front door, "that could also be suicide." He walked straight into Len.

The older man burst into tears, grabbing hold of Dan.

"He's fine, liefling," said Conrad and with effort, pried Len's arms off Dan.

"I'm fine, my friend." Dan smiled at Len, and dashed around him. "Gotta go."

"She's going to do everything in her power to get to Mlilo, to all three of us," said Amira, "to regain power over the bone. It's suicide not to."

"Daniel," everyone stopped at the booming voice from Len at the front door. "Before you and your friends run toward certain doom. You *have to* set your wand," he said firmly. The moon is nearly gone for the night and the full moon is the ideal time for wand rites."

Dan nodded, rushed outside and into the rondavel, sweeping only his essential effects together and back to the waiting arms of Len now at the kitchen door.

"The field at the end of the road. Two minute's walk."

Len turned to Amira and Mlilo and added, "You three have the magic you need for this. Trust one another. Use one another. Together."

Mlilo was fanning the flames of his fire while, over a metre away, Dan did the same to his. Amira placed the last small bundle of twigs and thick, dry grass between them and sat down watching her friends.

They were in the field Len had told them about, surrounded by a handful of trees a few metres away in a clearing of long grass and patches of sand.

Dan looked to the western horizon, the moon nearly touching the dark hills in the distance.

"What time do you have, Amira," he asked.

"Three thirty-four," she replied.

Dan stopped adding kindling to his fire. "Are you telling me it has only been twenty-four hours since we started this kak?"

Mlilo laughed.

"I feel way older than one day, I can tell you that."

The fires were well on their way. Dan stood in the space between them, checked Amira's spot, nodded and turned to ask Mlilo to sit directly opposite her. "Holding the space," he said with two thumbs up to his friends. "We pass between the two fires, summoning protection in the natural and supernatural realms."

Dan sat on his haunches, looking his branch over. Mlilo passed him his small knife from his boot.

"We call on the elements of fire, water, earth and air. Bless this grove."

He began by curving the blade around the circumference of the thickest end, turning until a deep score had been made, placed the branch on his knee and gently snapped it in two. He repeated the process over a hand's breadth from the first, snapping it away to reveal the full wand taking shape. Swift, sharp movements of the knife in his right hand, the blade occasionally glinting in the low moonlight, exposed the pale wood beneath the rough bark. The inner wood was already drying and hardening.

Dan's left hand felt the rough grip of the branch, the opposite sensation to Fagus and its smooth white polished shaft. This felt right. He continued the whittling of the top half of the stick, like a stake. The dark brown of the handle contrasted to the starkness of the fresh cut wood. This was what he wanted. This was what this wand wanted to become.

Dan stopped cutting. Around him in the dirt lay the splinters and wood fibres. He placed the wand next to the flames of the fire while he gathered all the remains, separated them into two and stood between the fires. He took a deep breath and dropped them into each fire. The damp wood crackled and sparked.

"Aren't you taking the rest of the bark off," asked Mlilo.

Dan returned to his haunches and picked up the wand, feeling its weight, passing it from hand to hand. "Nope. This one is from this land and this is what it wants to be. A tree is never dead. You can touch a living tree. A tree communicates with you and with its own. The roots run deep in the ground, and like whale-song through the earth, they resonate with one another. This is what this one has told me."

Dan placed it horizontally on his left forefinger and right forefinger.

"Now we name it," he said and looked from Amira to Mlilo. "Something Len said resonated with me."

"What's that," asked Amira.

"Together," he said, gazing at the wooden stick then back at his friends. "We did this all, we got back here, together. And we are about to go into battle."

"Together," Amira and Mlilo echoed.

"Hlangana kwempi," reiterated Mlilo.

"United, no matter where," agreed Dan.

"uKuhlangana," Mlilo emphasised the last syllable.

Dan thought for a moment, conjuring up the ogham symbols representing the letters of the name. He plotted out the spacing with faint notched in the bark. When he was satisfied, he began the fine, gentle carving.

"We all seem to have had some adventures of our own."

"Pfft," said Amira.

"No kidding," said Mlilo.

"Something happened to me that I'm not sure about," Dan said and blew some of the wood filings away. He took a deep breath and continued, "One of Oom Sol's henchmen tried to slit my throat with a knife."

"Shit," said Amira.

"Is that when you–"

"No. That's the funny part, if there was a funny part. That was early on in the," he took a breath, "interrogation. Anyway, when he tried to, as soon as the blade touched my neck, my skin, there was this hectic light and heat and sound. Imagine a welding job exploding in your face."

"And?" Asked Amira.

"And nothing. I was fine." Dan blew the stick. "The other oke, not so much."

"You must've done something," said Mlilo. "Tapped into something."

"I hadn't. It wasn't my magic or anything emanating from inside me."

The three friends were quiet while Dan continued his carving in silence.

"Hmm," mused Mlilo after a while. "Remember the boat ride with Haiseb."

"The happy boatman, sure," said Dan. "How pissed was he when–"

"You dared touch his river water," interrupted Mlilo.

Dan stopped his cutting.

"What are you taking about," asked Amira.

"You two have heard of the river Styx and Achilles, right?"

Dan nodded.

"Yes," Amira said and rolled her eyes, waving her hand for him to get to the point. "Achilles' mother dipped him in the protective powers of the river, making the mistake of not doing his entire body in the protective waters."

"Exactly. We are talking about an ancient river here, a river that goes beyond Greek mythology. And to Haiseb's horror you dipped your left hand in and splashed water over your neck and face."

"What," Dan asked, clearly not getting the idea.

"Daniel," said Amira throwing her hands up. "Those two areas of your body are immune."

"Whoa," he whispered. "So why don't we go now and douse ourselves in the waters and get permanent immunity?"

"Because, smart arse," Mlilo said, "if it were that easy, everyone would do it. And besides, Haiseb is the only one who it doesn't prevent from harming you."

"Or killing you if he found out," said Dan thoughtfully.

"Correct. He was this close," Mlilo said with his thumb and forefinger together in Dan's face, "to smiting you, Dan."

Dan shrugged. "The oke needs better rules for his river guided tours."

He dusted the piece of wood off and gave it a satisfied once over. He removed a twig at the edge of the fire, patted the glowing embers out and crushed the black charcoal in his free hand. Taking the wand, he gripped it in his blackened palm and slowly pulled it through, twisting the soot over and around the entire shaft and pale tip. The dusty brown wand was nearly done, the ogham script stark against the bark.

"Here." Amira withdrew a small container from her tunic pocket and handed it to Dan. "Kajal paste. Protecting against negativity."

Dan took the small vial, opened the lid and wiped his finger through the black paste. He smeared it steadily over the carvings, filling the spaces inside the wood, darkening the etched markings.

He held his new wand gently in both his open palms, his face flushed and tears welled up.

He took a deep breath, and stood up, with a fire in front and a fire behind him. His friends sat transfixed to his left and right.

Dan closed his eyes and listened and smelled. He began his breathing, connecting and let the rhythm take over.

His body tingled.

"Awen," he said. Crackling filled the air around him.

He opened his eyes and looked down at his hands and the wand. Blue tendrils of sparks had wrapped around the wooden object, holding it a centimetre above his palms. He gently turned his palms over to the sides, suspending the wand in midair and said, "Cleanse, consecrate and bless this wand that it may be used for your service and the service of humanity. May it wield love, wisdom, and power. I so name this wand _uKuhlangana_. I name it so that it may serve me in good stead and honour you."

"Awen," he whispered finally.

He picked the wand out of the air and in one swift movement, down to his knees in the sand, slammed the butt of the wand into the ground.

Dan was surprised. Rather than the blue white light he had expected, the blue tendrils from his hand and fingers melded with a red glow pulsing from the wood.

Branches of purple energy grew outward.

"uMnganam," he heard Mlilo whisper amazement.

The lightening continued to expand, the tree-like form taking shape and growing upward.

Dan maintained the power running out of him and through uKuhlangana, the tip rising to an elongated spike crackling into the night air.

In the distance, Dan became aware of another sound like incoming rain. He kept his gaze steadfast on the energy in his hand, knowing full well that there had been no storm approaching them.

The noise grew into a sound like crackling leaves.

"What the–" he heard Mlilo say.

In an instant, Dan was engulfed in a swirling vortex of insects.

Flying ants.

The harmless creatures, attracted by the light on a summer's night, flittered around the pulsating wand. Electric charges snapped at their wings and small bodies as they flew around the wand. Dan extended his hand, holding the wand up like a beacon.

The rattling, glimmering wings of the insects glowed with his energy, growing more frenetic and the sound more deafening.

He noticed both Amira and Mlilo were on their feet, transfixed by the spectacle.

And just as suddenly as they had appeared, they began flying up into the night sky like fireflies.

Dan allowed his light to fade and the sound of the ants dissipated. He looked to the dark western horizon, the moon finally behind the hills.

"Come," said Mlilo and pointed to the ground in front of him. "Time for amathambo."

He sat side on and smoothed the sand and bits of grass and stones away while Amira and Dan came over to the spots he had pointed out and settled in. He placed his leather bag on the cleared ground and took a deep breath.

Dan watched as, one by one, Mlilo removed and placed his objects in the sand in front of him.

The first were familiar to Dan: three porcupine quills, the shinbone, the Morrígan's feather, and the cracked pod of red lucky beans plus three dried leaves from uNomkhubulwane. Next was a conical sea shell and, finally, untying a leather cord from his wrist Mlilo placed two strange looking beads alongside the other objects.

Satisfied, Mlilo picked them up, returning them to his bag and said a few words under his breath. A final deep breath and he blew into the pouch.

Mlilo upended the contents, scattering them onto the floor.

Dan watched his friend mull the pattern over. Prodding a quill, lifting the shell and turning it over and replacing it as it had been.

It was the sight of the broken quill lying across the other two and the feather than caused a sharp intake of air through Mlilo's clenched teeth.

"What," asked Dan.

Mlilo raised a finger for quiet and shook his head. He pointed to the seedpod, all three red seeds exposed from inside their hard casing. "That is a good thing," he whispered.

Mlilo clapping his hands caused Dan and Amira to jump, and he gathered his object up in the pouch once more, leaving the dried leaves and the seedpod in the sand.

"It's not going to be easy," he said to his friends and pulled his knees up to his chest for comfort. "But we have to do this."

Dan relaxed with a sigh. "We'll survive then?"

Mlilo shrugged. "A hard fight is what I see."

The three sat in silence as the fires slowly dwindled around them, the chill of morning setting in.

"You dream of a certain life for yourself," said Amira softly, "then you get it and you don't realise it and you think our life is bland or unexciting. But you're in your dream and you don't even know it."

"Seriously," said Mlilo, "I need you guys in my life. I've come to realise you are there to support me."

Amira nodded. "I learned I actually don't need things to give me power. I'm pretty capable. Remind me to tell you about that later."

"And I'm able to tap into anything I want," Dan patted the ground, "here."

"Yes," agreed Mlilo. "This land is full of gods and powers. It's our duty to tap into everything we have at our fingertips. Amadlozi guide me. Amadlozi are part of me. I've said to you, our ancestors are there helping us whether we ask for it or not."

"Runes, talismans, symbols," added Dan, "all open the same doors. We can kick some hyena ass."

"This is an ancient goddess, an African goddess," said Amira. "It's not always a happy ending. You don't just complete five tasks and go home. We might not get out of this alive, Daniel."

Mlilo picked up the seedpod, poked and pulled at the hard outer casing. He reached over and handed Amira one of the seeds, and another to Dan. He picked up the fragile dried leaves, giving them a blow to remove any dust and proceeded to close his hand over them, crunching and crushing them. He held up the third seed and, heat building in his open palm, the remains of the leaves began to smoke and crackle. He gently placed his seed into the warm, glowing heat of his palm. They all watched as the smoke rose into the night air and Mlilo gave the embers a soft blow, sending the pungent aromas around the three friends.

Finally, the only thing that remained in Mlilo's open hand was a large coffee-bean sized seed.

He picked it up and said, "uKuhlangana."

"uKuhlangana," they echoed.

"I know where this will be planted," said Dan eyeing out the red seed. "My grove is in need of more sacred trees." He raised a finger as if remembering something then pulled out his own pouch and dug out a wooden rune. He placed it in his left palm, along with the seed, and closed his hand.

"Aren't you going to look at it," asked Amira. "Tell us what you drew?"

"Nah," Dan shook his head. "I'm going to trust whatever comes our way, and use this extra power."

A strange, high pitched hissing sound emanated from behind Amira, who jumped up and pivoted, ready with her wand for any threat.

A pinprick of white light in midair appeared two metres from her and split in two, drawing a faint arch down to the ground. Ornate patterns and swirls fanned out like doorway pillars while the central space shimmered. A silhouette appeared in the archway and stepped out into their field.

"Sita," said a shocked Amira and lowered her wand.

Mlilo and Dan were on either side of her, guarded.

"Amira," said the goddess and smiled warmly at them all. "It is good to see you three together."

Sita looked around the clearing and up at the blue sky and fading stars. "It has been an age since I was in your world."

"Why are you here?" Asked Amira.

Sita looked back at her. "A woman walked into my world seeking something for herself. She was left empty handed," said Sita taking a step closer. Amira tensed but remained where she was. "That same woman came to her friend's aid. With nothing but your wits, Amira, and your ever-growing power from within, you ran headlong into danger for someone else." Sita stopped and looked at the two men beside Amira. "You all have."

Sita gently lifted up her right hand.

Tiny bursts of white and golden light speckled in the space between Amira and the goddess, pulling horizontally and curving outward.

Amira's eyes widened.

"You have been found worthy to now wield the mighty Chandrahas, Amira," said Sita and gestured for Amira to take the glowing sword before them.

Amira hesitated, then reached out and felt the warm touch of the metal hilt, her left hand touching the decorative, crescent blade.

Sita moved around to Amira's right, Dan and Mlilo stepping away. The goddess put her arms around Amira and slowly pulled them back around her waist. Amira stared in disbelief at the belt and sheath now glowing around her abdomen. She took a final admiring glance at the sword, admiring the fine engravings, and sheathed the sacred object at her right side.

Sita moved back to her glowing arch and said to the trio staring at her, "You may step through my doorway." She turned to Mlilo. "It will take you to where it is you desire to be."

Amira watched, dumbfounded as the goddess walked into the light and disappeared.

"You went into the underworld for a sword," asked Dan.

"Yes," said Amira and turned proudly to the two men. "I was beaten by a horde of crabs that turned out to be–"

"Tokoloshe!"

"Korrigan?"

"Yakshas," Amira said to the two men with a frown. "They took me prisoner. The king set me free when he realised I was after his bastard half-brother's sword. A yakshini lieutenant and I fought off the storm bird and Sita refused to give me this. Chandrahas."

Mlilo and Dan looked at each other, wide-eyed.

"What did you do for the past twenty-four hours, Dan," Dan asked himself. "Oh, you know, kidnapped and tortured. Passed out into Abaphansi because the pain was unbearable in the real world. How about you, Mlilo?"

"With the help of my one friends, I saved my other sarcastic friend's ass from the god of the dead."

It took a moment and they all burst out laughing.

CHAPTER 34

The nhaa-nhaa-ha-ha-ha, crybaby call of a flock of a dozen or more trumpeter hornbills flying through the trees filled the dark skies above Amira, in single file between her two friends. The nasal wailing of the birds finally faded off into the valley.

"What's the strategy," asked Amira touching the shimmering breastplate of the armour that she had successfully summoned.

Since exiting the waterfall down in the valley over ten minutes ago, Amira had practiced the incantation. This time she put herself back in the mass of attacking yaksha bodies and imagined the feelings she had felt. Helpless. Defenceless. She allowed those emotions to dissipate. Then, the storm bird attack upon Kubera's chariot platform. The final moments without the breastplate. Exposed. She had recognised the new feeling that welled up; that force from within herself. She had focused on that as she uttered the final words.

The full weight of the iridescent armour, unwavering, was reassuring.

Through the shadowy, valley forest they ducked under thick trunks of mossy vines and creepers, over gnarled exposed roots and rocks, winding their way up the valley to the looming mountains in the distance.

"uNosithwalangcengce is powerful," said Mlilo leading the way. "Dan and I barely got away from the porcupine and her children through that portal in the waterfall."

"And we have no idea who or how many creatures are hankering to destroy us," said Dan.

"So, aiming to kill her is a risk?"

"And this time we're not risking anything," said Dan. "Right, Mlilo?"

"Mhm," Mlilo agreed. "Our simplest bet is to take or destroy her bone. Do everything we can to get it away from her.

"And if that's destroyed, she will never regain her full power," said Amira.

"Yep," Mlilo said with a sigh. "Killing her is a bonus."

"Possibly a fight for another time," agreed Amira and glanced back at Dan coming up behind her.

He was flexing his fist, opening and closing with the rune and seed in his grasp. "I have a score to settle with nGungumbane."

"No matter what is waiting for us up in the caves," said Amira, "the Hyena queen will be gunning for Mlilo. It's what's been driving her lately. How we take her on is key and even though you think you may be able to handle her on your own, we are in her domain."

"And," added Mlilo, "she's more than likely going to split us up, reduce our combined forces."

"We will have to make sure we keep it together if that happens."

"uKuhlangana," said Dan.

Mlilo stumbled over the loose shale rock. The terrain had changed, the foliage less dense than the path up the valley. More conducive to fighting.

The three companions wound their way through the thicket of ironwood that was thinning out around the large boulders. A Lebombo Krantz Ash, a medium sized tree growing from a rocky outcrop, caught Mlilo's eye.

The characteristic seeds, made of a papery, ellipsoid wing enveloping the seed itself, provided a unique dispersal mechanism for the species. Mlilo could see the tree was in a dry autumnal phase, and the seeds dark brown and beige.

He couldn't help himself but pound the butt of his palm into the trunk.

Dozens of seeds bumped and rustled off their fragile stems through the bare branches. As they made it into the open air, they began their distinct spiralling downward. Just as they would have landed on the ground a gust, from up the valley behind Amira and Dan, lifted the flittering objects over the tree-line.

They paused to watch the spectacle of the seeds, like a flock of birds, twisting and undulating away.

"I think we're nearly there," whispered Mlilo.

The other two companions turned to him as he pointed to two large boulders twenty metres up ahead.

"That ledge of rocks peaking above the boulders over there," he continued, indicating a level line, over fifty metres wide, of stones and large rocks curving along the side of the mountaintop and obscured by the occasional bushel and boulder. "That's more than likely the entrance platform to the hyena's den. We aren't going to get a better view to know exactly what the layout is without exposing ourselves. So, if we crawl behind those two rocks, we can take a moment before we climb over. But let's assume we're here."

"Wait." Amira held up a hand. "We can't just *climb over* into god knows what, Mlilo."

"What do you suggest," asked Dan.

"Once we're behind the rocks, I'll sneak up to the edge and see if I can get a glimpse of the lay of the land."

Mlilo thought for a moment.

"Better than charging ahead," Amira said through clenched teeth.

"Fine," said Mlilo and lead the way.

They instinctively hunched down and edged slowly to the safety of the boulders, Mlilo and Amira taking the left.

They pressed their backs up against the rocks, an understanding of silence passing between them, and listened.

Mlilo could make out low murmurings.

Amira didn't wait for a signal and slipped between the boulders, silently and steadily climbing over the stones and rocks and positioning herself, squatting below the ridge.

She looked to Mlilo then to Dan for assurance. All they could do was nod in response.

Centimetre by centimetre, Amira craned her neck until a flicker of firelight reflected off her glossy hair and forehead. She held it for a second or two then slowly ducked down.

Back behind the shelter of the rocks the three friends huddled together as Amira drew in the dirt with her left forefinger and whispered, "I count four porcupine creatures, plus that weasel you call Chakide, and the hyena. The platform curves away from a roughly twenty-metre central cave mouth, for at least another twenty either side of exposed rock face and platform. No cover other than the curving back of the mountain. At the cave entrance there are two porcupines on the left, and one on the right. The fourth, bigger porcupine, is pacing about inside to the right of a central raging fire pit, while Chakide is lounging on the left of it. I can't make out clearly through the flames, but beyond that, in the other half of the cave, say, ten metres in, there's a large beast, larger than that porcupine, reclining on a wide bench or throne thing. They are the ones doing the talking we can hear."

The two men nodded.

"Sounds doable," said Dan.

"My suggestion, chaps," said Amira, "is Dan and I take a flank each, crawl along the bottom of the ridge and come up where they can't see us, and stick to the side. Mlilo, you take the middle, pretty much where I was sitting."

"Mhm," he agreed, "I'll be able to see the two of you approaching," Mlilo said nodding.

"We'll get in position," said Amira easing her sword out the sheath with her left hand and raising her khaṭvāṅga in her right, "and as soon as you decide, hop up and we'll be right beside you."

"Yasas," said Dan. "This is all suddenly very real."

The blood was rushing in Mlilo's ears as he carefully looked over the edge at the wide cavern reaching at least eight metres high.

Just as Amira had described it.

The warm tones of the setting sun, directly opposite in the west, enhanced the colouring of the banded layers of faulting, clay-rich sandstone walls gently curving from either side and seamlessly into the depths of the fire-lit chamber.

Mlilo hunched down looking back at the sweeping view of the world below. He estimated they were nearly half a kilometre up from the riverbeds of the valley leading to the Great River, while the escarpment rim of the mountaintop was only thirty metres above the rock shelter itself, covered with small bushes and rocks.

He chanced another glance at the platform. Built out and away from the mountain rock with sand, soil and rubble, it was soft compared with the worn, smooth looking ground leading inwards.

A check to the left and right confirmed Amira and Dan were at their positions, ready for him.

He ducked down, took a deep breath, feeling the warmth flowing over his palms and fingers, and hefted himself up.

Mlilo roared as he bound onto the edge of the platform, giving Amira the cue to engage. Moments before, she and Dan had locked eyes, nodded and waited for the signal that was finally here.

From her wand she planted two rapid-fire pulses, booming sounds resonating around the mountaintop and inside the cavern, at the unsuspecting porcupines on the left of the entrance.

Horizontal columns of orange-red flames from Mlilo streamed into the centre of the cave, pummelling the larger of the porcupines away from the stunned hyena queen and into the right interior wall, and burning and blasting a yelping Chakide deep into the inmost part of the cave. The fourth porcupine was twitching and writhing, held in an unending, purple electric grasp from Dan's wand.

One of Amira's porcupines rolled left and in a flash was on its feet charging at her. A blast boomed into it, shifting its trajectory away from her, giving her the opportunity to swiftly slice with Chandrahas across its middle. She felt the pull of flesh and the cutting of quills through the hilt.

A howl screamed out over the mountains.

Amira stood side on, glancing left and right: new threat stalking her sword arm, while the right porcupine forced itself onto it legs. Blood seeped from its side and forearm but it would be on her again.

Mlilo was building up his fire for another torrent.

Dan's beam of lightening was not keeping the porcupine in its grasp back. It was enduring the pain of the energy coursing through its tough hide, pushing against it closer and closer.

Amira turned khaṭvāṅga away from her injured assailant and blasted at Dan's. A mistake.

The pulse of energy dislodges the porcupine, momentarily slammed against the outside wall, from Dan's hold on it. Purple branches licked up and around the cave roof as Dan teetered backward, also feeling the impact of Amira's power.

"Bring me their bodies!" The hyena queen, propped on her left elbow, hissed the command from her stone bench.

On cue, the two porcupines, each facing Amira and Dan, lunged at them.

Rather than feeling the immediate impact against the ground, Amira's world turned dark, and a tearing noise filled her ears.

Then the wind was knocked out of her.

Mlilo checked behind him. Nothing but an injured porcupine, hardly a threat. No sign of Amira or Dan anywhere. Then he saw them: two deep holes in the ground.

They had taken his friends somewhere out of this world.

He was alone.

Chakide's whines and intermittent snarls could be heard from behind the slab of uNosithwalangcengce's throne.

nGungumbane, on this right, growled low, the sound of her quills rattling filled the chamber. The relentless noise grew unbearable in the space. She was on her feet, shadowy form bristling behind the flames of the fire as she circled around toward Mlilo.

He side-stepped left, mirroring her movements, studying her posture and trying to predict her next move.

He narrowed his eyes, grinning, and lifted a hand.

The pop of the exploding log, the sparks and burst of flame, had nGungumbane leap backward.

Chakide, circling from the left, cackled their delight at the warning shot.

uNosithwalangcengce had not moved from her position but he knew she was locked on Mlilo.

"This is most unexpected, mortal," the rumbling voice of the hyena queen was smoother than he had anticipated. It commanded attention. She patted her hand to nGungumbane and Chakide to wait. "Finally, we are alone, fire bringer."

Mlilo checked his surrounding, watching for threats unseen, understanding the environment he found himself in.

Vertical streaks of groundwater, seeping through cracks and fissures, enhanced the reds and oranges tearing down the rough stone face of the den chamber.

He traced the horizontal layers of rock faults from the exterior walls coming into the chamber, and realising how they became grooved and carved. But it was the intricate triangular patterns, tiny circles and square glyphs chiselled between the lines, like script in a massive book, which almost took his breath away.

isiBheqe soHlamvu writing.

"If I could have foreseen you would come to me, to supplicate, I would have rather bided my time." uNosithwalangcengce's laugh brought Mlilo's attention back to the threats edging closer to him.

"No one is supplicating, uNosithwalangcengce," he addressed the massive being for the first time.

The wide stone bench was curved like a hand cradling the huge hyena queen. uNosithwalangcengce was resting on her left elbow, and her forearm and fist clutched at her left breast.

"Accept the inevitable," she laughed, "rather than needlessly attempting to evade me or my minions."

The left space, occupied by the snake Chakide on other side of the throne, led to the back of the cave. A large, central archway was flanked by two smaller ones, leading into subterranean tunnels beyond.

Although her body, covered in the rich blacks and golden yellows of her thick coat and more vibrant than any hyena he had ever seen, the hair around her left shoulder and chest was grey with bald patches of equally grey skin visible.

"Hmm," she mused, "you see the mark your ancestor made all those eons ago."

"Say her name," Mlilo said through tightened jaw. "Zandile!"

The queen's fur bristled at the name echoing through her chambers.

Out of the confusing darkness from a moment before, Dan tumbled onto a dusty ochre ground, kicking and pushing the porcupine away from him.

He flicked himself up onto his haunches and steadied himself as the frantic animal hissed and spluttered in anger.

Dan's eyes darted around, taking in the setting, looking for cover and obstacles.

Both adversaries snapped their heads to Dan's right as the sound of Amira grunting and shouting caught their attention.

He realised they were standing in a stretch of land covered in clusters of small, ancient pagodas as far as he could see, sloping conical-shaped structures at least five to eight metres high, with narrow doorways leading inside. Tufts of foliage, stone mounds and trees overgrown in pockets were given an added richness by the early morning sunlight. It was strangely familiar and it conjured up images of sacred spaces he had seen in India or Myanmar.

A cloud of the orange-red dust puffed around one of the structures from Amira's direction.

Dan's porcupine leaped at him, two large spear-like quills in each claw.

Dan stepped right, narrowly missing the tip of one of the spikes, and sent a burst of purple light into the animal's back. It slammed into a pagoda, loosing a torrent of sand brick and mortar on the porcupine.

Dan didn't waste time. He focused another hit from uKuhlangana, this time aiming for the creature's feet, knocking it down before it had a chance to charge at him again.

The clang and ping of metal on stone, and occasional booms meant Amira remained on her feet. Dan skipped backward towards the commotion while keeping his eyes locked on his adversary.

With distance between them he darted around a corner to find a writhing, screaming porcupine being elevated off the ground. Dan stood frozen with shock as Amira, sword in her left hand, held against her chest and gleaming breastplate, while her wand in her right was using its rumbling, invisible kinetic force to move the helpless enemy through the air.

Then he saw the objective.

The pagoda nearest the rising animal had a steel axial pole at its peak. A spike.

Amira steadied the animal directly over the deadly decoration, and Dan held his breath.

But as Amira released her hold on the terrified creature, Dan was sideswiped with a winding tackle into the dirt. They slammed into another pagoda sending rubble on top of them. Pain flared in his eyes with a blow to the back of his head, but he rolled away a second before two quills stabbed deep in the dirt next to his exposed face.

His wand was aimed and blasting the animal away, but not far enough to counter it diving on top of him.

Amira's sword twanged useless against the rows of quills on the porcupine's back but a backup blast pummelled it off and away from Dan.

Immediately they both send a wave of their respective powers at the creature as it yelped and dashed away, ducking behind a bushel and disappearing around more pagodas. Amira gave Dan a nod and the two friends followed on its heels, wands and sword at the ready.

They came around where they assumed the porcupine would be but all they could see were more pagodas.

"It's gone back through one of those," Amira pointed to four archways, at least four potential portals.

"You take number one on the left and I'll take number three," said Dan rushing into the doorway.

"It must be infuriating to be trapped here,"

"No one is trapped!" nGungumbane raspy voice growled as she watched Mlilo's every move, guarding her queen.

"Zandile fended you off, ambushed in her own home. Imagine what I can do, prepared and with you weak and festering in your crumbling throne room."

The hyena laughed.

"Do not take my physical weakness as weakness. I have bided my time over these trifling centuries to gather my forces. The time is right to release them on all the worlds."

Chakide cackles.

Mlilo sidled over to the left wall, pretending to inspect the carved designs. He picked at a wad of thick moss from an oozing column of groundwater.

"A once resplendent room for a hyena queen," he said and slapped the wet mass on the ground. "I see you are no longer the mighty queen, the goddess to your people, who once faced off with my ancestor, Zandile. Your defeat has endured the decades and centuries, uNosithwalangcengce. That," he pointed at his feet, "is the hate and rot that you allowed to set in. Seeking more and more power comes at a cost. Use your own inner abilities rather than feeding off others. Diminishing others."

"But look at you, fire bringer," she said, her teeth glinting in the firelight. "You wish to destroy me."

"A lifetime ago I did. Now?" He shook his head. "No, I wish to stop you from overcoming others. I do not wish to crush you. I will defeat you and leave you to carry on rotting in this dark hovel."

The hyena queen let out a guttural laugh and said, "Unlike your modern gods, we are who we are. We were never created in an image imagined by mortal men. We walked the earth both in this world and your world. We owe you nothing. While others desperately try to remain relevant to exist, we don't need your veneration to survive."

Mlilo turned his attention to the lithe form of Chakide, pent up and ready to strike at a moment's notice.

"Sawubona, uHlakanyana," said Mlilo.

The animal froze at the sudden attention.

"What deals have you made? Whose allegiance do you truly hold?"

They twitched and glanced at uNosithwalangcengce then back at Mlilo.

"What has your crafty, treacherous mind been up to since I last kicked your arse out of my world?"

"Nothing. Nothing much. Nothing really," they muttered quickly. "Nothing important. Nothing that important. Nothing that can be a problem. Nothing that's a big problem. Nothing to worry about. Nothing to worry a lot about."

"So, nothing of substance, then?" Mlilo screwed up his face with disgust.

"Nothing."

"You can gather all the forces you wish," he said to the hyena queen, "all the underlings you can tempt over to your side, but in the end, you are unable to wreak your usual havoc in my world." Mlilo looked from Chakide to the bristling nGungumbane with a wry smile. "And right now, I'm surrounded by troglodytes."

The hyena queen let out a groan. "I see you have not come to give your blessing, to hand over what is rightfully mine, part of *my* body. Death will be its only release."

"Death is *your* only release."

A few seconds of blackness and dizzying atmosphere and Amira burst out of a tall arch onto a paved path. The sun was high in the bright blue sky hanging over a lush green valley before her. Temple buildings peaked out from huge trees, pathways and small walk-bridges, visible between bushes and hedges snaked their way up towards Amira's location.

She turned to get a look at the arch she had come through and had to take a step back from fright.

At least twenty metres up the green hillside protruded a giant, square white head staring out over the valley.

Glancing down at the arch, she realised she had exited into this world through giant, sculpted hands held together. The head's huge hands.

"The Ghost King," she whispered to herself with disbelief. "China?"

Dan stood baffled. He had come out on a raised, stone platform, with the sprawling orange desert he was now scanning. The dry landscape was littered with huge rocky outcrops.

"Oh, come on," he shouted into the icy desert air. The sky in the east was a predawn, deep blue.

He turned back, taking a second to glance at the four storey high facade, hand-carved into the red sandstone, like Petra in Jordan, but a single, freestanding rock.

Impressive.

He hurried into the dark, decorative archway.

"Let's try again."

Amira had already returned to the pagodas, searching for the right portal.

"Wrong," shouted Dan.

"Me too," she said under her breath. "Here." She was pointing at the ground in front of the second doorway.

"Footprints," said Dan seeing the disturbed sand. "We've got to hurry, who knows how long Mlilo's been stuck in there by himself."

Amira gripped his shoulder. "We need to be ready for whatever is waiting for us on the other side."

They nodded and Amira, sword raised, leaped inside.

Looking out of the long cave mouth, nGungumbane had planted half a dozen of her large quills, half a metre apart starting at the left wall.

Mlilo understood the makeshift barrier was narrowing entry to the chamber. And exit. He had kept his back to the right wall, needing only a couple of leaps to get out, should he need to.

Chakide was at his left, at the feet of the hyena queen, plans flitting behind their darting eyes.

"One day," uNosithwalangcengce was saying, "I have dreamt it, the Moon will come down to the Earth and kiss it with its icy coolness. Its pale light will nourish and caress the dying soil of the land laid bare and exposed by those who ignore its true power. I will liberate the Earth from you mortals. Man has had long enough and man has squandered it."

Chakide, feigning indifference, yawned and seated themselves on the polished stone floor of the chamber. They stretched their lean limbs, the muscles quivering with pleasure and the hair bristling.

Mlilo stepped towards the cave entrance. Something was shifting in the air. A flurry of air at his ears, followed by the murmur, a whisper, "Qaphela."

He looked right, but the injured porcupine, on the platform, was well out of reach of him. Something stirred in the ground. nGungumbane stepped between two of her planted quills and readied herself, a quill in her right fist, near one of the holes made by her offspring at the edge of the cavern.

It was strange to witness a porcupine, effortlessly bound up and out of the dirty burrow.

The porcupine mother gave a satisfied grunt and turned back to her barrier as the retiring animal sniffed around on its haunches, checking the situation.

"You underestimated Zandile, a mortal," said Mlilo taking another step closer to the opening. "You paid for that. But obviously you have not paid enough. You gather these petty thieves as disciples, using your hate, lies and empty promises. But hate does not unify. Hate hates, always. Hate detests anything other than itself."

The hyena queen growled low in the centre of the room. "Petulance and arrogance," she said through clenched jaws and slapped a huge hand against her stone throne. The vibrations dissipated and she added, "You've come to a fight with your magic and amathambo, when you should have come with an army."

uNosithwalangcengce drew in a long breath, her body rising slightly from her reclining position, and let out a deafening hyena whoop-whoop-whoop that boomed outward, amplified by the shape of her den chamber, echoing over the valleys and mountaintops.

The three porcupines roared their approval. Chakide, up on their feet, tittered and paced side-to-side, ready for anything.

Mlilo's body continued to shiver from the sudden noise and vibrations as the last murmurs of the queen's call subsided.

An eerie stillness descended over the world around him. Apart from the crackling fire, nothing stirred.

Something to his left. He glanced at Chakide but there was a soft din, building, beyond Chakide, from the arched tunnels.

Clearer now, it was a response call. Another hyena bark erupted from the opposite tunnel entrance. Mlilo's skin goosebumped and he moved his hands, circular movements, over one another, building the heat and flame.

Chakide's chattering reached fever-pitch, like a hyena's on the hunt. Mlilo had nGungumbane out the corner of his eye to the right.

"The magic I call upon," Mlilo raised his voice over the growing noise, "from within and from without, is sufficient to defeat any army, of any size, or any ruler thinking they must create an outside force to enforce their ways on others. My fight begins in here." He pounded a flaming fist against his chest, sparks bursting outward, adding, "and ends with your defeat."

Two shadowy forms bound out of each flanking tunnel behind the queen's throne, a yowl emanating from each as the large hyenas came to a synchronised stop on either side of uNosithwalangcengce.

Their queen gave a snort of approval.

Mlilo was at the cave entrance, softer soil under his feet, while the injured porcupine had made its way alongside its sibling opposite him.

"My people have survived your guns and bullets, tanks and teargas," said Mlilo checking the other pit for any threats, "and your armies marching across the landscape, blotting out magic. All for a singular ideology that does not allow for free individuals. My people have survived because of the truth and justice within us."

The two porcupine siblings stiffened and focused on the hole, three metres from them, that the one had emerged from minutes earlier.

There was a shimmer of gold and purple as Amira dived out, immediately rolling to the side, followed by the grey form of Dan, flickering his wand defensively.

Mlilo held his fiery hands ready and breathed a sigh of relief.

"Our people," Mlilo gestured to his friends getting to their feet, "overcame your hate. Our people are a people of truth. Our people are the ones who fight for freedom not ruled by a festering few."

The three friends rumbled, crackled and burned with their energies.

"Our force comes from within ourselves. And it is that magic that will destroy you, Hyena Queen. Your filth has oozed into our world for too long. You will not be the last but you stop, now. You are the troglodytes hiding in shadowy caves rather than growing for the greater good."

Mlilo had barely uttered the last word when bedlam broke out.

The two cleared the fire pit and focused all their teeth and claws on Mlilo, while the three porcupines descended on Amira and Dan.

Chakide dashed from left to right, choosing his fight, looking for a gap.

Flames leaked out around Mlilo and the tearing claws of the dogs pinning him in the dirt. He could feel the pulse of Amira's roaring kinetic force pummelling and Dan's purple electric energy lighting up the cliff face.

Singeing, burning fur filled Mlilo's nostrils and throat. Pain seared into him from all angles. His adrenaline burned in his veins as he concentrated a blast of fire from his chest.

The explosion sent the two hyenas staggering back, one evidently receiving the brunt of Mlilo's force. It fell limply to the ground and the second yelped and charged back at him.

Mlilo caught a glimpse of Amira's flashing sword, finding its home in the exposed chest of the previously injured porcupine. Down on its knees, it was done.

Mlilo burned a single column of flame at the hyena in midair, slowing it enough for him to step away and watch it tumble beyond the platform edge into the boulders and bushels below, but not in time to counter the attack from the conniving Chakide. Claws ripped his left shoulder and spun him around, disorienting him, and slammed him to the ground.

The cackle was right in his ears.

Dan's wand pushed against the raging nGungumbane, while his left hand, drawing from the rune and seed gripped within, scattered lightening in front of him and Amira, barely enough to weaken the third and only remaining porcupine offspring.

A rumble of Amira's force hit both porcupines, sending them a few paces back.

Dan looked over at Mlilo, his friend in a dusty brawl with the dog Chakide. If he released uKuhlangana's hold, even for a moment to help Mlilo, the porcupines would be on them.

All he could do was scream up into the sky.

Mlilo managed a blast at his adversary, sending Chakide tumbling through the dirt.

In that moment everything darkened. Flitting shadows filled the air around them.

Dan froze, and it dawned on him. The Morrígan.

"Welcome to the fray, Morrígan," hissed uNosithwalangcengce.

The three friends regrouped while the stunned enemy drew their lines at the cavern mouth. Chakide, nGungumbane and her last child stood ready.

"Was that it?" Mlilo screamed above the racket. "Was that all you've got?"

Rather than materialise into her female form, the Morrígan's voice from the cloud of birds said, "An army approaches, Mlilo."

Dan saw his shocked friend look at the undulating mass around him. "What?"

"uNosithwalangcengce, the Hyena Queen, has sounded the rallying call of her hyena army. Like the beasts you dispatched only moments ago, these are no ordinary dogs, no ordinary hyenas. These are the imposing cave hyenas of old."

In response, uNosithwalangcengce let out her whooping cry once again.

The rustling wings of the Morrígan seemed to quiet down and an unnerving sound moved up through the valley, from the mountains and on the air. Deep howls, bellows and yowls drifted up to the cave entrance.

"Without uNosithwalangcengce at her true power," said the Morrígan, "these creatures cannot leave this world. But rest assured this is what will spill over into your world should you fail."

"No pressure," said Dan.

"These matters do not concern you, crow," growled the Hyena Queen from within her den chamber.

"Amira, Dan, Mlilo. We will keep the hyena hordes at bay. Your fight is here with this *queen*," she hissed the last word and with that, the birds dissipated into the starry skies above.

"Enough," roared uNosithwalangcengce.

The three enemies took their cue: Chakide sprinted at Mlilo, and the two porcupines dived at Amira and Dan.

"Finally, some quiet. Now, bring me their bones."

The quiet, predawn streets of Durban pounded with the sound of bodies hitting earth.

The glow from the spotlights reflecting off the neo-Baroque-style City Hall, its impressive central dome rising nearly fifty metres into the morning sky, was enough for Amira to make out their location and the shadowy forms ready to pounce on her and Dan once again.

They had clearly emerged from the creatures' portal pits in the war memorial gardens in the square between Kaseme and Lembede Streets.

Out the corner of her eye she could see Dan checking his location, followed suddenly by a shriek. Amira whipped her head over her shoulder and back at the imposing porcupines circling them.

"A statue," whispered Amira with irritation. "The threat is in front of us."

Dan had caught a glimpse of the Durban Volunteers memorial angel statue five or six metres up, her hands held out with flowers in her right and flanked by two weathered, bronze reclining lions.

The stars were fading and the sun had yet to rise but the sky was growing pale. Fatigue would quickly set in here in our world.

Chandrahas in her left hand and her khaṭvāṅga in her right, Amira stood side on, ready.

The younger porcupine was first to attack, wielding a long quill as a spear at Amira.

nGungumbane took the cue and ran at Dan, low to the ground and sweeping him, flailing, up through the air.

Amira parried the blows of her porcupine, deflecting enough for her to buffet Dan's landing with a boom of her power, away from the hard, paved ground. She watched him roll to the side, near the single, wide pit of pulverised soil and grass where the four of them had emerged earlier.

Amira pivoted, the dark grey City Hall at her back, and paced into the middle of the open paved square.

The younger porcupine was at her again, bounding towards her, raging and twirling its quill with style. Off behind it, its mother was stalking the hunched form of Dan.

Amira took a deep breath and shouted, "Dan."

nGungumbane's shock showed as she froze for a moment then ran at Amira's friend.

Not waiting for the porcupine to get to her, Amira dashed, facing the attack head on. Hoping it would do exactly what she hoped, the animal leaped through the air, bringing the quill up like a broadsword ready to stab. She dropped to her knees and slid beneath the shadow form above her.

Holding for the right position she raised her wand and sent a thunderous force into the animal's abdomen.

Without waiting for it to land, she kept the kinetic energy rolling out of her and sending the beast slamming into the angel statue, almost toppling it from its solid concrete plinth. The outstretched flowers, covered in red liquid, protruded from the impaled and writhing porcupine trying to free itself.

In the space below, Dan was barely holding nGungumbane off him, her quills swiping centimetres from his straining face, as he pushed against her with his wand and lightening.

"nGungumbane!" Amira's scream stunned the large porcupine and gave Dan a moment's respite. "Let's fight like real girls, shall we?"

Assuming she would take the bait immediately, Amira was shocked to watch nGungumbane launch her quill at Dan.

But he was ready. His wand was there, blasting a crackling bolt into the sharp projectile, holding it frozen in mid-air before it shattered into dozens of shards.

nGungumbane wasted no time and launched herself in Amira's direction. One, two, three and four quills pulled out from her massive back. Amira could feel the weight of the monster, beating through the hard ground, heading her way.

Quill number one flew at her. Amira ducked and moved left, having to bring up her wand to push the second, hurtling close behind the first, clinking and clattering away onto the nearby curved stairs. It was about to be close combat against the remaining two quill spears and a relentless beast.

Amira blasted her energy at the advancing, spiney mass, doing little to slow her but rather enraging her further.

The dark animal closed the ten-metre gap in a second but Amira used nGungumbane's momentum against her.

Instead of blasting her energy outward, to repel, Amira pushed then, planting her feet firm, grabbed and yanked, like a giant fist pulling the massive porcupine towards her.

With the rumbling sounds of a brewing storm, nGungumbane helpless in an invisible hold, Amira swivelled and pushed, sending the massive porcupine rolling out of the open, paved square, across Lembede Street, and smashing into the Royal Hotel foyer. The bunting and glass of the wooden doors shattered and splintered with the impact.

"I've got a plan," yelled Dan coming up alongside Amira.

"Through that archway down there," he pointed back to the intersection visible through an arch at the corner of the gardens. "You'll know when to pummel her."

She nodded to her friend as he skipped backward, getting in position.

nGungumbane smashed out of the wreckage, charging toward Amira.

Now near the far end of the square, Dan sent a flash of purple lightening into a nearby palm tree causing the massive porcupine to duck to her left, away from Amira and towards Dan's position. Its head snapped at the source of the blast, refocussing its anger on the druid, but not before it took a giant leap through the air. The spiky form of nGungumbane twisted at the wide shoulders, followed by her waist.

With only a split second to react, Amira crouched and sliced her sword through the air barely catching the tips of the three large quills, like arrows, flying at her. The dull shafts landed their intended blows, one deflecting from her right glove and the others against the side of her breastplate, whacking her to the ground.

"Welcome to my world," Chakide seethed and spat with fury.

The dizzying earthquake of the shapeshifter's teleportation had Mlilo reeling to steady his mind, the all-consuming sound pushing like gusts of air against his eardrums. This was unlike any portal between worlds he had ever experienced.

The wavering light and shadows coalesced but remained wobbly like being rattled in a glass jar. Mlilo barely recognised the dark, blurry surroundings of Durban harbour, the lampposts of the promenade a few metres away to his left and the neat grass of the gardens beneath him, but at least he was away from other threats.

He forced his focus on the animal pinning him to the ground and clawing at his arms, tearing at the fire he instinctively burned from his clenched fists protecting his chest.

Boom.

Enough of a force was released to push Chakide off him and back a pace or two, shaking the impact off and grinning wide-eyed at Mlilo.

Mlilo toppled over the moment he tried to stagger to his feet. Everything shifted and the shake was relentless.

"Shapeshifting," said Chakide with a raised clawed palm, disdain sneering through their teeth. "Bending it to my will. I'll bend you until you break." Their palm snapped closed and Mlilo's body was compressed by an invisible force, crushing from all sides, winding him.

Mlilo pushed everything he had against it, his fire licking upward from his neck, past his face in a vertical stream. Another wobble of the bubble of Chakide's energy and he stumbled to his knees, held fast. His intense heat leaked down, through Chakide's bubble of energy, scorching the patch of grass under Mlilo.

He had to think. He was pushing everything he had everywhere, to find a weakness.

That was it. Focus.

Rather than blowing up and out, Mlilo channelled his fiery force into his right hand alone, to his fingertips. He released his clenched fist and flattened his palm.

A triangular blade of fire grew outward, emerging like a solid, sharpened instrument.

He thrust his arm out in a short rapid jab.

Chakide howled in response, Mlilo feeling his body freed and slumped to the ground for a split second. He was back on his uneven footing, but breathing and no longer restrained.

Chakide's cackle was no longer that of derision, by hysteria. They circled Mlilo, body and muscles ready to lunge.

"Shifting," they uttered.

Mlilo's stomach lurched but he remained fixed on the unpredictable creature, his fiery blade held out at his adversary. The air in his eardrums reverberated once again and the world shook.

Mlilo stood his ground but his outstretched hand wavered and warped before his eyes. He looked at his legs and feet to centre himself and get a grip on reality, but they seemed to be twisting into the ground, melding with Chakide's sphere of shimmering energy and undulating shadows.

That moment's hesitation was all the trickster needed. They ploughed into him, scuttling them both against the wrought iron railing of the harbour promenade. Clang.

Teeth pierced Mlilo's shoulder and a claw gripped his impande. Chakide tore downward, nails slicing Mlilo's leopard-print vest and chest and snapping one of the red strings of beads.

Before the tiny charms could clatter to the paving, Mlilo brought up his right hand. A wavering heat momentarily levitated the objects and with a snap of his fingers they were transformed into searing hot shrapnel shooting at the trickster. Mlilo didn't falter, instead using the painful distraction peppering the animal to tap into the adrenaline pulsing through him, and sent a wave of heat outward, barely singeing the ravenous animal cowering from the burning bullets. The iron bannister, warping out and away from its cement bonds gave them the opportunity to lunge at him.

Mlilo had barely enough time to shake off the searing pain in his skin before he was launched, bodily into the night air. Like a slow-motion crash, his world twisted and upended but he pushed his heat through his right hand once again.

Chakide's enveloping energy softened the impact of pounding into the shallow, muddy salt water of the harbour.

Mlilo didn't wait for the water to settle or to get his bearings; instead, he lunged at the floundering Chakide gasping for air.

The animal was scuttling back on their elbows, a deep wound visible at their ribcage oozing dark liquid. Their warping world was gone and Mlilo stood firm, towering over the hysterical animal.

He sucked in a sharp breath, readying himself, and smacked his lips.

"Hmm. Salt water," Mlilo said with a wry smile. The whites of Chakide's widening eyes glowed in the dark as realisation dawned on them.

"My amadlozi have landed my bum in the proverbial butter, hey, uHlakanyana."

Chakide yelped and whimpered, holding a shaking claw up to Mlilo.

The water at Mlilo's feet bubbled, the energy rising from the dirty liquid, up his legs. Flickers of blue flame encircling him converged at his knees and grew upward becoming a golden yellow orange.

The damp surface of Mlilo's skin crackled and sparkled, the seawater instantly drying, leaving white salt crystals powdering his skin.

He kept his focus, staring intently at Chakide's shifting forms, now in a crouch, but his world rumbled in a familiar way.

The dog was going to escape.

"Not today, uchakide," said Mlilo and leaped, an explosion of water and light and flame charging with him into the shimmering force building around the stunned creature.

Dan dashed to the left, skipped over the chain barrier and onto the pavement below, the rattling sound of the incoming monster thundered close on his heels. He heard nGungumbane ram into the green, iron bollard, snapping the thick chain fence and stumbling down the stairs into a large palm tree.

Dan ran, turning sharp left at the corner, past the archway leading back up to the gardens and Amira standing ready, and ducked through the wrought iron gate down the flight of stairs into the public toilets below street level.

He heard a blast and a rumble through the ground, followed by a roar. Amira had hit her mark.

He knew he was trapped but he had a plan. He moved from the bottom of the stairs, back against the wall facing the row of urinals to his left, and the toilet stalls on the far right, and held his breath.

The entrance gate above was slammed against the thick walls, shattering plaster and concrete shards everywhere.

Dan pushed up against his wall, keeping an eye on the growing shadow to his right, but taking the moment to focus all his energy to his wand gripped in both hands.

nGungumbane was inside the confined space in a split second, head darting left and right, searching; Dan going unseen in the dark corner behind her.

He held on until she was at the far end of the room, then stepped forward.

The giant porcupine, realising her mistake too late, had barely enough time to pivot as the white streak of lightening slammed her against the far wall, white tiles shattering around her black form. Dan's energy didn't abate, instead it branched out, licking along the grey floor tiles and walls to the left and right. A crackle filled the air.

The tendrils of purple-white light had found the water pipes of the urinals on the left wall. Inside the flapping doors of the toilet stalls on the right erupted the song of porcelain cracking and falling.

Dan moved back to the bottom of the stairs, holding his arms straight out, energy pulsing from his wand. One final surge and nGungumbane was engulfed in a torrent of water, masonry and wooden panels from the splintering doors.

Dan pivoted and bound two, three steps at a time as the water rushed up the stairs behind him.

Amira was standing, stunned at the commotion building below her.

Dan leaped through the entrance, grabbed the iron gate behind him and slammed it closed. "Keep her down there," he shouted above the mayhem.

Immediately Amira raised her khaṭvāṅga in her left hand, Dan could feel her kinetic force push against and past him as his wand and clenched left fist, drawing from the rune and seed firmly in its grasp, worked on melting the iron gate to its frame. He edged out of Amira's firing line, pushing at whatever might be coming up the stairs, just as the bubbling water burst over the sides of the barred walls onto the pavement.

The two companions stepped back, onto the street. Waiting.

The force that hit the iron barrier cracked the outer walls but they didn't budge.

"Harder," shouted Dan sending a blaze of light into the middle of the raging porcupine thrashings at the top of the stairs, trapped.

Amira took a step forward, leaning her weight into the energy being emitted from her hands.

For a brief moment the geyser of water hung in midair, not spilling down onto the ground, and nGungumbane was thrust back against the stairwell wall. The next moment she was under the water.

Another blast from Dan and another step forward from Amira. nGungumbane didn't surface. The hissing water poured around the sides of their forcefields, finding any way to escape the pressure from below. But no porcupine.

Then the ground rumbled. And again.

"She's going to pound her way out of there," shouted Amira above the racket. "If she gets to the soil below the concrete foundations, she's gone."

"Keep holding," screamed Dan. He ran over to one of the palm trees lining the pavement, uttered some quick words, and gripped its rough trunk. The power that surged through Dan cracked through the concrete paving, rippled up the walls of the building, sending a thunderclap of light and sound down into the depths of the raging waters.

Stunned, Dan looked to Amira, thrown to her knees but holding her barrier in place.

The buffeting sound had stopped.

Slowly the waters abated, trickling around them and finding their way into the gutters and drains.

Everything became quiet.

Amira eased her power down but they both kept their hands, wands tightly gripped, at the ready, expecting anything.

They moved closer to the open bars enclosing the side wall, the water retreating inch by inch down the stairs. The lights had long since blown themselves out, leaving indiscernible shadows undulating in the murky darkness.

Dan flinched. Amira took a sharp breath.

Black spines protruded from the water. Gradually the thick quills emerged, but the body of nGungumbane was motionless in the subsiding water.

A splitting shriek of terror vibrated through Dan's ears.

He and Amira turned just in time to dodge the last of the porcupine's offspring lunging at them. Amira brought her sword up in time to stab its left shoulder, giving them the opportunity to blast their energy at it, slamming the writhing roaring creature back into a parked car. It peeled itself away, leaving two bloodied quills protruding from the shattered vehicle.

They backed away, as the animal readied itself for another attack, holding its injured arm at its side.

"Back to the garden," Amira whispered to Dan.

Confusion passed over his face, then he realised what she wanted to do.

Mock charging. Amira buffeted it back. Dan flashed lightening along the ground between them and the frothing beast.

They stepped back onto the pavement, the stairs leading up into the gardens a metre behind them.

"Now," shouted Amira.

They both sent a blast of energy at the animal, giving themselves the time they needed to dash up the stairs and onto the torn-up soil where they had come into the real world. Feet planted solidly, Amira held her sword in one hand and khaṭvāṅga defensively in the other while Dan pointed his wand and with his other hand crackling with blue sparks in anticipation. The animal leaped the distance of the stairs in a single bound, relentlessly charging at them.

Amira's khaṭvāṅga released a thud of force, stopping the porcupine in its tracks, grabbing hold of it while Dan's both hands shimmered with light out into the middle of the beast's chest. They were holding it.

Together they moved it inch by inch over the hole, and without prompting, leaped at the stunned creature, tackling it into the dirty void.

Chakide had taken the brunt of Mlilo's blast as they had emerged at the mouth of the hyena queen's cavern. The panting animal was dragging themselves along the dirt platform.

Mlilo didn't see it coming.

An iron grip wrapped around Mlilo's neck and wrenched him off his feet. uNosithwalangcengce had been ready and waiting, standing at the entrance to her den chamber, hoping Mlilo, or at the very least, his companions, would be brought back kicking and screaming. This was no longer the huddled and injured looking queen hyena. This was the muscled and bristling eight-foot frame of a queen.

She held him up with her right hand; her left in the same position clasping something and firm against her chest. He had misjudged the extent of her injury. It had not weakened her.

"You can have all the skilled warriors in all the realms," she growled and held Mlilo at her eye level, struggling for air, "but you have to settle things yourself."

Her rows of white fangs gleamed in the firelight as she paused.

"Listen, Mlilo," she said and held her breath.

Mlilo could now make out the roaring and yelping of the approaching hyena army, close by, maybe just around the corner or below the platform.

uNosithwalangcengce waited a moment longer and then he saw them. They were everywhere. Massive shadows bound over the rocky ledge, peeled in from both sides. Yellow-white eyes and teeth flashed in the dusty black faces.

Relief flooded over him as the hyena queen lifted him up and stepped into the cave. His boots and pants scraped over the fire-pit, heat licking around him. He tried to use it but the hyena only squeezed tighter.

She was taking him to the back of the cave.

A commotion of yowling and yelping behind him signalled the return of his friends. Or their bodies. His stomach lurched at the thought. But the howls that followed and the recognisable lights and sounds gave him hope.

uNosithwalangcengce, glancing back at the clatter, moved around her wide slab of a throne and headed towards the central archway in the back wall.

"I will finally cross through into your world as I squeeze the life out of you, fire man."

uNosithwalangcengce shoved Mlilo into her course hairy chest, face pressed up against the scabbed and scarred wound. Giving Mlilo a moment to breath, she released the tight grip of her right hand and immediately wrapped him in a chokehold with her left arm.

It was the first time in what felt like an age that Mlilo laid eyes on the stark white breastbone, bright between the black claws of the hyena queen. It was right there.

The commotion at the mouth of the cave was growing to a fever pitch, giving uNosithwalangcengce a moment's hesitation. But she was determined.

Birds swarmed in, flitting and scratching around Mlilo and the hyena, but she roared and moved closer to the dark archway. Her right arm was stretched out, reaching into the dark void beyond, her grip on Mlilo's neck like a vice cutting off the blood to his head.

Patches of black appeared in his vision, and sparkles of golden light quivered around uNosithwalangcengce outstretched claws. It was happening. Mlilo's life was fading and the hyena queen's full strength was returning.

Screams erupted. The black shapes became birds pecking and squawking their anger. Purple light flashed. The golden rays were up to uNosithwalangcengce's forearm.

Mlilo tried with everything he had but he was weakening.

Dan and Amira had not anticipated the onslaught as soon as they emerged through the pit with the limp body of the last porcupine.

Huge hyenas were flooding up the hill and mountain side, a river of black weaving through thickets of bush and scrub-forest, clattering over shale and rocks to get to their queen.

Even with the Morrígan back to fend them off, Dan and Amira were using everything they had to repel the onslaught.

Dan could feel the tightening, constricting, of his left hand, as if the previous injury from nGungumbane was cramping and slowing him down, but the energy he was pulling from the rune and seed in its grip was unending.

"She's going through to the other side," screamed Amira as she and Dan backed further into the cave. Dan could not take a second to glance back at his friend. He blasted all he had into the mass of bodies.

"You have to help your friend," said the voice of the Morrígan. "The hyena queen must be stopped at all costs."

She was right. If Mlilo died it was all over. Their energy focused on the terror attacking them was wasted if she succeeded.

"She's right," screamed Amira. "Now!"

They simultaneously sent a burst of their energies into the oncoming wave of hyena soldiers, giving them the second or two they needed to run into the cave.

Nausea hit Dan's gut at sight of Mlilo's limp body hanging from the massive form of the hyena queen.

A thundering boom blasted from Amira and Dan followed it up with his own crackle of lightening.

It was enough to slam uNosithwalangcengce against the cave wall, stunning her into dropping their friend.

Amira pummelled her again while Dan swooped in and grabbed Mlilo under an arm. He pulled his friend across the smooth floor randomly aiming his wand with zaps at anything coming at him.

Relief washed over him as Mlilo roused himself into a crouch position.

Amira blasted the hyena queen back against the wall and retreated to the two men, but uNosithwalangcengce would be on them soon enough.

"You two need to trust me," she yelled in their faces, "and do exactly what I say."

Mlilo was wide-eyed and alert as Dan and Amira hefted him onto his feet. She stood between, them facing the inevitable attack from the hyena queen.

uNosithwalangcengce shook off the effects of the attack and roared with anger. She had been so close but she had failed.

Glancing over her shoulders at Mlilo to her left and Dan to her right, Amira shouted her orders. "You have to blast your magic, with everything you've got, but through me!"

"What?" They screamed back at her in unison.

"As long as your target, the intention of your magic, is that hyena monster in front of us, and *not* me, trust me."

Dan looked at Mlilo, shrugged, and raised his wand hand. Mlilo turned his balled-up hands over one another.

Amira's rumbling sound grew.

"Now," she shouted.

The initial blast nearly knocked them all off their feet, but it slammed uNosithwalangcengce into the cave rock face sending rubble and dust scattering down onto her.

It had worked.

"Again!"

This time they maintained their energy and Dan watched in amazement as his purple lightening slivered into Amira's right shoulder blade. Instead of harming and tearing at her clothes and body it was absorbed and pushed out, thundering through Amira's khaṭvāṅga, at something like a tenfold force.

"How's Amira doing this?" Mlilo screamed.

Dan looked to his left and saw Mlilo's bright, golden-red column of flames blasting into Amira's left side. The crescent sword, Chandrahas, glowed white-hot with the energy it expelled.

"It's like she's pulling our energy out of us, using its fullest potency."

Both men watched as the sound, light and heat waves from Amira beat against the roaring abdomen of uNosithwalangcengce. The barrage of energy pounded at uNosithwalangcengce's muscles and bones, holding her back but the hyena queen was not dying.

"The bone," screamed Mlilo. "Focus on the bone."

Amira hunkered down and steadily brought Mlilo's fiery force from the left, the smell of uNosithwalangcengce singeing chest hair and burning flesh filled the air, while the right, Dan's electric pulse, twitched and convulsed the muscles beneath the skin of the hyena's left arm. uNosithwalangcengce moved her arm outward trying to evade the stream of magic, her clenched fist flinching and shaking. Amira pummelled the hyena queen's arm against the cracking wall, exposing the breastbone in her grasp for a split second. It was the one second Amira needed to combine both streams of energy and push them out with all her might into the hyena's fist. The tearing sound of lightening through air, the scream of fire sucking the oxygen out of the atmosphere, and the thunderclap of the ever-expanding kinetic force from the three companions combined to obliterate uNosithwalangcengce's left arm.

Immediately the pandemonium of the battle around them died down.

A guttural moan emanated from the bloodied form of the hyena queen doubling over in pain onto the cavern floor.

"It's done," whispered Mlilo.

A hyena yelped.

Dan looked to the mouth of the cave. The sight of large hyena bodies piled up took his breath away.

In a flash the Morrígan materialised nearby the dwindling coals of the fire pit, and said, "You three need to go."

Amira was already leaping over the stone throne and Mlilo staggered around and grabbed Dan by his coat.

A blast from Amira gave them the space they needed to climb over the animal bodies. As they made it onto the platform, the remaining weary and confused hyena soldiers watching the three companions, Mlilo stopped his friends.

"We may not be able to kill uNosithwalangcengce," he said and pointed to the cave, "but we've got to put her down."

Amira took up her central position and brought a steady blast into the cave roof.

Dan, followed by Mlilo to the right, sent their magic flowing into Amira's back.

Within seconds the mountain was quaking. A crack split from the outside and quickly travelled through the cave roof.

The three friends halted their blasts as the massive den chamber imploded.

The clatter of rubble and dust gave them the cover they needed to climb down the platform ledge and begin their mountain descent at a sprint.

Mlilo imagined the scene from a birds-eye view: the mountainside and thickening forest dropping to the valley below flooded with the shadowy mass of hyena hordes chasing down the fleeing trio. Intermittent thunderous booms and incandescent bursts of light and fire lit up the gloom around the increasingly dense shrubs, trees and rocks as they fended off a new relentless barrage from the hyena queen's army.

Mlilo held the rear, relying on Dan and Amira's frantic silhouettes ahead of him to dictate his next manoeuvre, when to duck, when to leap.

He ignored the thorns and branches scraping at him, righted his gait with the twisting of an ankle. Caught his breath after he bumped and knocked against boulders and trunks. His focus was on the fires he was throwing out at anything that moved next to or behind him. He used the foliage as cover, burning the brittle branches in an explosion of sparks and light.

They had to get to the portal.

CHAPTER 35

Amira stood, heaving to catch her breath, the sounds of animals echoing in her ears. Relief was slowing seeping in as her body calmed and her throbbing heart eased off. She slid Chandrahas back in its sheath but kept a hold on her khaṭvāṅga and its warm, reassuring metal.

They had made it into the waterfall they had emerged from before their climb to the hyena queen's den chamber.

"Where are we now," she asked, staring out at the first rays of the morning sun peaking over a mountainous landscape.

"Oh cool," said Dan panting and jogging to a stop beside her. "uNomkhubulwane."

"Yoh."

The two friends turned to look at Mlilo, checking himself over. Clothes mended and his body intact. He looked up at them and gave a wide grin.

Amira looked at Dan with a raised eyebrow and said, "Is he smiling?"

"Indeed." Dan nodded with his hands on his hips. "Durban would've been better, bru."

Mlilo strode over to them. "You should know by now that a certain someone brings us here, not me."

"If you smart arses don't tell me how we get off this mountain," Amira began.

"Good work back there, Amira," said Mlilo.

"Don't tell me," Dan said coming around to face her. "Things you learned from your adventures in Abaphansi?"

Amira twirled her wand in the air, caught it and folded her arms with a wry smile. She looked down at Dan's hands and gave a puzzled look.

"What," he asked. "Whoa."

Mlilo came over to them and saw the network of roots spindling out over Dan's clenched fist.

Dan eased his hand open to reveal the small, crinkled, bright green shoot sprouting from the red seed. The roots had grown around the wooden rune stone, becoming part of it, and in between Dan's fingers.

"That's what I could feel during the mountaintop fight," he said in awe of the little resilient plant. Dan gently peeled the vine-like roots away from his palm and knuckles, and turned the rune over to look at the burned engraved glyph for the first time.

"Mannaz," he whispered as Amira and Mlilo huddled closer to get a glimpse of the rune symbol, like two conjoined Ps, "The self."

"That's pretty apt," aid Amira.

Dan placed the interwoven objects into his rune bag and said, "For planting later."

"Well, bard," Mlilo said and held Dan's shoulder, "you now have a tale of your own. A helluva tale to tell and a legendary tapestry to weave."

The friends were silent for a moment. Amira sensed something in the air. "Is it me or is mist coming in?"

"It's okay," whispered Mlilo reassuringly. "You're about to meet uNomkhubulwane."

Mlilo watched the pale mist become gloomy as it cleared away to reveal the recognisable night-time landscape and vast lake.

Amira let out a breath of surprise.

The giant, watery-speckled form of the goddess towered above them.

"As you gain more and more abilities, magic and powers," said uNomkhubulwane, "the Earth is going to call on you for ever more assistance, young ones. You have to step up. This is the role of isangoma, druid, warrior and the symbiotic dance with the planet you draw your energies from. It is an exchange. A duality of purpose. The circular flow of that energy for the greater good."

"uNomkhubulwane," said Mlilo. "Siyabonga. For all your help."

"Thank you," whispered a stunned Amira.

Dan raised his wand in his hand and said, "Thank you."

"It was you," she said. Her form rippled and sparkled, lowering down into the inky waters of her lake, closer to the three friends standing in awe. "Individuals trusting themselves. Trust within allowed you to trust one another."

The calm, dark waters of the lake began to rise, edging up the shallow shore and gently trickling over their toes and feet. The sound of pouring rain engulfed them.

"There is more to come."

Warm sunlight hit Mlilo's face and the sound of crashing waves was all around him. He stood, eyes closed, frozen in place for a moment. He took a deep breath and opened his eyes to the bright morning sun over the ocean stretching out to the horizon.

"Durban," he whispered with relief.

"Almond, anyone?" Dan, to Mlilo's left, held out a pile of orange-brown seeds in his open palm. "Who's up for a cup of rooibos at my place?"

Mlilo took one and popped it in his mouth. "I need more than a couple of almonds and a cup of tea for the hunger in my gut, mfowethu."

"What did she mean by _more to come_, Mlilo?" asked Amira to his right.

"Angazi," he said and shook his head.

A moment past and all three mobiles bleeped in each of their pockets.

Mlilo gave an irritated growl. "Back to reality."

"What does that even mean, Anathi," said Amira at the text on her mobile screen.

"What do they have to say," asked Dan.

"||_Khwai-hem is threatening the desert lands_." Amira gave a shrug in confusion.

"Who," said Dan.

"Hmm, _Khwdi-hemm_," said Mlilo. "The all-devourer."

"Why does that sound familiar," Dan said thoughtfully.

"You know our porcupine friend nGungumbane?" Mlilo asked Amira. "Her dad.. The monster that devoured a nation."

"Oh, great," said Dan.

>>>END<<<

GLOSSARY

Traditional Beliefs (in order of importance)

Idlozi / Amadlozi (pl) – 'Ancestors', spirits. Those who were never living on Earth.

Amathongo – 'Ancestors' who were once living people, relatives, on Earth, now sleepers.

Kwelabaphansi – Ancestral place. "In that (country) of those (people) below."

Abaphansi – The ancestral realm, beneath the water. Relating to the setting sun, descending past the line of the horizon over the water's edge.

Inyanga / iZinyanga (pl) – More than a 'traditional healer'. The connectors between the healing and the spirits.

Uhlanya / iZinhlanya (pl) – Broad term for initiates and diviners, who are then categorised by the method of initiation (see iSangoma, Abalozi, iSanusi below).

Isangoma / iZangoma – One of the various forms of healing initiates. Trained through dancing and music.

Abalozi – One of the various forms of healing initiates. Trained through the whistles.

Isanusi – The highest level in African healing. Seer and prophet.

Ukuthwasa – The initiation process. iThwasa is an initiate.

Amathambo – 'Bones' or sacred objects used for divination.

uMuthi – Traditional, plant-based, medical formulation or herbal remedy used for healing. uMuthi, 'tree'.

Mphepho - Dried plant, Helichrysum odoratissmum, which is burned for the cleansing smoke.

iSigodlo – Structure where a healer practices.

uMqombothi – Homemade beer made with fermented maize.

Amazulu – The Heavens.

Camagu / ǀGammãgu / ǀAmmãkua – Givers of water. The line between the known and the unknown. A statement or invocation of peace, gratitude, or a respectful greeting.

Language and Colloquialisms:

Bru – Slang for brother. Anglicised from Afrikaans 'broer'.

Charna – Slang for mate/friend.

Chop – Idiot.

uDadewethu – Sister.

uDadewethu omkhulu – Big sister.

Dankie – Thanks.

nGiyabonga – Thank you.

Kak – Afrikaans slang for crap.

uKhanyisa – Illuminate.

nKosazana – Miss.

nKosikazi – Madam.

uMfowethu – Brother.

uMfowethu omncane – Little brother.

uMnganam – Friend.

uMnumzana – Sir.

Moenie – Don't.

Moer – Damn or Hit (Afrikaans).

uMsizi – Helper.

Sawubona – Hello.

Skattie/Skat – Treasure, term of endearment.

Yasas – Anglicised slang equivalent of Afrikaans 'Jesus'.

Yirra – Slang for Lord.

ACKNOWLEDGEMENTS

Through the three lead characters I was (and still am) able to work through my own stuff that began building since 2016. Mlilo's depression, isolation and tendency to self-reliance were part of my journey with Bones & Runes. The single sentence I had in bold at the top of my notes document read "Mlilo's depression is your depression. Use it." As is the roller-coaster of life, I was served up more real-world situations and emotions for my characters to encounter. Catharsis is a relief.

I'd spent most of my early adult life feeling like I was alone on a spiritual journey (of the self and of a higher calling), then being on that journey with Riley for the past twenty years has given me a travel partner willing to go into the dark as well as the light. No matter what. It's all good to have those close to you say "We believe in you" but to have someone really know what you're about, say: "I believe in you, I believe in this thing you are doing, go and do it," is quite something else altogether. Bones & Runes feels like a side-quest we've shared, levelled-up, and then diving headlong into the next, together.

My kids. Treycin and Kaylin. These two beautiful beings were heading into their adulthood when I began the idea of Bones & Runes. I wanted to write for them and draw from my early adult life. Like the characters in the story, they were, and now are, experiencing the ups and downs of the "real" world. I hope you keep the magic in your hearts as you journey through all realms. You have me, no matter where I may be, loving and supporting you. And you have one another.

Nthombi Memela, for pointing me in the right direction and helping me really kick off my research, and the importance of practising my isiZulu. And one simple suggestion of who to speak with next meant everything that followed below was able to happen.

A huge thanks and appreciation go out to Professor "Gugu" Precious Thokozani Gugulethu Mkhize – the Linguist, the Cosmologist. With multiple meet-ups, always beaming with enthusiasm to share. Patience at my questions relating to this fantasy novel idea and figuring things out in real-time. Emails during the pandemic. Shining a light on things I only knew on the surface – and so much more in an ongoing discovery of isiZulu, the traditions and all its beauty. Gugu was truly the beginning of my journey into the world of "Bones & Runes".

Elliot Ndlovu – the Inyanga, the iSangoma and the Herbalist. Elliot shared his personal experience of becoming an isangoma with Riley and I, but most importantly his love of the land that provides the essential herbs and materials that make being an inyanga possible. Respect – whether it be the ancestors or the provisions nurtured by nature – respect is the key tenet for how I've tackled all the sacred beliefs and traditions portrayed in my work. Live it. Speak with those knowledgeable. Educate yourself. Something that stood out for me was Elliot's belief that it doesn't matter who you are, isangoma is for anyone willing to take that step, to listen to your calling, your ancestors, and live true to that.

Dr Velaphi "VVO" Mkhize – the abalozi and teacher. Spending a few hours enraptured by this man, along with a lecture hall brimming with eager students, was a highlight of my research. His Umsamo Institute, his publications and podcasts are vital for anyone interested in the intricacies of African and, specifically, Nguni divination.

Geoff Ryman for his support and encouragement during peak lockdown. Always nudging to keep writing and putting words down on paper.

Samantha Ramdheo, peppered by my random questions, always happy to share her knowledge of her traditions. Such details and nuances you cannot readily find other than through conversation.

Pule kaJanolintji for going beyond with your translations and linguistics. You saw, understood and believed in what "Bones & Runes" is: its multilayers of traditions, philosophies and, most importantly, the true significance and power of every single word. We need more literature in African languages. IAmmākua.

My brother Michael, doing what big brothers do but on another level. We were on wobbly ground and you and Cecilia gave a calm, peaceful oasis to get our life together. Always checking in, giving a "don't stress" reassurance for me to do what I need to and do the creative things I love. Being with you as this all came together was phenomenal to share.

My father Rob, and stepmother Morena. Your words of encouragement, words of love and words from life experience gave me two people who knew what I was going through. Your regular check-ins were appreciated and needed.

Jane and John Smith. Your love and support gave us stability just when everything was upside down. You also watched as this book came to fruition.

Onyeka Nwelue's unwavering enthusiasm and support for "Bones & Runes" got it out to the world. And for so much more, I am grateful.

Let's see where the journey into Abaphansi takes me next…

ǁAmmākua *(Camagu)*